BOOK ONE IN THE WOMAN OF SIN TRILOGY

WOMAN *of* SIN

DEBRA B. DIAZ

First e-book publication 2010
First printing 2015

Scripture references and quotations are directly from the King James Version of the Holy Bible or paraphrased by the author.

Except for historical figures and events, the characters and events in this novel are fictitious. Any resemblance to persons living or dead is coincidental.

Cover Design by 100Covers.com
Interior Design by FormattedBooks.com

REVIEWS OF "*WOMAN OF SIN*"

"Author Debra B. Diaz elegantly and beautifully weaves an unforgettable story . . . Filled with suspense and romance, this novel will . . . lead you on a journey that is so real you will not want it to end. A true masterpiece!"

—CBM Book Reviews

"It is a great book and Diaz is a very good fiction writer. She has eloquently captured the life and politics of first-century Jerusalem, and the empire, and has spun a terrific story around one of the Bible's most mysterious characters."

"Personal and compelling, very solidly based on biblical events and history."

"I am a hospice nurse and sit with people who are dying . . . your book has changed my life. It is the best book I have ever read!"

"I really like biblical fiction and this author produces some of the best."

"I loved this book and could not put it down. . . A very well-written story."

REVIEWS OF THE "*WOMAN OF SIN*" TRILOGY

"Excitement, romance, suspense, and pure story telling—everything a story should have is here."

"This is absolutely one of the better reads! . . . These people are portrayed so realistically that you become involved and are able to draw parallels to our present time and lifestyle."

"An enduring gift to your soul. Beautifully written."

"I fell in love with the characters, and the books gave much food for thought about the early believers, their passion in sharing the good news, and their willingness to lay down their lives. The author did an excellent job at telling the story."

"Great books for seekers—couldn't put them down."

"Poetic, literary music."

"One of the best portraits of Jesus I have ever known . . . I was truly touched for a lifetime."

IN GRATEFUL ACKNOWLEDGMENT

I want to convey my deep gratitude to readers who enjoy my books and make it possible for me to keep writing. You are so much appreciated and I write with you in mind, for your pleasure and, hopefully, inspiration!

The teachings of many men of God have influenced the writing of my biblical novels. I can't name them all here but would like to extend special recognition to the witness and teaching of Dr. Billy Graham, Dr. Adrian Rogers, and Dr. Charles Stanley.

Special thanks to others (who wished not to be named) who edited and helped contribute to the former publication of this book.

CONTENTS

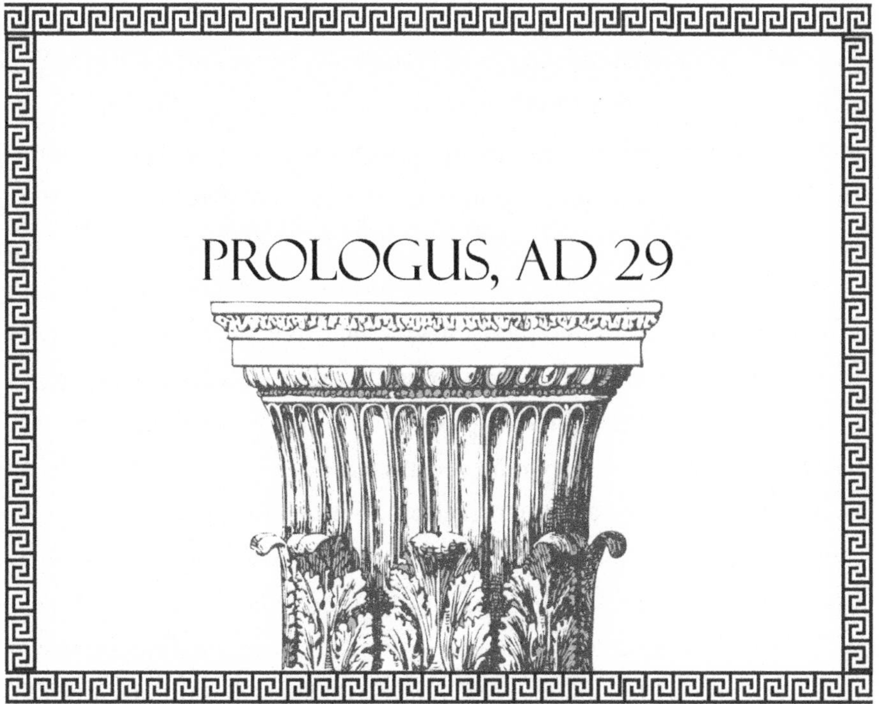

PROLOGUS, AD 29

The streets of Rome seemed alive, twisting and writhing like some tortured serpent. Its massive human coils swelled and clotted the narrow roads channeling into the forum, like tributaries rushing toward the sea. The white draped figures of aristocrats mingled with the simpler garb of the plebeians; the covered litters of the wealthy vied for passage alongside vagrants and beggars. Some had to squint and put up their hands to shade their eyes against the dazzling whiteness of the buildings beneath the hot July sun, but their progress was little impeded. Market pavilions spilled over with more than the usual number of hawkers and their wares. A slave ship had recently made port, attracting the curious as well as those who had intentions of making a purchase.

It was a busy day in the busiest city of the world.

Rome's progression from mud to marble had taken only a few centuries. Her little group of colonies spread along the Tiber River sprouted into city-states; her rule changed from chieftains to kings, to the semblance of a republic, to the present-day empire. She had more than survived; she had prospered. Secure in her military superiority, she became caught up in what she perceived to be her destiny—mistress of the world—and proceeded to fulfill it.

She was as majestic as she was malodorous, as splendid as she was squalid, as full of color and pageantry as she was white marble and dull rituals. Half of her population was composed of slaves, some of them men and women brought as captives from remote provinces. Others had been unwise in money matters and were forced to sell themselves until they could buy back their freedom. Some had been of such poor judgment as to be born to slaves . . . and there were the luckless ones who simply fell victim to the paranoia of those who ruled.

The first emperor, Augustus, had gone far toward healing the scars caused by the civil wars both preceding and following the murder of Julius Caesar, that famed general who had conquered Gaul and ultimately destroyed the Republic. Augustus was an affable man and a brilliant administrator—though some said too strict and old-fashioned—and he had died much too soon. The people had been as fond of Augustus as they were baffled by his successor, Tiberius.

At first the stepson of Augustus had governed well. He guarded the borders and kept the frontiers safe from the barbarian hordes; he handled the finances with frugality; he improved the highways and thus stimulated trade and commerce. But he was melancholy by nature, and almost wholly indifferent to the games and amusements that were of vital interest to everyone else. Always reclusive, he had finally removed himself to the nearby island of Capri where he lived in a virtual, self-imposed state of exile.

Rumors abounded—of wild sexual orgies and an obsession with the afterlife. As the years passed, he grew shorter of temper and slower of speech. He had never had any rapport with the public; it was said even Augustus despised him and had only named Tiberius his successor due the machinations of his wife, Tiberius' mother. He now all but ignored the Senate and often sent the dignitaries scurrying whenever they ventured to visit him at Capri.

Rome whispered that he was insane. She further whispered, a bit louder, that he ought to at least make a pretense of running the government—who was really in control, anyway? But Rome didn't long trouble herself. As long as there was food to eat, wine to drink, and races and gladiatorial contests to attend, life was good.

A few knew the answer as to who was in control, but there was nothing anyone could do about it. Aelius Sejanus, the emperor's chief advisor, had played upon the fears and suspicions of the old man with amazing success. Sejanus craftily set about ridding Tiberius of all his critics—who usually happened to be critics of himself as well. Hundreds were executed or exiled, or sold into slavery. Even senators and their families were not immune.

Strangely, much of this internal discord resulted from the fact that it was a time of peace throughout most of the empire. Though struggles against Roman rule broke out on occasion, other countries recognized the wisdom of at least a temporary submission. And without wars to occupy his mind, Tiberius was free to wonder who might be plotting against him. Peace could find no place in the emperor's soul, though he sought it with diligence. His thoughts turned often to religion. There were gods and goddesses to suit any disposition, but such tailor-made deities did little to earn the respect of men, especially the man who ruled the world.

Yet there was *one*, one that his own astrologers spoke of who would be called the King of kings. They were vague as to his origin. The prophets of the Jews were more particular, perhaps because this man was to be born in their country, in Bethlehem of Judea. He would "shine like a light in darkness," they said. He would be called the "prince of peace," and "of the increase of his government and of peace there would be no end." He would arrive "in the fullness of time."

This unknown king struck a fear into the emperor that exceeded even his dread of assassination. There was to be something supernatural about this king, and Tiberius did not know how to fight him, or even how to recognize him. How was Rome to mass her armies against a prince of peace who was supposed to live forever?

Sejanus assured him that it was only superstition, that the Jews had always been "crying for a messiah."

"If it were just a Jewish belief it would not concern me," the emperor said testily. "The world's most learned astrologers have seen his star in the heavens! And we know what that fool Herod did about it. Killed everybody else and let the one child get away! The one child, Aelius Sejanus, born in Bethlehem on the day in question and who, I have heard, was identified by some sort of otherworldly light that hovered directly above him."

"Augustus gave no credence to those Arabian stargazers," Sejanus said calmly. "He allowed none of it to be officially recorded, even Herod's little tantrum. Besides, what are a few Jewish infants? It was nothing!"

"Augustus didn't record it because it reflected poorly on him," grumbled Tiberius. "The Arabians and the child escaped. Not to mention he had a lunatic ruling Palestine. But it is enough for me that Herod took it seriously. If there was one thing he knew how to do, it was to hold on to his throne! It is plain that he believed the child to be a threat."

"But as you say, Herod was a madman. Brilliant in some ways we must admit, but mad at the end."

The emperor glared. "It's been thirty years. The child is a man now. And my astrologers tell me the sign of a coming king is still there, written in the stars."

"It is your own star they have seen!" proclaimed Sejanus. "You are the greatest of all kings, the greatest of all gods!"

Tiberius told his chief counselor to go and take a bounding leap into the Tiber. Sejanus chose not to heed the advice but prudently removed himself from the emperor's presence, while that one dourly resumed contemplating how to defeat his future rival.

As for Rome, she eagerly set forth on a most exciting day—an auction in the morning and races in the afternoon . . .

CHAPTER I

Within the tent Alysia stood dazed and silent, her face set in lines that gave little hint of the emotions surging beneath it. Outrage wrestled with utter disbelief. This was a nightmare from which she couldn't seem to awaken. Slow-moving scenes played over and over in her mind, shrouded in the fog of horror—her father taken away, the slave ship, the gradual realization that her life, as she had always known it, was over.

Frantic activity surrounded her as other female slaves, skilled in the arts of fashion and hairdressing, prepared these for public sale. Her clothes had been snatched away, but she stood straight and perfectly still, not cowering and crying as some of the others were. She was too dazed to cry, too humiliated to even acknowledge those who came and looked, whispered together, and left. From the noise that assaulted her ears there must be hundreds in the crowd outside. A man's sweating face appeared at the edge of the curtained alcove in which she stood.

"Are they ready?" he barked impatiently, a glint appearing in his eyes as he thought of the hefty profit he would make this day. Some of these women possessed beauty and grace; others had a look that bespoke of a lifetime of hard work and discipline. Each, in her own way, would serve her master well.

"Almost," replied one of the hired women, glancing up in frustration. "You haven't told us, Felix, which ones to send out for the private sale."

The slave merchant, bald and wearing a dull white toga, stepped into the alcove. His gaze roamed over the naked bodies, then he pointed at Alysia. "That one. The red gown."

Someone thrust a freshly laundered garment into her arms. Alysia hurriedly put it on. Its cut was close and clinging, with the left side drawn up and draped over her shoulder, leaving the other shoulder bare. Another woman stepped forward and rubbed rouge onto her face and lips, then arranged her long, softly curling black hair to sweep over the bare shoulder.

"Follow that slave in the gray tunic," the woman said, giving her a slight push. Alysia and two other women were ushered through a rear opening and guided through a maze of tents to a huge, canopy-covered platform surrounded by a high, wooden wall. On the platform, separated from the spectators by a heavy curtain, stood a dozen or so women ranging from about twelve to twenty years of age. Even the private auction, open only to the wealthiest citizens, would be held outdoors today because of the fine weather and the unusually large number of potential buyers.

Alysia had thought, in those first unbelievable days, that she must be in the grip of some strange and powerful hallucination. Could it have been only a month ago she'd been in Athens, in her own home—spacious and comfortable, filled with fine furniture, employing half a dozen loyal and indulged servants? She couldn't remember now what she'd been doing when the soldiers came to the door, speaking in a crude mixture of Latin and Greek that she could barely understand. Her father had joined her. She heard the word *treason* and gradually began to understand they were accusing her father, a physician, of aiding a wounded revolutionary. He did not deny it and had gone with them quietly, saying to his daughter with dignity and ominous finality, "The gods have mercy on you, my child."

Bewildered, Alysia followed him to the door, calling after him. Two more soldiers appeared and dragged her outside, thrusting her ruthlessly into a horse-drawn wagon covered with wood siding, a leather roof, and with a tiny window that allowed for ventilation. What happened to her father, she did not know, nor what became of her house and belongings. Probably the entire estate was sold and the money placed in the imperial treasury, a treasury now bloated with the assets of "traitors."

The short, bumpy ride ended at the harbor, where a Roman ship rocked and creaked upon the swells of the Aegean Sea. Two brawny arms lowered her into the dark hold of the ship, where thin rays of light showed through the planking above her head. She was not alone. The compartment reeked of close-packed bodies, human waste, and the results of violent seasickness.

Even then she couldn't believe it. A mistake had been made, and soon some official would appear to claim her and to beg her pardon. She could *not* be on a stinking slave ship bound for Rome with these—these criminals! She was the only child of the most sought-after physician in Athens. She had done nothing wrong!

By the time the ship made port at Ostia she was half-starved and covered with filth. Stunned and blinking in the sunlight, the slaves were herded out from the bowels of the ship and transported in wagons to a building somewhere in the depths of the city. For days they were fed and groomed for the sale. The same wagons took them to the forum where a long row of gaudily colored tents had been hastily assembled. Alysia had wished for a storm, or an earthquake, or some other catastrophic event . . . but the sun rose on Friday as surely as it had risen since time began.

After she and the other two women had climbed the steps of the platform to join the others, a small, wiry man came forward and directed the new slaves to form into a line. A man waited for them with a bucketful of white chalk that he poured over their feet, marking them as imported goods ready to be sold. Beyond the curtain, the slave merchant's voice rumbled out the attributes of the first young woman, whose pallid face, sweating brow, and shaking limbs were much at variance with the smiling confidence of the merchant.

"From Sparta comes this pretty damsel! An innkeeper's daughter, she knows well the art of serving . . ."

Alysia heard men's voices calling out bids; a drunken voice demanded a closer view. Someone behind her gibbered a hasty prayer to the gods. Another young girl was wailing over the loss of her amulet. Alysia heard a distinct slap and the girl was silent. She had never believed in amulets or charms, and she no longer believed in the gods—for she had beseeched them to save her and they had not listened.

"This is a dream," she told herself, closing her eyes for a moment. "I will wake up and it will have been—just a dream."

Someone shoved her forward into stabbing sunlight. Realizing she was on the verge of exhibiting the same, quivering dread shown by the innkeeper's daughter, she took a deep breath and held it for a moment. A strange sensation overtook her, as if her mind were leaving her body in a desperate attempt to cope with something that could not be borne. Her eyes gradually grew accustomed to the brightness of the area before her. The front of the platform stood directly in front of a massive stone building so that no one could view the sale but those prosperous-looking Romans within the ground-level enclosure.

"A beauty from Athens," Felix called loudly, consulting a roll of papyrus he held in his hands. "A virgin, cultured and educated in all the womanly virtues, what will you bid for this daughter of a Greek physician? No ordinary physician, but one of great learning and repute!"

Voices belonging to faceless bodies answered—raucous and eager voices, others stern and dispassionate. Alysia felt something touch her leg and looked down from the platform to see a man fumbling at the hem of her gown. She shook herself from her strange lethargy and tried to pull away. The cloth parted with a loud ripping sound. The man gave a high-pitched chortle and grabbed the gown again, deliberately tearing it to above her knee.

Without thinking, Alysia placed one bare foot against the man's head and sent him toppling backward, leaving the white print of her foot upon his forehead. His comrades surrounded him, trying to hold him up, some stifling their laughter and some guffawing unashamedly. Other, more sedate-looking men, merely frowned at the spectacle.

The slave merchant came toward her in a fury. "You fool! He is the son of a senator!" He drew back his hand to strike her.

A commanding voice called out over the laughter: "CEASE!"

The man whirled, his hand upraised. A Roman soldier had approached the side of the platform, just outside the wooden barrier. He sat tall upon a magnificent dark gray horse, his tawny hair ruffled with the breeze. He returned Alysia's defiant stare with indifference, then fixed his eyes on the merchant.

"Since when, Felix, have you felt the need to beat your slaves into submission?"

"Legate!" Felix began to sputter. "You do not understand! She has assaulted the son of Senator Eustacius!"

The soldier regarded the wronged party with an expression of wry amusement mixed with contempt. The man rocked dizzily back and forth and seemed to have trouble focusing his eyes, much to the entertainment of his comrades, who howled with laughter and clapped him heartily on the back.

"I doubt that our friend Magnus will remember the incident by nightfall," the legate said smoothly. He spoke suddenly to Alysia. "What is your name?"

The very sight of his uniform was enough to curdle her blood with rage! For a moment she wished she could hurl some insult at him as well, but she had no doubt Felix would strike her to the ground if she did so. She lifted her chin and murmured her name.

"What did you say?" he persisted, speaking in perfect Greek.

She tightened her jaw and repeated it, loud and clear over the clamor. His eyes swept over her, and he glanced at Felix. "How much?"

"The last bid was two thousand denarii, sir."

"I will give you four thousand if you will stop the bidding."

Felix, reflecting briefly that this woman meant trouble and he would do well to be rid of her at the first opportunity, promptly affected an air of obsequiousness. "Sir, would you like to take her inside one of the tents for a closer inspection?"

Alysia's stomach tightened into a hideous knot as she waited for his reply. Again the soldier's gaze swept her, and she heard him say, "That will not be necessary."

"Sold to Legate Paulus Valerius Maximus for four thousand denarii!"

"What is your age?" Again the piercing blue eyes turned to Alysia.

She had to force herself to answer him. "I am eighteen years, my lord."

"My sister is in need of a maid. She is your own age and recently lost a slave to illness. I'll send a litter for you—no doubt you are weak and not able to walk a great distance. When you arrive at the house ask for Calista, the housekeeper. Tell her that I have purchased you for my sister." He paused for a moment. "Do you understand?"

She managed a demure, "Yes, my lord," as he inscribed his name on a sheet of papyrus brought out to him by one of Felix's assistants.

He sat looking at her from the great height of his horse. He seemed to be assessing her, looking beyond her face and form into her mind, a man accustomed to learning the attributes of those beneath him. She refused to look away and knew he could see her resentment, the tears of anger in her eyes. Then he inclined his head and turned the horse, disappearing as unceremoniously as he had appeared.

Alysia was shaking as she turned to walk behind the thick curtain, relieved that this part of her ordeal was over—and yet apprehensive about what was still to come. She wondered what this man's sister would be like, for she had a feeling that *he*, at least, was a person of considerable importance.

Paulus Valerius made his way with as much patience as he could muster through the masses thronging the forum. Most people took one look at his uniform and scurried out of his way. The street was hot and smelly and he fervently wished himself elsewhere. He became aware that someone on foot had caught up with him and was keeping pace with his horse. Glancing down, he recognized an acquaintance of his, a lawyer named Tacitus.

"What have you done, Paulus?" the lawyer asked, with a knowing smile. "Too much spirit for a slave. I haven't laughed so hard since that grandnephew of Tiberius was posturing about at the theater and fell backward off the stage. You could just see his boots sticking up—gave a whole new meaning to his nickname! A pity it didn't break his—well, never mind. Tell me, Legate, how are you going to tame so wild a creature?"

"She belongs to my sister, and so I leave the discipline to her," Paulus answered lightly, though he felt a jab of uneasiness he didn't show as he considered what the slave had done. Magnus was an idiot, but his father had considerable influence. Not that Paulus' own position didn't carry as much authority—but there could still be trouble.

Tacitus seemed to follow his thoughts. "I wouldn't worry. After all, you are the city prefect." He added, still smiling, "At the moment."

Paulus' mouth quirked good-naturedly; it was a truth he'd come to terms with and was prepared to accept—for a season. The route he had traveled to arrive at his current position had not been the route of his choosing, and the story behind it was almost as complex and convoluted as the history of Rome.

It was common to begin one's career with military service, though it was usually a superficial form of service that only lasted until the man could gain a civilian position and begin to work his way up the political ladder. But Paulus actually *liked* the army. After spending a year as quaestor, during which he had many administrative duties that he found boring—not to mention constant exposure to the "give and take" practices inherent in politics, which he found reprehensible—Paulus asked permission of the Senate to be allowed to return to the army and stay there.

The Senate did not recall ever having been accosted by a man who had so little ambition as to prefer the battlefield over politics, and referred the matter to Tiberius. It so happened that, for several reasons, Tiberius held Paulus in great favor. First, Paulus' mother was a good friend of the emperor's first wife, whom Tiberius had been forced to divorce in order to make a more politically advantageous union with Augustus' daughter, Julia (who had later, in fact, been banished from Rome by her own father for gross immorality); second, Paulus' late father had been a close advisor to Augustus and an esteemed member of the Senate—things that once upon a time Tiberius had respected; and third, Paulus had once saved the emperor's life.

It happened during one of Tiberius' rare public appearances aimed to dispel rumors of his demise, before his "retirement" to Capri. Paulus had been appointed to oversee his personal bodyguards, and during the procession observed a would-be assassin aiming an arrow at the oblivious and scowling sovereign. Acting swiftly, he managed to pull Tiberius out of his sedan just as the arrow thudded deeply into the chair's back. After his initial fright, the emperor was overwrought with gratitude.

Paulus' request to return to the army was granted. He already had an outstanding military record, and now, to the chagrin of Aelius Sejanus, he began to exceed it.

As a junior officer in one of the African provinces he distinguished himself during a minor revolt by taking over for one of the legates, who lost control of his bowels when he saw the painted warriors whooping in savage fury toward his ill-prepared troops. The horrified commander ran into a clump of bushes and paid a heavy toll for his lack of valor when a Numidian spear impaled his brain. The other officers were shouting in helpless terror when Paulus rallied the men and succeeded in driving the revolters back, until the general and fresh troops arrived.

He didn't know, himself, where his courage and recklessness came from—he only knew that he felt doubly alive on the battlefield, that all his senses quickened, that he could think clearly when many others could not, and that in the midst of mortal combat his sword became like an extension of his own body.

Although Aelius Sejanus expended mighty efforts to prevent it, Paulus' successes again came to the attention of the emperor. Tiberius appointed him to the rank of legate and he was sent to quell rebellions in imperial provinces from Hispania to Palestine. His excellent use of strategy, and his firm but moderate treatment of the vanquished, earned him a reputation that any general with political ambition would give his right arm to possess.

Sejanus concluded, at this point, that Paulus must be permitted to go no further. The legate must not be advanced in rank; to do so, he told Tiberius with great solemnity, would be to invite disaster. Paulus made it no secret that he favored the Republic. If, with his immense popularity, he decided to march on Rome and overthrow the monarchy, he might actually be successful. (No doubt many members of the Senate would think that an excellent idea, but none would have the courage to say so.) Sejanus could not easily dispose of the man when he was currently in the emperor's favor—*currently*, because Tiberius did not long remain enamored of anyone. But until Paulus did something to displease him, Sejanus would have to bide his time.

He managed to convince Tiberius that the legate should be kept in Rome where Sejanus could watch him. Tiberius saw the wisdom of this but wanted Paulus to be able to choose his new position and offered him everything from second prefect of the Praetorian Guard to the governing of a nearby province. Paulus refused them all and asserted as tactfully as he could that he did not wish to be involved in politics, wondering if and when Tiberius would lose patience and either force some position on him or chop off his head.

At last, Tiberius decided to make him prefect of engineers. Paulus had studied engineering before his marriage. His immediate improvements to the roads and bridges, as well as some inventive planning that eased the congestion on the Tiber River, infuriated Sejanus. He hinted to the emperor that Paulus was opening a way for rebel factions to get inside Rome.

Tiberius scoffed at the idea, but after a few months of brooding on the matter, allowed Sejanus to remove him from the office. "Put him over the police and fire brigades," Tiberius ordered glumly. "Temporarily, of course. He ranks too high for it to be a permanent position. That will keep him too busy to think about anything else."

"But the city prefect—" Sejanus began.

"Has enough to do without the police brigade!"

"Well, at least it will keep him in Rome," Sejanus replied. "No traveling about looking for opportunities to oppose you, Caesar."

"As you say," Tiberius grumbled. "And I hope that is all I will hear from you about Paulus Valerius Maximus." He said the full name slyly because he knew Paulus' nickname, meaning *greatest*, irritated his chief counselor; indeed, the army always referred to the legate as "Maximus."

Sejanus was quiet, until the crime rate dropped significantly and there was order even in the poorest and most dangerous sections of the city. The number of fires dropped as well. He waited until he knew Tiberius had one of his severe headaches and would be less likely to argue.

"Caesar, the legate Paulus Valerius must be removed from his appointment. There are over four thousand men now in the police brigade. My spies say he meets with them regularly and has an unusual control over them."

But Sejanus had misjudged the emperor's mood.

"Of course he meets with them, idiot! He is their commander. In fact, I want you to make him prefect of the city. I know he didn't want that position, but there are some things that need fixing!"

Sejanus was horror-struck. "Sir, he will not accept such a political—"

"I am telling you for the last time to hold your tongue or I will take great pleasure in pulling it out with my garden shears. I have never had any reason to suspect Paulus Valerius of any misdoing! He saved my life and has served Rome well. You are jealous of him, Aelius Sejanus. You should be. If he were more a cutthroat, I would give him your position. I fear he is too honest to be of much use to me."

Sejanus fumed but did as he was told. Paulus then had oversight of not only the police and fire brigades, but stores, banks, theaters, and even some authority over the courts. He didn't like his new appointment; it involved too much intercourse with politicians. Sejanus' schemes had amused him for a while, but now Paulus was ready to return to his legion. Even though Tiberius had allowed him to retain his position and he still wore the uniform of a legate, it wasn't the same as being in the field—and away from Rome. Someday, soon, he would have a talk with the emperor.

"But as I was saying," Tacitus went on, squinting up at the legate, "your stepbrother will no doubt have something to say about this slave's assault on Magnus. You know, I suppose, that they are close friends."

"Lucius' friendships are no concern of mine," Paulus said, becoming impatient with the conversation. "The girl will be disciplined for what she did to Magnus Eustacius. Although, I am tempted to reward her."

Paulus stopped his horse for a moment and looked straight at the lawyer. "You can pass that around in your circles, Tacitus. I won't hear any complaints on the matter. Good day to you."

Tacitus watched as the legate urged his horse forward and noticed how a passing group of soldiers stopped to salute and respectfully wait for him to pass. The lawyer hitched up his toga and had a fleeting thought that, for whatever reason Sejanus feared Paulus and kept moving him about like a pawn in some sort of game, it was probably wise to do so.

CHAPTER II

Even had she managed to concoct some plan of escape, it would have been impossible under the steely gaze of the two muscular men who carried the heavily curtained litter. They wore tunics rather than uniforms; Alysia didn't know if they were soldiers, or part of the police brigade, or even slaves. Within, she sat on a hard cushion and braced herself against the constant jostling. It grew hot, and finally she pushed back a corner of the curtain. A welcome breeze rushed in to cool her, swirling her gown and hair.

It seemed to take a long time. She heard the sounds of people rushing past, women talking, men yelling, dogs barking, the slap of sandaled feet against the fitted stones of the pavement—all the noise of city traffic. She could tell when they began ascending a hill. Peeking past the curtain she saw a long, tree-lined road, at the end of which stood a large house of brick and stucco with a red-tiled roof.

She felt the men lower the litter roughly to the ground. The curtain opened but no one extended a hand to help her. Alysia got stiffly to her feet and glared at the men, but they only stared stoically back at her. Not wanting them to see how anxious she was, she didn't hesitate but made her way to the stone steps and pillars of the portico. She was about to knock on the door when it opened unexpectedly. A man looked down at her in surprise, tall and swarthy with curly black hair and dark eyes that, in spite of his surprise, managed to convey a look of perpetual boredom.

As he noticed her attire, one eyebrow went up and a subtle smirk touched his handsome mouth. "What have we here?" he drawled, his eyes lazily taking in everything from her bare, chalk-whitened feet to her wind-tossed hair. She stood uncertainly and wondered how she was to address him, noticing that he wore the uniform of a military tribune.

"I have just been purchased by the legate for his sister. I am to see Calista."

"Ah," he said, without moving. "The new slave. Slaves use the side entrance."

She raised her chin and was about to turn when he gave a low laugh. "Wait. Just this once, we shall make an exception."

Still, he made no move to allow her to pass. Did he expect her to squeeze past him? Well, he could stand there staring all day as far as she was concerned! In fact, she would rather seek the other entrance, and was about to do so when a horse trotted up the drive. She turned to see the legate dismount easily, handing the reins to a slave. Alysia sensed the man next to her stiffen and draw back.

"Hello, Paulus. I suppose you've come to look over your new—acquisition."

The legate replied with a chill in his voice that did not escape Alysia. "I've come to instruct Calista about the disposition of the slave before Selena returns tomorrow."

His words stabbed like a knife as the realization struck her that these men did not regard her as a person, but as a piece of property. She was "the acquisition." She was "the slave." They talked about her as if she weren't there, as if she were a dumb animal!

"I'm glad you're here, Lucius," the legate was saying. "You can tell Magnus Eustacius to keep his head. She's my sister's property and he would do well to stay away."

"What has Magnus to do with her?" the dark man asked.

"You will know soon enough. I don't anticipate any trouble from old man Eustacius, but Magnus is a fool. Come with me, Alysia."

Lucius was forced to step back as Paulus went through the doorway, leaving Alysia no choice but to follow him. "I suppose you mean an altercation of some sort. If she has insulted Magnus, the slave will have to answer for it," he said, all traces of civility wiped from his face. "If you won't see to it, Paulus—I will."

The legate turned to look at the other man. Alysia stood between them, and in the pause that followed, knew that something passed between the two men, something ugly and almost frightening. Then Paulus gave a slight shrug and said, "I won't tell you how to be a good tribune, Lucius—and don't tell me how to be a good master."

The scene froze for a moment, and then broke apart as the legate gestured for her to follow him. She tossed a glance over her shoulder at the scowling man as she hurried forward, and wondered at the look of unconcealed hatred on his face.

"You're pale," the legate said unexpectedly. "Are you unwell?"

Alysia could only marvel that he would ask such a question. He must have some idea of what she had experienced in the past weeks, and yet he thought it strange that she didn't look well! It was on the edge of her tongue to give him some sarcastic reply—although she *did* feel tired, and ill. But she would die before saying so.

"I am perfectly well," she answered, refusing to look at him.

He paused and then continued leading the way through the door into a short hall, his footsteps ringing on the mosaic-tiled floor. The interior of the house was dim and cool. They entered the large atrium, its walls covered in frescoes and extending to a great height. Marble columns supported the roof, and its open center poured sunlight into the brightly colored, rectangular pool below. An artfully draped statue bent over the pool, holding a marble vase. Grecian urns and large potted plants reposing on ornate pedestals occupied every corner, except the one with a little table bearing images of the household gods. Chairs of citrus wood, tables inlaid with ivory, alcoves from which peered statues and busts, all filled her vision in the moments it took to follow the legate across the atrium.

Other rooms were visible from here as well. All the curtains and latticed doors had been thrown open to allow the cooled air from the atrium to circulate throughout the house. From a turn of the passageway a petite, elegantly clad woman ambled toward them. Her stola flowed about her, accented by the brilliant jewels adorning her neck, wrists, and ears. Her blonde hair was arranged with three rows of braids at the crown of her head, with the rest braided and piled on top, and it too was interspersed with jewels.

"Paulus, dear!" she exclaimed.

"Hello, Mother." The legate bent to kiss the woman on the cheek.

Antonia Pulchra smiled at him with affection, and then glanced at Alysia, cutting her eyes back toward her son with a raised eyebrow. "Who is that?"

"Her name is Alysia. She's Selena's new handmaid."

"Did you get her? Where is she from?"

He answered his mother's questions while Alysia stood motionless, forgetting to feel resentful, as a strange, unpleasant sensation of warmth began to spread over her body. Her head felt as though it were spinning, and she took a deep breath. She hadn't been able to eat much that morning, in spite of the fact that she'd been ravenously hungry for weeks.

Antonia looked sideways at the slave, privately judging her too thin and pale, though most slaves looked like that when they first arrived. But her eyes were exquisite, blue-violet in color and almost startling against the blackness of her hair. The girl's face wouldn't be considered perfect by Roman standards, for it was elliptical in shape and her features were slim and finely molded. Round and plump faces were the favored look these days. And generous noses were preferred over slim ones.

Antonia was nothing if not a woman of fashion. Since it wasn't fashionable to remain unmarried, she had acquired her third husband, Decius Aquilinus, who had lost his own wife when a drunken slave drove her coach over a cliff. Paulus' father had died while giving a particularly heated address in the Senate, and Antonia's second husband had languished with a lung ailment before descending to the river Styx.

She'd also acquired a stepson whom she did not like; he was a tribune and spent his days idling about and doing the gods knew what. She only knew he made much of his title and did little, if anything, to earn it. He'd been appointed by Sejanus and served in some sort of administrative role; oh, dear, everything was so irregular these days!

Paulus and Lucius had both been sixteen years old when she married Decius; they even shared the same birthday, which she had, at the time, considered a good omen. She had been wrong. The two young men had instantly disliked each other, and as the years passed Lucius became more and more antagonistic. Paulus, in turn, didn't bother to hide his contempt for his stepbrother.

Staff tribunes often had little or no military experience but loved to strut about and give orders to their subordinates. Lucius was no exception; he wore the uniform of the military tribune and appeared to have some authority, also bestowed upon him by Sejanus, but it was ambiguous in nature and no one seemed to know how far it extended. Lucius contented himself by keeping the lower-ranking officers running hither and yon on various errands, and he created an illusion of being much more experienced than he actually was; in reality, he had never been near a battle, nor made any study of military tactics or maneuvers. He was, however, highly skilled in the use of a sword—something he proved often in mock exhibitions of swordplay in the gladiatorial training arena.

Lucius' relationship with Antonia's daughter, Selena, fared little better, for Selena bestowed no cordiality upon anyone who failed to admire her brother. Their conversations often escalated from idle talk to Selena's outrage and Lucius' vast amusement. It was an unhappy situation, to be sure, but Antonia had no idea what to do about it. She had simply shrugged mentally, turned her attention to her prize-winning gardens and frequent parties, and prayed to the gods to keep them all from killing each other.

Alysia knew the older woman was scrutinizing her, but she suddenly felt too sick to care. Without warning the room seemed to darken, and the floor dropped away. The legate turned as she began to fall and instinctively reached out to catch her. Through the fog of semi-consciousness she heard the woman say, "Don't touch her, Paulus—I hope she isn't sickly . . ."

She was floating, the walls were gliding past her and the legate's hard leather cuirass was pressing uncomfortably into her side. Her arms dangled awkwardly but she refused to raise them to his shoulders. He didn't look at her; he seemed almost angry about something. He easily climbed a short set of stairs, entered another room, and lowered her onto a couch. She scrambled up and tried to get to her feet, but again the world seemed to reel and she stood swaying as he grabbed her and set her down again.

"I'm not going to hurt you," he said impatiently. "Be still."

Her eyes fell upon the knotted red sash that hung down the center of the breastplate; she stared at it as if hypnotized. She had no idea what to expect now . . . or what was expected of her.

"Master Paulus, your mother said you have need of me."

A plump, elderly woman with tight curls all over her head stood in the doorway. She looked at Alysia and then moved toward her, clucking like a hen. "Oh, but that gown, my dear! We shall have to get you some clothes. The other maid's things won't fit you at all. She was much heavier in the—"

"Calista, may I have a word with you?"

The legate walked back to the door. Alysia's eyes flitted over the room, noting the fine, colored panels of the walls, the rich wood of the chests, the bed with its linen covering, and the shadowed antechamber that would no doubt be hers. She sank back against the cushions of the couch, still half-believing this was a dream. Here she sat, in a strange land, in a strange house, no longer a person but the property of Romans.

Romans had taken her father. Romans had destroyed her life.

Calista scurried toward the legate, and though he spoke in low tones, Alysia could hear everything he said. His words didn't leave her with any great feeling of reassurance.

"Give her something to eat. Let her rest until tomorrow." He hesitated, and his eyes went over her thoughtfully. "Above all, see that she is kept away from my stepbrother, and his friends."

She woke abruptly, alarmed by the quiet solitude in the room. She wasn't accustomed to quiet. She climbed out of the narrow bed and stood blinking in the tiny, almost dark room. Now she remembered; she'd eaten what Calista had brought her—bread and some kind of fish soup—and then she had lay down on the bed in the little room and fallen into a profound sleep.

Alysia peeked into the adjoining bedroom. No one was there. She moved lightly to the window and threw open the latticed shutters.

The late morning sun slanted through the window and she leaned far over the sill to take in the view. Because the house topped a steep hill, she thought she must be able to see half the city. Markets, temples, the red tile roofs of other mansions, aqueducts, trees, and paved roads spread in all directions below. Looking toward her right, she could see the glint of the Tiber River and the hills beyond. A narrow road, apparently for private use, ran almost directly beneath the window and appeared to connect with another house some distance away.

Rome wasn't at all like Athens, she decided. Athens was a peaceful place, tranquil, lost in its memories of days gone by. There, the agora was a place where men who had nothing better to do gathered to discuss the exploits of Pericles, the philosophies of Plato, Socrates, Aristotle. She had been to Corinth once, and it was like Rome—all noise and activity, overpopulated and abused.

She stretched and was about to move away when she heard the clip-clop of a horse's hooves on pavement. Looking downward, she saw the legate in full uniform, a dark red tunic, over which he wore the leather kilt and cuirass. She'd always thought men of high rank wore white tunics with purple borders, but he seemed to prefer the crimson. His hair shone in the sun, a light, tawny brown with pale streaks from much time spent outdoors. It was somewhat longer than the current fashion of close-cropped curls and was straight with a natural fullness.

The sleek horse and the man moved with rhythmic precision, somehow conveying an air of mutual respect between the two. There was, she thought reluctantly, something of the strength and grace of the man that reminded her of an animal. Once, in one of the agoras of Athens, she'd seen a captured lion on display. The beast had awed her in its magnificence, its sheer power. The Roman, too, was strong and agile and proud. She remembered how he had carried her as effortlessly as if she were a child. No doubt he was as fierce and deadly as a lion; no doubt he had killed many men.

He spoke cheerfully to someone on the grounds and glanced up at the window as he passed, as though he could feel her watching him. Their eyes met. She made herself look away and retreated slowly until the diminishing hoof beats told her he was out of sight. She felt her heart beating hard with anger and resentment.

"My brother is very handsome, is he not?" A proud, feminine voice spoke from behind her.

Startled, Alysia whirled and stared at the voice's owner. She was a young woman of her own age, of the same tall stature and slender form. She had golden hair piled atop her head, woven into intricate curls and gaily decorated with ribbons to match the pale rose and cream gown she wore. Large, dark eyes regarded her solemnly, but in their depths something much like mischief sparkled.

"I am Selena. My real name is Valeria, of course, but no one ever calls me that." The girl moved with liquid ease further back into the room, as if expecting her slave to follow. "And you are Alysia. The name suits you. I don't expect I'll change it."

Alysia remained where she stood, her eyes on the floor. Change her name, indeed!

"I allowed you to sleep late because my brother said you were ill yesterday. You are feeling better, I hope?"

"Yes." Alysia struggled with a wave of rebellious thoughts. She was accustomed to servants doing her own bidding, and now she must take orders from this girl, this *Roman*!

"I have arranged for you to—" Selena paused delicately, "bathe. I shall go through some of my old clothes and select some for you. I don't like my slaves going around in dark colors. I'm sure they'll fit you. My other maid—the one who died—was much shorter of stature."

Alysia was silent. She certainly did not owe these Romans her thanks! Selena seemed unperturbed by her lack of gratitude.

"Tell me, what sort of things do you do?"

Alysia looked puzzled. "What do you mean?"

"Do you sing, dance? Tell stories?" Again, mischief sparkled in the dark brown eyes. "What can you do to entertain me?"

"My father, before he was murdered, was a man of means. His daughter was not versed in the art of entertaining. If you think I am going to amuse you, you'd best send me out to work in the fields."

"Oh, but you do amuse me!" Selena seemed to restrain herself from a burst of laughter. "And believe me, you wouldn't be happy working in the fields."

"As happy, I'm sure, as I will be serving you."

The young woman gazed at her for a moment, the hint of laughter disappearing. "You may address me as 'lady.' I'll leave you alone now. Calista has brought you a light breakfast. I'll send someone in with a tub and water." As she was leaving, she said over her shoulder, "We will discuss your duties later."

Alysia ate the bread and cheese, drank the water lightly laced with wine, and did feel a little better. The bronze tub was brought in and filled with water by two youths. A sour-looking young woman left a linen towel and a pile of clothes on a table. She looked as though she'd been sucking lemons. Alysia wondered if *she* looked that way too.

Hastily she stripped off the torn red gown and stepped into the water. Though she had been vigorously washed by the women preparing her for the auction, she scrubbed again at her sore skin as if she might erase every trace of the slave ship. She washed her hair, pouring clean water over it from a pitcher. When she had dried herself with the towel, she examined the clothes. There was a sleeveless shift of an off-white color, a tunic of pale green, and an outer skirt—the Romans called it a palla—of deep sea green. A soft leather girdle bound her slender hips and there were dark green sandals that fit her narrow feet perfectly. Alysia supposed that, wearing the cast-offs of the legate's sister, she would be the best-dressed slave in the empire!

She quickly plaited her hair, allowing the waist-length braid to hang down her back. On the table where the clothes had been was Selena's mirror, a large, round bit of pottery into the center of which had been poured metal and glass. She lifted it carefully and stared at her reflection.

It was a striking face, remembered by those who beheld it. Finely sculpted cheekbones gave balance and distinction to her slender features; her eyes tilted slightly upward and were accented by curving black brows and a thick fringe of long, dark lashes. Her lips were full and well-shaped and, once upon a time, could curve into an engaging smile. Her teeth, in spite of their recent neglect, were even and white and showed no signs of imminent departure.

She felt vaguely surprised by the familiarity of her face. How could she remain unchanged, after all that had happened to her?

The door to Selena's bedroom opened. "Come, Alysia," Selena said, smiling. "There is much to teach you."

CHAPTER III

Alysia felt as if she were becoming another person. She wasn't rude by nature; she had always been civil to everyone, even to her servants. But after having the midday meal at the rear of the house with the other slaves, she discovered that she was pointedly ignoring them and didn't know why. It was as if by refusing to acknowledge them, she could somehow refuse to acknowledge that she was one of them.

The girl who had brought her clothes did not attempt to be friendly. There were two boys, who stared at her, and a female cook, unusually fresh looking and lithe of figure; it was Alysia's experience that cooks were often overweight and out of sorts. There was a silent Egyptian who she learned was the butler; he gave her a solemn nod. Others drifted in and out. They were all quiet but looked at her curiously.

Afterward, Selena came and escorted her into the library, where she received an outline of her duties in stony silence. It seemed that her sole function in life was to be Selena's shadow, attending to her every need and comfort. She must always stand straight unless given permission to sit, must never speak unless spoken to, and she must always be at the beck and call of her owner. She was to see that Selena's clothes were laundered and laid out each day; she was to help her dress; and she was to be trained in the art of hairdressing so that she might create an enviable coiffure at a moment's notice.

Now she sat listlessly as Selena slept with a volume of poetry on her chest that moved slowly up and down with her breathing. It was the Roman custom to nap in the afternoon, Selena had told her—wasn't it that way in Greece? But Alysia must not even close her eyes— "unless, of course," Selena said with a wink, "you think you can get away with it." She'd been sleeping for a long time, and before that had read for a long time. Alysia was so bored she could have chewed up the book and spit it out. That should prove very entertaining!

From far away she heard the sound of the knocker at the front door, and presently she saw the Egyptian, whose name she had learned was Omari, pass down the hallway. Selena stirred and sat up at the sound of voices.

Omari appeared in the doorway and bowed stiffly. "My lady, your sister-in-law has arrived."

Before Selena could reply, a woman fanned into the room, her scarlet gown billowing and trailing the scent of a strong perfume. Omari disappeared on silent feet.

"Megara, what a lovely surprise," Selena said, stifling a yawn.

The woman sat down, looking at Alysia without speaking. Selena followed her gaze and frowned disapprovingly. Alysia remembered she was to stand in their presence, unless given permission to do otherwise. She made a motion to rise and stopped, resentment flooding her once again. She pretended not to see Selena's glance.

"Where is Phoebe?" Selena asked quickly, as Megara delicately arranged the folds of her palla about her.

"Sick—again! I left her at home." Megara seemed disgusted by the absent Phoebe. "She's the laziest slave I've ever seen, and I may sell her to those Arabian merchants I saw in the forum today. It would serve her right, having to live in a tent and be in their—harems, or whatever you call them."

Selena giggled. Megara again cast a questioning eye in Alysia's direction, and again Selena hastened to speak. "How is Paulus? I only saw him for a moment this morning. I spent yesterday with Cornelius' family in the country."

The other woman sighed. "I wouldn't know. Probably I see less of my husband than you do."

Alysia glanced up sharply, regarding the woman with more interest. From what the legate had said yesterday, she had assumed that Lucius was his stepbrother and had mistakenly concluded that this woman must be Lucius' wife. There was something about Megara that brought Lucius to mind, a kind of alert wariness that made you feel you were not quite to be trusted. She didn't seem suited to Paulus somehow, though she was very beautiful, with red hair—probably dyed—adorned with jewels set in a tiara, and large, light brown eyes, almost topaz, which were rather cold and remote. She was slightly taller than Alysia and, she guessed, about ten years older. She had a rich, throaty voice and spoke with precise enunciation. "I see you have a replacement for—what was her name?"

"Lydia. Yes, this is Alysia. Paulus got her for me yesterday."

"Indeed?" Megara's face became very still, but something in her eyes leaped into life.

Selena said, with deliberate nonchalance, "Paulus must have been much impressed. He despises slave auctions, you know, but I begged until he gave in. I don't like to go myself, and I don't trust anyone else. I expected him to buy the first one he saw, so I could hardly believe it when I saw she was so elegant, and such a beauty."

Megara smiled. "How brotherly of him. I trust you didn't pay more than a few hundred denarii?"

"He wouldn't tell me, though I suspect it was much more than that. He gave her to me as a gift."

For a moment, the other person Alysia had become hated them both, hated them so fiercely she thought she might be sick upon the white cushions of the couch. She almost wished she *would*, just to see their horror-struck expressions. They would certainly think her elegant then!

Why am I thinking this way? she asked herself, dismayed to realize how bitter she had become in so short a time. She jumped when Selena called her name. "Alysia, go and have Nerva prepare a tray of honey cakes."

Alysia's jaw tightened. She saw the contemptuous way Megara regarded her and, for some reason, this gave her the impetus to stand and walk stiffly from the room.

Megara watched her departure. The slave did have an uncommon beauty, and it was easy to see why Paulus had been attracted to her. It was not unusual for a man to free a female slave and set her up as his mistress. The wives of such men usually shrugged and pretended not to care, many really didn't care and promptly found lovers of their own. Never mind that Augustus had once made adultery a state crime; it was an old-fashioned statute that no one paid any attention to these days.

But Megara did not intend to share Paulus with a slave. She knew he'd had a few affairs but always very discreetly and with ladies of breeding. Never let it be said that he preferred a slave to his own wife!

"She's not very pleasant," Megara said. "I shouldn't think you'd want her."

"Oh, she's still indignant about losing her station in life. But she will recover. I remember Lydia was that way for a while."

"If she's proud, she'll never make a good body-slave. You'll do well to get rid of her, and find some girl simple-minded enough not to care about a meaningless existence."

"Meaningless—oh really, Megara! We treat our slaves very well. If she's loyal she can live a very good life, and I might even free her someday."

Megara sighed again. "She's a troublemaker. I can tell by looking at her. If you change your mind, my household manager will dispose of her for you and even get you another maid."

"No, thank you. I intend to keep her, if only because Paulus went to the trouble of finding her for me. Here she comes . . ."

Alysia returned with a tray prepared by the cook and passed it to the two women. She set the tray on a table and went to stand beside Selena, not knowing where to look, and finally focused her eyes on a painting of a woman covering the opposite wall. The woman's almond-shaped black eyes stared impassively back at her.

The afternoon wore on. A trip to the theater was planned. There was a wedding to attend next week. The women discussed a chariot race to be held the following week—the chief attraction of which seemed to be one of the drivers, known for his handsome face and his skill on the track.

"I'm betting very heavily on him," Selena said. "I swear he is a Hercules, Megara, and yet he handles those horses as if they were kittens!"

"I know, and he's thoroughly conceited. I've met him."

"Oh, Megara, do give a party and invite him! I'd give anything to meet him!"

"I wouldn't have him at my table. Don't you know his parents were slaves? Decius is having a banquet day after tomorrow. Tell *him* to invite your Hercules."

"He wouldn't either." Selena frowned. "But I'll find a way. Maybe Paulus can arrange it."

"Do you think Paulus would introduce his precious sister to such a rascal? The man has a veritable stable of women."

Selena was wide-eyed with curiosity, and the conversation turned into a recital of names and places associated with the apparently tireless chariot-racer. Alysia was able to relax and listen with some interest, for her presence had been completely forgotten.

A cool, if somewhat noisome breeze drifted in from the Tiber as the day arrived for Decius' dinner party. He had enjoyed a profitable day collecting his rents, had spent a relaxing afternoon at the baths, and he was in a festive mood. Slaves had been cleaning and cooking since dawn. In the kitchen, waiting to be served course by course, were platters and silver trays of roasted pheasant, clams, mussels, assorted fruits and melons, baskets of smoking breads and dainty pastries, and pitchers of fragrant wine mixed with honey.

The Greek gardener had cut some of Antonia's tall, vigorous roses, ranging in color from almost white to garnet, and they held various posts of honor throughout the dining room in delicate blue and white vases. In a darkened corner, three hired musicians plucked their instruments in a soothing cadence. Just outside the room, Selena gave instructions to Alysia, looking rather anxious. "There will be a steward overseeing things and two boys serving the table. But Decius wants you to serve the wine."

"Why?" Alysia asked, trying not to betray her own nervousness.

"Because you are beautiful, of course, and a credit to his household. It's a simple task, but you must be vigilant."

"By that you mean that no one should have to ask for more—I should simply pour it?"

"Not only that, but before the pitchers are empty, send the boys back to get them filled. Don't go into the kitchen yourself. It's hot and you'd come back smelling of garlic and fish sauce."

They entered the dining room and Alysia took her place beside the wine table. It was a long room, edged with marble pillars, behind which were large, square panels of varying colors. The floor was tiled in black and white, and the couches were covered in some heavily padded material the color of peaches. Bronze lamps hung in chains from the ceiling and burned with perfumed oil. The two serving boys were singing softly and moving nimbly about, setting out seasonings and little bowls of water and lemon.

Two senators were already present with their wives. The men, Camillus and Laurentius, were elderly; their wives were considerably younger. Megara had arrived without her husband. Soon another man arrived, also a senator—middle-aged, overweight, his toga rumpled and his mostly bald pate edged with feathery wisps of gray hair.

Alysia began pouring wine. The fat man was drinking it as if it were water. Then Lucius arrived with another man and two women who appeared to be their wives. Lucius' wife was attractive and plump with a quick, nervous air; the other woman was plain and hardly said a word. Alysia's eyes widened when she looked again, for the second man was the very one she had kicked at the slave auction. Magnus apparently suffered from poor eyesight and failed to recognize her as he was seated, but Lucius was smirking in her direction and she felt certain he'd brought Magnus for some perverse reason of his own.

She tried to become part of the wall.

"Decius, when are you going to reveal the occasion?" demanded one of the guests, the drinking one, his huge girth pressed tight against the edge of his couch.

"No occasion, Eustacius! My genuine affection for you is the sole reason you are here tonight!"

The massive senator bellowed with laughter, as if that were quite a joke.

"Why, Father," said Magnus. "I swear the only time I see you is at other people's parties."

"Seems so, my boy, seems so!" Eustacius yelled. He, apparently, suffered from poor hearing.

After a few more inanities, Decius turned the conversation to other topics—the dwindling water supply and whether or not the rains might be plentiful this winter, and did they think the Tiber might flood in the spring? Had they seen the repairs made to a basilica near the business district? An earthquake had damaged it years ago, surely the senators remembered . . .

"Megara," said Senator Laurentius, when a brief silence fell, "I heard something about Paulus today that I hope you will speak with him about."

"Indeed?" Megara said cautiously.

"There are many who would like to see him elected consul. When we approached him about it, he only said that consuls aren't elected anymore—they're *selected*, by Sejanus and Tiberius, in that order. You know how sardonic he can be. But today there was some serious talk about it. I think that Tiberius would approve."

Megara didn't speak, but her eyes were snapping with interest.

"My son is a little young for the consulship, isn't he?" Antonia said, but she looked pleased. "He is only thirty-one."

"It might not happen for several years," answered the senator. "We merely want him to start thinking along those lines. He needs to gain more political experience, though he does have some as city prefect. Besides, age is no longer a strict requirement. Things have changed somewhat, haven't they? As his wife, Megara, perhaps you could convince him."

Megara said slowly, "My husband loves the army. I fear he would never consider leaving it—at least voluntarily."

"Of course, he could still command an army as consul. We like him in the Senate. We feel he could do a great service to Rome. Though there are those who would thwart us, Tiberius seems to hold him in favor."

"You have forgotten how my stepbrother hates politics," said Lucius boredly. "If he had his way he'd send the entire government into exile, especially you senators, and start a new one. A republic, mind you. And would probably free all the slaves too."

The legate entered the room at that moment, and since he was looking at Lucius it seemed obvious he had heard the remarks. He still wore his uniform. He apologized for his tardiness, handed his mantle to one of the serving boys, and went to an ornate table in the corner to wash his hands.

"Isn't that so, Paulus?" Lucius said, smiling coldly.

"Is it true that I hate politics? As much as I hate hypocrisy and pandering and unctuous speeches. Forgive me, Senators Laurentius and Camillus," he added dryly. "The statement is general and not directed toward you." He pointedly did not mention Senator Eustacius, who sat staring at him without comprehension.

"About the *slaves*, I mean."

Paulus wiped his hands and eyed his stepbrother with mock gravity. "There are certain aspects of slavery I find objectionable, but a mass freeing of slaves would achieve nothing but chaos. Especially since they outnumber their owners twice over."

Decius looked puzzled. "See here, Paulus, we couldn't survive without—"

"Slaves," muttered Magnus thickly, having partaken of the wine almost as liberally as his father. "And where is that vixen you bought the other day? Kicked me in the head, then before I could stand up straight she was gone."

Paulus stood perfectly still, having just noticed Magnus, for that one had been slumping over his plate and was hidden by his father's bulk. Everyone seemed to think they had misunderstood the remark. It was unfortunate that Eustacius chose that moment to demand more wine. Alysia had completely forgotten her task until he thumped his couch and bawled, "I say, more wine! Is your slave *deaf*?"

The dining room steward, a stout Thracian who had remained almost invisible all evening, suddenly froze and looked terrified. Selena grew pale and gestured at Alysia, whispering, "More wine for everyone."

Magnus giggled. "Father's beastly drunk!"

Alysia moved forward, trying to remain as unobtrusive as possible. But Magnus was peering at her, his eyes squinted, his nose wrinkled and his mouth open, and she knew with a sinking heart what he was about to say.

"That's her—by Jupiter! She kicked me in the face!"

"Alysia?" Antonia cried. "When?"

"At the sale!" Magnus hiccupped and continued, "I hope you gave her a wall—walloping, Legate!"

Alysia paused, but Selena nervously waved her on, and she began to pour the wine. Her hands shook, and as she filled Magnus' cup the wine splashed against the sides of the cup and onto Magnus' bejeweled fingers. He swore and shook them, flinging droplets across the table, then rose unsteadily from his couch and whipped his hand across her cheek.

Burning tears rushed into her eyes. Amid a chorus of horrified gasps, she tossed the entire contents of the pitcher into Magnus' face. Magnus dropped back into his seat, spluttered, and shook his head like a wet dog. He grabbed Alysia's hand in a surprisingly strong grip, twisting it until she cried out and fell across the table before him. She had a blurred glimpse of his face coming toward her, and to her disgusted amazement he pressed a wet, loathsome bite upon her throat. She clenched both her fists and was about to send them flying against his ears when he was yanked abruptly from his couch. When Magnus could focus his eyes, he saw the legate towering over him with a dark scowl on his face.

"This is my mother's house," Paulus said evenly. "It is a house of honor, and you have assaulted the property of my sister."

It was too much for Magnus. His eyes rolled in his head and he slid slowly to the floor, where he sprawled atop a pool of wine. His father had preceded him in slumber, having dropped his head into his plate immediately after demanding the refilling of his cup. His snores punctuated the music, which—after an uncertain pause—played serenely on.

Everyone stared at Paulus, who said with a heavy inflection of mock politeness, "I'll leave him now to the ministrations of those who love him." His eyes found Alysia, who had risen to a sitting position on the table. "Come with me."

Lucius began, "The slave will have to answer for—"

The legate didn't wait to hear the rest, striding from the room with Alysia reluctantly following behind. They crossed the atrium and entered one of the reception rooms at the front of the house.

Lamps set into the walls burned dimly. Paulus turned and she saw that he was angry, but she couldn't tell if his wrath was directed toward her or Magnus.

"Slaves have been killed for lesser offenses," he said. "Perhaps you have a death wish?"

"Did you think I should have stood there while that—that jackal beat me? He's not even human, he's an animal!"

"From the moment he struck you, you should have assumed complete submission. I would have stopped him from doing any further harm."

"How was I to know that? Would you stoop to defend a slave?"

"You have complicated a situation that was already—complicated."

"Through no fault of my own!"

"You should *not* have done what you did."

Alysia caught her breath and tried to speak calmly. "So I am to remain still, and do absolutely nothing, and allow myself to be abused or even killed?"

"As long as there is someone to defend you, yes. As I said before, slaves have been killed for doing less. In this household, abuse of slaves is not tolerated."

Alysia turned away from him, overwhelmed with a feeling of despair. "You don't understand how—" she began, but no more words would come. It didn't matter. She was only a piece of property to him, and he must protect his property. She said more clearly, "Maybe I do have a death wish."

"I suppose I don't understand," he said quietly. "But I cannot spend the rest of my life interceding in your behalf. Why do you inflict this misery on yourself? Why not accept what has happened? As a slave you have great value and will be treated well. If you were free, where would you go? I happen to know that you have no family left. Have you any means to support yourself?"

"Do you know what happened to my father?" she asked suddenly.

He looked into her eyes. "I only know that he's dead," he answered in a low voice. "Felix had it written in his records. I don't know—how. He was accused of treason."

"A false accusation! My father was a good and honorable man."

"Good men often die these days. I can only say I'm sorry."

She turned her back and felt his hand on her arm.

"Alysia."

When she heard him speak her name, it was almost as if he'd done something kind and intimate, and it was too much to bear. She would rather he stayed angry with her! She refused to look at him and felt his hand tighten on her arm.

"Paulus?" A voice from the doorway broke the silence.

He turned slowly. "Come in, Megara. Alysia, go to my sister. She probably thinks I've killed you by now."

"My dear husband, you did not look as if you were going to kill her," Megara said flatly, giving Alysia a cold stare as she hurried out.

Alysia paused outside the door. She was frightened now, as the folly of what she had done began to be clear to her. She could be stripped and flogged, or worse, as a lesson to all. Listening hard, she heard only a murmur of voices. Down the long hallway she could hear Magnus' wife crying and the rumble of Decius' deep voice speaking in conciliatory tones. She couldn't go back there—someone else could pour the wine, and Selena didn't need her. She went upstairs to Selena's room and entered her own tiny chamber.

She sat for a long time staring at the wall. At last she heard Selena come in, moving about and then getting into bed and growing quiet. The fact that she didn't say anything seemed far more ominous than had she flown in with screams and remonstrations.

Alysia slowly undressed and lay down on the bed. *The legate will protect me,* she thought. He was of high rank; he was prefect of the city. He took care of his property, and that of his family. Only that comforting thought allowed her to finally drift off to sleep.

CHAPTER IV

Alysia sat up, awakened by a rough hand upon her arm. She recognized two of the yard slaves crouching in the predawn light.

"What do you want?" she demanded, half-asleep and more irritated than alarmed by their presence.

"You are to come with us, by order of the legate."

"For what purpose?"

The men seemed nervous and apparently had no liking for the errand they had been set upon. "We don't know," said the older one, a small man with a dark, seamed face. "You are to make haste."

She looked from one to the other and couldn't see their expressions clearly. As her mind cleared from the fog of sleep, a vague feeling of trepidation stole over her.

"Shall I be allowed to dress?"

The slave shook his head. "The legate said to come at once."

She threw back the linens and followed the two men from the room, wearing only a white, short-sleeved nightgown. They went quietly past Selena, who didn't stir, and passed the garden room, a formal dining room with wall murals depicting various flowers and plants, and the smaller dining room where last night's disastrous supper had been held. They went through the peristyle, with its colorfully painted colonnade, its graveled pathways and flower beds lined with box and other well-trimmed shrubs. This connected with a larger version of the portico that stood at the front of the house, and outward from the portico spread a court with benches and a fish pond with a fountain in its center.

The slaves stopped. Alysia looked up. A low wall surrounded this back area of the house and, beyond it, the legate stood waiting. The sun had begun slanting over the distant hills, casting a golden glow upon his tall frame. Some distance away she could see his horse, saddled and waiting. When she saw his expression, her sense of impending doom was complete. If they had been cast in stone his features couldn't have been more cold and hard.

Wordlessly he handed a length of rope to the older slave, while the younger gently pushed her backward until she stood beneath two close-set columns of the portico. She looked at the men, puzzled, but they avoided her gaze. They took her arms and stretched them apart, tying them deftly to the slim columns on either side of her.

Alysia looked at Paulus and read her sentence in his eyes. He reached inside his tunic and withdrew a sheet of papyrus, through which a string had been drawn and tied with a knot. He walked closer to her and held it up for her to see. "Can you read this?"

The words were written in Greek: "Guilty of Disrespect."

"I hate you," she gritted through clenched teeth, her eyes filling with tears of rage and humiliation.

"You will stand here until sunset," he said calmly. "Maybe after today you will display more discretion."

He placed the papyrus over her shoulders, causing it to hang down over her torso. She closed her eyes for a moment so she wouldn't have to look at him. He was going to leave her here to swelter in the sun and suffer this indignity—she had been a fool to think he was different from any other Roman!

The other two slaves melted away into the shadows. The legate remained behind her. "Don't move," he said. She heard a sound like a knife slipping from its sheathe and felt him lift away the back of her nightgown. She couldn't have moved; she was paralyzed with fear. The cloth of her gown ripped as he slit it with his dagger.

He said, close to her ear, "It will look as though you have been lashed. Play the part well, Alysia." He strode away from her, mounted his horse, and left without a backward glance.

Alysia stood stiffly erect, too outraged to pretend to be the drooping victim of a whipping. The stone steps before her led down to the pond. The fountain splashed merrily; it was made like the head of a bearded man, or maybe a god, with water gushing from its mouth and running down different levels of bronze steps into the pond. It seemed to grin at her. A huge carp swam lazily among the water lilies; the minnows flashed back and forth, glinting in the sunlight. She watched them for a while, until the house came alive. As word of her punishment spread, almost all the slaves came out to view her shame. She stared straight ahead as if oblivious to everything and burned with mortification.

By mid-morning she had begun to sag against the rope. It bit into her flesh relentlessly, scraping it raw. Gnats began to swarm over the sores. By midday, not a thread of her gown remained dry as the heat bore down upon her. Her hair curled wetly about her face. The arch above the portico partially shaded her from the sun, but there was no relief from its heat. Every muscle in her body screamed to be relaxed; every bone seemed ready to pierce through her skin.

She had finally ceased to be the center of attention. The slaves now seemed to be avoiding the courtyard, as if not wishing to be reminded the same thing could happen to them. But when she heard Lucius' voice inside the house, something inside her shriveled; panic surged up from the pit of her stomach and flooded across her mind. Then the hatred returned, a hatred of all Romans, and the panic evaporated.

She heard footsteps cross the tessellated pavement behind her. He came around the columns and a shadow fell over her. Lifting her head, she looked directly into his eyes.

Lucius' gloating grin froze and disappeared when he saw her face filled with loathing and recognized in her eyes an obvious and barely restrained desire to kill him. Lucius had never been the recipient of such a look, especially from a woman. His eyes narrowed until they were two dark slits, and his lips curled back in a sneer.

"Good afternoon," he said mockingly. "But the fair Alysia is looking a bit bedraggled today. Perhaps you didn't sleep well. Or could it be this beautiful Italian sun does not agree with you?"

She stared at him unflinchingly, remaining silent. He stood quite close, and with her feet unbound it would be a simple maneuver to give him a swift kick in a tender spot. But he wasn't worth dying for!

He stepped quickly away as if reading her mind. "From now on, slave, you will obey commands, and if you ever insult a friend of mine, you will answer to me. I will not be so lenient with you."

She didn't answer, refusing to rise to his baiting words. He gave her a last, cold perusal and walked away. Alysia became aware for the first time that the Egyptian slave, Omari, had been standing across the portico, half-hidden behind a cypress tree. When Lucius departed, Omari also took his leave, unfolding his arms and disappearing into the depths of the house.

She forgot them both as her discomfort became acute, almost wrenching a groan from her. The moments wore on until her entire body became numb. She ceased to care about her bleeding wrists or her swollen feet or the humiliation she had endured. She felt no hate, nor anger, nor fear. Time no longer existed. She had always been tied to these columns and always would be . . .

Much later, she felt a cool hand upon her cheek. She opened her eyes and focused slowly on the Egyptian. Something cold and wet touched her lips, and she drank as swiftly as her benumbed muscles would allow. When she had drunk all the water, she looked up at the other slave.

"You will bring trouble upon yourself," she said hoarsely.

"The legate instructed me to watch over you," he answered. He loosed her bonds and she was allowed a brief respite before he tied her again and left.

Was the legate never going to come? Did he intend for her to die as a lesson to all rebellious slaves? Well, she wouldn't do it! She was going to live, and she was going to make certain he was sorry he had ever done this to her. Let the dull-witted Romans tie her up to bake in the sun. She was no puny weakling and the blood of Greek warriors flowed in her veins!

Her head drooped forward again as evening approached. The frogs and insects began such a clamor of croaking and chirping that she couldn't hear anything else. The moonlight gave the white stone of the portico an eerie cast.

At last, she collapsed against the rope and felt it dig afresh into her wrists. She hung there, half-fainting, until a strong arm came around her waist, supporting her as the rope was cut. She fell into someone's arms, and she didn't have to open her eyes to know it was the legate. He carried her across the courtyard and into a place that smelled of hay and horses. She felt herself being lowered onto a pile of straw. The relief at being able to lie down was so great she felt tears begin to slide down her face.

Only half-conscious, she realized he was rubbing salve on her bleeding wrists, and he helped her drink water from a tall cup. She must be delirious! Surely none of this was real. As soon as her head touched the straw again, everything went black and she knew no more . . .

Alysia opened her eyes, aware of unfamiliar sounds and smells. A horse whinnied somewhere near.

Name of the gods, she thought, staring at the sunlight through the wooden rafters over her head, *what am I doing in the stable?*

Then the blurred images crowded back into her memory. She moaned and attempted to sit up. Her body felt as heavy as a wagon-load of bricks. Cautiously she tried turning her head and saw a water pitcher where the legate had left it. She reached for it and drank thirstily, not even using the cup.

So last night hadn't been a dream. Odd that she could feel no hatred for him now. All she felt were intense humiliation and a bitter sense of injustice. Magnus, who had been the cause of the whole sorry business, went on his merry way, whereas she—being innocent of any crime—was made to suffer what should have been his punishment!

Footsteps sounded outside the stable door and quickly she closed her eyes, feigning sleep. Someone knelt beside her for a moment, and then an arm slipped beneath her shoulders and another beneath her knees, lifting her. Immediately she came to life, pummeling the arms that held her and writhing from their grasp. She looked up into the legate's sea-colored eyes.

"You jackass!" she cried before she thought, but he looked more amused than affronted. She knelt on the straw, glaring at him, her nightgown askew and her hair wildly tangled. Unexpectedly, he sat down on a stool next to her.

"Maybe you would have preferred a flogging," he said conversationally. "Tell me, have you ever seen a Roman flagellum? I thought not. It's made up of a number of straps, each of which are weighted with bits of lead and bone. It can tear a man's back to ribbons in less time than it takes to tie the laces of a shoe."

She said nothing and he cocked an eyebrow at her. "Or you could have been banished to one of Decius' farms, where you could grind at the mill all day. Perhaps you would have liked being branded. Or would you have preferred hanging? Maybe that would have been more dignified."

She leaped to her feet in a high rage, forgetting her stiff and sore muscles. "I should have been let alone! It was Magnus Eustacius who—"

"Magnus is a Roman citizen," he interrupted smoothly. "You are a Greek captive. A slave. You chose to commit—"

"I didn't choose anything! I simply defended myself!"

He rose and stood looking at her thoughtfully. "Alysia, heed my words. Eustacius is not without influence in the Senate, and if he decides to pursue this matter there is little I can do about it. You assaulted his son—this is punishable by death. As it is, he will hear of your punishment and maybe that will satisfy him."

Her resentment faded as she looked up at him; she felt suddenly overwhelmed by his presence. It was too quiet here in the stable, too isolated. She began to back slowly toward the door, her heart hammering against her ribs. "May I go?"

"No," he said, halting her surreptitious retreat. "I hope you have learned a very serious lesson."

She answered without hesitation, "I have learned there is no justice in the world, and I can trust no one."

"Bitterness is not becoming in one so young."

"The Romans have robbed me of my youth!"

Something passed between them, almost like a shared knowledge, but it was tenuous and slid quickly away. Paulus said slowly, "And so you will know this, Alysia—slaves have not only been killed for what you did, but all the other servants in the household were slain along with the guilty one. I don't think you want to be responsible for anyone's death, do you?"

She swallowed nervously. He added, "Also, it is customary to make the guilty one hang suspended with weights attached to his feet. As much as you may hate me for this, it could have been much worse."

"Then I shall try to be grateful that you lessened a barbarous custom on my behalf, my lord. Just as I will take comfort in the knowledge that slaves in this house are never abused. May I go?"

He paused and inclined his head. She met his eyes for one last moment and turned to leave the stable. Her entrance into the house didn't seem to be noted by anyone; the slave girl with the sour face was digging around an herb garden in the peristyle, and the two kitchen boys were quarreling. Selena wasn't in her room and Alysia wondered why she cared; surely she could expect no sympathy from her owner, who no doubt had given approval to her brother's idea of discipline.

The bronze tub was in the room, filled with water. Alysia didn't know if it was intended for her or Selena, but she was going to use it! She pulled a screen around the tub, bathed herself, dressed, didn't know what else to do, and sat waiting for Selena to come back.

"Oh, here you are." Calista bustled into the room, not meeting her eyes. Calista had been one of the few who hadn't come out and stared at her. "Master Paulus said to give you this." She set a platter on the dressing table and scampered away. Alysia looked it over; there were figs, cut-up pieces of watermelon, and a small loaf of bread. She thought about sending it back to the kitchen. But then, Lord Legate Paulus Valerius Maximus had probably left by now and would never know about her little act of defiance. And she really was very hungry.

The sun blazed down from a flat, blue-gray sky as Alysia walked briskly down the street toward the shops and markets. The heat of late summer had become almost intolerable. Decius owned a villa in the country to which his family usually escaped, but she had learned that a new wing was being added and they would have to forego its comforts this year.

The legate also owned a villa, but though Megara went for a few weeks he stayed in the city. On the few occasions she saw him, she sensed a tenseness about him, almost as if he were waiting for something to happen. The hostility she'd detected between him and his stepbrother was now a tangible thing. They had become like two preying animals—lion and panther—circling each other, each deliberating on the right moment to pounce.

She'd heard Decius and Antonia discussing in low tones the fact that Magnus' father had complained loudly in the Senate about "that slave's" behavior toward his son, but he was swiftly assured by his colleagues that the legate had severely punished the slave and that certainly ought to be enough to satisfy the senator . . . after all, Magnus had assaulted the property of the legate's sister, and that sort of behavior was not kindly looked upon in aristocratic families. Do what you liked with your own slave, but leave your neighbor's alone.

Paulus hadn't spoken to her since the day in the stable. But whenever he was in the house her stomach began to flutter, and she became so nervous she dropped everything she picked up. Although, everyone was affected by his presence; everyone's attention went to him as soon as he walked into a room with that long, military stride. Selena and Antonia were drawn to him like plants leaning toward the sun. Decius seemed to enjoy his company, even more so than his own son's; in fact, he didn't seem to like Lucius very much. All the more reason for Lucius to hate his stepbrother!

Today Selena had sent her to purchase a bundle of Chinese silk for a shawl she wanted to make. Alysia spent more time than was warranted in the shop, poring over the beautiful things she once would have purchased for herself: tinted glass figurines and exquisite linens from Alexandria, spices and perfumes from Arabia, fragrant Sicilian herbs, combs inlaid with African ivory, necklaces and bracelets from faraway India . . . luxuries she had taken for granted and, she supposed, would never be hers again.

When she left, she saw with dismay that the sun had disappeared behind a mass of leaden clouds. She hurried past the brightly colored signs of the shops, looking carefully about to make sure she wasn't lost. The first time she'd ventured into the city without Calista she'd taken a wrong turn and found herself in the *insula*, a large section of cheap, multistoried buildings so close-packed she could barely tell where one ended and another began. There were people idling about and even lying in the streets. The air stank of hot, dirty pavement and unwashed bodies.

She had hastened to retrace her path, and for days afterward she'd felt humbled as she considered that she was far better off than those poor wretches in the tenements. But in time she managed to overcome this moment of weakness. At least *they* were free to go out and earn their own living, if they chose, whereas she must ever bend to the will of another.

She reached the private, uphill road that led to her owner's house. A gusty wind began to blow, snatching at her long skirt and pulling at her hair. Loosened from its pins, it tumbled in black waves down her back. A few large drops of rain pelted her and she tucked the package into a fold of her skirt.

It seemed as if the sky opened; torrents of rain poured down and a rumble of thunder vibrated the ground beneath her feet. She began to run. Hearing swift hoof beats behind her, she stopped in exasperation so that the horseman might pass. Instead, he reined in so quickly that the animal rose on its hind legs, pawing the air. She looked up through the drenching rain and recognized the legate.

"Give me your arm!" he shouted over the downpour.

"I cannot—I'm only a slave!" she replied, unable to control the defiance in her tone.

His brows drew together and he reached down, skillfully controlling his great horse at the same time. He took the bundle from her and tucked it into a leather bag that hung from his saddle, then caught her around the waist and hoisted her roughly to sit sideways before him, his arms braced on either side of her, his hands holding the reins. He urged the horse forward at a trot. The well-trained animal moved so smoothly she hardly bounced at all, though she held tightly to the bar of the saddle at her side. Her rain-soaked bosom kept touching his arm—which was certainly intolerable—she must do something to distract his attention from it.

"May I speak?" she asked, raising her voice over the rain and intermittent bursts of thunder.

"Please do."

"Aren't you afraid of what people will say?"

He shrugged his wide shoulders negligently. "Whatever they say won't be within my hearing, I assure you."

She reflected that there was no haughtiness in the remark; it was a mere statement of fact. Unlike Lucius, she'd never known the legate to display arrogance or conceit.

She twisted her head to glance at him. "Are you so feared then, my lord?"

"If men fear me it is because they do not know me—they know only what they have heard."

"The stories of battles in faraway places, and all the crowns you've received—they're true then? Is that how you got that scar?" She nodded toward the white line that traced from the throat of his tunic to his left ear.

The rain began to slacken and Paulus lowered his voice. "Stories of battles often get greatly embellished in the telling, especially if they're told by a younger sister—and I'm assuming it was Selena? As a soldier I've had a duty to perform and have done it to the best of my ability." He paused and added, "The scar is the result of a youthful overconfidence that nearly cost me my head."

She raised her eyebrows. "If you were so successful in the army, why did you leave it?"

"I haven't left it. The emperor gave me my current appointment, but I'm still in command of my legion."

Her mouth fell open. "You've spoken with the emperor?"

"On occasion."

He must be far more important than she had realized. She didn't know anyone who had even seen, much less talked to, the reclusive Tiberius. The conversation seemed to have ended, so she searched her mind for another topic. She knew slaves weren't supposed to gabble on, but she couldn't seem to stop herself.

"I've been wondering why your sister isn't married."

"She's been betrothed since childhood to our cousin, Cornelius. He's a tribune. They plan to be married when he obtains a civilian position. It's taken him a bit longer than most, that's all." She felt him looking down at her. "And you? I assume you were betrothed as well?"

Alysia shook her head. "My father wouldn't go against my wishes, and there was no one I wanted to marry."

The rain stopped as they arrived at the stable. Paulus dismounted easily, then reached up to swing her to the wet ground as if she weighed no more than a feather.

"My thanks, Legate," she murmured and started to move past him, completely forgetting Selena's parcel. His hand on her arm detained her.

"Alysia," he said, his voice serious. "I would have a word with you."

"Yes?" In spite of herself, her breath quickened at his touch and her voice came out in a whisper.

"Selena tells me she is unhappy with your attitude, that you seem resentful and cold. She's uncomfortable. She believes that you hate her."

Alysia stiffened. "I didn't know that I was expected to love my enemies."

"She is not your enemy," he said earnestly. "She wants to be your friend, or as nearly a friend as possible, under the circumstances. She can't live with your hatred. She owns you. You could find yourself once again at the slave market."

Alysia stared at him dumbly, unable to think of a suitable retort. She couldn't believe she was being rebuked for not showing affection toward the very people who had wrecked her life!

He watched her, seeming unaware of her mounting indignation. "I can see that you won't take my words to heart," he said, then added pointedly, "but you do realize there are people who do not treat slaves well."

Suddenly, everything hit her with such force it was like a physical blow—her fear and helplessness, her sense of loss, her mixed feelings for this Roman soldier, the utter injustice of her predicament. As always, rage wiped all caution from her mind.

She kicked him, barely feeling the pain as her foot struck the iron hardness of his leg. "You dare say that to me after what you did!"

He caught her thrashing fists in his hands. "Stop, you young tigress," he commanded, struggling with her. She writhed violently, tears stinging her eyes. For this moment she didn't care if she lived or died, and now that she had let loose her wrath it refused to be stilled but poured forth as torrentially as had the rain from the sky. She stamped her foot like a bucking calf, splattering mud over both of them. He fought to restrain her, for she was strong and in her temper like a young Fury. She twisted so that he couldn't keep a grip on her, and he swore when she sank her teeth into his hand.

"Go ahead, flog me!" she cried, her body contorting to escape his binding arms. "Beat me until I'm dead, I do not care! Kill me! I want to die, you—you—" She couldn't think of a scathing enough insult. Somewhere in the back of her mind she knew she had completely lost control, but it was too late. She made a tremendous lunge, unable to move either forward or backward.

"Stop it, have you lost your senses, woman? Stop, before I—" His words were cut off as the wet skin of her arm enabled her to pull it free, and her hand laid resoundingly across his face. Without hesitation, he grabbed both her arms, pinioning them to her sides. This time he was not lax in his grip. He pulled her so close she seemed to become part of him. Then he bent his head and his lips came down hard upon her own.

A rush of hot wind swirled over them, and it was as if the wind were inside her, soaring through her nerves, touching her everywhere at once. Alysia felt the wild anger die, replaced by a new emotion, something different and yet as violent and uncontrollable. Paulus placed one hand behind her head, closing it over her streaming hair, his mouth like a fiery brand upon hers. *His slave*, she thought, somewhere in the back of her mind, somewhere small and vague and distant from the all-consuming sensations that were sweeping over her—his slave, his property.

A sudden crack of thunder shattered the stillness, and a flare of lightning briefly illuminated their merging figures. The rain began again in a steady deluge. Alysia pulled away with a gasp, and meeting his gaze for a fleeting moment, whirled to run toward the house. Paulus was upon her in an instant, his hands catching her shoulders, forcing her to look at him.

"Alysia, wait!" he shouted over the tumult of the storm, his eyes blazing.

"No! Leave me alone! I hate you! Don't ever touch me again or I will kill you, do you hear? I would rather die—I would rather rot in jail than have you touch me!"

He looked at her searchingly, and though the rain drove into his face, the intensity of his expression did not falter. Then, slowly and deliberately, his hands dropped from her shoulders. She turned and walked away from him, her head up, her shoulders straight. She entered the house through one of the side doors; she walked, dripping, through the center hall and up the stairs, into Selena's empty bedroom, and went as if in a trance to the unshuttered window.

Paulus had just mounted his horse and swung around toward his own house. Alysia watched him pause and look slowly up at her, as if he knew she would be there. Without conscious thought her hand moved to her still-pounding heart. She was struck by the gravity of his expression and wondered, with a strange detachment, what it meant.

She kept standing there long after he was gone. For the first time since her trouble began, a tear of grief rolled down her cheek, and then another, and she wept—wept for her murdered father, for the loss of her home, her freedom, and for the loss of her own will. He was a Roman soldier, he was her enemy, and yet she had lied when she said she hated him. And he had known it was a lie.

CHAPTER V

The Circus Maximus seated more than a hundred thousand people, and surely there were at least that many here, all in a hurry to procure the best seats—seats that might have to be relinquished when someone with more wealth or authority made a tardy entrance.

The colossal amphitheater nestled in a valley between two of Rome's seven hills. Shaped like an elongated circle, one end was open where chariots stood in readiness for the last spectacle of the day. The sand-covered arena was bisected by a low wall, on which hung seven bronze dolphins that would be raised up or down to indicate the number of laps the chariots had made around the track.

A wooden arcade containing dozens of small shops completely surrounded the outside of the arena; spectators had to pass through the arcade to gain access to their seats. Vendors hawked a tempting array of refreshments—water and wine, cheeses, breads, nuts. People thronged and pushed in the aisles. Common courtesy had flown away with the doves that had been released into the sapphire-blue sky a few moments ago, signifying that the festivities were about to begin.

Fascinated, Alysia gripped the sunshades, cushions, and fans she carried and looked around her. This marked the first day of a celebration in honor of the god, Jupiter. It seemed to her that Rome lived for such occasions—Selena and her friends had talked of nothing else for days. Glancing furtively here and there, she felt strangely disappointed that the legate was nowhere to be seen. She had thought he would sit with his family.

"You won't see my brother here today," Selena said, with a knowing gaze on Alysia's face. "Someone must stay and keep order in the city. Besides, he doesn't like the games. He always has someone else attend in his place."

Unwilling to admit any interest in Paulus, Alysia began to voice a protest but Selena had turned her attention elsewhere as she called to a friend, her eyes shining with excitement. Everyone seemed gripped by the same fervor, faces animated and eager, voices loud and high pitched. Over the din, Alysia could hear the roaring of the animals that would be exhibited in one of the events before the race, and an occasional wayward breeze brought reassurance of their presence somewhere behind the moat separating them from the spectators.

Selena turned to her again. "Here, leave me those fans and a parasol, and two of those cushions. You'll have to wait in the slave section. Oh, there's Cornelius—" She moved away to be embraced by a man in a tribune's uniform, and they disappeared into the crowd. Alysia looked toward the place where Selena had pointed and made her way slowly to the section reserved for those who awaited their masters.

It was only the beginning of a day of disappointments. The section was small, for most slaves were sent home. There were no seats and very little view; a wall obscured all but a corner of the arena. A religious procession honoring Jupiter was first on the agenda, and this she missed completely. By the time the wrestling and boxing matches began, someone moved and she was in a better position to watch the rather indifferent performance; it was nothing like the athletic events she was accustomed to seeing in Greece. Then the animals paraded out—monkeys doing tricks, lions, zebras, elephants . . .

The longer she watched the more depressed she became, exactly the opposite mood that dominated the huge crowd, whose roar was almost deafening. The races were about to start. Alysia didn't want to witness a spectacular crash; she didn't want to see some unlucky driver get thrown from his chariot and trampled by horses or dragged around behind his own chariot, having been caught in the reins. These, according to Selena, were common occurrences and a day at the races just wouldn't be quite the same without them!

What was she doing here, waiting in the hot sun for no other purpose than to carry things for an ungrateful young woman who was perfectly capable of carrying her own fans and cushions? How utterly futile her life had become, and tiresome, and such a waste of her youth!

A feeling of desperation seized her, a darkness of spirit that set her feet suddenly moving. She took a path through the arcade and all at once found herself outside the amphitheater, crossing street after street, passing temples and great arches and forums, passing men and women whose eyes didn't even touch her. It was as though she did not exist.

She always felt pressed in, here in the center of the city, a city crowded with buildings and people, the buildings crowded with statues and huge columns. There were steps and stairways leading away in all directions. Searching for she knew not what, she went inside a basilica; it was cool and dim as she walked among the aisles of seats, her footsteps soft on the marble floor. There was a meeting of some kind at the front, and when the men turned to look at her she quickly left, encountering hawkers on the steps outside selling food to passersby.

She passed markets and taverns; she passed shops—one piled high with wicker baskets and furniture, one selling rugs, others she barely looked at. She stopped at a bakery, drawn by the aroma of rolls and cakes. She realized she was ravenous and bought a sweet bun and a fruit tart. She always had a purse with a few coins in it.

She walked until darkness fell and finally sat down on the steps of a deserted temple.

Ha! The Temple of Fortuna, goddess of luck. Fortuna had not been kind to her. For a moment Alysia wished she believed in the gods so she might curse them.

In the past weeks the idea of escape, however vague, had lurked reassuringly in her mind. Someday, she'd thought, someday she would run away and start her life over again. But now that she'd taken that first step she had come to a dead end, banishing whatever hope the thought of escape had held for her. She didn't know where to go. There *was* nowhere to go. How was she to leave Rome? How would she support herself?

She looked up at the moon, half obscured by clouds. *I've been a fool*, she thought, with a mild sense of surprise and self-reproach. *All this time I've been thinking this was a mistake—that someone would see it was a mistake, and rescue me. I've thought I could get away with things because of who I am, or was. But no one is going to rescue me. This is forever. I am a slave.*

It seemed remarkable that people kept passing by without even a glance at her when she had reached such a crucial moment, such a dreadful precipice in her mind that one more step would surely send her into a pit of darkness from which there was no return. For a moment she wavered there, half-wishing she would fall into that pit. But something stopped her, causing her to step back and turn her mind's eye first to the past, then to the future.

Her life, as she had known it, was over. Everything dear and familiar to her had been erased in that single moment when Roman soldiers thrust open the door of her father's house. Now she was someone else, someone who was not able to come and go as she liked, who was not free to say what she felt, whose future comfort was no longer assured. Long years of lonely servitude loomed before her.

She said aloud, "I've been an arrogant, stupid fool."

Not only had she refused to accept her condition, she'd been deliberately rude to everyone, even her fellow slaves, because she was the victim of injustice and wanted everyone to know it. The trouble was that they *did* know it, but there was nothing anyone could do about it—even if they cared to. Clearly, she wasn't the center of anyone's world but her own.

Alysia got slowly to her feet, swept by waves of shame and remorse and hopelessness. And something like a sense of nostalgia, for things that *might* have happened, but now never would.

It must have been near midnight when she returned to the Aquilinus house. She walked softly across the outer courtyard and let herself in the side door. After crossing the atrium, she was a good distance down the corridor when she heard someone hiss, "Alysia!"

Startled, she turned and saw Selena standing within the shadows of Decius' study. Selena gestured for her to enter and she did so with an air of resignation. She'd already made up a story about feeling ill and leaving the amphitheater, then getting lost and wandering about all day.

A lamp burned on the desk and another on a large wooden stand, casting great shadows on the walls. Selena stood just inside the entrance, her brown eyes worried, her hair glowing like spun gold.

"Alysia, where have you been? I didn't dare tell anyone you'd disappeared, except Paulus. He's been out looking for you—" She stopped and turned toward the door.

Alysia waited in weary silence as they listened to the approaching footsteps. Paulus stalked into the room, his eyes searching until they found her in the gloom. He said nothing but his gaze went over her swiftly, as though the reason for her disappearance might somehow be on her person. Or maybe he was assessing her for damage, she thought cynically. After all, she had cost him four thousand denarii.

"Where have you been?" Selena asked again, perturbed by her slave's lack of response. "Alysia, I've endured much from you simply because my brother—"

Paulus came further into the room, saying, "Selena, would you leave us alone?"

His sister hesitated, then lightly touched his arm. "Yes, thank you, Paulus. Goodnight."

When she had gone, Alysia turned and looked at him warily. He moved closer, the lamplight exposing lines of worry and anger on his face. "I'm beginning to think you enjoy being punished," he said.

She could find no words and went to stand before the window, where a faint gleam of moonlight made a halo around her head. He came still nearer, so she could see the vivid blueness of his eyes. She braced herself for the question Selena had asked, but instead he said, "Why did you come back?"

For a moment she could only look at him blankly. At last she shrugged. "Because there was nowhere else to go."

He remained silent for so long that she moved and sat down in a chair opposite him, forgetting that it was improper for her to do so. A faint, gnawing fear was driving a wedge into her apathy. What was he thinking? Had he decided to get rid of her? Was he really going to punish her?

"I want to know," he said, his eyes fastened on hers, "if you meant what you said a few days ago—when you told me you never wanted me to touch you again."

Her heart did a strange little flop in her chest. "I—I meant it when I said it."

He continued to watch her with an intentness that puzzled her. "How would you like to leave this house?"

"Leave?" she repeated. "Are you going to sell me to someone else?"

"No, Alysia. The house would be yours. You would have your own clothes, your own servants. But you would belong to me." He paused. "I want to buy you back from Selena."

She stared at him. With the attraction between them that she could not deny, his meaning was all too clear. His *liberta,* his concubine!

She hid her uncertainty beneath a heavy inflection of sarcasm. "Is this indeed a request, my lord, or a command?"

His look did not waver. "I would not want to keep you against your will."

Alysia managed a brittle laugh. "You wouldn't keep me against my will, and yet I am your slave, as much as I am your sister's and everyone else's. You contradict yourself, Legate!"

He came abruptly toward her, his hand reaching out and pulling her to her feet. "We won't quarrel again over your status as slave," he said sternly. "You know what I mean. An unwilling woman, held prisoner in her own house, is not what I had in mind."

Unable to speak, she merely looked at him with her mouth half open. His ire slowly vanished. "I'll not ask you to give your answer tonight. And be certain of it when you decide. I won't punish you—in any way—if you say no, and if the answer is yes—" He stopped and said quietly, "If the answer is yes, I'll expect more from you than the obedience of a slave."

Her pale cheeks colored under his steady gaze. Sexual knowledge was not uncommon among girls her age, and in fact such things were openly discussed so she was not completely ignorant as to his expectations. It was impossible not to notice the eroticism that saturated both Roman and Greek society, for it was in every form of art, from graffiti scrawled upon walls and buildings to even household dishes. Not to mention that any time one turned almost any corner there stood a statue of a god—and the gods seldom bothered to wear clothes. Even the lamp on the desk before her had a little naked figure perched on top of it.

She knew she must speak. Her voice was soft but clear. "I—I am sorry. I've been acting like a child. I haven't been myself. Believe me, I haven't always gone about screaming and kicking people. It's only—" She stopped, thinking her words might seem like a plea for sympathy. She didn't want sympathy or pity. She wanted only to be herself again.

A flicker of surprise went over his face at her words. He put his hand on her cheek and turned up her chin so that he could look more closely into her eyes. She met his gaze soberly and, for the first time, without rancor or resentment. His hand moved from her chin and both arms went around her, pulling her close against him.

"You have suffered many things," he said quietly. "Things I cannot change, Alysia. But you can start over again. Never again as you were, but I promise you, things will be better."

His cheek was against the top of her head, and she nodded because she couldn't trust herself to speak. No one had ever held her like this, so that she felt safe and strangely comforted. She let her arms slide around his belted waist. He raised his head and she never knew what he was going to do because the comforting silence was broken by a familiar and unwelcome voice.

"What, Paulus? Another conquest?"

Alysia jumped and stumbled back into the shadows. She and Paulus turned simultaneously to see Lucius standing in the doorway, his arms crossed and a glittering smile upon his face. The wavering light upon his swarthy countenance gave him a strange, unearthly appearance, as though he'd just been conjured from the underworld.

"And the elusive Alysia at that. Quite a triumph for you, I'm sure!"

"What," Paulus said, his posture relaxed but with an unpleasant glint in his eyes, "are you doing here?"

"I've been visiting my father, if it's any of your business, and as I was leaving I heard voices, not to mention other strangely muffled sounds. And, being the stalwart soul that I am, came to investigate. For all I knew it could have been—" he paused and grinned wickedly "—a slave rebellion."

He stepped into the room and sat down casually on a chair. "But Alysia doesn't seem very inclined toward rebellion tonight, does she, Paulus?"

"What do you want, Lucius?"

"Alysia, my poor innocent." Lucius ignored his stepbrother and leaned back in the chair, laughing softly. "It really wouldn't be wise to give yourself to Paulus. He has a certain reputation with women, or haven't you heard? It's hardly one of lasting commitment. What will you do when you're as fat as Calista and he begins to look elsewhere for his pleasure? Well, I suppose you are too young to be wise."

Alysia felt her temper rising with his baiting words. She had long carried in her head a tidy speech for Lucius, and ignoring Paulus' warning look she unburdened herself of it.

"Here is a word of wisdom for *you*, Tribune," she said, her voice low but fierce, her chin held high. "You are a vain and cowardly man, accepting a title you don't deserve and doing nothing to make yourself worthy. You are envious of your stepbrother because he has earned the honor and esteem shown him. Even your own father has more respect for him than for you!"

Lucius came slowly to his feet, his face white. "You will regret, Paulus, that you have allowed this slave to speak in this manner."

Paulus took a step forward. "Take heed, Lucius. I've told you before you are never to take matters concerning Alysia into your own hands."

Lucius replied, without looking at Alysia. "Guard her well, then, and keep her from my sight. This is no idle threat. She will pay for what she has said."

"And this is no idle warning. Her master alone has the authority to punish her."

"You are not her master—yet." Lucius turned on his heel and stalked out. They heard the front door open and close with a bang.

Paulus looked at Alysia with exasperation. "I wish you hadn't made an open enemy of Lucius. He'll never forgive you for that, or forget it."

"I couldn't help it. He is insufferable!"

"You must control your temper, Alysia. This is no game of wits. He will find a way to avenge himself, mark my words."

"What can he do, when you are my protector?"

"You have too much faith in me and too little experience with a mind like his."

He seemed to think for a moment. "I'm sailing for Cyprus on a business matter tomorrow afternoon. I have a farm there. I think you'd better come with me. Even if you haven't yet made your decision."

Taken by surprise, she didn't know what to say. Instead of answering, she asked, "What about your wife?"

"She's not going. Ours was an arranged marriage, Alysia. If it were otherwise . . ." He shrugged a little and said, "I can assure you, she doesn't care."

Another moment of silence went by, and she made up her mind. *Better a mistress than a slave.* She felt strangely detached, as though this scene in a dimly lit room had merged into the dream her life had become.

"I have decided. And I will go with you to Cyprus, my lord."

"My name," he said, "is Paulus."

"Paulus," she repeated, and smiled at him. "Paulus Maximus."

He looked into her eyes and slowly returned the smile. "I'll come for you in the morning. I'll explain things to Selena."

"Yes."

"Goodnight, Alysia."

He walked past her, pausing to look quizzically into her eyes, but he didn't speak or try to touch her, and left the house. Alysia sat down abruptly, her legs weak.

What had she done? She, the pampered daughter, the proud Athenian, who had never met a man she wished to marry—to be a kept woman! Free, but not really free. It was still slavery, wasn't it, of a different kind. Slavery to a man who stirred her emotions as no one else ever had, a man she should hate and despise simply because he was a Roman. But, she reasoned, his had not been the hand that slew her father. Nor had his been the command to cause her father's slaying.

Slowly she pulled herself up to walk to her tiny room. *What will tomorrow hold?* she wondered. *Tomorrow night?* The only thing she was sure of was that she would no longer be bored.

"I don't know how you could have embarrassed me so!" Selena pouted as Alysia painstakingly combed and pinned her owner's golden hair. Despite the lessons she had received from one of the best hairdressers in the city, Alysia had not become quite proficient. Selena went on, "I waited for you, and when you never came I had to tell everyone I sent you home because you were ill. One of Cornelius' servants had to carry my things."

Alysia said nothing, increasing her owner's vexation. Her mind was on other matters. She had spent quite some time before Selena woke packing her clothes into a drawstring bag she'd found in a storage closet, and every time she heard a door open somewhere, she thought it might be Paulus. She had dressed carefully in a lavender gown, and her raven black braid fell smoothly to her hips. She didn't know that her cheeks were rosy with excitement and that her eyes shone like crystals.

"What's the matter with you?" Selena asked. "What did Paulus say to you last night?"

Alysia hesitated. "He—I—he said *he* wanted to tell you about it."

"He wants to make you his mistress, doesn't he?"

Alysia dropped a comb with a clatter and bent quickly to retrieve it. "Yes."

"Yes," Selena repeated, stretching out her arm and looking at her fingernails. "He'll find someone else for me, of course. It's just as well. I don't think you and I were going to be friends. Oh, do brush that out, Alysia, and start over."

Alysia felt a twinge of resentment, but she knew Selena was right. She had rebuffed any overtures of friendship. She wondered if she would ever be able to open herself to friendship again.

"Megara will hate you. I've never understood Megara. She doesn't care a whit for anyone but she's terribly jealous. And you are very fortunate, Alysia. Many women have desired to be in your place. Paulus has always been quite discreet—and discriminating. People talk, though. There are no secrets in Rome, not really. You will do well to remember that."

Alysia stared at her curiously. "What do you mean?"

"You have no idea what all this means, have you? You will not only be his lover but his confidant—he may tell you things that you must never repeat to others. You may get to know a large circle of people, but you cannot ever be one of them. Do you understand what I'm trying to say?"

"That I mustn't forget that I'm nothing but a freed slave?" Alysia's teeth clamped together and she slammed a drawer with unnecessary vehemence.

Selena shrugged. "Still, you are fortunate and don't seem to know it. We've given you everything—every opportunity to make something of yourself—"

"Given me everything! You have *taken* everything!" Alysia felt tears of rage stinging her eyes and she flung the brush she was holding onto the dressing table, causing Selena to jump and stare at her in astonishment. A stray tendril of blonde hair fell from the mass piled on top of her head and dangled over her face.

Alysia flounced from the room, the hot tears blinding her. Why couldn't people leave her alone and stop telling her how grateful she ought to be? Complacent in their wealth and secure in Paulus' high position, they could have no conception of what she had endured!

She ran down the hallway to the stairs, then to the portico, seeking the peaceful, symmetrical beauty of the courtyard, seeking solitude and fresh air . . . and ran directly into the presence of Lucius and Magnus.

CHAPTER VI

Both men saw her at the same time.

Having obviously just returned from some late-night revelry, Lucius lounged unsteadily against a marble bench, a large cup swinging from his hand. Magnus crouched on the ground in illustration of a ribald story and they were laughing uproariously.

With surprising dexterity Magnus leaped up and grabbed her arm, preventing her retreat. "Look who has come to greet me," he called out to Lucius. "She seems in a great hurry—I believe she's missed me!"

Alysia looked hastily behind her to see who might come to her aid, but saw only Nerva's head poking out of the kitchen. It withdrew at once.

Magnus flung her toward Lucius, who rose and caught her against his hard body and stared into her eyes with a look of hatred. He pushed her back at Magnus. Her attempts to flee were constantly thwarted, and their roughness was leaving red streaks on her arms. She tried to call for help but each push knocked the breath from her lungs.

Then Magnus' face changed; it became mean and lustful, intent on a single purpose. He tried to force her away from the courtyard and toward the stable. Alysia braced her arms against him in an attempt to hold him back, but in spite of his thin frame he was strong and agile.

Desperate, her fleeting gaze fell on Lucius' sword where he had carelessly dropped it on the pavement. At the same moment, Magnus got one leg behind her and caused her to fall to the ground. She managed to wriggle far enough away to grasp the sword, only to find it too heavy to lift from her prone position. In a slurred voice Lucius called out a warning, and when Magnus turned to glance at him Alysia pushed him away and scrambled to her feet. She lifted the sword with both hands and held it out before her.

"I'll kill you!" she cried, struggling to catch her breath. "If you don't stop, I swear I will kill you!"

Magnus laughed and lunged toward her. He must have expected her to either drop the sword or back away—when she did neither it was too late to halt the impetus with which he'd launched himself. Alysia felt a strange, grinding sensation as the blade pierced Magnus' chest and, sickened, she released it at once. The heavy end pulled downward and the sword clattered to the pavement.

Her attacker made an odd, groaning sound and slowly dropped to his knees. He swayed back and forth, then fell with a fearful thud, his head twisted to the side. "She's slain me," he said, with a look of great astonishment. His eyes became staring and empty and he did not move again.

"Now you've done it!" Lucius shouted. Somehow he'd held on to his cup during the entire spectacle and now he hurled it in fury across the courtyard. "Murderer!"

Alysia heard running footsteps and whirled, half-expecting to be killed on the spot. Paulus stood there, taking in the scene with one sweeping look: her disheveled appearance, Magnus staring upward with a fixed expression of stunned disbelief.

"Your slave killed him!" Lucius roared, but underneath his rage there was something very much like smugness. "She murdered him!"

Alysia, panting, looked up to see Paulus' cold gaze full upon her.

"This time you have gone too far," he said, in a tone that sent a shiver through her body. "Punishment is out of my hands."

He took her arm, leading her back into the house, almost lifting her with his strength. Once inside, Alysia wrenched away and faced him. "You must believe me! He was going to—"

Paulus' manner had changed abruptly. "Do you realize what you've done? They'll tear you to pieces—Lucius was a witness and he'll never let this go. You must leave Rome at once."

"Leave . . . but where . . . how—"

Pushing her swiftly toward the front of the house, he said, "The ship I chartered is waiting in port. I'll send a letter bidding them leave at once. Omari will take you to the ship."

"Please, I must explain—"

"I can guess what he was about to do. I don't blame you for killing him. Now go and get your clothes. Hurry!"

She flew down the hall and up the stairs, thankful to find that Selena had left the room—probably to complain to her mother about Alysia's behavior. She grabbed the bag she had already packed, thrust a few more things into it, and when she emerged from the room Paulus stood waiting for her, holding a purse tight with coins. He led her toward one of the side doors of the house. A horrified scream came from the courtyard, followed by Lucius' loud proclamation of Alysia's guilt. His voice drew nearer as he sought them. They heard a door opening and Selena's anxious voice questioning him.

"Here is some money," Paulus said, pressing the bag of coins into her free hand. "Find an inn and stay there. I'll come for you."

The silent Egyptian appeared and stood waiting.

"Go now. He knows where the ship is docked. It's a small ship—it sails straight from Rome rather than Ostia. Here's the letter for the captain—Omari will explain to him. I'll come as soon as this can be settled."

"They'll blame you, I can't go—" she began.

"You're as good as dead if you stay." He gave her a none-too-gentle push. "Go!"

He watched them until they had rounded the corner of the long drive and disappeared. Then he went inside to confront Lucius and to prevent him, bodily if necessary, from following.

The shores of Italy were miles behind them and the island of Crete had been sighted. Alysia sat alone in the cramped cabin reserved for Paulus, her thoughts going round and round as if they were horses on a track from which there was no exit. In all her exhausted reasoning, she could feel no remorse for killing Magnus. It was all a blur in her mind, in spite of the fact that each moment had, at the time, held acute clarity, so that the sharpness of images and impressions had seemed to slow the very passage of time. But looking back, it was as though everything happened all at once and she only vaguely remembered it. Her concern now was for Paulus and how he was to explain the fact that his slave had killed a man and mysteriously disappeared under his very nose.

Omari had whisked her to a wharf on the Tiber in a two-passenger van he had rented in the forum, complete with a gaunt but very fast horse. He had stayed with her among the warehouses and dock workers until the captain of the ship could be found. The captain read Paulus' letter and looked Alysia over with a frown.

"This is rather unusual," he muttered. "Although this is the legate's seal."

"If you will permit me to speak," Omari said, "I am the servant of the legate's mother. This young woman is going to his estate as a guest of his mother."

"Ah." The captain's eyes took on a faint gleam. "I see." He all but snorted with what he considered a worldly understanding of the situation.

Omari seemed apologetic as he bade her good-bye, adding in his deep, accented voice, "May the gods grant you good fortune."

"Thank you, Omari," she said, almost in tears of gratitude as she boarded the ship.

She stayed to herself in the cabin, rarely venturing onto the deck. She had plenty of time to think. What would her life be like once Paulus came for her? What if he *didn't* come for her? She hadn't committed murder when he made his proposal! And if he did still want her, he'd have to keep her in hiding, wouldn't he?

Everything was different now. Even with all his authority Paulus couldn't change or deny the fact that she, a slave, had killed a Roman citizen, an aristocrat, the son of a senator. No one would care why she had done it and Lucius would no doubt lie. He could say that Alysia had deliberately and maliciously attacked Magnus while he was sitting there minding his own business!

Yes, Paulus would have to hide her away. And what would happen as she grew older and he grew tired of hiding her? Would he then desert her and find someone else? What if she had a baby? Would he welcome a child? The child would be in danger too!

What was to become of her?

Round and round, round and round . . . At first, the exit was glimpsed as from a great distance. The closer she drew to it the more she recoiled, but it was the only way off this mental track that went nowhere. She must not go to Cyprus. Even if she felt assured that their life together would be happy—which she didn't—she could not put Paulus in danger. And if he were found with her, the authorities would know that he had helped her escape.

She thought, with a strange sadness, that any relationship they might have had was doomed from the beginning. She hated Rome; he was a Roman. He was an aristocrat; she was a slave. His feelings for her were based on physical desire; hers were . . . what? She didn't understand her feelings. She only knew that they were deep and powerful and she had no control over them.

I must not go to Cyprus.

Paulus had been generous; he had given her enough money to live on for months. She would go somewhere and hire herself out as a servant, or even as a laborer in the fields. It didn't matter. Nothing really mattered, except that Paulus must never find her.

The thought of freedom should fill her with relief, shouldn't it? She should be happy that she need never see him again, need never have her heart quicken and her hands tremble in his presence. But she was neither relieved nor happy. She felt as if a large rock had settled in the pit of her stomach.

After another night spent in sleepless twisting and turning, the need for fresh air sent her onto the deck. The sea was dark and stretched far and away until somewhere, indiscernibly, it touched an equally dark sky. Black clouds boiled overhead, split by streaks of lightning and racked by reverberating peals of thunder. A strong, steady wind arose, making the whitecaps rise in the air and lap ominously against the side of the ship. Alysia clung to the wooden railing as men rushed to and fro around her, heaving ropes and shouting at one another. She looked over the side at the tumultuous waves. The wind snatched at her gown and hair, taking her breath away.

The water would do that, she thought, would take her breath away just so, and in a moment she would never have to think of Paulus again, never have to worry or think of anything again . . .

A hand clasped roughly about her arm and a voice shouted into her ear, "The legate would want you below, young woman. Come with me . . ." and she was thrust back inside the little cabin. The ship began to pitch back and forth.

She got down on her knees and held on to the cot, which some farsighted craftsman had bolted to the floor. Her bag of clothes and the pouch of coins rolled about the tiny room, but there was no sound except for the howl of the wind and the roar of the sea.

Much later, Alysia woke with her head on the bed, conscious of a strange stillness. She stumbled to the door, feeling as off-balance as if the ship still tossed wildly about. She opened the door. The sky was a queer yellowish color. She could hear two men talking quietly.

"We'll make port at Crete for repairs. I don't think the storm blew us very far off course."

"See that the repairs are done quickly."

"But the weather—"

"You heard me . . ." The voices moved and faded away.

The unscheduled stop at Crete was brief indeed, lasting just long enough to seal a few cracks and mend the mainsail. Believing the worst of the storm to be over, the captain ordered the crew to cast off again. The pale young woman who walked purposefully down the steps to the pier and disappeared, went unnoticed.

The ship bound for Cyprus never reached its destination, for the storm erupted with more fury than ever and battered the vessel until it broke apart, drowning everyone on board.

Alysia watched with rising fascination as the distant shoreline came nearer and nearer. Some miles back it had seemed a long, even curve, but now she could see the jagged indentations and stretches of smooth, sandy beach. The buildings of the city seemed to rise magically out of the sea. It was a beautiful sight, the land sloping upward to a great height and covered by rows of terraced gardens and houses. Beyond them stretched a long, blue line of hills and mountains.

"Have a care there, young woman," said the kindly old captain as she leaned over the rail. "There's man-eating fish in these waters."

She smiled at him and moved back. The two nights she had spent at Crete had rested and revived her. She could hardly believe she'd considered jumping into the sea and killing herself! She was alive and young; she had a healthy body and a full purse, and she could go anywhere she wanted to go.

But she had quickly discovered she couldn't go *anywhere*, for of the three passenger ships docked at Crete, one was bound for Rome and one for Athens. She couldn't return to Athens any more than she could return to Rome. Besides, Paulus might seek her there. The third ship was sailing for Alexandria. But there would be many Romans and Greeks in Alexandria, a city noted for its scholars and multitudes of travelers.

At last she found a merchant ship whose captain allowed people needing passage to purchase a spot on deck, as long as they had their own provisions. The ship was bound for Palestine. She knew little about that country or its people, except that they had a strict religious and moral code. That, for some reason, seemed appealing and offered a sense of security. And surely there wouldn't be many Romans in so obscure a country. After shopping for a blanket and cushions, as well as some dried meat and fruit, she bought passage and boarded the ship.

The harbor at Joppa was really no harbor; the ships had to weigh anchor some distance from land while smaller boats came out to pick up passengers and commodities. Several miles up the coast, Caesarea was the main port city with, it was said, the finest harbor in all the empire.

Alysia gathered her belongings from her station on deck and carefully climbed down the ladder to the waiting boat rowed by slaves. At last they reached the landing, and she climbed another ladder to begin her walk down a creaking pier full of rotting boards. In spite of her new optimism, she had to admit to herself that she was frightened and uncertain. But what else could she do but set her chin, propel herself forward, and see what the day would hold?

In spite of its lack of actual docks and berths for ships, Joppa was a busy port city. Its highway was the main connection for merchants and pilgrims to the larger city of Jerusalem. As she made her way down the platform, she was jostled and practically forced along by the sheer number of people hurrying to and fro.

Alysia looked back for a moment at the turquoise waters sparkling under the midday sun. Several ships drifted at anchor, their sails and masts starkly outlined against the azure sky. Maybe it was the last time she'd have this view of the sea—the Great Sea that led to Rome, and to a man she couldn't seem to put out of her mind.

Don't look back, she told herself. *Never look back.*

Again she lifted her chin and tried to decide which of the narrow, winding streets to enter. She saw rows of flat-topped adobe houses; another way led to a section where carpenters and stone masons were at work, either building or refurbishing. Joppa wasn't nearly as attractive on land as it was by sea.

Laden camels and ox-carts were moving slowly toward another road, and she reasoned that this must be the main highway. She fell in with the throngs of people going in that direction. They were, for the most part, plainly dressed, many of them barefoot. She couldn't help but feel a bit superior to these people scurrying about in this unsavory city. They didn't show much intelligence, squawking back and forth at each other in their heathen tongue. How was she going to make them understand her? She thought the whole world spoke Greek. What could she do to earn a living here?

She would just have to find a comfortable inn, if one could be found, and spend more time planning a course of action. She needed to learn something of the towns and cities of this country; she must be able to make a rational decision about where she was to live.

The marketplace opened suddenly before her, filled with people, camels, donkeys, and mules. Large bazaars shaded by awnings lined the edges of the street, and the merchants either sat with their goods surrounding them or stood behind long tables bearing samples of cloth or pottery or woodwork. The odors of food and of the mementoes left by the beasts of burden filled her nostrils, and loud voices, creaking wagons, and assorted clankings and rattlings created a din of confusion.

She made her way cautiously through the crowd, not noticing a small boy who followed her closely. She caught a glimpse of him when she dropped her bag and bent at once to pick it up, but thought nothing of the fact that he seemed to be watching her. She walked on, and a moment later heard a man's voice speaking in Greek. When she turned, surprised, she saw the boy again. The instant their eyes met the boy lunged forward, jerked the linen bag out of her hand and darted away, disappearing into the morass of people and animals.

"Stop!" she cried, beginning to run after him. At once the tall, muscular man who had spoken in Greek caught her arm and said, "Wait, I will catch him."

Alysia hesitated. The man pushed his way into the crowd. She would never have been able to do that and she'd already lost sight of the boy. The man's companion waited beside her with a reassuring nod. People jostled past them and they moved to stand beneath an awning stretched over a stall, from which issued chopping sounds and a disagreeable smell of fish. Alysia waited in an agony of confusion and suspense. Were these men part of the thievery, or were they really trying to help her? And why should they try to help her, a stranger?

"You are traveling alone?" the man asked, also speaking in Greek and exhibiting a kindly interest.

"Y—yes," she answered slowly, but she could see no threat in the dark eyes. He was a thin man, dressed in a plain robe and sandals, with black hair and a long, thin nose. She supposed him to be between thirty and forty years of age.

"This is my sister," the man said, as if to put her at ease, and for the first time Alysia noticed a young girl standing behind him. Her petite frame was clad in an ankle-length gown belted at the waist, and a long cloth headdress covered most of her dark hair. She had delicate features with large, dark eyes expressing sympathy and concern. At that moment the other man returned, sweating and breathing hard. He was holding her bag.

"I found this but the boy was too quick for me. The clothes were scattered. I replaced them, but perhaps he took something—did you have money?"

Alysia searched frantically for the purse she'd stuffed down into the bottom of the bag. Clothes, blanket, a little food . . . the purse was gone.

She couldn't believe it; she was penniless, poorer even than that wretched beggar across the street with his cup full of coins. She had not even a cup to beg with! The others observed her expression and looked at each other uncertainly.

Finally, Alysia cleared her throat and murmured, "I am grateful for your help. I—I have nothing but these clothes. Maybe I can sell them here in the market."

The two men again exchanged glances, almost as if they could communicate without speaking. The one who had chased the young thief said, "My name is Nathan, and these are my cousins, Lazarus and Mary. We live in Bethany of Judea, a town some distance from here. May I ask your name, and if you are alone?"

"My name is Alysia. And yes, I am alone."

"Do you have friends or relatives nearby?"

"No. Not nearby. I'm traveling—I've only just arrived."

Nathan had a pleasant face, with curly, copper-colored hair and eyes almost the same shade. He gave her a long, appraising look that wasn't like the crude and lustful stares to which she had become accustomed. He said, "I think it would be folly to leave you without any means. You would not get much for the clothes, knowing the merchants here."

Lazarus added, "Would you like to accompany us to Bethany? Mary and my other sister live with me. You could stay with us, if you like, until you decide what to do."

This unexpected kindness brought more tears to her eyes. She brushed them away and glanced at both men. They had honest, open faces. She felt a hand on her arm. The young girl was looking at her and nodding, as though she understood what was being said.

Maybe it was fate that these people had come along just now. Maybe she *should* get away from the coast and disappear into the country.

"Yes," she said quietly. "Thank you all. I will come with you."

Nathan said, "We were almost ready to go. Our wagon is this way."

They walked across the street and into an area where wagons were being loaded with various items. They approached one of them, where a husky youth was tucking a blanket securely about the sides. Nathan spoke to the youth, gave him some coins, and watched until he had gone out of sight.

Nathan drove; the others would walk. The two donkeys pulling the wagon plodded slowly forward. The hard road had been beaten smooth by the hooves of animals and the wheels of all manner of conveyances. The outer edge of the town was surrounded by orange orchards and wheat fields, and as they left the plain they began a gentle descent through a long valley with rolling hills on either side. Heavily laden camels and ox-carts travailed before and behind them.

Soon the road began ascending, with the surrounding hills becoming steeper. The pass was dark and seemed threatening, somehow, and Alysia felt relieved when they emerged onto a higher and wider portion of road, and the mountains seemed not to press so closely about them. Trees dotted the landscape—cedars, firs, pines, and oak. Thick, thorny bushes sprouted from everywhere.

Unexpectedly they encountered a Roman watchtower constructed of huge bricks, which reared atop a plateau high above the road. The lone sentry glanced down at them as they passed. Alysia almost held her breath until she saw him turn and face the opposite direction, taking little interest in such a small entourage that included two women. The men remained silent as they passed the watchtower. She received the peculiar impression that they were as uneasy as she.

Some miles further, the men guided the donkeys to the side of the road and stopped beneath the widespread shade of an enormous fig tree. Mary began unpacking a satchel that she pulled from beneath the seat of the wagon, removing from it a long loaf of bread, a covered dish full of olives, and a corked bottle of water. The few times that she spoke it was in a different language; it seemed she knew very little Greek. As Alysia helped her pour the water into cups, the men fed the donkeys a mixture of oats and chopped hay. They took out jugs of water and emptied them into a bucket for the animals to drink.

When the meal was ready they all sat beneath the tree. Lazarus recited something like a prayer and they began eating. Alysia tried to watch and behave as they did.

"Where did you say you live?" she asked Nathan.

Nathan looked up. "Bethany. It's about two miles east of our holy city, Jerusalem, a two-day journey from Joppa. There's an inn further on where we'll stay the night. And, if you don't mind my asking, how is it that you are traveling with no companion?"

Alysia busily wiped crumbs from her lap. "There was a—a death in the family. I had to leave rather quickly."

"Where are you from? Do you have any family here?"

Alysia had been thinking along the journey about what she would tell them when the questions inevitably came. They seemed to believe she was a Greek-speaking Jew—there were many of them in Athens and, indeed, everywhere. Why they should make such an assumption she didn't know; yet, why else would she have come here, to Palestine?

"My parents have been long dead," she began, hating to lie to them but not knowing what else to do. She would tell the story once and hope never to repeat it. "I lived with my aunt and uncle in Cyprus. My uncle died last year, and my aunt a few weeks ago. They were from Jerusalem." (That was the only Jewish city she'd ever heard of.) "I've never been there, and as far as I know I have no other relatives. But I didn't wish to stay in Cyprus, and so I thought

I would come here. I did have some money, but—I was hoping to find work."

"You never came to Jerusalem, even during the festivals?" Lazarus asked.

"My uncle was an invalid. We were not able to travel."

Alysia kept her gaze on her food, not knowing if they watched her. She tried to think of something to say to divert the attention from herself.

"And you—you are from Bethany and yet you speak perfect Greek."

"Growing up in Cyprus you would not be familiar with our ways. We're taught Greek and Latin in school, in addition to Hebrew and Aramaic." Nathan and the others began packing what was left of the food into the satchel. "In a land so occupied by foreign invaders, it is necessary to know more than one language."

There was an almost passionate bitterness in Nathan's voice and Alysia looked at him in surprise, having taken him for a quiet, mild-mannered man. She noticed how strong his hands looked and how his square jaw was set in lines that could only be called purposeful.

He turned abruptly. "Forgive me, I did not mean to bring up unpleasant things."

She tried to smile, but felt compelled to ask, "Are there many Romans here?"

"Not in the smaller towns," he answered. "But in Jerusalem, yes. There's a Roman fort there. You may know that Caesarea is their headquarters. There are soldiers as well as Roman merchants and their families in many of the larger cities."

"I see."

He watched her expectantly and she added, "I was hoping not to see many reminders of Rome. The Romans have not been kind to my family."

Nathan did not reply, but Lazarus smiled a little and said, "If you have come here to avoid Romans, Alysia, you have come to the wrong place."

CHAPTER VII

Before darkness fell, they came to a town called Emmaus and stopped at an inn for the night. It was small, lacking in many comforts, and consisting only of the innkeeper's living quarters and an open courtyard surrounded by a low wall where travelers could put down their pallets. Fortunately, Alysia still had her blanket and cushion, and she and Mary lay on one side of the courtyard, with Nathan and Lazarus on the other. She lay awake for a long while thinking about what Lazarus had said. There were many Romans here—well, they were everywhere! That didn't mean she'd come to the wrong place, did it? She would just have to be careful. No one here could possibly know what she had done.

For some reason she felt at ease with these people; she trusted them. It seemed right to travel far inland and dwell in a small village.

Maybe she could find work there. At last she drifted into a peaceful sleep . . .

They rose early in the morning and were on their way again. The inclines became steeper, the sun hotter, and the men quieter. The cart creaked and rattled. The grass had turned brown in the summer's heat, but the rolling landscape was still beautiful against the blue-ridged backdrop of mountains, which drew nearer and nearer.

"Will we go through the city of Jerusalem?" Alysia asked, wondering if she should be concerned about the presence of soldiers there. Surely there was no one in this entire country who would recognize her!

"We will pass around it on the north side," Nathan answered. "You've seen what our roads and highways are like—only the military roads are paved. Some are wide and smooth like this one; others are little more than paths. We will take the easiest route. It will probably be dark by the time we reach Jerusalem."

She would have asked more questions but she was tired and hot. They stopped several times to drink and water the donkeys. She had never in her life fallen asleep while sitting up but she must have done so, for she had climbed into the wagon before they approached the "holy city," and the next thing she knew it was dark with a great moon and they were climbing up a rock-strewn road toward a cluster of houses perched on the edge of a mountain. The road was lined with trees as they passed within the gate of the village, and the small houses glowed with lamplight from within.

Alysia sat up straighter. The wagon continued a short distance until they came to an imposing house made of brick, with a staircase running up two stories to the roof. The shadows of trees loomed blacker than the darkness. Mary jumped down from the wagon and ran to the house, throwing open the large, wooden door and revealing an inner courtyard.

Mary came out again, accompanied by an older woman who was smiling, but she eyed Alysia's attire with a wondering expression. She had a motherly face and wisps of gray hair escaped the loose confines of her head covering. Lazarus introduced her as his sister, Martha, and then spoke in Aramaic as if explaining Alysia's presence.

Finally he said kindly, "Come, let's go inside. I know you are tired."

Nathan had busied himself unhitching the donkeys from the wagon. Alysia followed the others inside.

The spacious house had an atmosphere of comfort and hospitality. The couches, tables, and chairs were plain but of excellent quality; handsome rugs and cushions were scattered over the floors. Bronze lamps hung from the ceilings and oval-shaped clay ones were set in niches in the walls. Martha had gone to see to the preparation of food, and Alysia was left alone with Mary and Lazarus. Nathan soon joined them.

"You have been very good to me," she said, over a strange lump in her throat. "I don't know how to thank you."

"Have you any plans?" Nathan asked.

Alysia shook her head. "I suppose I shall go tomorrow and try to find work."

"What sort of work can you do?" Lazarus asked, with sober practicality.

She remembered her earlier expectation of tutoring the ignorant rabble and felt foolish, considering that these Jews were more learned in languages than she.

"I've had experience doing domestic work."

Nathan rubbed his chin. "I know of no one around here who requires another servant, unless it is you, Lazarus. Maybe in Jerusalem—"

"There will be time enough to decide what you are going to do," Lazarus said to her. "You may stay here as long as you wish."

Martha returned to announce that the food was ready, then she and Mary descended upon Alysia as if she were a child, removing her shoes, helping her to wash and serving her a plate, all without saying a word.

Lazarus and his sisters seemed content to have her stay with them, and the longer she stayed the more firmly established she became as a permanent resident. The language barrier receded a bit more every day until Alysia was reasonably conversant in Aramaic, an ancient language that differed significantly from the original Hebrew, and of which there were several dialects. The Judean women were just as quickly learning Greek. By mixing the two languages, everyone managed to make themselves understood.

She learned that Martha was a widow and that Lazarus had lost his wife and son in childbirth several years ago. Mary was of marriageable age but not yet betrothed; she didn't seem interested in marriage, though she loved children and often helped care for the children of Lazarus' servants. They were not slaves but were paid what they must consider generous wages, for they seemed to be content.

She shared Mary's large bedroom and found Mary to be very devout, praying often and reading the works of the Jewish prophets. Alysia shrugged off her opinion that religious belief was the height of stupidity and decided that if Mary found comfort in it—that was well and good. She almost wished she could believe in something of a higher order than what she had seen of the world!

Lazarus was a man of considerable wealth. His was the largest house in the village. He owned several orchards and olive presses that were managed by paid overseers. Although Lazarus objected, Alysia insisted on working for her keep and labored alongside several other men and women in his olive groves, beating the branches of the heavy-laden trees with a stick and collecting the ripe olives in baskets. She didn't mind working, now that she wasn't forced to do it. She also helped with the housekeeping and cooking. Still, she was treated neither as slave nor servant, but as a member of the family. Hospitality seemed almost a sacred tradition here.

The heavy rains of autumn came, and the winter saw a light fall of snow. Spring arrived and the first drafts of warm air came to thaw the town and renew spirits dampened by the unpleasant weather.

Alysia's presence seemed to be accepted with a cautious friendliness by most of the town, though no one besides Mary and Martha made any overtures toward becoming a close friend. All of the young women were civil to her, but she noticed them casting furtive, curious glances her way as she went about her tasks. She supposed it was because no one really knew much about her; everyone supposed her to be a Grecian Jew who had lost her family, been robbed upon landing in Joppa, and had been practically adopted by Lazarus and his sisters.

Lazarus seemed to regard her as if she were another sister. None of them asked questions of a personal nature for it was considered rude. It saved her from having to fabricate some tale to account for her previous life, for which she was grateful. She hated lying, especially to these people who had been so kind.

Nathan, Lazarus' younger cousin, lived on the next street in a much smaller and plainer house. The handsome stonemason was plainly considered a good catch for some enterprising young woman, though he spent almost all his time on sporadic travels throughout the province. That spring, however, he traveled less and more of his leisure hours were passed at Lazarus' house. His interest in

Alysia was growing conspicuous and had become a budding cause of general feminine resentment.

The more Alysia learned about Jewish traditions and beliefs, the more secure she felt that she would not be compromised or forced to do anything against her will. Women had little social standing but they were respected and their chastity well-guarded. She didn't know if all Jews were alike, but she could find no fault with Lazarus and his family.

She liked Nathan. Maybe once she could have loved him. But there was a man she could not forget, and whenever she thought of him desolation swept over her like a relentless shadow, and she longed with all her heart to see his face, to hear his voice, to feel his arms around her once again. But it was not to be. By now, he knew that she had not gone to wait for him in Cyprus. He had probably stopped looking for her.

In fact, he had probably forgotten all about her.

The voice of the emperor's secretary was low and respectful. "I will inform the emperor that you are here, Lord Valerius."

Paulus nodded and resigned himself to an interminable wait.

The Isle of Capri was a tiny, steeply-inclined island a few miles south of Rome. Tiberius' main villa overlooked the sea, situated high upon a rocky bluff. Inside the central hall Paulus looked at the mammoth columns, the high-ceilinged corridors leading in all directions, the endless rooms, the extravagant silk curtains and tapestries, the profligate use of gold and silver and jewels, and thought what a waste it was . . . a pitiful waste that one man lived alone here, alone with his servants and guards and his bitter thoughts.

On the wall across from him was a painting of a nude couple in a somewhat dubious position, and he pondered briefly on the rumors of Tiberius' bizarre sexual habits. There might be some truth in the stories, though they were probably greatly exaggerated. After all, the emperor was getting up in years and it was doubtful that even a man accustomed to such excesses could continually live up to his reputation!

But despite his alleged bent toward debauchery, Tiberius had been in his day a capable military leader. He might have possibly been an equally capable ruler, but too often he had listened to the unwise counsel of those hungry for power, too often he had fallen victim to his own morbid and brooding nature.

Paulus eyed an uninviting marble bench and wondered how much longer Tiberius would keep him waiting. He wasn't certain why he had been summoned, unless it involved his written request for a new appointment. He also wondered if Aelius Sejanus would be present, although as far as he knew the man was still in Rome. If Sejanus had finally convinced the emperor that Paulus had sinister intentions in regard to the empire, he would no doubt be facing a trial for treason, probably as soon as the next day. And treason trials almost always ended in conviction. The few who were acquitted were usually later found dead—of "suicide."

"My lord, the emperor will see you now."

The soft-spoken secretary waited for him to follow. Paulus turned sharply, his sword slapping against his thigh as he walked with confident steps into the emperor's chamber.

Tiberius Caesar peered myopically from his chair. His once straight shoulders had a weary slump, and his tall body drooped as he sat wrapped in a thick robe, though the weather was warm and humid. His thinning hair had turned a dull yellow, and his frowning face was tired and drained of the vigor of youth. Sagging lines of dissipation marred the once handsome features. His eyes were restless and roving, never lingering on any object. Any aura of past dignity and authority had disappeared.

"Let us not be formal, Paulus," said the ruler of the Roman Empire. "I will call you Paulus, as we are old acquaintances, are we not? Sit down. You will dine with me."

Paulus inclined his head. "I am honored, sir."

A table had been drawn up to his chair so the emperor could eat while sitting up; he had become too stiff and his digestion too fragile for reclining. Paulus sat in the chair opposite him, noting that his plate had already been served and there was no one else in the room. He was surprised by that, as well as by the fact that his sword had not been taken from him before entering the room.

"There aren't many men I would trust alone with me," Tiberius said, as if guessing his thoughts. He spoke slowly and with great effort. Words had never come easily to this Caesar. "Aelius Sejanus didn't want me to see you. He doesn't like you, you know. Thinks you want to dethrone me or some such nonsense."

"Sejanus and I have clashed many times over the years," Paulus said mildly. "Rest assured, sir, I have no desire to sit in your place."

"Eh, and why not?"

"There are too many problems inherent in a monarchy, sir."

"Well, Sejanus hasn't gone so far as to say you want to do away with me. But admit it; you do want the Republic back. I, too, once favored the Republic, but the fates decreed otherwise. Fate has always been against me . . ." Tiberius' eyes wandered gloomily across the room and he mumbled, "They wait for me to die. I suppose I have disappointed them. They compare me to my stepfather, the great Augustus, who 'found Rome a city of brick and left it marble'!"

He chuckled mirthlessly. "A bit of an exaggeration, but an improvement, nevertheless. I live upon this island like a hermit. My only contribution has been to keep the frontiers safe and tighten up the purse strings, which I might add has done nothing to increase my popularity."

"Future generations will no doubt profit by your foresightedness."

Tiberius nodded, but went on in a sullen tone, "How long shall I be remembered? What monument will serve as a memorial to me, besides these villas I build, this whole wretched island?" He regarded Paulus ruefully. "Of course, the emperor is supposed to be immortal, but I do not deceive myself. I pretend to believe in the gods because it amuses me, but there are no gods, Paulus, and there is no afterlife. A dismal thought to be sure, but one that must be faced at some point in a man's life. Master of the world one day, a rotting corpse the next."

The emperor's weary brown eyes turned expectantly toward him but Paulus held his peace. He knew better than to voice an opinion to the old man, who was likely to change his mind within the hour and would only recall that Paulus did not consider him of Olympian virtue. He'd been known to have slobbering fits of rage when not shown the proper respect and the culprits generally disappeared from the island, never to be seen again. On the other hand, he detested any overt show of flattery and had once fallen over backward trying to escape an overly enthused admirer. The less said in the presence of the emperor, the better.

"You're not drinking much wine," Tiberius said. "It's quite safe, I believe. After all, Sejanus is not here to poison it. Neither is my mother."

Paulus met his gaze inquisitively. The emperor nodded. "Yes. My mother ruined my life, Paulus Valerius—may she be eaten by worms! She and her—ambitions. She's ancient now and rumors are she's not getting on very well. She needn't expect any honors from me. Wants me to make her a goddess! Well, she's not the woman Rome thinks she is, believe me!"

Paulus raised his eyebrows but made no rejoinder.

"Go ahead, drink more wine. Taste the fish. It's from the Sea of Galilee, the best in the world. Ah, that reminds me. I've almost forgotten the point of your visit!" His frown was, for an instant, replaced by the shadow of a smile.

"You have been to Judea, have you not?"

"Yes. Several years ago."

"Tell me about it. You met Pontius Pilate, of course?"

"Yes, sir."

"And you are familiar with the language and customs?"

"Enough to get by."

"I have need of you there." Tiberius coughed. "The position is an important one, as you will see, but could be handled by a tribune. Some would say this is a relegation."

Paulus shrugged. "I am ready to go wherever I am needed."

The emperor looked at him with sudden sharpness. "It seems as though you are eager to leave Rome behind you, come what may."

Paulus nodded, saying nothing.

"Well, it so happens you are needed in Jerusalem. I want someone there I can trust. I'm putting you in charge of the fort and you will be the superior officer in all of Judea. Pilate will retain his position as prefect, which means you will be subordinate only to him. He spends most of his time in Caesarea. Pilate, in turn, is subordinate to the governor of Syria, who spends most of *his* time in Rome."

"I understand."

Tiberius eyed him curiously. "Your rank is equal to that of Pilate, except for the fact that he is governor. But in social position you are superior to him—he is only a knight. I would like to know why you would even consider such an appointment."

Paulus didn't answer for a moment. Rome had become intolerable, his own life was empty and equally intolerable, and filled with regret and hopelessness. They were emotions that he masked, that no one knew of, but they were there all the same.

He said slowly, "I feel the need for—challenge."

"It will be challenging, all right! Pontius Pilate has caused any number of problems for Rome. He has no tact. I may not have any great abundance of it myself, but at least I learn from my mistakes!"

Paulus nodded again but continued to look quizzical.

"All I need is an excuse, Legate. Give him enough rope to hang himself. Sejanus likes him and I seldom oppose Sejanus. I have my own reasons for that. Ha–except when it came to you! I had many a good laugh over the look on his face whenever I gave you an appointment. But—one more mistake and Pilate is finished. I want you to watch him. As soon as he makes a misstep, you will report directly to me."

Paulus hesitated only an instant. "I have no wish to be employed as a spy, sir."

At last Tiberius appeared on the verge of losing his famous temper. He pounded the table with his fist so hard the plates rattled and a guard stuck his head in the door. Tiberius drew in a gulp of air and yelled, "Get out!"

The guard disappeared. Paulus sat unmoving.

"By the infernal gods! I am your emperor! You will do as I say!"

In the silence that followed, Tiberius strove to stop an involuntary shaking and finally collected himself enough to say with a degree of calm, "You are not to interfere with Pilate's treatment of the Jews. Let him make a mistake. In so doing you will prevent more loss of life, for he will be instantly removed. You can put your own man in his place. Anyone, even yourself, if you ever get over your aversion to politics."

Paulus remained carefully calm. "Yes, Caesar."

The emperor went on as if there had been no outburst. "There is a strong group of rebels there—Zealots, they are called. No doubt you are aware of this. You may deal with them as you will when Pilate is absent. They are fanatics, and I hear the Jews are expecting a leader to rise up among them to release them from Rome."

"That is true of the common people, but the Jewish government is not looking for such a man. They have no quarrel with Rome and are very much enjoying the freedom you have given them."

"Ah, but my own soothsayers tell me that a man will come from the east who will be called the King of kings, that he will be both human and divine. What do you think of that?"

"I would advise the emperor not to lose sleep over the pronouncements of prophets and soothsayers."

Tiberius stared at him, then burst into laughter. "If you only knew how much sleep I have lost over it!" He sobered just as suddenly and said, "Nevertheless, I want you to watch. Ah, I know what you're thinking. It's been said I don't like my position, so why should I mind losing it? One grows accustomed to power, Paulus—and I am the most powerful man in the world! You can never have enough of it. But it has been the ruin of many a man."

Tiberius sighed. "I don't know why I speak with you so frankly, Paulus Valerius Maximus. Are you really the honest man my gut tells me you are, or just another of the self-seeking villains I must cope with constantly? I suppose it is because you remind me of my brother. Drusus was an honorable man, which is why he's dead."

Paulus took a sip of wine and again refrained from comment, lest Tiberius proceed with a confession of some sort and then decide that Paulus must not live with such knowledge. The emperor was becoming drowsy and seemed half in another world.

"No, it's Germanicus," he muttered. "My nephew. It's Germanicus you remind me of. He was—good. He should have been—" He looked at Paulus and said, unexpectedly, "Are you Germanicus?"

Paulus was taken aback. "No, Caesar."

"No. No, of course you aren't. He's been dead for years." Tiberius shook his large head and refocused his eyes, looking sheepish. "Er, what of your wife? Will she go with you?"

"I assume so."

"Very well. She can reside at Herod's palace, if she doesn't wish to stay at the fort. The palace is very grand, I hear. I know little of your family situation. Are there children?"

"No."

"Eh?" The heavy eyebrows arched. "My stepfather would not approve. Populating Rome was one of his pet projects." Tiberius gave a wry chuckle, then narrowed his eyes. "What about that slave of yours that killed young Eustacius? Did they catch her?"

There was another short pause. "She perished in a shipwreck."

"Shipwreck? Did you recover the body?"

"No, sir. Only two or three bodies were found."

"Then she might still be alive. The search will go on, of course."

"I examined the wreckage myself. There were no survivors."

"Perhaps you would have us believe that, Legate. Sejanus says you helped her escape."

"Magnus Eustacius was about to rape her. There was a struggle with the weapon."

"Surely you don't try to defend a slave, and a stupid one at that! Better to be raped than to die, or to live your life a hunted criminal."

Paulus' jaw hardened but he said nothing.

"I am tired. You may go, Paulus Maximus. Ha—Sejanus hates it when I call you that! Make your preparations and be ready to leave before the end of the summer."

"Thank you, sir."

The emperor's eyelids drooped, and there was an even more pronounced slump to his shoulders. But he roused once more and seemed impressed by some distant memory. "You should have lived, Germanicus. You should be ruler of Rome! I hate this place! I hate my life, and yet I'm grateful to you for saving it." His gaze was turned inward, his eyes glazed with sudden fear, and he seemed hardly aware that he was speaking.

"I hate the world, and yet I'm terrified of leaving it."

Again he was confusing Paulus with his dead nephew. The Claudian side of the family, no doubt—everyone knew half the Claudii were mad. But his words touched something in Paulus, something almost of commiseration.

As he took his leave, he thought, *He's nothing but a slave. The most enslaved man in the empire.*

CHAPTER VIII

Martha was quiet, not like herself, as she and Alysia sat on low stools in the courtyard, grinding grain to make bread. It was a chore that everyone shared for it was a constant necessity. The morning sun warmed the pavement and reflected off the yellowed stone of the house. Daisies and poppies were in full bloom around the outer edges of the courtyard. The latticed roof and inner walls threw a band of shade over the women and a gentle wind blew, playing with the edges of their long robes and mantles.

Alysia had sold her Roman gowns to a traveling peddler and purchased clothes of the Jewish fashion. She wore a blue, ankle-length gown, called a chiton, gathered in with a belt just above her waist. A mantle, called a himation, was worn over the gown and was also raised to cover a woman's head when she appeared in public. Alysia didn't usually cover her head while around the house, though Martha and Mary did; she privately considered them a little too modest. She also chose brighter colors and shoes and sandals that were more elaborately made than the other two women wore.

But today, for some reason, Martha had asked her to cover her hair, and while Alysia didn't like it she always did what they asked, out of gratitude and respect for their ways. She wondered what was on Martha's mind. Their task was certainly tedious and tiring, so maybe she was thinking of nothing in particular.

The grinding mill was made of two circular, flat stones, one atop the other, with a wooden handle. It required two people to operate, as both had to place their hands on the handle and turn while one of them, with her free hand, took the wheat from the basket and dropped it into the top of the mill. Alysia had just put in a handful when a voice from the outer doorway startled her.

"Peace be unto you!"

The women turned to see Nathan striding toward them, his copper hair bright in the sunlight. Alysia cast down her eyes as she knew was expected of her.

"I have just spoken to Lazarus," Nathan said.

Martha glanced at him and a look of dawning came into her face. As if she had just remembered, she said quickly, "Oh! Oh, I did leave something baking, didn't I?" She struggled to her feet and bustled into the house. Alysia stood and looked after her in bemusement.

"May I speak with you?" Nathan asked, with a serious expression.

Alysia looked around, noting that everyone, even the servants, had disappeared. Nathan led the way up the outer steps to the flat roof of the house. Most Jewish families utilized this area of their houses, and Martha had furnished it with couches and chairs, straw mats, potted plants, and even a swing covered with colorful cushions. Alysia went to a wicker chair and sat down.

Nathan couldn't keep himself from staring at her. How beautiful she was, how exquisite her violet eyes and how mysterious, for they seemed to hide some secret sadness that he wanted to draw out so that they might sparkle with mirth. He wanted to hear the sound of her carefree laughter. Alysia grew nervous as she began to have an inkling of his purpose. She looked at him directly, but seeing that this had an unusual effect on him—to the extent that he seemed to lose his train of thought and was speechless—she lowered her gaze and waited for him to begin.

"How do you find this place?" he asked finally. "Bethany, I mean."

"It is a lovely place," she answered, not looking up. "I have enjoyed living here."

"Enough to stay here, as my wife?"

Her head came up in pretended surprise. Before she could speak, he went on, "I have been fortunate to prosper at my trade. I can provide for you. I have paid the bride price to Lazarus, and he has agreed to provide a dowry for you. He is, after all, considered your guardian. He is very fond of you. He's giving you an interest in one of his groves."

Alysia's mind flew down this unexpected path. She had never seriously thought this would happen, since she wasn't Jewish; she always had to remind herself that they had all assumed she was Jewish, and she had let them believe it. But it *had* happened! Here was a man she had affection for, who was willing to give her a home when she had no home, who was willing to provide for all the social traditions, and who clearly had deep feelings for her. How could she refuse?

Already she had begun to wonder how much longer she should remain a guest of Lazarus and his family, for no matter how firmly they professed their fondness for her, she didn't belong here. She needed her own home, her own family. But she also needed to be honest with this man who was offering so much.

She began hesitantly, "Nathan, you know nothing of my past, and I—"

He interrupted, "Maybe we both have secrets, Alysia. If you wish things about your past to remain unspoken, I will respect that. As for me, there is something you should know before you answer."

He turned to look out over the town, squinting in the sun. "I am what they call a Zealot. There are many factions, and I belong to one of them. We hate the Romans and we cause trouble for them whenever we can." He added quietly, "You see, Romans killed my parents. I was a child. I was here when it happened. It was just after Martha's husband died and she had moved here to live with Lazarus. In fact, it was Martha who raised me after my parents died."

Alysia watched him, seeing the way his hands gripped the top of the low wall that surrounded the rooftop. "They were traveling. They came upon some soldiers who tried to compel my father to carry some of their equipment. He resisted. When my mother tried to intervene, the soldiers killed them both. There was a relative traveling behind them who witnessed it all."

"I'm sorry, Nathan." After a moment, she said, "And this group you speak of—it's very dangerous, is it not?"

"Yes, of course. I could be killed. But in these uncertain times I could be killed for any reason, Alysia. I know that you will be secure in the friendship of Lazarus and his sisters if anything should happen to me."

She put her hand over one of his. "I told you that I too have reason to hate Rome. I cannot fault you for this part of your life. There is a part of my life that, if it is discovered, could bring danger to you."

He put his other hand on top of hers and looked into her eyes. "Danger, like grief, may be more bearable when it is shared. You can bring no more of it to me, Alysia, than I have already brought myself."

"Do you wish me to tell you of it?"

"No," he said at once. "Because I want nothing to interfere with my intent to marry you. For Jews there are certain—well, I must have no reason to turn away from you. Do you understand what I am saying?"

"Yes, I think so."

"Have you never wondered what Lazarus and I were doing in Joppa? I was collecting a shipment of supplies—weapons."

"Oh, is Lazarus—"

"No, Lazarus is not one of us. It's true that his health has not been good for some time, but even if he were able, he would not support our cause. He hates what the Romans have done but he doesn't share our idea that violence should be met with violence. He's never given money to us, or aided us."

"Then, did he not know—"

"He went with me that day, at great risk to himself, so that I wouldn't be alone if anything went wrong. The man who was supposed to accompany me was indisposed. Lazarus purchased some supplies for his business, and I hid the weapons in the bottom of the wagon. He's a gentle man, but not lacking in bravery. As for Mary, she wanted to come at the last moment and we could think of no reason to dissuade her. I think she knew, though; I think she believed her presence would cause us not to be examined so closely. And Lazarus simply said that he trusted God to take care of her."

"I see."

"I have spoken enough of unpleasant things." Nathan spread out his arms. "And I am not very good at speaking words of love. Alysia, will you marry me?"

Her eyes moved and lifted. She could see the entire town from here, with its sunbaked houses and terraced gardens, its narrow streets, the undulating land covered with rocks and date palms. There were no Romans here; once in a great while a soldier or two rode through, but there was a wider road that went around the village that was better suited to horses.

No one would ever search for her in Bethany of Judea. Paulus would never come here.

"Nathan, I would be honored to become your wife."

The summer had aged into its last month as the Roman vessel sped smoothly across the sea. The night was lit with twinkling stars and a yellow moon that cast an eerie light upon the black water.

Paulus stood alone on the foredeck, one hand resting on the rail before him and another clasping the rigging that stretched down from the mast. The moon and its reflection on the water cast a wavering light across his features as he gazed seaward. A breeze caught the ends of his tawny hair, even as it invisibly urged the ship on its way. He stared unseeingly across the endless expanse of ocean, his mind as far away as the distant horizon, indistinguishable now in the darkness. His thoughts were of a dark-haired slave girl, dead for almost the full year past.

He could not forget her, and why this should be he didn't know. It was more than feeling responsible for her death. He could scarcely believe that she *was* dead, yet it was impossible that she had survived. He had viewed what was left of the ship, beaten against the rocks surrounding Crete where the wind and waves had left it. He had meant to make things right for her. She had suffered greatly through no fault of her own and now she was gone forever. He himself had sent her to her doom.

Paulus sensed a presence behind him and turned quickly to see Simon, a slave who had come into his possession through his marriage to Megara. Simon, who was half Jew and half Greek, had been a merchant living in the city of Cyrene until the Roman authorities had confiscated his property and sold him into slavery. Paulus didn't know the details; he didn't ask.

"Your wife requests your presence at supper, sir," Simon said, in a pleasant voice. He was not a sullen slave, seeming resigned to his fate with some good cheer. He was almost as tall as Paulus and several years younger, with a dark complexion and thick, raven-black hair.

"Tell her I will join her presently."

"Yes, sir." Simon retreated into the shadows.

Paulus' mind resumed its former gloomy path, his humor little restored by the summons from his wife. Their relationship, which had never been intimate, was steadily deteriorating. They had nothing in common with each other. He had learned, in a most unpleasant altercation soon after their marriage, that she didn't want children—in fact, she quite vehemently didn't want them because she loathed "brats" and had no intention of losing her fine figure.

"I've been taking precautions," she had told him, knowing full well that, for him, childbearing was the main function of marriage.

He'd been surprised but strangely unmoved by her outburst, thinking privately that it was a good thing; he would pity any child of hers. That had set the tone for their marriage throughout the years. For the most part they lived in peace, for she knew when to have her say and when to remain silent. At least, she used to know. Lately she had become more and more combative. He didn't know why, but it had begun not long after he had purchased Alysia.

His wife had been first shocked and then outraged when he announced his decision to leave Rome. She'd called him a fool. He shrugged and said that perhaps he was. She had told him that if he were planning to leave her behind he was an even greater fool, for she would not appear before her family and friends as a woman deserted by her husband.

She was vain, obstinate, and seldom had a kind word to say to anyone—unless she wanted something. Legally, it would be easy to divorce her. But what a fight she would put up, he had no doubt! She would probably sue him for everything he owned, though she'd have little chance of getting it—even if her father was a man of considerable influence *and* distantly related to the Caesars.

He had never cared enough to divorce her; he cared even less now. Nor did it matter if she stayed in Rome or chose to follow him about with that odd, single-minded possessiveness of hers. As long as she stayed out of his way and made no demands on him, she could do what she liked.

In Caesarea they were greeted by the staff of the governor, as Pilate was not currently in the city. They would rest for a day or two from the sea voyage before continuing to Jerusalem—in deference to Megara, for Paulus needed no rest and was eager to press on.

He never failed to marvel at the ingenuity of the harbor King Herod had built here, along with the city he had named in honor of Augustus Caesar. In fact, Paulus had studied the details of its construction years ago when he first became interested in engineering. There being no suitable port from Joppa to the city of Dor, Herod had undertaken to build one by sinking a cementing mixture into the seabed to create a breakwater, and topping the walls with huge paving stones to make a wide, public walkway. The result was an artificial harbor of surpassing beauty, and large enough to accommodate three hundred ships.

Paulus could see that Megara was impressed, though she endeavored to retain her habitually stoic expression. They stepped off the ship directly onto the walkway, whereupon they entered a heavily cushioned coach and were borne away to the palace. They had been able to glimpse the palace from the sea, gleaming white in the sun and situated on a high bluff that jutted out over the swelling waves.

Several dignitaries were present to greet them, seeming anxious that the legate and his wife might not be affronted by Pilate's absence. Pilate, explained his second in command, had been called away to investigate a disturbance near the Jordan River where there were signs of a possible uprising. The prefect would write the legate a detailed letter concerning the situation upon his return.

Paulus knew that Pilate had not been overly concerned about a "possible uprising"; any number of his subordinates could have conducted such an investigation, including Paulus himself. Pilate no doubt resented Paulus' coming for two probable reasons: Paulus outranked him socially, as Tiberius had mentioned, and everyone knew it, just as everyone knew that Paulus had achieved considerable fame as an officer and was highly favored by his legion. Pilate's command over his own troops was for little more than appearances; as far as Paulus knew, he had practically no military experience. The governor of Syria had been overseeing Pilate's handling of his army.

The prefect may also have guessed that Paulus was being considered by Tiberius as his replacement should he somehow ever lose the support of Aelius Sejanus and fall from the slippery slope he currently stood upon. Several times, with obvious full awareness of what he was doing, he had offended the Jews to the point of what could have resulted in a full-scale massacre. He had, on one occasion, brought standards bearing the image of the emperor into Jerusalem during the dead of night so that they would be on display over the fort, Antonia, when the unsuspecting Jews woke in the morning. Their religious belief forbade the use or even the presence of anything bearing such an image. The hue and cry had been thunderous. When Pilate threatened to kill the protestors, they had bared their necks and waited for the swords to fall rather than submit to such a flagrant violation of their beliefs.

Disgusted, Pilate was forced to either back down or kill literally thousands. Prudently he gave the order to remove the standards, after giving a speech informing his recalcitrant subjects that he had merely been testing them and they should appreciate Rome's tolerance of their "peculiar" ways. But, he had said, be aware that Rome's generosity would only extend to a certain point. What that was, no one asked.

Another time he had outraged the people by diverting money from the Jews' sacred treasury, money intended for the upkeep of the Temple, toward the construction of an aqueduct. On that occasion, many of the Jews actually died in the ensuing tumult.

Paulus suspected that Pilate, like his mentor, Sejanus, secretly despised the Jews and would have liked to have seen them totally annihilated. After all, the land would be much easier to rule without their demands and whining over religious matters—which they couldn't even agree on themselves. No doubt the only thing that gave him pause was the fact that Tiberius had granted the Jews leniency concerning their religion and even their laws, so that they more or less had a form of self-government. The only authority they lacked was the right to put someone to death; for that they needed permission from Rome. Pilate was usually only too glad to grant it, no matter who howled in protest.

All things considered, Paulus could understand why Tiberius wanted Pilate watched; he could also understand Pilate's probable resentment. But as for being the man's successor, Paulus would rather be stripped of his rank completely. There was no satisfaction for him in thinking up new taxes and supervising their collection, nor of keeping dull accounts, nor of listening to domestic disputes. He'd had enough of that in Rome.

Planning and implementing new construction would be something Paulus could enjoy, but there was little of that to do in Caesarea, and he would have to involve himself in political wrangling to get the funds should he seek to improve the smaller cities. No, Paulus belonged in the army; leadership was in his blood, and he liked nothing better than to create strategies and outwit an enemy on the battlefield, though, thanks to Sejanus, it had been a few years since he had done so.

True, Alysia's death had for a time made him lose interest in everything. But now that he was here—in this restless land filled with bitterness and discontent—he actually began to anticipate a change in his life. There was a sense of excitement, of things about to happen. It would, at the very least, be a diversion.

CHAPTER IX

"It *is* breathtaking, isn't it?" Alysia said, spreading her arms and lifting her head as though she were seeing it again for the first time. She stood on the narrow road from Bethany on the sloping shoulder of Mount Olivet, looking across the valley at the city of Jerusalem. Crowning a high, rocky plateau, it seemed to have risen out of the earth by the word of some ancient worker of magic. The palatial homes of the wealthy spread out in elegant lines throughout the upper city, nestled in the rolling hills and interspersed with the majestic architecture of Herod the Great. The Temple Mount gleamed white and gold in the fading sunlight.

She, Lazarus, and Mary were returning from a visit to the lower city where they'd spent an enjoyable afternoon at the market. Lazarus had bought a wagonload of supplies, which would be delivered to his house in the next day or two. They'd eaten salted fish, fruit, and even a pastry at a little shop on Baker Street before leaving for home, and as they always did before reaching the distinct curve in the road, turned to look back at the view.

"You are not the first to stop and marvel at it," Lazarus said, smiling at her enthusiasm.

"If only it weren't so noisy and crowded," she added as they started walking again.

"Jerusalem is flawed, yes, but its history is so interesting," Mary began. Alysia gave her an indulgent smile but her mind wandered as Mary began to talk about the origins of the holy city. Mary seldom spoke of anything except history or religion. Besides, Alysia now knew most of it. Just after her formal betrothal to Nathan six months ago—and in spite of the fact that she'd been going to the synagogue almost since she'd arrived in Bethany—she had confessed to Mary that she knew practically nothing about their beliefs. Because, she had said, her family was not religious. Shocked, Mary hastened to rectify the matter and had been instructing her.

She had learned that the Jews believed in one God, and that he created the earth and mankind. There were beings of the spirit realm that God had also created, called angels, and one of them had rebelled against God's authority, gathered together untold numbers of followers, and instigated a war in heaven, the abode of God. As a result, this enemy of God, whom they called Satan, had been cast out of heaven along with his followers—but in the spirit world he still plotted and devised ways to destroy the human race, which God loved.

Satan had encouraged the first man and woman to follow his example and rebel against God. Hundreds of years later, the earth had become so corrupt that God decided to destroy it with a flood, saving only one family—a righteous man named Noah, his wife and three sons and their wives.

These stories were very old, Mary told her; some of the ancient Greek and Roman myths were based on these actual events. There were other accounts, written into what they called their "Scriptures"—Abraham had been called forth from his native land to become the man God designated to be the father of this race, the Jews; a man named Moses had led the Jews out of their bondage in Egypt, and God had given him a set of laws for the people to obey; David, a shepherd turned king, had seized Jerusalem from his enemies and made it his capital city. There were tales of violence, bloodshed, lust, and the wrath of God toward an unfaithful people. But there were also stories of love and beauty, the everlasting love of a God promising to save and bless his people in spite of their unfaithfulness—though not without punishment.

That love was the single, main thread woven into the beliefs of the Jews, the undisputed core of their religion, and that love was in the form of a Deliverer. God would send a man to rescue them from all the troubles that had plagued them for so many centuries. They called him "Messiah," or "Christ" in the Greek language, and believed that he would eventually rule the world in a kingdom of peace and good will.

It all sounded strange to Alysia but something about it made sense, unlike the wild and improbable escapades of the Greek gods. It was singularly comforting to immerse herself in this remarkable education. It gave her new things to think about and opened a new world for discovery.

The day had grown steadily hotter. Alysia tugged at the mantle covering her head, a requirement for a betrothed woman, and the movement brought to mind the day she had promised to marry Nathan. They'd gone into the house and Lazarus had read aloud the marriage contract, wherein Nathan had promised to protect and provide for her. Nathan had given her a gold ring and they had shared a cup of wine. Her acceptance of the cup was a symbolic way of accepting his proposal. And suddenly, they were betrothed.

Alysia hadn't seen much of him since then; it was the custom for a man to immediately begin to prepare a bridal chamber for his intended bride and they were to remain apart until the wedding. Nathan was adding a room to his house for her but he did manage to visit Lazarus and his sisters on occasion, especially when it was time for supper. Sometimes Alysia remained in her bedroom, and sometimes Lazarus came to her with a wink and asked her to join them.

When Lazarus, as her guardian, decided that the bridal chamber was satisfactorily completed and that the time was right, he would tell Nathan to come for his bride. Usually this occurred late at night about a year after the betrothal, so Alysia was supposed to remain ready at all times. Her wedding clothes were to be laid out; the blankets and linens she sewed, with Martha's help, were to be packed and waiting. It was meant to be a time of anticipation and excitement. And sometimes she did feel excited; sometimes she did look forward to leaving Lazarus' house and having a home of her own.

As long as she didn't let herself think about Paulus.

Lazarus and Mary were still discussing some aspect of history involving a woman named Esther when Lazarus stopped suddenly and held up his hand, as if listening.

"What is it?" Alysia asked.

"Horses. Don't you hear them?"

They all stopped and listened, and presently the sounds of rhythmic hoof beats and men's voices were clearly audible.

"Get back from the road," Lazarus said quickly.

Alysia felt a familiar revulsion as she saw the group of Roman soldiers top the rock-strewn incline before them, each one close behind the other. There were five of them, with their bowl-shaped helmets reflecting the dying sun's rays and their short, red mantles blowing out behind them. They were all drunk it seemed, and the centurion in front was no less drunk than his men—probably more so, judging from the droop of his posture. They halted as they observed the three people on the side of the road, drawing their swords with comical unsteadiness.

"What! An unlikely band of highwaymen!" roared the centurion, sheathing his sword with difficulty. "Two girls and a scrawny man!"

"Be wary, sir," said one of the soldiers, with a lopsided leer. "It could be three scrawny men in disguise!"

A bellow of laughter met that remark, and the centurion said, "No, Servius. Have you not eyes?"

The men crowded their horses about the women and inspected both minutely. Their stares returned to Alysia, who breathed rapidly with suppressed anger.

"She'd be a fine one to take to the barracks, wouldn't she?" commented the man named Servius. "Remember, Marcus, we wagered the others on who would bring back the best-looking wench—and the new commander is not due for another week."

Lazarus stepped to her side. "She is not going anywhere."

"Show some respect to Rome, Jew," growled the centurion, only momentarily diverted.

"I show no disrespect, sir, though your authority is perhaps only temporary."

"What do you mean by that?"

"He means that one day we shall fall and *his* people will be in authority!" shouted one of the other soldiers.

Servius raised his brows. He was a thin, dark man with a prominent nose and small, shrewd eyes. "It seems that we have a Zealot on our hands."

"Maybe they are all Zealots, out to set an ambush as we passed!" cried the other man and guffawed at his own words.

"Let's take both the women," suggested another soldier eagerly.

The centurion, who had a handsome but dissipated face, glanced at Mary. "She's too scared to be any use." He said to Alysia, "What say you to our invitation to Jerusalem? We'll show you a good time and pay you well."

Mary gasped and Lazarus pressed closer to Alysia, his body tense with outrage.

"I would say, sir, that I would rather be torn asunder by jackals than to play the harlot for a lot of drunken fools."

She had spoken so mildly and with such gravity that at first the men merely stared at her, their grins frozen on their faces. Then the centurion's brows drew down in a scowl.

"I say you come with us!"

"I will not!"

The centurion's face suffused with red and he seemed to have trouble gathering his thoughts. Servius leaned forward and said coldly, "Will you come, or must we take your Zealot friend and have him executed?"

"I am not a Zealot," said Lazarus. "You have no evidence of such a claim."

"We need no evidence." Servius chuckled. He gave Alysia a raking glance and said, "Is it a bargain? Your company, for his life?"

"She will not go with you. If you think her to be a harlot for hire you are mistaken. She is under my guardianship, and I will take this matter before the law."

Lazarus' words seemed to have no effect on the soldiers; in fact, only the centurion seemed to half hear them for he said thickly, "We are the law here."

Alysia thought, *With luck I will soon have a chance to escape them.* She couldn't let them kill Lazarus, and she had no doubt they could, and would!

Her voice was steady. "I will come."

"No, Alysia!" Lazarus reached out to grasp her arm. Mary screamed as one of the soldiers hefted his sword.

"We'll take her anyway," Servius announced, "and what use will you be to her, dead?"

He shoved his foot into Lazarus' chest, knocking him to the ground. Before he could get to his feet and stop her, Alysia moved toward the centurion, who pulled her up to sit before him. She managed to poke her elbow in his ribs before he urged the horse forward with a grunt and they started up the stony path. She caught a glimpse of Mary's shocked, white face and heard Lazarus shout, "I'll find Nathan—we'll come for you!" and then there were only the sounds of clattering hooves and men laughing and jeering.

The pathway descended at a steep incline through the Kidron Valley, then began to rise as they traversed the long, Roman-built row of steps leading up the hill to the southeastern gate. One by one the horses trotted through the gate, which was dim and cool within the thick city wall. On the other side a publican gathered up his day's collection of coins and gave them a look of bored curiosity.

For the second time that day Alysia passed through the lower section of the city, with its hills and slopes and streets running in every direction, its bazaars and shops of all manner of craftsmen—potters, weavers, bakers, carpenters, perfume-makers. Here stood the close-packed houses of the poor and those of moderate means. The heavy traffic of the morning and afternoon had all but disappeared. There were few pedestrians, and a pack of half-wild dogs snarled at them from a foul-smelling gutter. A bridge spanned yet another deep valley and they ascended into the upper section—the well laid-out streets, many of them paved, the homes of Roman officials, the mansions of wealthy and powerful Jews.

Alysia rode in icy silence, though her heart pounded sickeningly, and she tried to be alert for any possible means of escape. But her skirts were caught under the centurion's legs and he kept one arm tight around her. The men had tried to draw her into conversation and, failing that, fell to giving lusty appraisals of her face and figure. Cringing inwardly, she wondered what horrors the night would hold for her. Was there no one to help her? If only Nathan would come, but he was away on one of his mysterious trips. It wasn't possible that Lazarus would find him in time. And what could he or Lazarus or anyone do against these brutish soldiers?

Passing beneath an arched viaduct, they went around the huge platform on which sat the Temple and began climbing a wide ramp that ascended sharply to the Roman fortress. It was almost dark now, and Alysia could see nothing but the outer wall. The centurion guided his horse onto the ramp and she saw a colossal wooden door that began to swing open as they approached.

They entered a courtyard, riding beneath another arched bridge connecting the fortress to what she assumed was the Temple area. Looking up, she could barely see the sentries on the wall between the battlements as another door opened; they climbed another ramp to an area enclosing the soldiers' barracks and several other buildings.

Alysia had hoped to see superior officers or others in authority who would stop these men. But there were only guards, who saluted the centurion as if he were the one in charge. A deep panic gripped her, much like the feeling she'd had when she'd first been taken from her home in Athens—that familiar sense of unreality, that this could not be happening! She felt the centurion slide off the horse, then he reached up and pulled her toward him. Distantly she heard the men arguing, haggling over her; she lashed out and scratched one of them. The centurion grabbed her arm and pulled her into one of the buildings. It seemed almost like a palace, with a long flight of stairs leading to other rooms. The foyer was empty and dimly lit by a single lamp hanging from the ceiling.

The centurion may have been drunk but he was strong. When he began to pull her toward the stairs Alysia came alive, struggling, kicking and scratching, but either he was too intoxicated to feel her efforts or his body was made of iron, for he gave her little heed. She tried to grasp his dagger but he laughed and twisted her hand away. Could she bring herself to kill another man? She would never escape without being killed herself!

They stumbled into another room, a bedroom. The soldier slammed the door shut and shoved a bolt into place. Alysia ran to the opposite side of the room. He turned and with a leering grin started toward her. Seeing a heavy oil lamp beside the bed, she plunged toward it, her hand closing over the thick handle. It flew through the air to graze the side of his graying head. He yelped with pain; his grin turned into a grimace and he lurched forward.

Alysia retreated until she felt the wall at her back. She could smell the heavy, fermented drink on his breath. Then he grunted loudly, hiccupped, and with a slow, weaving motion dropped to the floor. His eyes closed and he began to snore.

She stared at him for a moment, hardly daring to breathe lest she wake him from this unexpected repose. He didn't move and she finally forced her shaking limbs to step over the inert form. She unbolted the door and pushed against it, but it didn't budge against her wildly pressing hands. Someone had barred it from the outside to prevent her escape. She slid the bolt again as the centurion had done. Casting her gaze frantically around the room she saw there was no window, and there was nothing she could use for a weapon. Except—one of the clay shards of the broken lamp had a jagged edge. She picked it up gingerly.

She felt overcome with weariness. Every bone and muscle ached from tension and the long ride through the city. She dragged a blanket from the bed and sat down in a corner of the room, concealing her improvised weapon underneath the blanket. She didn't know if she would be able to use it, but it gave her a small sense of satisfaction.

She whispered, and didn't know if she meant it, "God of Abraham, if you are really there, protect me and see me safely home."

A strange moaning sound woke her. The centurion sat on the bed, elbows on his knees, head in his hands, with a chamber pot on the floor before him. He slowly ran his hands through his thinning gray hair and turned to look at her through swollen eyelids. Alysia shrank from his gaze and pulled the blanket up to her chin, clutching the shard of pottery in her other hand. He made a noncommittal sound and turned away, as if annoyed by her presence.

During the night she had heard someone knocking at the door; she'd heard voices and then one of the other soldiers had called, "Marcus, let us in! You've had her long enough!" She waited in horrific suspense, but the centurion snored on and never moved. She heard the men mumbling and clattering back down the stairs. They had not returned and somehow she had slept.

She rose hesitantly, quickly adjusted her garments, and ran her fingers through her tangled black hair. Her mantle had long since been ripped from her and she felt strangely bare without it, though she held onto the blanket. Her movements brought the centurion's eyes back to her and she stopped, paralyzed.

Could it be that he looked—ashamed? He refused to look directly into her eyes and a slow red crept into the greenish tint of his face.

Reaching up, he unhooked his red cloak and dropped it onto the floor, then promptly heaved the contents of his stomach into the chamber pot. Alysia's eyes widened and she shrank still further into the blanket, which she held against her as if it were a magic shield.

After a while, the soldier shifted position, wiped his face with the cloak and cleared his throat.

"Young woman, it occurs to me you have been somewhat—misused. My men had no right to force you to come with us." He paused and peered painfully at her. "For whatever happened last night you have my apology."

She could only stare at him with her mouth open.

"I must get you out of this fort. Not only for your own protection, but—for other reasons. If I agree to see that you are escorted safely home, do I have your word you will say nothing of this to anyone?"

Alysia saw no need to make promises to him, since obviously he had to get her home somehow. "I—I cannot say that I will not discuss it with anyone, but I will not seek to charge any of you with a crime. Nothing good would come of making this widely known. I should not like for anyone to know about it."

"I am not exactly . . . rational when I am drunk. And I remember very little. Weren't you with someone when you were taken?"

"My family."

"What will they do?"

"The man to whom I am betrothed will be very angry."

The centurion winced. "I believe we must have thought you were a prostitute. You are . . . uncommonly beautiful."

She looked down and said nothing.

"I must have your word. There is a man I know, a diplomat, who can take you home and perhaps reassure your family. But he is at Herod's palace. If I take you there, you must remain silent and allow me to explain the situation to him. If you break your word, we will all swear you are lying; we will say that you propositioned us. Do you understand?"

"I understand very well, Centurion."

He waited a moment, then drew himself up with a grimace and staggered to the door. He slid back the bolt and bellowed for a sentry, holding his head as if it might fall off at any moment. The door was unbarred and without a backward glance the centurion left the room.

It seemed a long time later that he returned and escorted her from the upper hall into one of the reception rooms below. He had washed himself and straightened his uniform. Three of the other men had gathered there—she supposed the fourth was lying insensible in his quarters. They were subdued and eyed her gloomily, as if she were responsible for the present situation.

"Go and make yourself presentable," the centurion said irritably. "And get rid of that," he added, snatching away the blanket she still held against her. With a disgusted air he threw it on the floor.

Alysia saw her mantle lying on the tiled floor near the blanket. She retrieved it and marched angrily toward the room indicated by the soldier. It proved to be a washroom, with a large basin of water on a marble pedestal, linens, and a bronze mirror hanging on the wall. She washed her hands and face and tried to repair her appearance.

In the other room, the centurion looked from one surly face to another. "Don't tell me you're unhappy because I bolted the door! You would be in far worse trouble had I not done so."

Servius said, "Are you not overly concerned, Marcus? Just send her home and be done with her."

"This is your fault, Servius, and by the gods I'll never listen to you again! First I let you talk me into visiting Herodium, and then drinking all the way back! The Jews in her town could bring trouble over this. It will require more diplomacy than I can offer. I will leave her with a friend of mine, one of Herod's advisors whose task it is to smooth things over with the Jews. He will see to her well-being. And some monetary recompense may be necessary—more than I can provide."

"You are making too much of this," said the other man coldly. "She is not important—it is nothing. Send her home, or get rid of her somehow. Don't involve anyone else."

"As I said, Saltus is a friend. He will know the best course of action."

"You've grown soft over the girl," Servius muttered, with a smile that didn't reach his eyes.

The centurion allowed the remark to pass. "This is a serious problem. The new commander is due to arrive in the next few days and this must be resolved beforehand. Pontius Pilate doesn't mind making trouble for the Jews, but this Paulus Valerius has a reputation for exacting justice no matter who it involves, and he will not let the incident go without an investigation. Where would we stand then? We could only say we were too drunk to know what we were doing. I doubt that will exonerate us in his eyes!"

No one said anything. Alysia came back into the room.

"She has given her word that she will say nothing, in exchange for being returned safely home."

"And you believe her?" Servius almost sneered.

"She has her own reputation to protect," Marcus replied. He looked at Alysia. "Let's go."

She fell in step behind him, only too glad to be leaving the company of the other soldiers who stared after her like dogs thwarted of a bone. The centurion now wore a crested helmet and a fresh mantle over his uniform. Alysia followed him down a flight of stairs, across a courtyard, and this time went through a less conspicuous doorway to the street below. Other soldiers and guards watched them curiously and she was careful to draw her mantle over her head and half over her face.

It was a cloudy day and uncomfortably warm. Marcus told her to walk in front of him. "And don't try to run away," he growled. "Keep walking straight ahead until I tell you to stop."

A viaduct ran directly from the Temple area to Herod's palace, but the soldier chose not to use it. Instead they walked on the street level, mingling with many others who hurried here and there and paid them no mind. They passed several houses of exquisite design, some of which looked like palaces. On they went until they came to another upraised platform, similar to the one the Jewish Temple had been built upon. It, too, was walled all around, with towers standing at each end. They were now in a large market area, quite different from that of the lower city; here were the gold and silversmiths, the jewel and silk merchants, the master tailors. The people were aristocrats, well dressed, moving about more sedately than those she had seen yesterday.

Suddenly, the centurion stopped and stood completely still for a moment, staring up at the entrance gate. He seemed to be debating upon his course of action. Alysia held her breath, then his heavily creased face took on a look of resignation and he gestured for her to precede him. She climbed a steep flight of steps and stopped short as she came in direct view of a long row of Roman guards. Paralyzed, she saw the centurion speak to one of them. He nodded toward her, frowning, and she followed him through the gate.

Alysia's mouth dropped open. Never had she seen anything so magnificent, even in Rome. An immense courtyard spread out before them, with a Roman-tiled floor decorated by mosaics of pomegranate leaves and other designs. Lush rose gardens, groves of trees, and clipped hedges surrounded it, along with marble benches and bronze fountains. A huge pond with a fountain dominated its center. At either end stood two villas, all marble and gold; between them were other stately buildings. Columned porticoes lined the other two sides of the pavilion. Sentries stood at their appointed places, and slaves in their native dress hurried importantly on their errands. Here and there groups of people were gathered in conversation.

"Yes," said Marcus, noticing her stunned expression. "Rich as Croesus."

Alysia swallowed and whispered nervously, "What if this friend of yours has better things to do than taking care of me?"

"There is little choice in the matter. And he owes me a favor."

Alysia forced herself to remain still and clasped her hands together. Marcus spoke to one of the other guards. The guard consulted briefly with a man who sat at a desk beneath the portico across from them, then returned at a brisk pace.

"Ambassador Saltus has left for Caesarea, Centurion. He sails for Rome tomorrow."

Alysia's heart sank and she looked quickly at Marcus, sensing his quandary. "I will return to Bethany alone."

"That is absurd. Do you know your way through this city? If something were to happen to you, my men and I would be worse off than before."

She had had enough of him thinking only of himself, as if she were responsible for his predicament! As always, her patience ended abruptly and her temper soared out of control.

"Then what do you propose, my gallant Roman?" she gritted out, her voice heavy with sarcasm.

The centurion shrugged his shoulders, unaware of her foul mood. "We will return to the fort and make other arrangements."

"No!"

Looking at her face, Marcus was filled with alarm. All activity stopped at the sound of the angry and vehement voice.

"I will not return with you to your men! And you cannot force me!"

"You are mad," he said, glancing uneasily at the spectators now staring at them with amused interest.

"Leave me alone! I will find my own way back." Alysia whirled, then felt him grab her arm.

"Have you no gratitude, woman?" he snarled and she saw a trace of the meanness in him that had been so manifest the day before.

"Gratitude! After what you have done?"

Her words reverberated throughout the courtyard. Alysia stopped, aware that she had become the center of attention. She saw out of the corner of her eye that several people were coming toward her.

"Now see what you've done!" Marcus whispered harshly, but Alysia only snatched her arm out of his grasp.

"What goes here, Centurion?"

Marcus abruptly came to attention. Alysia saw a rather short man, surrounded by slaves or bodyguards, with a florid face in which were set small, brown eyes. His graying hair fell in oily curls; he wore a scarlet robe over which hung a black cloak, heavily embroidered with gold threads. Jewelry adorned his thick neck, arms, and fingers. His gray-streaked beard came to a point on his chin.

"What have you done to put this young woman into such a fine rage?"

"My, er, slave—"

"I am not his slave!" Alysia cried. "This Roman and his contemptible soldiers took me against my will from my friends on the road to Bethany!"

The oily man fixed the centurion with a stern look. "Is this true?"

Marcus licked his lips. "With respect, Herod Antipas, this matter does not fall within your jurisdiction."

Herod smiled benignly. "Quite true, Centurion, but perhaps you would not like the incident to come before the new commander. I am certain I can be of service." He turned to a guard and ordered crisply, "Escort these two to my receiving chambers."

The ruler of Galilee marched sedately ahead, followed by his retinue. Marcus and Alysia were obliged to trail after him. The people around them had gone back to their own pursuits as if such occurrences were not unusual. She was regretting her outburst, although she did hope the centurion was suitably anxious for his own welfare.

They reached the massive building at the north end of the great court and found themselves in a marble-walled chamber, furnished with chairs and couches, statues, tapestries, and a thick Persian carpet. Herod seated himself in a throne-like chair in the center of the room. His attendants disappeared, but two more emerged from an arched doorway to stand over him and wave huge palm leaves, stirring the still, warm air.

Herod regarded his visitors with a sober eye. "And what is the complaint, Centurion?"

Marcus opened his mouth but Alysia had already begun. She told the story in detail, with a vivid description of the drunken state of Marcus and his men when they abducted her. The centurion groaned inwardly, then widened his eyes in surprise. She was taking care to tell of his consideration toward her after he had regained his senses.

"I cannot blame you, Centurion, for your rashness when under the influence of strong drink—and such beauty. However, neither can I condone your actions. You did well to bring her to me. I shall say nothing to Pontius Pilate, nor to your superior officers. I shall see that the matter is handled with tact. There is no reason for you to remain here."

Alysia was surprised when Marcus hesitated and she saw him glance at her with almost a look of pity. But then he moved with a clatter of his sword, nodded briefly, and left without another word.

"What is your name, child?"

She told him.

"Where is your family?"

"I have no real family. I am living with friends in Bethany."

"And they, I presume, will be looking for you?"

"Yes."

"My dear, you must not hold the actions of a few simple-minded soldiers against the entire garrison. The important thing is that you are quite safe now, and you must allow me to—compensate you in some way."

She supposed he meant money. Before she could haughtily refuse, he said, "There is a storm coming in from the west. A bit early this year for storms, but as you can see, it is already raining." His head moved smoothly toward the window; there was indeed a fine sheet of rain spattering onto the pavement outside. Thunder rumbled with the threat of more to come.

"You must stay overnight as my guest. I have a stepdaughter about your age whom you will enjoy meeting."

His words caught her off guard. "No—I will not trouble you. Could you send a messenger to Bethany so my friends may come for me?"

"I will send a messenger, yes—to say that you are safe and will arrive in the next few days. Neither your friends nor you should venture out in this storm. As for my messenger, he is used to such danger. And he has a very fast horse."

Without waiting for a reply, Herod smiled and clapped his hands. The heavy bronze door swung open and a bald, Germanic-looking slave waited expectantly.

"Show this young woman to a room near Salome's. Have one of the women find her some clothes. Of course, Alysia, you must keep whatever they give you as your own."

Alysia perceived that she was being bribed, and there was something else—she didn't like the way he looked at her. In fact, she didn't like anything about this king, or whatever he called himself. He might be rich and important, but that didn't mean she had to obey him. Especially since he governed Galilee, not Judea.

The slave bowed. As Alysia opened her mouth to protest, Herod said, "There will be a feast tonight. I have invited many guests; most of them are already here. I wish you would attend. I would deem it a returned favor."

A burst of thunder startled her and before she could speak Herod turned away and left the room, swift as a fox into its den. She gave a sigh of frustration and followed the slave.

The apartments to which she was led proved no less magnificent than the rest of the palace. The bedroom was brightly lit against the darkness of the approaching storm. A jewel-studded, purple silk canopy covered the enormous bed. Small cedar boxes reposed on an ornately carved table drawn close to the window. When she looked inside, she saw they were filled with jars of balsam, powdered rouge, kohl for lining the eyes, and salve to redden the lips. Clothes in the Roman fashion and shoes of every description stuffed the closets.

Beyond the bedroom was a large sitting room with a lounge for reclining and benches to accommodate guests. To the left, hidden by a screen made of reeds, stood a huge marble bathtub. An open cedar chest revealed thick towels and bottles of scented oils.

Alysia caught her breath. The shutters had been closed at the window and she pushed them slightly open. Rain was pouring down now, but she could still see the vague outline of the Judean mountains in the distance.

She closed the shutter and returned to the bedroom where she sat upon the bed. Something wasn't right. She should not have agreed to stay here—although, with all this luxury, it was certainly tempting.

She was incredibly tired. Her powers of reasoning seemed to have deserted her, nor did she feel capable of analyzing the situation in which she now found herself. She would think about it later, after she'd had just a few moments' rest . . .

The first rain of the season had wet the city as Paulus and his wife arrived in Jerusalem. It had been a four-day journey over roads that left much to be desired; the Jews were not road builders and only a few had been paved by the Romans. As they entered the city through one of the north gates, the smell of wet, dirty streets and gutters, food, and the smoke from extinguished cooking fires filled the air. This, and the sight of the skull-shaped hill where executions were carried out, were unfortunately the first impressions Megara received of her new home. The splendid sight of the Temple was hidden behind the Antonia Fortress from this angle, and not until they had proceeded some distance could she see the buildings erected by Herod the Great, the father of Antipas. Her indignant frown began to lift somewhat as they drew near Herod's palace where she was to reside.

Some miles back—and soon to her chagrin—she had abandoned her carriage, choosing to arrive in a fashionable, covered litter carried by slaves. Paulus rode on horseback, as he had the entire way, and behind them marched a detachment of legionaries in full military dress but bearing no standards. Their shields were plain but prominently displayed, along with their swords and javelins. Without wanting to antagonize the Jews, Paulus felt it wise to emphasize the strength and readiness of his troops.

An unexpected storm had spoiled Megara's grand entrance, for her slaves were now dripping and bedraggled, and her canopy was sodden and drooping. The dampness had even found its way inside the litter and her hair had fallen as limp as her clothes. Paulus' uniform was soaked but his hair was almost dry, and he hadn't minded the rain since it had cooled the air considerably.

He dismounted from his horse and handed the reins to a servant. He helped his wife emerge from her litter and restrained a smile at her puffed lips and glowering eyes. As they entered the courtyard they were greeted by a rush of dignitaries and staff.

Megara said in a low voice only he could hear, "I am afraid this city has a most unpleasant odor."

"It's an affliction common to large cities—Rome especially—if you'd ever been away and then returned. You might as well smooth out that patrician nose of yours. Besides, you can't deny that some of these buildings overshadow anything we have in Rome."

Megara answered him with a glare. He treated her like a child! He had changed. She couldn't quite put her finger on what was different but she was convinced it had something to do with that Greek slave who had drowned.

He, of course, had told her nothing, but Megara had very efficient spies. She knew that, after Alysia had murdered Magnus, Paulus had spirited her away on a ship that had sunk somewhere between Crete and Cyprus. Where once he had been merely quiet and slightly reserved, he had become taciturn and brooding—except when he was conversing with that Cyrenian slave, Simon, to whom she had taken an active dislike. Paulus never knew how to put slaves in their place.

Their entourage stopped in one of the great halls of the palace, and after seeing that Megara was ushered off to her apartments, Paulus took his leave before Herod Antipas himself made an appearance. He would meet the tetrarch soon enough and as usual he had no patience for political posturing.

On horseback and accompanied by the legionaries he turned back toward the Antonia, built by Herod the Great and fawningly named after the Roman general, Mark Antony. The fort was highly visible even from several blocks away, so tall and formidable looking that it appeared to be one single tower, though each of three corners boasted its own tower while the fourth, overlooking the Temple area, reared up higher than all.

A huge ramp spanned a ravine on the west side, which was the main entrance to the fortress. Paulus went up first, accompanied by twelve rows of legionaries marching four abreast. These men would stay overnight, then return to Caesarea. There were six thousand men stationed here, now under Paulus' authority. During the periods of Jewish festivals, there was ample room to host hundreds more, who came from Caesarea and other forts to "enforce" the peace.

He entered the main courtyard, noting the bridge as well as a set of stairs that connected the fort to the Temple. He went through a wooden doorway, up another much narrower ramp, to the area above. It looked like a small city.

Along each wall were the soldiers' barracks; there were residences for visitors, baths, a parade ground, a temple, the judgment hall where criminals were brought (and its whipping post), and in the midst stood the praetorium, almost a small palace. Paulus knew that underneath the fort were dungeons to house prisoners; there was also, somewhere underneath, a secret passage connecting the fort with the interior of the Temple. All around were trees growing in pots, well-tended shrubbery, and statues of Roman athletes.

Immediately a servant took his horse and led it away to the stable. A young man introduced himself as Petrus, the temporary commander, explaining that he had been away and only just returned, but would Paulus like to inspect the troops . . . he had just lined them up on the parade ground . . . ?

Paulus answered affirmatively and took his measure of the troops, thinking that for all their smart appearance he detected a certain lack of discipline that would have to be dealt with promptly. The soldiers regarded Paulus with respect and some unease, for his reputation had preceded him. He was known as being rigid but fair, ruthless in battle, outspoken regarding military matters, and close-mouthed about everything else. This Paulus Valerius Maximus did not strut about and shout his orders as the former commander had done, but he had a naturally compelling air that seemed to make a silent demand for obedience.

And he was liked by Tiberius and disliked by Sejanus, a lethal combination—yet he was still alive. The question as to why he had been appointed to command a fort in a Jewish province, under the governorship of a man who was not even his social equal, had already provoked much speculation.

Paulus gave them a short, improvised speech—he hadn't anticipated doing so until tomorrow—and finally was able to retire to the praetorium, where his living quarters would be. Simon helped him remove his cuirass; he got into a dry tunic, found a comfortable chair, sat back with a sigh, and propped his feet on a stool. A servant brought a tray of fresh figs stuffed with pistachios, a slab of goat cheese, and a pitcher of wine.

He motioned for Simon to sit down. "Here, have some figs—they're delicious. Tell me, Simon, have you ever been here before?"

"No, sir. My father was Greek, so we never made the pilgrimage. It's rather like Rome, is it not, sir?" Simon did sit, but very straight, and he only partook of two figs. Although he liked Paulus, he never forgot he was a slave.

"I can see why you would think so. Herod tried to turn it into a Roman city. You won't find as much of the . . . decadence, shall we say, that you find in Rome. At least it doesn't show outwardly—among the Jews. And you will find no statues of gods and Caesars, except in the Roman quarters. Graven images, you see. Their God would not approve. Most of them take their religion very seriously and to make jokes about him as we do our gods would be blasphemy."

"Do you know much of their religion, sir?"

Paulus leaned his head on the back of the cushioned chair and stared meditatively at the gilded ceiling. "I know that there is a reverence about it that I find impressive." After a pause he added, looking at his slave with a gleam of amusement in his eyes, "But don't misunderstand me, Simon. I speak of the people, not their leaders. The Sadducees are more political than religious and would kiss the back end of a donkey to retain their current position of importance.

"And as for the Pharisees . . . they won't even associate with anyone who doesn't observe their so-called rules of purification. They would rather walk into a wall than look at a woman on the street, which makes you wonder if their thoughts are as they should be to begin with! They're forever counting up their good deeds to make sure they outnumber any sins they may have unwittingly committed. And you will see some, Simon, who display such humility they look as if their beards are growing to their chests."

Simon was chuckling and Paulus grinned. "It would be interesting to see someone of their own faith take them down a peg or two. But it would take a very brave man."

"You paint an interesting picture, sir, but I'm not very familiar with the functions of these—whatever you called them. In fact, though my mother was Jewish, she died when I was very young, so I know little of Jewish ways or their past."

"Well, I will give you a brief lesson, then." Paulus put a fig in his mouth. "I think they have soaked these in honey and lemon juice—here, have another. Now where shall I begin?"

"How about when Pompey conquered the land a hundred years ago? I do know Roman history."

"Very well. You may be aware that the word *Palestine* comes from *Philistine*, which was the name of the original inhabitants—as far as our historians have discovered. Then the Israelites, or Jews as we call them, moved in—and believe me, their history has been anything but peaceful. After our conquest, Rome made the first Herod king over the whole country; he was very shrewd politically and had many powerful friends.

"But the Jews hated him. He was an Edomite; we Romans call the region Idumea. The Edomites are of mixed races, so naturally the Jews despise them, and Herod had an Arabian mother—so he was doubly cursed. You are probably familiar with the antics of Herod. He committed as many murders as any good throne-seeker in Rome, and many of them were of his own family."

"But obviously," Simon said, with a droll look, "a master builder."

"Indeed. The Jewish Temple, this fortress, all those palaces . . . you should see the one near Bethlehem. Amphitheaters, too, and race courses. He wanted to impress the Jews and at the same time seduce them into the Roman way of life.

"He died at last, and Rome divided his kingdom between three of his sons. Archelaus had Samaria and Judea, Antipas has Galilee and Perea, and Philip has a territory east of the Sea of Galilee. But Archelaus turned out to be too much like his father and so Judea is now ruled by procurators. Though Pilate is just a prefect because of his lack of military experience."

"But you were called prefect of Rome, sir."

"That, Simon, is a complicated situation that I'll have to pass over for now. Back to your original question—Rome allows the Jews a great deal of freedom, both political and religious. Their government is presided over by a supreme council called the Sanhedrin.

There are about seventy men or so on this council; their headquarters are here in Jerusalem. And these seventy are composed of Sadducees, who are aristocrats, and Pharisees, who are of the middle classes. They have beliefs that differ somewhat from each other, so there are often conflicts and squabbles. One thing they all agree on, though, is that they enjoy their freedom and don't want to give Rome any reason to take it away."

"It is surprising to me, sir, that Rome tolerates this self-government."

Paulus shrugged. "They're impossible to rule otherwise. They'd rather be slaughtered than make concessions regarding their religion. The people I mean—I'm not too sure about the priests. And I forgot to mention the elders and the scribes, the scribes being experts in Jewish law, and the elders are supposedly descendants of the ancient ruling families. Most of them are quite wealthy."

"And so this council governs all of Palestine?" Simon asked.

"Well, there are local courts throughout the provinces, but they all answer to the Sanhedrin. It's when they can't handle their own affairs that Rome must get involved, but that's Pilate's problem, not mine."

A curt knock on the door interrupted them. The guard opened it to admit a centurion, who saluted briefly. Paulus got to his feet and acknowledged the salute as Simon rose to stand across the room.

"Welcome to Jerusalem, sir. The cohort commander asked that I make a report." He was nervously grasping two sheets of heavily scribbled on papyrus.

"Thank you, Centurion. Your name?"

"Marcus Terentias, sir. I am the senior centurion. I regret that I wasn't present at the inspection earlier. I was occupied elsewhere."

Paulus wondered at the man's obvious unease and noticed that Marcus' hands were shaking. His bloodshot eyes and red face indicated a possible habituation to strong drink.

"I will serve on your administrative staff, sir, as we are short of tribunes here. We will be ready to assemble at your command. I understand you're particularly interested in Zealot activity."

"That is correct. The staff will meet in the morning an hour after sunrise. I would like to see all the reports you have, as well as a map of known meeting places and recent attacks."

"I am afraid not much is known, sir, as they strike without warning and then disappear. Their leaders are unknown to us."

"Do we have any in prison?"

"No, sir." The centurion looked uncomfortable, but then brightened. "There is a man you may wish to interview. Herod has him in prison at the fort in Machaerus. He claims not to be a Zealot, but he has amassed a strong following."

"What is his claim, then, that others should follow him?"

"He is said to be a religious prophet."

Paulus raised an eyebrow. "For what reason did Herod imprison him?"

The centurion succeeded in looking even more uncomfortable. "That is largely a matter of gossip, sir, but it was for religious reasons. It is said that Herod's wife was enraged because this man openly denounced her, and the tetrarch, for committing adultery."

"Ah," Paulus said, with a wry look at Simon. "As I recall, she divorced his brother, Philip, to marry Antipas. This prophet had better look out, if Herodias' temper is all it's rumored to be. What is his name? I might be interested in speaking with him."

"John, called the Baptizer, because he baptizes his disciples in the Jordan River. Our sources say his followers number in the thousands. There is another man, called Jesus of Nazareth, who is also gathering a following. So far he has confined himself to Galilee."

"I will, of course, adhere to the Roman custom of allowing certain religious liberties, but you may continue to watch these men and include their activities in your reports. I suspect, though, that this baptizer's days are numbered. Is that all, Centurion?"

"Sir, a messenger was sent to say that Herod Antipas extends his welcome and would like you and your wife to attend a feast tonight to celebrate your arrival. He is very sorry he was not able to greet you earlier today."

"You may send word we will be present, providing my wife is feeling well."

When the centurion had gone, Paulus looked at his slave with humor. "Sounds as if Herod had better get himself back to Galilee, if only to make sure he's not overrun with prophets. Or at least send Herodias. She'll make short work of them, no doubt."

Simon stifled a laugh, not sure if he should go so far as to imply mockery of the tetrarch's wife—it was all very well for the legate to do so. Instead he said, "It sounds as though you will have a busy evening, sir."

Paulus sighed. "One I'm not looking forward to, Simon, I assure you."

CHAPTER X

The sound of feminine giggling roused Alysia from a light sleep. Two young slave girls entered the room with pails of water and began to prepare a bath. They chattered to each other in some foreign tongue, eyeing her with shy curiosity. Glancing out the window she saw that night had fallen, and, listening for rain, she decided it had stopped. The room glowed yellow with lamplight.

Alysia managed to make the girls understand that she wished to bathe alone and they left after replacing the screen around the marble tub. When she stepped out of the tub and onto a wicker mat, she found the slaves had left clothes for her—delicately sewn undergarments, a cream-colored gown embellished with gold thread, and shoes with ribbons for lacing around her ankles. She eyed the box of cosmetics and at last could not resist them, but she applied them lightly. The slaves had also laid out a thick necklace inlaid with amethysts and gold beads and a matching pair of long earrings. She wound her hair in a knot and pinned it back.

Surveying herself in a mirror, she was almost startled to see the image of her former self, Alysia of Athens, daughter of a wealthy physician. It seemed a hundred years ago. She had never thought to see herself this way again.

She felt as if she had become two people. Alysia of Bethany did not belong here—should leave at once! There was nothing to justify her presence at Herod's party, no reason for it, except that apparently it would please him and was no doubt intended to assuage her indignation.

The other Alysia, this ghost of her former self, liked the way she looked and thought with longing of being a guest of the king, in the king's palace. She would be admired, as she had always been before, and she would be able to talk with people who had similar backgrounds to her own and who wouldn't look down upon her as a slave or a foreigner.

Yes, she admitted to herself, it was a struggle with her vanity, and the old Alysia won. She could only hope there would be no one present who would recognize her as a fugitive from Roman justice! True, the world was getting smaller all the time, but it was beyond credibility that she would be seen here by someone who would know her face and what she had done. Besides, she looked quite different than she had in Rome.

A soft knock on the door caused her to jerk away from the mirror. A young woman opened the door and came boldly inside, looking at her with sharp curiosity. "I am Salome, Herod's stepdaughter. You must be Alysia."

"Yes." Alysia couldn't help staring at the other woman. Salome wore a gown of diaphanous yellow cloth and beneath it only the briefest of undergarments. She had jewels in her long hair, which was obviously dyed blonde and had been frizzled with curling tongs, giving her a wild, licentious appearance. Her face was artfully painted in the manner of the Egyptians.

Salome smiled. "He sent me to find you. Won't you come with me?"

Alysia followed her into the corridor and Salome paused so she could walk beside her. She gave Alysia a sidewise glance that took in everything from her hair to the tips of her shoes.

The corridor was full of people, all well dressed and perfumed, who seemed to be heading for the same destination. In a moment they arrived at a great banquet hall. The music of harps, reed pipes, and cymbals played from shadowy corners and competed with the noise made by hundreds of talking, laughing people.

Alysia felt deceitful somehow, as if she were pretending to be someone she was not. *And that,* she thought suddenly, *is exactly what I am doing.*

Salome reached out to take a cup of wine from a tray, handed it to Alysia, and took another for herself. "This is your first time?" she asked, sipping her wine.

"My first time?" Alysia repeated blankly.

"That is, your first time here at the palace. Your first association with my stepfather?"

"Oh, yes. I met him this morning."

She caught a glimpse of Herod parading about in his stately robes, a large chalice held in one bejeweled hand. His face was flushed and jovial. Looking around, she saw a woman who must be Herod's wife, dressed in scarlet with a huge, ruby-studded headdress. Heavy earrings dangled from her ears and rings glittered coldly on her thin fingers. A massive gold necklace hung around her long, thin neck and seemed to slightly stoop her shoulders.

A slurred voice near her ear startled her and she turned to see the leering face of the tetrarch. "What fortune is mine," he whispered conspiratorially, "to have the two fairest women on earth grace my kingdom!"

Alysia thought it futile to remind him they were in Judea, not Galilee. Nor was she certain how to respond, so she merely said with a forced smile, "You are overkind, my lord."

"Overkind?" Herod gurgled with laughter. "No one has ever accused me of that before!" He leaned close to her. "Your head is much too lovely to roll in the dust, my dear. For your sake I shall forgive the insult."

When the king had wobbled on his way, Salome gave her a mysterious look and giggled. Then abruptly she straightened, drawing in her breath. "There he is—that must be him! The new commander, of course."

"What?"

"Just coming through the door. He has a woman with him, his wife I suppose. Mother's talking to her, so she must be important. I wonder if that red hair is her own—oh, but *he* is magnificent!"

Alysia smiled without turning. "Adonis?" she said lightly, wondering how she might escape. She didn't belong here; she'd been a fool to come.

"No . . . He is Mars, the god of war. Oh, to be his Aphrodite!" Alysia began to turn but Salome caught her arm. "Don't look now. He is staring at us."

Alysia had to laugh, amused by the young woman's flair for drama. But as Salome proceeded to describe the object of her attention, she stopped laughing.

"From his uniform he is a legate or a general. He's half a head taller than most of the others. Perhaps thirty or thirty and five. Light hair, long for a Roman, blue or green eyes—I can tell even from this distance . . ."

Alysia stiffened, feeling the blood drain from her face. How many other Roman legates could claim that description, and with a red-haired wife!

The Roman paused and stared at the woman in the cream-colored gown who stood with her back to him. There was a striking familiarity about the set of her shoulders, the curve of her back . . .

Alysia! Then he scoffed at himself. Impossible! And yet . . .

The young woman inclined her head to listen to her companion, and the well-known gesture brought a flare of unexpected pain to his heart. He started toward her but a flock of people crossed in front of him, blocking his way. The woman seemed to become rigid, as if feeling his eyes upon her, and Paulus knew then who she was, with a sureness he could never have explained.

Alysia turned slowly, and as she did all the music, the noise, the chatter receded, until she was deaf and dumb and lost in a world where there were only two people, herself and the tall man across the room. Their gazes collided in mutual amazement.

She was alive! Paulus didn't know how or why, but she was here and fate had led him to her. Then, on the heels of that thought another one struck him. She must have been here all these months and had not communicated with him, had not even let him know she was alive. Someone had taken his arm, and he tore his eyes away from the wide, dark violet ones to look into the ruddy face of the tetrarch, who led him straight toward Alysia and the woman beside her.

"Legate Paulus Maximus, er, I forgot the other name—it is a pleasure and an honor to have your presence here. Let me introduce you to my step-Salome."

Alysia began to quake as Herod rambled drunkenly. She had never expected to see Paulus again. He would think her heartless and dishonest to have run away after he had gone to such lengths to help her. How could she make him understand?

"I saw you staring, and who would not!" Herod cackled with good humor.

Paulus acknowledged the introduction and Salome's gaze scanned him boldly.

"Welcome to Judea, Legate," she said silkily.

"And, er, what is your name again?" Herod inquired of Alysia.

"It—I—" she stuttered, incapable of speech.

"Alysia," said Paulus. "I believe we have met before."

Paulus' gaze seemed to mock her with its calm. He had an innate self-possession that never seemed threatened, no matter what he saw or heard. She couldn't know of the inner turmoil surging inside him, kept at bay by strength born of a lifetime of carefully leashed emotions.

Alysia found her voice. "It is possible, sir."

Salome did not seem pleased that Paulus and Alysia knew each other. A man touched her arm and she turned away, even as someone refilled Herod's goblet and he was off again to make his rounds. Alysia became aware of a familiar voice calling Paulus' name. They turned simultaneously and she stood face-to-face with Megara.

Megara stopped. She blinked. A slender hand slid to her throat where a pulse began to beat spasmodically.

"You—" she breathed in a harsh whisper. The look in her eyes could have chiseled granite. A striking gong momentarily drowned out every sound and people began to move en masse toward an adjoining room. Alysia was swept along behind Paulus and Megara.

Herodias had arranged the great hall in imitation of a Roman banquet, with the tables arranged in groups of three and with several dining couches drawn up to them. A slave ushered Alysia to the king's table, where Paulus and his wife were also being seated. Paulus' rank had, no doubt, earned him the honor, but Alysia wondered why she had been so chosen. Salome also reclined at the table, beside her mother.

She was never to remember much about the feast. Platters were loaded with viands and delicacies of every description, from wild boar to lobster; those with more exotic tastes sampled the flamingo tongues and peacock brains. She was vaguely aware of an elderly man, an advisor to Herod, who reclined next to her and showered her with compliments—and saliva from his toothless gums.

She was conscious only of Paulus. He talked and laughed with some of his officers, yet Alysia knew he was keenly aware of her presence. She lost count of the number of times she looked up to find his eyes upon her.

Megara became sullen and withdrawn. "Why couldn't the sea have swallowed you, sorceress?" she raved silently. "Now you will weave your spell over Paulus all over again. Well, we shall see what happens when it is discovered what you did in Rome!"

The meal seemed to last for an eternity. At intervals, some of the guests staggered from the room to regurgitate what they had consumed so they might continue eating with more gusto. When the servants had cleared the tables of everything except the wine, Herod clapped his hands for silence. The roar of noise gradually diminished and faces turned toward him expectantly.

"We will have dancing!" he cried, his face bright with excitement.

At once, a primitive beat of drums began at a mad tempo and a score of gyrating dancers burst into the room. Alysia had seen and heard enough of Roman banquets to know what to expect; the dancing would be quite sexually suggestive, the drinking and merry-making would increase, and—*what was I thinking to come here?*

Herod laughed at some crude jest and, turning, caught Alysia's eye and winked boldly. He gestured for a slave to refill her cup.

She glanced quickly away and noticed that Paulus had seen this exchange. Something flickered in his eyes she could not interpret. Disgust? Jealousy? She would have given anything to know his feelings. Unable to sit still any longer, she rose and made her way unhindered to the arched doorway. She knew Paulus turned his head; she felt his eyes burning into her back with every step she took.

She found her way to an empty room that opened onto a balcony and walked across it to the railing, letting the breeze cool her flushed cheeks. Torches flared and smoked at each corner of the balcony, and her gaze lifted toward the great, shining moon.

At last the sound of the drums ceased, followed by the patter of bare feet as the dancers scampered from the room. A scraping of couches and chairs told her there was to be a pause in the entertainment. Footsteps sounded in the hallway, a single set of footsteps that paused now and again, as if searching. Was Herod looking for her?

She turned and looked up to see Paulus walking slowly toward her.

"You seem to know your way around the palace," he said, standing against the marble balustrade. "How long have you been here?"

"Only since this morning." Her voice was unnaturally high pitched, and she pressed her hands together to keep them from shaking.

Paulus waited. His own mind was still struggling to accept the fact that she now stood before him, flesh and blood and stunningly beautiful.

"You see, I—I was brought here against my will." Briefly she related the events of yesterday and this morning.

A muscle twitched in his cheek. "I assure you that the men responsible will be punished. Is that all you would like to tell me?"

"Yes. I mean, no. I suppose you are wondering why I didn't go to Cyprus."

At his nod, she went on. "There had been a storm, and the ship stopped at Crete. And then I—didn't get back on. I boarded a different one. I was afraid. And I wanted to be free. Free to live, and to marry, as I chose."

After a moment he said, "That is understandable."

"Are you—am I still your slave?"

"I acquired someone else for Selena. I suppose now you do . . . belong to me."

He paused and she felt the suspense mount until she thought she would suffocate if her breathing didn't return to normal. Finally he said, "But I have no use for another slave. I won't take your freedom from you a second time. I can put it in writing if you like."

She shook her head quickly. The last thing she wanted was for someone to find evidence of her former bondage.

"Thank you. I can pay you. Not all at once, but—"

He interrupted. "No. You owe me nothing."

"Sir—"

"You were to call me Paulus. Remember?"

"Paulus," she almost whispered, "would you have someone you trust take me home in the morning?"

"In the morning," he said, "might be too late."

"What do you mean?"

"Alysia." For a moment she saw the former Paulus, saw caring and concern in his eyes. "Why do you think that perverted old fool wants you to stay here?"

"Because—" She stopped, and saw his meaning. "I suppose I didn't think. With everything that's happened, I—I just assumed he was trying to smooth my feelings, so that I wouldn't cause trouble."

"Maybe you didn't see the way he looked at you."

She glanced down at the floor, embarrassed. "I am the one who is a fool."

"How could you know?" he said quietly. "I've heard his usual method is to lure young women into the palace under certain pretenses, then get them drunk. Then they are too ashamed to tell anyone, or even if they did, he is the king. Rome cares nothing about his habits—Rome has worse habits."

"But why? He could have any number of slaves or mistresses. Why would he risk such a thing?"

"Boredom. The thrill of the risk."

"I must get out of here tonight!"

"Yes, you must." She looked up to see a kind, half-smile on his face. "Come, Alysia. I will take you home."

Paulus had gone to get his horse. There were more guests in the corridors. Most had partaken too liberally of wine and were being escorted by slaves to their bedchambers. Alysia tried in vain to find the room she'd been given; the palace was like a city, with hallways leading in every direction. She stopped looking, afraid she would see Herod Antipas rounding a corner at any moment. Besides, hadn't he told her to keep the clothes? She would just have to leave her own things behind.

But she wouldn't keep the jewelry. Passing through one of the many vestibules, she removed the necklace and earrings and left them atop a pedestal bearing a small statue of Eros—a fitting gesture, she thought. Through a window she glimpsed the main courtyard, found a doorway leading to it, and stepped out into the night. There were guards standing here and there but before she could speak with one of them a man stepped out of the shadows and came toward her. As he approached one of the torches that burned nearby, she saw that he had dark hair and a sober expression that was at variance with the twinkle in his eyes.

"My name is Simon," he said. "Do you remember me?"

"Yes, you're Paulus' . . ."

"Slave." He smiled when she hesitated. "He thought it best for you not to be seen together, for your sake. He'll be waiting for you at the southeast gate."

As they descended the steps to the street below, two slaves in short, dark tunics appeared, bearing a covered palanquin. Alysia turned and looked at Simon.

"It is for you," he said. "The legate's orders."

The slaves lowered the conveyance and Simon helped her inside and drew the curtains. "I'll follow you. Don't be afraid."

Alysia hadn't been afraid since the moment she saw Paulus, but it did feel strange to travel this way. In Athens she had always walked or ridden in carriages, and the litter that had carried her to the Aquilinus house had not been nearly as luxurious as this one, with its padded seats and armrests. The curtains were almost transparent and she could see the streets gleaming in the moonlight. There were few people about at this hour.

Down the sloping streets and the many long flights of stairs they went to the lower city, then through the same gate Alysia had entered with the soldiers. She felt the litter touch the ground and the curtains opened to reveal Simon, who gave her his hand. He gestured to the other slaves and they all disappeared within the city gate.

Paulus stood waiting for her, holding the reins of his horse. "Walk or ride?" he asked.

Glancing at him sideways, she remembered too well the last time they had ridden together; she remembered too well his sea blue eyes, his face tanned to bronze, the sun-streaked mane of tawny hair . . .

"Walk," she said hastily.

Paulus made no reply, and with him leading his horse they fell into step together. The narrow road barely gave them room to walk side by side, and the egg-shaped moon shone brightly down on the white rocks lining the valley. She hadn't realized her teeth were chattering until he wordlessly removed his white mantle and laid it across her shoulders. It warmed her at once.

"Thank you," she murmured. "The nights are often cold here."

Why didn't he say something?

"I've never known you to wear the white uniform," she said lightly.

"It is only for tonight. Sometimes it is wise to . . . make a statement," he answered obliquely, and fell silent again.

"I suppose Herod Antipas will be furious with me," she said.

"I think I will have a talk with the good king of Galilee," he replied, and, glancing at her, he asked, "Tell me again about these men who took you; what were their names? Did they . . . hurt you?"

"No." Alysia felt herself flush; she hated speaking of it. "The centurion—his name was Marcus—took me to a room and fell asleep before anything happened. Another was called Servius. I didn't hear the other three called by name."

"I assure you they will be punished."

"You won't . . . kill them, will you?"

"They deserve to die. Their intention was very clear, whether or not it was carried out."

"Please don't! They do deserve to be punished but the centurion made things right, or tried to. I don't want anyone to die because of me."

They had emerged from the Kidron Valley and began climbing toward the shoulder of the Mount of Olives. Alysia had to hold up her long gown and step carefully in the thin shoes. A low brick wall ran alongside to their right, and to their left the moon revealed a deep, shadowed forest.

Paulus said at last, "As you wish."

Another silence fell, except for the insects and their own footsteps, and the rhythmic clip-clop of the horse's hooves. She stumbled; he caught her arm and asked, "Why don't you ride?"

"No, I want to walk."

"So," he said, after a moment, "you are living with the Jews. Have you accepted their religion?"

"I—I am not certain yet. Do you know that they believe in one great, all-powerful God? That he created the world and—"

"Yes, I am aware of their beliefs," he interrupted, with the slightest edge to his voice. "Their writings go back to the beginning of time. Many of our Greek and Roman myths are based on them."

"Oh, but they're very different."

"Different in the sense that our gods are silly and perverse, but the ideas come from the Jews, who wrote of strange and perverse creatures that existed before the great flood, matings between humans and the so-called fallen angels—" He broke off and shook his head. "I'm not in the mood for a discussion of religion, Alysia."

"And what is your mood, Paulus?"

When he didn't answer she rushed on, knowing she owed him an explanation. But first there were things *she* needed to know.

"Paulus, whatever happened about Magnus?"

"There was an investigation by the Senate. Lucius swore you murdered Magnus, deliberately and with premeditation. I told them what really happened, but it wouldn't matter much, even if they believed me. I reported that you were believed dead but Magnus' family doesn't trust me. You are still being sought by authorities in Rome, and in Greece as well."

She was puzzled. "Why did you think I was dead?"

Again he hesitated. "The ship to Cyprus was capsized by the storm you spoke of. Everyone was killed."

Stunned, Alysia stared straight ahead. He'd gone a whole year believing her dead! He certainly hadn't appeared to be overjoyed when he saw her tonight. It seemed obvious he had no real feelings for her.

She said, in a cooler tone, "You risked much when you helped me escape."

"The risk was mine to take."

Shivering again, she pulled his mantle closer. "How did you come to be here?"

"I was appointed by Tiberius to command the Antonia. Fate, wouldn't you say?"

It was her turn to remain silent.

Paulus said, "Now I would like to ask you a few questions. At the palace you spoke of marriage. Are you married? I see that you're wearing a ring."

"I am betrothed. His name is Nathan bar Samuel. He's a stonemason living in Bethany."

"And he hasn't sought you?" Paulus asked sharply. "Does he know you were taken?"

"He is away, out of the province. A friend is trying to get word to him."

"Would you tell me how you came to Bethany?"

She told him about Joppa and the boy who had stolen her money, *his* money, and how Lazarus and Nathan had come to her rescue. He listened to her attentively and her words trailed off; she could think of nothing more to explain her own actions. She wanted to tell him how she felt, how she had wanted only to save him, but she couldn't. She dared not.

They reached the tall, wooden structure in the middle of the wall surrounding the town. It was after midnight and the watchman was nowhere to be seen. Slowly she removed Paulus' mantle from her shoulders and handed it to him, her eyes taking in his white tunic, the dark leather cuirass, the brown leather boots, the heavy sword at his side. Salome's words rang in her head: "*He is Mars, the god of war.*"

"Alysia," he said quietly, "do not marry this man."

Her eyes widened. "What?"

"I want you to marry me."

At least ten heartbeats must have gone by, though she could have sworn her heart had stopped beating at all. She whispered, "What did you say?"

"You heard me. I am asking you to marry me."

"Paulus, I am a slave, an escaped *murderer*. There is no future for you if you marry me."

"I will resign my position. It's not as important to me anymore. There are other things I can do—carpentry, farming. I will make a living for us, I promise you."

Alysia could only stare at him. If he were willing to do that, he must . . .

Sounds carried clearly and they had to speak very low. Paulus said, "I will divorce Megara. She may seem to be jealous but she doesn't care."

Alysia swallowed over the renewed thudding of her heart. "And do you . . . care so much for me?"

His eyes moved over her face, ethereal in moonlight so bright that it cast shadows of the date palms on the wall behind her. His hands moved slowly up her arms and drew her closer to him. "I could never stop thinking about you," he said, with a depth of emotion in his voice she had never heard before. "When I saw you tonight it was as if I were the one who had been dead, and had come alive again."

For the second time that night she seemed to step out of herself, so that she was two people—bound together and yet relentlessly opposed to each other. A vista of years appeared before her, and in those years she and Paulus lived a life of hiding, of being forced to move and hide again. Paulus would grow more and more dissatisfied, more frustrated. She, without him, could exist in anonymity. Together, they were more likely to be discovered. She was wanted for murder and he would be accused of aiding her.

It seemed a long time had passed, but it hadn't. Paulus must have read her eyes, for he said, "We can find a place where no one knows us, where no one will search. We *can* be happy."

"No," she said breathlessly, before she could change her mind. "I won't let you do this. You belong to the army! Do you think I could ever be happy, knowing what you have given up because of me?"

"Can you tell me that you do not love me? Can you tell me that you love this other man?"

"Whether I love him or not, I am going to marry him."

"Don't make this choice in haste, Alysia."

Her voice was unsteady, but she managed to speak the words. "I was afraid for you, Paulus. That was why I didn't go to Cyprus. I was afraid that if you were caught helping me, you would be imprisoned, or killed. And that is why I cannot marry you, now or ever."

She had a sudden sense of irretrievable loss, but she had finally made him understand. "Besides, Jewish betrothals can only be broken by divorce. Nathan and I are as good as married. I cannot dishonor him."

He stepped closer, his eyes holding hers. "I don't know how to convince you that I mean what I say. I would gladly give up my profession for you. There are other things more important. And I am well aware of the risk if we are discovered. Death is certain for everyone, Alysia, and at least we would be together."

She lowered her gaze, bowing her head. "I cannot."

He touched her face, making her look up at him. His thumb traced a tear sliding down her cheek. "You may believe you have sound reasons for your decision, but I happen to disagree with them."

The wooden door within the gate swung slowly open and there stood the night watchman, an elderly man with a cheap-looking sword in his hand. "What goes here?" he demanded, before he caught sight of Paulus' uniform. His jaw dropped.

Paulus had stepped casually away from Alysia. "There was a matter of urgency that compelled this young woman to leave Jerusalem. I have escorted her this far. I trust you will see her safely home."

"I—yes, yes, General—er, my lord."

"And you will say nothing of it to anyone."

"No, my lord General!"

The man turned back to allow Alysia to precede him through the gate. But she remained for a moment where she stood.

"Good-bye, Paulus," she whispered.

He spoke low, but she had no trouble hearing his words.

"It is not over between us, Alysia. We will meet again, and we will see how long we can deny what was meant to be."

CHAPTER XI

Alysia had been in Lazarus' house only a few hours when he and Nathan returned, with Nathan so wildly incensed that she feared he was going to storm the garrison single-handedly. Lazarus had sought him out, going from village to village until someone had been able to tell him where the stonemason could be found—although Alysia strongly suspected Nathan's absence had more to do with activities *other* than a building project.

A servant had let her into the house, crying out and bringing everyone running to the door. Mary wept with relief, saying she hadn't stopped praying for Alysia's safety since the moment she was taken. Martha had helped Alysia into her nightgown and tucked her into bed.

At dawn, a door flinging open and slamming shut again wakened everyone. She heard men's voices speaking with the servants and immediately Nathan bounded into her room. He knelt beside the bed and grabbed her shoulders. "To think that they . . . did they . . ." His face turned scarlet with rage and he couldn't find the words he wanted to say.

Alysia sat up on the edge of the bed, pulling a blanket over her shoulders. "They did not harm me. Nathan, listen to me," she said, and calmly told him what had happened. But she did not mention Herod's banquet, or who had brought her home. He stared at her, striving to control himself. Lazarus came into the room and sat down in a chair. His sisters stood in the doorway, listening and looking warily at their cousin. No one knew what he was going to do.

"Alysia, please forgive me," Lazarus said, with a pained expression. He looked extremely tired and pale. "I should have let them kill me before they took you. And then, I didn't know who to go to. I felt it was useless to go to the Romans. I do not trust the priests in Jerusalem . . . though they may have helped, I don't know. Perhaps I should have asked for an audience with Herod Antipas. It didn't occur to me. The best thing to do, I thought, was to find Nathan and talk things through. We had to think of your reputation and how this would look to others. I simply had to trust God to take care of you until then. We came here first, of course, and learned you had returned."

"You did exactly the right thing," Alysia told him. "And God did protect me. Nathan, you must not be so angry. As I have said, the centurion realized he had made a great mistake and that is why he took me to Herod's palace. He hoped things could be made right. It was only by chance that I was able to see Herod Antipas. He said he was sending a messenger to let you know I was safe."

Mary and Martha looked at each other. "There was no messenger," said Martha.

"I am not surprised, for I have heard about Herod's . . . well, he is not a man of honor. I do not think we owe him a debt, by any means."

"How were you able to return to Bethany?" Lazarus asked.

"I had to wait until the storm was over, and even after that I was kept waiting. Finally, a slave escorted me through Jerusalem to the city gate. I suppose I was not very important to those at the palace."

"Well, you are important to us!" Martha exclaimed, and wiped at a tear that slid down her motherly face.

For the first time since she had started talking, Nathan spoke. He was still now, and grim. His words sent a chill over her entire body, into her very heart.

"If it takes the rest of my life," he said, with blazing eyes, "I will see that the Romans pay for what they have done."

In the palace of Herod Antipas, Megara sat at an upstairs window looking down upon a small, private courtyard. She ate stoically from a bowl of orange slices and watched her husband converse with the tetrarch. Paulus clearly did not like Herod, and Herod clearly did not like what Paulus was saying to him, for he looked decidedly uncomfortable.

It has something to do with that slave, she thought. Last night, seeing her alive after months of believing her dead, was a blow from which Megara would not soon recover. But even "dead", Alysia had been a threat to her.

Paulus changed after the ship the slave had supposedly been traveling on had gone to the bottom of the sea. He seemed to care for nothing. He took on dangerous tasks, such as rooting out a gang of criminals in one of the most deadly districts of Rome. Every other city prefect had simply left them alone, but Paulus found out their hiding places and went, with a handful of soldiers and men from the police brigade, to either arrest them or execute them on the spot.

Then, before they left for Palestine, they had spent some time on Paulus' farm in the country. One day he'd gone with two men from neighboring farms in search of a wild boar that had killed at least two game hunters in recent weeks, equipped with only a bow, a quiver of arrows, and a spear. One of the men with him had supplied her with the details. Tracking the beast for miles, loping through the forest like some wild animal himself, Paulus had killed the huge boar single-handedly with his spear and had a long gash on his arm to show for it.

And then he had brought her to this place, with its strange customs and unfriendly populace. She had seen the hostile stares of the Jews as she was carried through the streets of Jerusalem. Megara couldn't even have the satisfaction of reporting Alysia's crime and exposing her as the criminal she was, for by doing so she would bring danger to Paulus and, by association, to herself. And besides that, Paulus had forbidden her to speak of it.

She had made the mistake of confronting her husband and assuming an injured air. "How long do you think you can hide her, Paulus? If you're seen with her, it will be the end of you."

"I will not discuss Alysia with you, Megara, for you have forfeit the right to do so. As far as I am concerned, she has done nothing wrong."

"Nothing wrong! She is a murderer and a harlot—"

She stopped at the look on his face. His Nile-blue eyes had frozen into two chips of ice and his brows drew together in a fierce scowl. "Bridle your slandering tongue, and if you betray her, I will defend her to my last breath—after I've killed you." He left her standing with her mouth open.

Well, she doubted he would kill her, but she would keep silent . . . at least for now.

Her face was stony as she watched Herod Antipas dip his head in the barest gesture of civility and creep into the palace like a whipped dog. Paulus immediately took his leave, passing through a doorway within the opposite colonnade.

She must be more careful. The gods forbid that he should decide to divorce her, making her an object of ridicule, or worse—pity. Somehow she had to find a means to get rid of Alysia, in a way that would bring no danger to Paulus. She did not intend to lose him, either by death or divorce.

Years ago, Megara had visited a famous sibyl just outside of Rome. She'd been a frightful sight, to be sure, hunched and wrinkled, with staring black eyes. The sibyl told her that Paulus had a great destiny before him . . . and that his influence would reach kings and kingdoms.

To Megara, that meant only one thing. And she intended to be part of it.

The winter months passed slowly for Alysia. And with the passing of each month, the day of her wedding drew nearer. At Nathan's insistence she did not venture outside the town, which was just as well since she had learned that there were Romans on almost every street corner in Jerusalem. And what if she should see Paulus? It was much easier to *not* risk catching a glimpse of him—to pretend that he was still in Rome and lost to her forever.

At least, it was easier for a while. Until she began to grow bored and restless and to feel as if she were a prisoner.

In the spring, Lazarus and his sisters began planning a trip to Galilee. There was a man there, a man they knew well, who had recently begun to preach. He was from the town of Nazareth; his name was Jesus. His fame had already reached Judea, for it was said he performed miracles, healing people without medicine or herbs, healing even the blind and deaf. Alysia wasn't particularly impressed; she had seen many charlatans and magicians in Athens who claimed to do the same things. It seemed the rest of the province was skeptical, too, for most Judeans were contemptuous of Galileans and especially of Nazareth, a town they considered uncultivated and uncouth. "Can anything good come out of Nazareth?" was the popular saying.

But that didn't stop her from wanting to go. She would have gone almost anywhere for diversion. One night, when Nathan was eating supper at Lazarus' house, she broached the subject with more than a little trepidation. She knew he would be opposed.

"Of course you cannot go," he said, not even looking up as he broke off a piece of bread.

She looked with dismay at Lazarus, who merely raised his eyebrows. He'd already told her she would have to abide by whatever Nathan decided.

"Why not?" she asked. This time, Nathan raised his brows.

"Have you forgotten what the soldiers did to you? What they would have done had not God intervened?"

"I'll be in the country. I won't go into any cities where there are Romans. Besides, it's ridiculous to think that could happen again."

"Why is it ridiculous? What has changed? The Romans are still without any sense of honor, and you are still a beautiful woman."

"Nathan, I will not spend the rest of my life afraid to venture outside the walls of Bethany! Everyone else at least is able to visit Jerusalem. I haven't been anywhere in months!"

Martha began picking up dishes and retreated to the kitchen. But Lazarus and Mary remained sitting at the table.

Nathan looked at his cousin. "Do you not agree with me, Lazarus?"

Lazarus thought a moment before he replied. "I was with Alysia when she was taken, and so I would not presume to promise you her safety. But I don't believe that such a thing will happen again."

"And about this man—Jesus of Nazareth. Maybe you know him well, Lazarus, but I do not! Why should Alysia risk so much to go and hear him speak?"

"We have been friends all our lives." Lazarus looked at Alysia and explained. "I was born and raised in Nazareth, but when I married I moved here to Bethany, so that my wife could be near her family. Not long after I lost my wife, Martha's husband also died, and she and Mary came here to live with me. Our parents had already been dead for some time, and Mary had been living with Martha."

Alysia nodded her understanding. Lazarus' dark eyes went back to Nathan. "Jesus was a good friend to me," he said again. "I was not a healthy child, and other children can be . . . unkind. He was several years younger than I, but whenever he was with me . . . for some reason there was no bullying from anyone, no cruel words. He's been a carpenter since his youth, and he taught me woodworking, light things that would not tire me. I know that he is a good man. If he feels that he has been anointed by God to preach, then it is so."

"You may not know this, Lazarus. The Romans are watching him. He has acquired a large following. And since the Romans are concerned, so is the Sanhedrin."

"As far as I know, he has said nothing against Rome."

Nathan said dryly, "That's what I don't like about him."

Unexpectedly Mary spoke, in her usual, gentle manner. "I wish you would let her go with us, Nathan. I know it must be tiresome, staying at home all the time. You could come, too."

"I cannot leave my work."

"Which work?" Alysia couldn't resist saying. "You do things of which I might not approve, and yet I am allowed to say nothing."

Nathan pushed his plate aside and crossed his arms on the table. "Alysia, I realize that you were raised differently, and you are not familiar with some of our ways. We've all been lenient in our expectations. And I will admit that some of the traditions are old-fashioned and not strictly followed anymore. At one time a betrothed young woman would be expected to stay secluded, never go anywhere, and not even see her prospective bridegroom for an entire year."

"But as you say, some traditions are old-fashioned."

Nathan paused for a moment, then gave a slow smile. "Well, it seems I am outnumbered. Lazarus, if some evil befalls Alysia perhaps your miracle-worker can save her."

"No evil will come to me," Alysia said, wishing she could be certain of that.

Lazarus also smiled. "Your concern is not without cause, Nathan. But if the Lord God is willing, I will bring her safely home to you."

Most Judeans hated Samaritans, even more than they despised the country-bred Galileans. If a Jew wanted to inflict the most scathing of insults upon another Jew, he called him a Samaritan. Besides the unforgivable act of being descendants of Gentiles who had intermarried with Jews, the Samaritans believed themselves to be racially superior to all other inhabitants of Palestine and had their own temple, their own priesthood, and their own holy city. Most Jews would not even pass through the province, going far out of their way to hug the western bank of the Jordan River, with many even crossing to the other side.

But Lazarus took a direct northern route, and on the second day they crossed into Samaria, where the hills of Judea lowered into a short plain and became the foothills of the Samaritan mountains. The highway passed through valleys, through rich, green vineyards and terraced fields and pastures covered with cattle. Close beside the road wild, thick vines ran along the ground, climbing posts, trees, and courtyard walls. Between the villages, scattered here and there, were quaint farms and the great barns of wealthy landowners.

After two more nights spent at roadside inns, they were joined by merchants and travelers from several other countries—Egyptians, Greeks, Arabians, Romans. The nearer they drew to Nazareth the more crowded the roads became, until their caravan was only one among many.

"The town of Nazareth is small," Lazarus told Alysia as they waited at a busy crossroad for an Arabian merchant to coax his balking camel into mobility. "But it is almost at the center of a very important trade route. In fact, this is the most used highway from Damascus to Joppa, and then by ship to Rome. I can say one thing for Rome—it has united almost the whole world with its system of roads."

"And a lot of good the roads do when you can't even pass," Martha grumbled, loud enough to be heard by the harried camel driver. She suffered immensely from the hard seat of the cart, in spite of the cushion she had placed there. In the other cart Mary talked quietly with the servant who drove and didn't seem to mind the jerking and jostling over rough ground.

They never reached Nazareth. After inquiring of fellow wayfarers where they might find the Nazarene preacher, they were directed to a point close by the northern shore of the Sea of Galilee—Lake

Gennesaret, as it was called by those who lived near it, or Lake Tiberias, as it was known by the Romans. The ground sloped uphill and was, as always, covered with rocks, some the size of boulders. Where the soil was more fertile, poppies and anemones provided vivid spots of color and beauty. To the east lay the city of Capernaum, known for its thriving fishing industry, and along the shoreline below sprawled Herod Antipas' capital city—Tiberias—as much a marvel of architecture as anything his father had built.

When they reached the top of the incline Alysia got off of the cart to walk—and had to stop and stare. A huge multitude of people, hundreds, perhaps a thousand or more, either sat or stood along the fringes of those sitting. Just above them a large stone jutted out from the brow of the hill, and upon it sat a man who was speaking to them. She could only see that he wore a light-colored robe and had dark hair, but his voice carried well in the clear air and from his vantage point surrounded by rocky hills.

Lazarus stopped the creaking carts. They all walked to the edge of the crowd and stood listening. Even sitting down this man was an arresting and dynamic figure. He spoke with a quiet simplicity, yet with such animation that the very words seemed to come alive. Alysia received the impression that he had been talking for some time. He began to quote from the Jewish Scriptures. She had no trouble understanding his Aramaic speech—almost a miracle in itself considering her limited vocabulary in that language.

At last he rose to his feet, walked along the ledge to a pathway running beside it, and came down to join his audience. All who had been sitting now stood up; several people surged toward him and he was lost from view. A middle-aged woman turned to Alysia with glowing eyes.

"No one has ever spoken as he does," she whispered. "He's not like the scribes or the Pharisees. He *knows* us."

Hundreds began taking their departure: women in plain homespun gowns, men in robes with long hair and beards, noisy children eager to play after being still for most of the afternoon. Many of them carried satchels and waterskins and began making their way toward Capernaum on the northern shore of the lake. Lazarus gestured and Alysia joined him and his sisters as they walked slowly upward.

Most of the crowd had dispersed. Now Alysia could see the Nazarene standing in a grove of fir trees to her right, talking to several other men. A light robe, open at the throat and belted at the waist, covered his tall and powerfully built frame. He moved about with a strength and agility that reminded Alysia of Paulus—indeed, both men had similar qualities of bearing and appeared to be about the same age. He wore his brown, shoulder-length hair loosely tied in the back. A beard molded closely with the contours of his face.

Then the Nazarene saw them. A sudden smile lit his face and he came quickly toward them, embracing them with great affection. Martha was in tears, but she remembered to take Alysia's arm and set her before their friend.

"This is Alysia. She is living with us now. She is betrothed to our cousin, Nathan."

The Nazarene spoke graciously to her in Greek, his dark eyes level and friendly upon her face. His voice was low now, but articulate, without the strong accent that characterized the speech of other Galileans she had met. She wondered why he had spoken to her in Greek.

"I speak your language," she said, in halting Aramaic. "That is, please don't feel that you must speak to me in Greek."

"You should hear the conversations at our house," Lazarus commented. "Half in Aramaic, half in Greek, with a little Latin and Hebrew thrown in for good measure. We've had more than one guest depart rather abruptly."

The general laughter lifted her feeling of nervousness and she listened as they all asked and answered questions of each other. There were four other men standing nearby who seemed to be friends of the Nazarene, and they were introduced as Simon Peter and his brother Andrew, and James with his apparently much younger brother, John.

Those who had chosen not to leave had begun to set up camps on the hillside, for it would soon be dark. Lazarus decided their group would do the same. By the time night had fallen myriads of small fires dotted the hills. Alysia sat just inside their tent; Mary and Martha were already asleep on their pallets. Another tent had been put up a short distance away for Lazarus and the servants who had accompanied them. She wrapped her arms around her knees and listened to Lazarus talking with the four friends of the Nazarene.

From what she could gather, Lazarus had known these men before he left Nazareth. Mary had already told her that these four—Peter, John, James, and Andrew—had been partners in a prosperous fishing business in Capernaum. They had left their livelihood to become disciples of this itinerant preacher called Jesus, who now lay stretched out on his side a little distance from the fire, fast asleep.

The other men lounged at various points around the fire. The one called Peter rose and retrieved a jug of water from a nearby cart. He was taller than the others, wide of shoulders; she could see the hard, corded muscles in his arms beneath the short sleeves of his robe. His dark brown hair was thick, curly, and seemingly windblown—even on this windless night. His eyes were black, and his skin was deeply tanned and creased about the mouth and forehead. Strands of gray streaked his short, dark beard. Of all of them, he was the most talkative and seldom stopped moving about.

His brother, Andrew, had a kind, ruddy face and seemed of a calmer disposition. John appeared to be not much older than herself and had a distinct, deliberate way of speaking. James was shaggy-haired with a deep, booming voice.

"Tell me, Peter," Lazarus urged, "tell me all that has happened since Jesus began to preach."

Peter relaxed for a moment against the trunk of a tree. "There is so much to tell, Lazarus, I don't know where to begin."

"Tell what happened yesterday," John suggested. "About the leper."

Peter gestured with his cup at the younger man. "You have a way with words. You tell him."

John waited a moment, as if gathering his thoughts. He gazed into the fire, drew his legs up and placed his elbows on his knees, and began.

"Yesterday morning, in the city, Jesus had been speaking to a gathering when a great cry went up and it was obvious that something was happening—for they were sounds of rage, and disgust. The crowd began to part, and we saw the leper. It was a very advanced stage of leprosy. It must have been a most painful and dangerous journey, for his feet were . . . well, they were hardly recognizable as feet. His clothes were like filthy rags hanging off of bare bones. What little flesh covered them was decaying, like that of a dead man. The stench was unbearable."

John paused. Alysia felt thankful they had arrived too late to see, and smell, this dreadful apparition.

"The people were bitterly indignant," he went on. "The poor man must have come from some leper's colony and had the audacity to approach a crowd of people and press his way in."

"They cleared a path for him fast enough," Peter added, with humor.

"Some of us drew closer to Jesus, as if we would protect him. Though I admit, should the man have proved hostile, I don't know if I could have brought myself to lay a hand on him."

The other men nodded in agreement.

"Jesus said to let him through. We tried to argue with him but he only repeated himself, so we fell back a little. The leper came face-to-face with Jesus. Everything became very quiet. It was a very moving sight…the crouching, diseased man and Jesus, tall and straight and completely self-possessed, not afraid or repulsed as we all were."

"Did the leper speak?" Lazarus asked.

"Yes. He said, very hoarsely, 'Sir, if you will, you can heal me.' And then he knelt down."

A silence fell, like the silence that must have fallen the day before as everyone stood staring, waiting, feeling the suspense mount. John's voice became unsteady.

"And Jesus said, 'I will. You are cured of your affliction'. And he reached out . . . and touched the leper."

Alysia sat up straighter, hugging her knees, her eyes locked on John's earnest young face.

"I was afraid to look. I must have been looking at the ground, because the first thing I noticed was his feet. Suddenly, where there had been two lumps of sores, there were two whole and healthy feet! And then I looked up. It was the same man, but a different man! This man's skin was as healthy as mine. This man was well nourished and bore no stench, though he was still in the same rags. This man was looking down at his arms and legs, and sobbing. This man was . . . well."

There was another long moment of silence as the men all looked at each other, each nodding and corroborating John's words. Finally Lazarus asked, "Is he here?"

John shook his head. "He left soon afterward. I suppose he returned to his family. Whoever they are, they had quite a surprise yesterday!"

The conversation went on until the campfire remained nothing more than a few embers glowing in the darkness. But Alysia heard no more. Her head was spinning, trying to make sense of what she heard. Such things were not possible! Her mind tried to tell her that it was trickery, but something within her rebelled at that. It would make the Nazarene a liar, nothing more than a magician practicing his craft—to gain what? Money, notoriety? He didn't seem like that kind of man to her. And what of these others—were they liars as well?

She had to admit she'd been strongly impressed by this man—by his sincerity, his unique ability to communicate with his listeners, his warmth and friendliness. They had been too late to hear most of his speech, but she had heard one thing, one simple statement, that resonated in her mind more than anything else he had said:

I have come to heal the broken-hearted . . .

CHAPTER XII

The Road of Death—The Bloody Way—they were not auspicious names for the road on which Paulus traveled. This highway was infamous for the bands of robbers and miscreants who lurked in the caves and behind the outcroppings, and many a wayfarer had met his end in this part of the Judean wilderness.

Three days ago he had received a missive with the emperor's seal directing him to inspect the Roman garrison at Jericho, a day's journey from Jerusalem, to ensure that it was efficient and well-staffed. He knew the order had come from Sejanus, not the emperor, but he had no choice but to obey. The reputation of this region was known even in Rome. No doubt Sejanus thought his plan amusing; no doubt he hoped Paulus would run afoul of robbers himself.

The city of Jericho was like an oasis in the desert…green and fertile, well-watered by numerous warm springs. Beneath a hazy blue sky, and beyond a horizon lined with palm groves and banana trees, ran the long range of the mountains of Moab. Herod the Great had built a winter palace here and left his signature upon the city with other fine buildings, as well as a small fortress.

Paulus found the fortress understaffed and had an unpleasant confrontation with its commander, who was obviously used to running things with little interference. The place was in poor repair and the men were, for the most part, surly and undisciplined. He sent the commander and several of the worst offenders off to Caesarea for Pilate to deal with, since the prefect had been responsible for their appointments. Paulus left one of his own tribunes in charge and ten of his best men, promising he would bring them back to the Antonia as soon as the Jericho fort met the standards of the Roman military.

The return to Jerusalem began as a gentle ascent, the road curving around an escarpment with the drop to their right gradually increasing until the slope became almost vertical. They had been climbing steadily for hours. Abrupt and unexpected turns often obstructed a view of the road ahead.

Sweating beneath the leather and armor of his uniform, Paulus drank from a waterskin and contemplated the area immediately before them. They were about to top a rise, which he remembered from the journey going down. Just beyond it was a wider expanse of road with a ledge above it, and above the ledge was a stretch of wilderness large enough to allow any attackers to escape. Beneath the ledge he remembered seeing deep caverns—excellent hiding places.

He hadn't had this feeling, this tingling up the spine, on the way to Jericho. But he had it now . . . and every time he had felt it before, something happened.

Paulus glanced back. He had brought with him, besides the men he'd left in Jericho, six mounted men who acted as his escort on expeditions such as this. Tiberius had assigned these men to guard him; normally only the governor traveled with an escort. (The emperor had written Paulus privately, saying that if Pilate was important enough to have bodyguards then the legate at Jerusalem must have them as well!) There were also ten regular cavalry and ten foot soldiers, as well as his cavalry commander, Silas—who now kicked his own horse to catch up with him.

"Won't you drop back and let your guard be in the lead, sir?" Silas asked. He was some ten years Paulus' senior, with thick, prematurely white hair.

"The men are tired," Paulus answered, not yet willing to reveal his uneasiness. "Tell them to stop, drink some water, and rest."

"Yes, sir." Silas turned and rode away to give the order.

Paulus deliberated the best course of action. Should he have the men retreat back to the fort for a day or two, thwarting the plans of any would-be attackers? And only on the basis of a "feeling" —he had no real reason to suspect an ambush. Or should they press on, even though they could only form a line of two abreast due to the narrowness of the road ahead? If they were attacked, they would be hard-pressed to defend themselves in such terrain. Still, they were tough and trained soldiers, and it was not the Roman way to turn back...even should the consequences be disastrous.

"Silas," he said, when the man rejoined him. "What do you think the chances are that someone lies in wait for us up there?" He inclined his head toward the top of the rise. Paulus respected the man's seniority and experience, and he had been at the Antonia for many years.

"Very slight," Silas answered with no hesitation. "But we could easily put to rout either thieves or rebels. It has a bad reputation, but

I've been on this road several times, sir, with no sign of trouble. Have you seen or heard something, sir?"

"No. And you are probably right. Nevertheless, we will take precautions. The men on foot will go first, cavalry in the rear. When we get to the top of this hill, shields up and swords in hand. There will not be room for anything but the sword, but the mounted men can use their javelins—or even their bows. After the first shot or two they may need to dismount quickly. Neither will there be room to organize ourselves in the usual manner. It will be almost impossible to retreat down the escarpment, so an attack must be met with full aggression. You and I will lead."

"But, sir, it is the duty of your escort to protect you," Silas objected. "You should ride in the rear with them."

"It is my nature to guard, rather than be guarded," Paulus said lightly. "If there is an ambush and I fall, they will be too occupied to notice. Just relay the orders, Silas, and try not to alarm the men. These are only measures of caution."

"Yes, Legate, it will be done."

Paulus put on his helmet, a signal to his men to do the same. He had permitted them to remove their helmets, for they absorbed the sun and were exceedingly uncomfortable.

Soon the men and horses began laboring upward again. Paulus looked back at them once more. They appeared more alert than apprehensive. That was good, for as disciplined as they were, it took only one man to start a panic. Paulus was the first one over the incline. His horse, the fine dark gray he had brought with him from Rome, twitched nervously and flung his head.

"Steady, Asbolus," he said, running his hand over the smooth muscular neck. But the horse only pricked up his ears—and Paulus knew, but too late. At the same instant, Silas made a muffled, wheezing sound. Paulus turned swiftly to see an arrow piercing the man's neck as he fell from his horse.

Armed men swarmed from their hiding places among the rocks, and more poured out of the dark caves just ahead. Paulus shouted a warning. With no time to dismount he wheeled his horse sharply and swung his sword at those trying to pull him from the saddle. The animal reared and stumbled backward, perilously close to the edge of the cliff. He was forced to drop his shield to control the horse. Shouts, outcries, and the clang of metal filled the air.

These men were Jews—Zealots—at least twice as many of them as there were Romans, and they fought with skill and fury.

His horse reared again, this time catching him off balance and throwing him to the ground. His head struck hard, knocking off his helmet. He sprang up. His sword clashed and rang with one blade after another, yet with every man he felled another leaped forward to take his place. He was not aware that he was covered with blood and most of it was his own; he didn't know that his head had been slashed, or that a great gash in his thigh spilled blood in a steady stream. He felt the blow from a club crack against his left arm but had no time to realize that it now hung broken and useless. The Zealots wielded swords and axes and stabbed with short daggers. From the ledge above, some were shooting arrows and heaving down large rocks.

He sensed that his bodyguards were trying to surround him, and also knew—without having to look—when they perished. The noise gradually began to diminish. Dead and groaning bodies were strewn over the rocky ground. Seeing movement within the caves, Paulus realized that there were more Zealots waiting to replace these when they tired.

His right arm began to grow numb. His wildly shifting gaze fixed on a man with blood-matted auburn hair who was heavily engaged with one of his men, and he raised his sword to split the man's skull. As he did so, one of the Jews shouted a warning: "Nathan bar Samuel, behind you!"

Paulus' sword paused in midair. His eyes met those of his foe. Although he had heard it only once, he recognized the name. The moment's hesitation confused the other man, and before he could strike, Paulus lifted his foot and sent the man sprawling in the dust. At once he was made cruelly aware of his wounded leg as a searing pain shot the length of it. Paulus staggered and caught himself, deflecting a sword thrust aimed at his neck. He killed another man, and another. Then he felt something, maybe a helmet, crash against his head and he fell to the ground, stunned. A Zealot pounced on him viciously, lifting his dagger to pierce the throat above the armored chest. Paulus caught his arm and they fought a silent battle, the Zealot straining, his eyes full of hate. Paulus grimaced, feeling his strength wane, knowing that in a moment the knife would rip open his throat.

Another man had climbed onto the ledge above them and doubled over, gasping for breath. "He's done for—let him suffer. Let's go."

The other Zealot wrenched his arm away from Paulus' vise-like grip. The man on the ledge held out his hand; the other took it and raised himself up. With a final sound of clanking metal, the entire army of rebels raced for the boulders where they had hidden their horses and rode furiously away from the scene of their victory.

Except for the groans and feeble coughs of the dying, there was utter silence. Paulus stirred, feeling the pulsating pain on the side of his head where blood ran in rivulets. One arm felt completely numb, the other throbbed mercilessly, and only by a Herculean effort did he manage to rise and stand with his weight on one leg, favoring the wounded one.

No stranger to gore and blood, he couldn't believe the sight that met his eyes. Bodies lined the road in macabre positions, a head stared at him from a gulley, an arm pointed gruesomely to the body from which it had been detached. Hemmed in as they were by the rocks, the narrow road behind them and the precipice beside them, they hadn't stood a chance to adequately defend themselves. And yet, another glance proved his men had taken a large number of Zealots in their own butchery.

A weak moan caught his attention, and stumbling over the bodies Paulus knelt beside a young legionary. He raised the man's head with as much gentleness as he could muster.

"Sir, there were too many. Too many—" He jerked spasmodically and then was still, his eyes glazing.

Paulus eased him upon the ground and stood, trying to brace his unsteady feet. He made his way painfully among the bodies. They were all dead. A horse lying on the ground quivered and rolled its eyes—one of its legs had been shattered with a club. Paulus knelt and gently cut the arteries of its neck.

As he stood, he felt the warmth of his own blood soaking into his boot and looked down to examine the long, jagged wound on his outer thigh. The flesh parted almost to the bone. He managed to tear a strip of cloth from someone's mantle and tie it around his leg. He would have to find help or bleed to death. He spied a broken javelin and, using it as a crutch, began to walk. It would be dark in a few hours and there would be little chance of anyone finding him. The horses surviving the massacre had all fled and Paulus seemed to be the only living creature in the vast Judean wilderness.

Bitterly he reproached himself for not obeying his instincts. The attack had been well planned, requiring a knowledge of the Romans' movements; it had been, in its ferocity, like an act of vengeance. The involvement of the man to whom Alysia was betrothed—if indeed, that was the man—was surely not a coincidence.

But he couldn't think of all this now. He didn't know how long he walked doggedly on until weakness overcame him. He stumbled and fell in a slow, graceful movement, like the lowering of a puppet on a string. For the second time his head struck against the hard earth, and the last thing he saw before consciousness left him was a huge black vulture circling in the serene sky above.

Alysia sat before the morning fire, absorbing into her soul the beauty and grandeur of this land. A mystic, almost supernatural light in soft, glorious shades of red, purple, and pink surrounded the hills and mountains. The cedars and fir trees were shrouded in black, and as the sun appeared they became tinged with a shimmering haze of gold, emerging from the darkness as if at that moment called into creation.

Below them, the road sloping down to the Sea of Galilee was lined with palm trees and the lake shone like a harp-shaped jewel, enclosed by gently undulating mountains. A layer of translucent clouds hung over the water, and slanting rays of light fell upon a single spot in the middle of the lake. Already there were dozens of fishing boats plying the waters. Down the sand-covered shoreline, the city of Tiberias' massive sea towers were a jarring reminder of reality—and Rome.

Martha and Mary were putting away the dishes from breakfast. She ought to join them but it was so pleasant to sit here and watch the sun rise, and to ponder the things she'd seen and heard since their arrival two days ago.

The first morning had been spent cooking and cleaning up the camp. The Nazarene had disappeared, and his disciples had said it was his custom to spend long hours in prayer. After the midday meal the Nazarene had begun to speak, and as the woman had said on their arrival, he spoke as no one ever had. Not only was it in the wisdom and even wit of his words, but his very manner of speaking made one want to believe in what he said. He *did* know people. The crowd grew; people seemed to come from everywhere.

The entire multitude sat still and listened as if hanging on his every word—all but the six, black-garbed Pharisees who stood along the edge of the crowd and shook their heads and muttered among themselves. The four disciples watched them. Peter and John looked angry and James offered to go and tell them to leave, at which point the more diplomatic Andrew said he would ask if they would like to speak personally with the *Rabboni*, an Aramaic word meaning "great teacher." But the Pharisees had left before anyone approached them. She saw that the Nazarene noticed their departure. A thoughtful, somehow regretful expression crossed his face for a moment.

He spoke, that day, of many things.

He stated the way to happiness: recognize one's need for God and for forgiveness; seek after righteousness; place one's strength, one's *self*, under control; be merciful to others; overcome evil with good; be straightforward and honest. And for these things, be willing to suffer persecution. He said that he had not come to abolish the law, but to fulfill it. Yes, he said, murder is wrong, but so is that hatred of one's fellow man that leads to it. Yes, adultery is wrong, but so is that lustful glance. Avoid judging the motives of others; be fair and use only a standard by which you would want to be judged. Have faith that God will provide. Treat others as *you* would like to be treated.

There was more, more than Alysia could take in all at once. Yet he spoke simply, illustrating his words by pointing out the rock-covered landscape, the birds flying overhead, the flowers in the fields, thorns and thistles buried in the brush.

The next day had been the strangest day of her life! The rattle of a wagon had interrupted the stillness of the morning. There was a shuffling about the camp with voices raised in what sounded like an argument. Alysia and Mary stood together, watching, and all around were other people emerging from their tents. The Nazarene came out from among the trees and called to Peter. That disciple came into view, closely followed by someone else. "I tried to tell them you weren't to be disturbed," he said testily. "I told them to come back la—"

"Come here," said Jesus. A man and woman pushed past Peter, shielding someone between them.

"Please, sir," said the woman piteously. "Have mercy on the boy! Nobody can help him! We heard of you in Magdala and followed you here."

"Can you help my son?" begged the man.

They were poorly dressed, pale, and desperate looking. The Nazarene lowered his eyes to the boy, as did everyone else. Someone gasped in horror.

He was about twelve years old. His eyes were unseeing with a fixed, vacuous expression. Fat, black flies swarmed over them. He didn't say anything, or even seem to hear, but as the Nazarene stepped close to him, he became very still, almost rigid. His face grew fearful.

"He wasn't born this way," the man said. "It happened gradually, over many months. First, he lost interest in everything, then he refused to speak, and then . . . his eyes…" The man's voice broke.

The Nazarene knelt on one knee. He bowed his head for a moment, raised it, and said something Alysia could not hear.

The flies scattered in every direction. The boy gave a piercing wail and fell down as if dead. As his mother screamed, Jesus caught the boy in his arms. The boy opened his eyes and looked slowly into his mother's face.

Gently, the Nazarene helped the boy stand up. For a moment he only stared at his mother, then he began to cry and threw his arms around her.

"He sees me!" the woman cried. "He hasn't seen anything for a year, nothing real, only horrible things no one else could see. Look at him, Zechariah! Look at him—he is healed!" Her husband fell to his knees and sobbed.

The Nazarene got to his feet, turning so that Alysia caught a look of anger struggling with compassion on his face.

"What did he say?" she asked Lazarus, who stood nearby.

Lazarus swallowed and there were tears on his own face. "He rebuked Satan for afflicting a child."

It was strange how hard it was to believe one's own eyes, strange how much she wanted to find a rational explanation for what had happened. But there was no denying it; no one could have staged such a thing. And today, gazing down at the lake below, she knew that the Nazarene was not like other men.

She knew she had crossed a great barrier in her thoughts . . . she had all but accepted a belief she'd never even dreamed of. The gods of Greece and Rome were easily dismissed and, until now, the God of the Jews had been half-real, dimly glimpsed, *possibly* the Creator, *possibly* an all-powerful figure existing in some other place, some other realm. But now, after what she had seen and heard—there must be a God, because *he* said so. God must care about his creation, because *he* told them so. And God must be very powerful, because *he* could work miracles.

That had been yesterday. Now Mary came and sat down next to her, smiling.

"Isn't it peaceful?" she said, nodding at the lake below. The sun glittered on the water as if diamonds danced on its surface. The shore was coming alive with fishermen wading out with their nets; more boats were starting out from the many small harbors. "And yet I've seen storms come upon it in the blink of an eye, storms so fierce as to terrify the most stout-hearted men. The winds gather around these surrounding hills and sweep off onto the lake and turn it into a cauldron."

"It must be an awesome sight," Alysia answered.

Mary was quiet for a moment. "There is something majestic about it—although I viewed it safely from a house in Capernaum! We used to visit there often, before traveling became so tiring for my sister. Alysia, tell me—what do you think about what happened yesterday?"

"I don't know," she said honestly. "What do you think, Mary?"

Her friend's voice was very low. "I think he is more than just a man."

"What do you mean?"

Mary shook her head. "Now it's my turn to say I don't know. But I think we should pray…pray that God will reveal to us who, and what, he is."

"But Lazarus has known Jesus all his life. How could he be anything but a man? Are you saying he is a god?"

"Not a god. Somehow, the same as God."

Shocked, Alysia said, "Mary, the priests would consider that blasphemy!"

Mary went on as if Alysia hadn't spoken. "Yes, Lazarus has always known him. And Lazarus says he is different. Did you know Jesus was born in Bethlehem?"

"What does that have to do with his being a man or a god?"

"Perhaps nothing," Mary said, with a cryptic smile. "Perhaps everything."

Paulus had often thought he would exit this world in the heat of battle, but not like this, lodged in a crevasse on a Jewish road in the middle of nowhere. He pushed himself out with the last bit of strength in him and fell full length in the dirt.

Somehow he had survived the night, spending most of it in a stupor of pain and fatigue. The rest was surely delirium. After rousing from unconsciousness, he had realized dark had fallen and that as soon as they caught his scent the carnivores would come. He concealed himself in a gap between two boulders, the tight fit holding him upright. The moon lit the night like a small sun, the utter stillness broken now and then by the howling of jackals and the strange chuckling calls of hyenas.

At some moment of lucidity, he opened his eyes to see four or five large, ungainly shapes with bristly manes. The beasts seemed to space themselves before him, showing strong, pointed teeth, sensing his weakness. He fumbled for his dagger. He hadn't much hope of killing one, much less all of them, but he intended to die fighting. In fact, he'd end his own life before giving it up to a cowardly hyena!

Growing bolder, they began to edge closer until he could smell them, a pungent death smell—they'd already been feeding on something. He cut the chest of one with his dagger. It slunk back, yelping, and then growled and showed its teeth, its feral eyes gleaming. The pack moved in slowly. All at once, for no reason that he could see, they began to yelp and snap at each other and then all skittered away in one direction.

Paulus stared, not believing what he saw. A huge, male lion crouched in the road, staring at him with an unblinking yellow gaze. It made no move to attack, showing no interest in him at all other than as an object of curiosity. The hyenas had withdrawn beyond the lion and finally slunk away in search of easier prey. The lion lay down in the road, almost as if to guard him from their return.

Now he dismissed it as a dream . . . a vision caused by fever and pain. He lay on the ground, feeling the sun's warmth on his skin. He had shivered all through the night. It was pleasant to lie here in the sun. Why bother to try to get up? It hurt too much . . .

He felt a gentle touch upon his fevered brow, and then grimaced with pain as the hand touched the deep laceration on the side of his head. He felt something cool and wet against his parched lips; he swallowed the water as if he could never have enough. He forced open his eyes. The sun stabbed into them mercilessly. He closed them, then opened them to slits and squinted upward. His vision gradually cleared to reveal a man garbed in the Jewish manner with a hood partially concealing his face.

"Who are you?" he managed to croak. As consciousness returned so did the throbbing aches and burning pains in his body.

"A friend," the stranger replied.

Paulus couldn't summon the strength to question him further. He thought of the lion but it was nowhere to be seen. The man placed him on the back of a horse, his face half-buried in its mane. The stranger mounted another horse and guided both animals forward. Paulus had no time to even ponder the identity of his silent benefactor before he slipped again into the world of restless dark.

The stranger left the wounded legate at the Antonia. He'd brought the half-dead man through the city streets and no one had dared to stop him. The officers of the fortress could only stare in amazement as he carried the long body of their commander inside the praetorium and placed him carefully on a bench. He left, silent, only half-seen because of the hood covering his face. Why he wasn't detained and questioned would always be part of the mystery surrounding him.

For days Paulus hovered between life and death. When he was told how he was brought back he could only vaguely remember the hooded man. The strangest part of all was that he had been returned on his own horse! How had the stranger found *his* horse, or was that only coincidence? He remembered the lion and thought maybe that hadn't been a dream after all. Perhaps the lion had already eaten its fill somewhere else, but regarded Paulus as a future meal and then was drawn by the smell of death further down the road.

A lion happened to be the symbol of his own legion—another coincidence?

He had many questions. Why had he been spared when all the rest had died? Why had he been rescued by a Jew, or at least a man dressed as a Jew? And this thought, above all: if he had died that night, would he have simply ceased to exist, or would a part of him survive to live forever in some unknown realm beyond time . . .

He'd never been afraid to die, but until now he'd not done much thinking about it. There were too many philosophies and myths concerning death and the afterlife. The Romans had borrowed from the Greeks, the Greeks from the Egyptians, the Egyptians from the Babylonians (or was that the other way around?) But all the stories, with their corruptions of names and fanciful additions, derived from a single source—the writings and oral traditions of the Jews.

According to these writings, there had been in the ancient past a great flood that had destroyed all the people on earth, except for one man and his family. This much Paulus believed, since every culture had a flood story; there were even some people who claimed their ancestors verbally passed down the memory of it from generation to generation. He knew people who claimed to have seen pieces of the great ark, in which the man Noah and his family had been saved, on the mountain where it had come to rest.

Mythology had changed the story into Noah's being a god; his time on the ark was like death; and his eventual departure from the ark onto dry ground was a rebirth. Oh, there were literally scores of versions. But they originated with the Jews, and later the law-giver, Moses, had written the account beginning with the creation of the earth.

As he recovered, he sought answers. He began reading the Torah, the five books written by Moses. He read the Jewish prophets. He read the Psalms by King David and the writings of David's son, Solomon. He read everything he could find, sending Simon almost daily to the library at the house of the High Priest. What Caiaphas thought about this pastime remained known only to Caiaphas who, in fact, secretly suspected the legate was about some spying mission and wondered if he should complain to Pilate.

Paulus' questions remained unanswered but his interest continued to grow. And he grew particularly interested in the prophecies concerning the Messiah, the so-called and long hoped-for rescuer of the Jewish people. After all, this was something that directly concerned him. The appearance of a "messiah" certainly didn't mean that prophecies were being fulfilled. Anyone could rise up and claim to be such a man, and, in fact, many had. They had all fallen by the wayside and been forgotten. But if and when such a leader appeared, he would be a direct threat to Roman authority.

And Paulus intended to be ready for him.

Lucius Aquilinus was bored. The debauchery of Rome no longer intrigued him and he was growing weary of his idle pastimes. His wife did nothing but grow fatter and more irascible. She doted completely on their two sons, who were as fat and irascible as their mother. And they were spoiled, unendurably so. Even Lucius' tantrums had not been so indulged.

He'd already been with every beautiful woman he cared to pursue; they, too, bored him. He was tired of the games and amusements, tired of pretending to like certain people when he despised them, and tired of politics. There was something in the wind concerning Sejanus; he wasn't sure just what it was but he was quite sure it was *not* something he wanted to "wait and see" about. He and Sejanus traveled in the same social circles and should anything happen . . . well, it would be good to be far away.

His mind took the same route more and more of late and he would remember a certain Athenian slave, a woman of striking face and slender form, of sharp wit and sharp tongue. He would think of her with mixed longing and hatred, and wished that if there were such a place as Hades that she was there and suffering indescribable torments for the murder she had committed. This desire was not prompted by grief for Magnus; it was simply that the deed itself had been a direct affront to Lucius.

She did it to spite me, he thought with oft-recurring fury. *Paulus turned her against me the day she set her foot in his mother's house because he coveted her beauty and wanted no competition for her favor.*

Then Lucius began to brood about Paulus, and his heart contracted with hatred and jealousy. He hoped that Paulus never recovered from the loss of his lover and that Megara, with her carping ways, would send the noble legate to an early grave. He deserved nothing less!

In fact, that might be an interesting thing to witness, he mused. *Certainly more interesting than anything around here.*

CHAPTER XIII

"The bridegroom is coming!"

The cry rang out long after dark had fallen, startling Alysia out of a pleasant half-sleep. The flat tones of a ram's horn rent the stillness of the April night.

"Behold!" the groomsman called again. "The bridegroom is coming!"

Mary was already up and lighting lamps. Martha ran into Alysia's room, still fully dressed, so Lazarus must have forewarned his excitable sister. Voices, laughing and amiable, could be heard on the street nearing the house.

Alysia jumped up and thought wildly, *What am I doing?* But all at once the room was full of giggling bridesmaids—they were all Mary's friends. Alysia was being dressed in a white gown and they were putting a wreath of flowers around her head. Her heart pounded fiercely; it was all happening so fast!

She was shoved good-naturedly out of the house, where she saw Nathan and his attendants and some fifty or more wedding guests waving myrtle branches and palm leaves. Some were singing to the accompaniment of drums and pipes and cymbals. Happy and excited, they helped Alysia climb into a palanquin and bore her gaily down the street, lighting the way with torches and oil lamps.

She'd known the time was near, but somehow she wasn't prepared. She tried not to think about the last time she'd ridden in such a conveyance—she tried hard to banish Paulus completely from her thoughts. He must have no place now, in her mind or in her heart.

The celebrants stopped when they reached Nathan's house. Alysia climbed out of the litter and Nathan, flushed and beaming and dressed in a white tunic, took her arm and turned to greet the guests. *Paulus had been wearing a white tunic that night, on the road to Bethany . . .*

As was the custom, Nathan read aloud their marriage contract in which he named the ways he would provide for her and proclaimed himself to be her husband and she his wife. Then he took his bride into the house, shut the door, and escorted her into the bridal chamber.

Breathless, Alysia looked at the room he had so carefully built and decorated. It was spacious, with a large bed laden with pillows. There were bright rugs on the floors and tapestries on the walls. Someone had already brought in her chests filled with her belongings and the things she had sewn.

"It is indeed fit for a queen," she whispered.

He seemed pleased, took her in his arms, and kissed her.

"She is like the budding rose in the springtime; her fairness dims the very sun!"

"Her hair is black as a raven's wing; her eyes like jewels, like amethysts; and her lips are as red as the anemones in the field."

"Solomon with his gilded tongue could not give justice to such beauty!"

Alysia didn't take the flattery too seriously, for it was all part of the wedding custom to compliment the bride and make her feel even more special at the end of the seven days of seclusion with her bridegroom. Now the couple had emerged to participate with their guests in the marriage feast, which was being held at Lazarus' much larger house.

Martha bustled about directing the servants. There was an abundance of food, the best wine, everyone seemed to think it was an excellent match—except for some of the unmarried young girls who eyed Nathan mournfully. *He* is *handsome and strong and kind*, Alysia thought. *Why am I not as happy as everyone else?*

It was, indeed, just a few weeks later that she knew she'd made a mistake. It was a completely insignificant moment except for that unwelcome revelation. She was standing outside at the oven, cooking supper—such a normal, everyday occurrence—but it was accompanied by a feeling of deep disappointment.

The house she now lived in was small and made of clay brick with a brick floor. It boasted four rooms: a kitchen, a bedroom—her bridal chamber—and two extra rooms; one was for storage and the other would be for the children they might have. She knew she should count herself fortunate, for many people lived in one-room houses with a dirt floor. The furniture had been skillfully crafted by the town carpenter.

A stairway ran up the outside of the house to the flat rooftop and they had furnished it with chairs and a table. She and Nathan spent whatever leisure time they had there, as did their neighbors on their own rooftops. It wasn't that she minded living in a small house with few luxuries. She would do that gladly, if circumstances were different.

What circumstances? she thought. But she knew.

She cautiously attempted to remove the spitted meat from the oven. The flames licked at her finger and she snatched her hand away, watching the meat fall with a triumphant hissing sound into the glowing embers. She fished it out with a wooden spoon and took it into the house, wiped the ashes from it, and put it on a plate. Nathan would be home soon and would be famished, as usual, and if he made one remark about the charred meat she would . . . well, she didn't know what she would do!

Now she knew how foolish she had been to think that Nathan, that anyone, could be a substitute for Paulus. Of course, she was fond of Nathan. She respected him and was grateful he had wanted to marry her in her penniless state—even though Lazarus had been good enough to provide a sizeable dowry. But she suspected that her husband's sense of loyalty to the Zealots surpassed his sense of duty to her, for many a night she was left alone while he went to secret meetings and plotted against the Romans. Worse still, his touch failed to stir her to the emotions so easily evoked by Paulus, who could take her breath away by merely looking at her.

Her thoughts ran rampant as she contemplated the burned meat and she felt overwhelmed with self-pity. For the first time since leaving Rome, a maddening sense of injustice filled her, making her want to scream with frustration, to fling herself on the floor and beat her heels against it like a thwarted child. Why was she denied happiness, when she had only tried to do what was right? But it was too late to change anything. It was all done now. She was doomed to feel lonely and unhappy for the rest of her life.

Yes, she was lonely . . . it was sympathy she needed, someone to whom she could pour out the whole story, from the beginning of her captivity to this moment. But there was no one she could tell who wouldn't be horrified, who wouldn't consider her immoral. Besides, the only person she really wanted to talk to was Paulus! He understood her, even when she was at her worst.

Alysia stared down at the table before her. Then she realized that Nathan was late…again…and his supper had grown cold.

"Enter," Paulus called in reply to the knock on the heavy wooden door. He stood beside the window on the second floor of the praetorium, gazing down at the turmoil in the streets of Jerusalem. The celebration of the Jews' main religious holiday, the Passover, was at hand. For days Jewish pilgrims had been pouring into the city from all over Palestine, from all over the empire, on foot, astride donkeys, in caravans. The surrounding towns were packed full; many had pitched tents in the public garden on the Mount of Olives; others thronged the streets looking for a place to stay. Some, for whom it was their first visit to Jerusalem, converged on the streets, wanting to see the fabled buildings and Herod's splendid amphitheater.

Paulus had tripled the number of legionaries patrolling the streets. He doubled the sentries overlooking the Temple and had soldiers on rooftops all over the city. After his experience with Zealots he was taking no chances.

In appearance he had made a complete recovery from the almost fatal attack over a month ago. His skin had resumed its healthy tan, his scars and broken arm were healing and his limp was gone. But something remained… a gruesome memory of his butchered men that would stay with him the rest of his life. And, but for some mysterious quirk of fate, he would have been among the dead.

In response to his call a servant entered, bowing stiffly. "The governor has arrived, sir."

Paulus descended the long row of stairs to the first floor and walked into the room where the prefect of Judea was handing his dusty mantle to a slave, while another swiftly bore upon them bearing a silver tray of wine and cheese.

Pontius Pilate turned to regard the legate with a wariness he tried to conceal. "Paulus." He accepted a cup from the tray and gestured with it. "Another for the commander. Sit down, Paulus. How are you? It's been a few years, hasn't it?"

Paulus noted the not-so-subtle air of authority Pilate was asserting instantly over both himself and the fortress—as was his right. He made a cordial reply and the two men sat facing each other. The prefect stretched out his legs and slouched forward as if to relieve the pressure of sitting.

"Tell me, Paulus, how do you like being back here? I confess I was surprised to hear of your appointment."

"It was time to leave Rome. I'm quite satisfied with the appointment."

"Indeed." Pilate looked disbelieving. He drank deeply and sighed. "Have you been outside? It's like Rome on a circus day."

"So far I haven't seen any signs of—trouble."

Pilate frowned. "The Jews are an obstinate race, as you well know. The potential for trouble is always there, but I hardly have to tell you that, eh? I see you have recovered from your little misadventure. Did you catch the men responsible?"

Paulus looked up as the servant brought more wine. "Some Zealots were caught and executed last week, but there was no way of knowing if they were involved in that particular attack. Most of them wouldn't talk even if offered their freedom."

The prefect nodded. "I've brought five hundred extra men. There is plenty of room in the barracks, as I recall. Herod planned for such contingencies when he built this place. I assume you've met the High Priest, and the members of the Sanhedrin?" He was looking at Paulus curiously. He wanted very much to know why the legate had been sent here—of course, everyone knew that Sejanus disliked him, so that *could* be the explanation.

"Yes," Paulus answered, looking faintly amused. "I've met the council, and Caiaphas, as well as his father-in-law, and I would say they give new meaning to the word 'arrogant.'"

"Ah, yes, but they play the game well. They've just never forgotten the priests used to be in control before we Romans spoiled things for them, and they still act as if they're running the country. In a way they are, since Caesar's policy is so tolerant of them. You need to make a show of force once in a while—show them who's really in charge."

It sounded like good advice from Aelius Sejanus. Paulus offered no comment.

"Believe me," Pilate went on, "if there ever is a hint of insurrection, the priests will be the first to put it down, if at all possible. Should they fail to do so they would be in danger of losing their power. And they have a great deal of power. They've gotten rich from the business of running the Temple. And no matter how contemptuous they are of the common man, they love to see the masses come into the city because these people spend money, and they give to the Temple treasury."

"You only confirm my high opinion of them," Paulus said. He already knew all this, but if Pilate wanted to share his knowledge it was always wise to listen.

"And I suppose you've been told that we hold the vestments of the High Priest here at the fort. They have to come and get them when it's time for one of their ceremonies. Our little way of keeping them in their place."

Before Paulus could reply a sharp rap sounded upon the door and it swung open to admit Megara, dressed in a gown of vibrant green with her red hair piled in the most fashionable of coiffures.

"I hope I'm not intruding," she said brightly.

"Pontius Pilate." Hiding his surprise, Paulus got to his feet and said, "May I present my wife. Megara, this is the prefect of Judea."

Megara smiled. "I came to visit my husband, and what a pleasant surprise to see that you have arrived. I am living at Herod's palace."

Pilate nodded, his dark eyes full of admiration. Megara studied him with interest. He wasn't as tall as Paulus, and somewhat heavier. The top of his head was bald, with close-cropped gray hair on either side. He wasn't handsome but he had an undeniable attractiveness, with lean, hawkish features, and when he spoke she thought his voice exceptionally well-modulated—rather like an actor's voice.

"I am delighted to meet you, Megara. I regret that my wife couldn't accompany me this year. I know you would have been great friends."

"I hope she isn't ill?"

"No. But extremely busy." Pilate did not elaborate on his wife's affairs.

Paulus surmised quickly that Megara had been waiting for Pilate's arrival so that she could meet him. After all, he was the highest-ranking official in the country, aside from the governor of Syria—and Megara was nothing if not ambitious. There was little chance Pilate would visit Herod's palace, for it was common knowledge that the two men disliked each other intensely.

"Oh, I envy her. I've almost forgotten what it's like to be busy." Megara ensconced herself in a comfortable chair as Paulus resumed his seat.

"So you find it as tedious here as I do?" Pilate chuckled and winked conspiratorially at Paulus.

"Well, tedious is perhaps not the right word. But there is only one good theater, and even it can't compare to those at home. Only the Greeks are any good at managing theater. And I find this city entirely lacking in good society. My husband doesn't understand. He has his duties to occupy him and I have nothing."

"But have you not met any of the other Roman matrons here?"

"My wife is rather particular about her friends," said Paulus blandly, when Megara hesitated to answer.

"And what's wrong with that?" she snapped suddenly, causing Pilate to raise his eyebrows. "I seem to recall that you used to be just as particular. At least I don't include among my friends a Cyrenian slave. Or a Greek—"

Megara stopped, for Paulus had a peculiar expression on his face and seemed to be daring her to continue. She looked appealingly at Pilate. "It's just that I'm so lonely. It's having a frightful effect on me. Why I hardly ever dare leave the palace with all that rabble outside."

"Oh, I don't think there is any danger to you." Pilate seemed amused. "I assume you have bodyguards?"

"Yes, of course, but what are they against so many? Look at what happened to my husband."

"But those were rebels who attacked your husband, because of his position."

Megara fell silent. Pilate said, "Come now, it's not as bad as all that. You must have made some friends here."

"Well, there is Herodias," she said reluctantly.

"Great Jove, I'd advise you to stay away from that woman! My wife despises her. And Herodias knows it, so it's not as if I'm telling tales. By the way, Paulus, what is the matter with Herod? We heard he was having some sort of collapse."

Megara hastened to explain. "I suppose you mean that preacher, the Baptizer. Yes, Herod is obsessed with him. He's been going to Machearus every few weeks to talk to him in prison. What about I'm sure I don't know, and Herodias is frantic to be rid of him."

"Yes, I've heard of this John the Baptizer. I was surprised it took so long for Herod Antipas to throw him into prison."

"There's another one as well," Paulus added. "He is connected to John somehow . . . there has been communication between their camps, so to speak."

"Another preacher? Isn't he afraid of Herodias?"

"He's not afraid of anything, from what I've heard," Paulus answered. "This Nazarene has openly criticized even the leaders of his own people. He must know he won't get very far with that. He has gained quite a following, though."

"I haven't heard of this one. What does he do?" Pilate almost flinched with regret at having made this admission; it raised a question of his competence. Well, he'd been overrun with administrative duties—probably there was a report somewhere on his desk.

"He travels with a band of disciples and I've heard rumors that he heals people, or pretends to. They say he was in Jerusalem earlier this year—I was incapacitated at the time—but he was rather quiet and left abruptly. Last year before my arrival he apparently created some kind of ruckus in the Temple. I would like to have seen it. But he has confined his activities to Galilee for the most part."

"Let him stay there, then." Pilate leaned back musingly, bending his elbows and placing his fingertips together. "Do the Jews think he is their—what do you call it—Messiah?"

"As far as I know he's made no such claim. If the Jews expect him to lead a revolt against Rome, I think they're mistaken. My sources say he talks of forgiveness and loving one's enemies."

"Well, the priests ought to like that. He won't be stirring things up they can't control."

"Oh, he's stirring things up. He has referred to them, and to the Pharisees in particular, as a lot of hypocrites—says they're too unbending, that they strain at gnats and swallow camels."

Pilate burst out laughing. "A bit indelicate, but I'll commend him for that. And what happened to loving his enemies?"

"I suppose they are an exception. He seems especially harsh toward men in authority who, in his opinion, mislead the people, or cause them to stumble over minute details and traditions they've supposedly added to their laws."

"Oh, I'm quite familiar with their washings and bathings and fastings, and how they can only walk a certain distance on their Sabbath. They are a ridiculous sight, bending over to say their prayers in the middle of the road! But the people love them, eh? They are far more popular than the Sadducees."

Megara said hurriedly, "Have you any news from Rome, sir? My father is such a poor correspondent."

The prefect didn't answer and a look of uneasiness crossed his face. Paulus guessed what was on his mind, for he had recently received a letter from a friend in Rome detailing the latest tumult; it involved Sejanus, to whom Pilate owed his governorship. Tiberius had at last grown suspicious of Sejanus' ambitions, or rather had decided to stop pretending he didn't know about them. He was apparently sending out signals of his displeasure to the Senate, attempting to ascertain the depth of their loyalty to his "co-ruler."

If Sejanus fell, there would be a full-scale investigation into his activities—and probably a bloodbath. Any and all of Sejanus' associates would be suspect, including the governor of Judea. Pilate would no doubt be keeping a much lower profile in the days to come. Anything he did to antagonize the Jews would go against him without Aelius Sejanus to support his actions.

Pilate recovered and said amicably, "The emperor remains at Capri and the world goes on . . . I've always said that no news from Rome is good news. Won't you tell *me*, Megara, the news of Jerusalem?"

Overcoming her earlier sullenness at being left out of the conversation, Megara launched into more criticism of Herod and praise of Herodias—notwithstanding Pilate's distaste for the subject, which was almost comically revealed by the subtle twist of his lips.

On a sweltering day in mid-summer the Nazarene came to Bethany. His arrival brought confusion and excitement as the entire town turned out to see the famed preacher. He was accompanied by his inner group of disciples, now numbering twelve. The men were tired and hungry and covered with white dust from the roads. All who could manage to get away from their occupations congregated at Lazarus' house where the men would be staying, in the hope of hearing a sermon or witnessing some miracle. It soon became apparent, however, that the Nazarene had not come to preach but to rest.

He sought seclusion in Bethany, and peace, but this time it was not to be so. Martha found herself hard put to feed all those who gathered on the courtyard to speak with Jesus and his friends. She, Alysia, and the servants roasted meat, boiled vegetables, and baked bread during the entire morning.

"Where is Mary?" Martha demanded irritably, her red face beaded with perspiration.

"I don't know." Alysia groaned under the weight of a huge pot as she pulled it from a shelf. She ran the back of her hand across her damp forehead. "The last time I saw her she was out on the courtyard."

Martha made a disgruntled sound. "Yes, as are all my friends, except you, Alysia. You would think they'd realize we need help in here."

"They haven't had the opportunity to hear him speak as we have, Martha."

"Mary has, and I'm going to call her at once!"

The older woman marched outside and halted until she spied Lazarus sitting a short distance away from the Nazarene, who didn't address the crowd but seemed to be answering individual questions. Next to her brother sat Mary, her young face rapt with attention. She was so concentrating on what Jesus was saying that she failed to hear her sister's voice until Martha practically screeched, "Mary!"

Everyone turned to stare at her, including Mary, who looked scandalized. Martha felt sick with embarrassment. She gave the Nazarene an imploring look. "Don't you care that Mary sits here while I do all the work? Tell her to come and help me!"

"Martha, Martha," he said, in a low voice, "don't trouble yourself so. Mary has found that which is important to her. Let us not take it from her."

Thus reproached, however kindly, Martha disappeared into the house where she sniffed ominously but continued preparing the food until it was taken outside and served. After the meal Alysia joined those who had overflowed the courtyard and now lined the street. The stifling heat of midday had lessened to a pleasant warmth, cooled by a breeze sweeping down the mountain.

She looked around to see if Nathan had come but didn't find him. He had obstinately refused to join her, saying there were repairs to be done around the house. She watched the Nazarene for a while, who was talking and laughing with several children. The children seemed drawn to him. Some perched upon his knees while others sat down at his feet.

She had a sudden, uncanny feeling that *she* was being watched and turned her head to look around. She caught a glimpse of a familiar face before the man nodded at her and turned abruptly to walk away.

Paulus! What was he doing here, and garbed as a Jew? She walked quickly after the retreating figure until she rounded a corner where they were hidden from the view of the townspeople.

He stopped and turned. His hair was longer and tousled and he wore a belted robe.

"Paulus!" she cried in amazement. "What are you doing here?"

He said only, "Alysia," and seemed to be at a loss for words. It had been almost a year since they had seen each other. She met his gaze and knew she must speak, must say something impersonal.

"You haven't answered my question, Paulus. And why are you dressed like this?"

He made his voice as casual as hers. "I couldn't very well appear here as a legate, could I?"

"I—suppose not."

"Alysia, there is something I must tell you."

His tone was serious and she felt a sudden apprehension. "What is it?"

"Lucius is in Jerusalem."

"Lucius!"

"Yes. He has no way of knowing you are here. I've warned Megara to say nothing. But you had better stay out of Jerusalem. And there is something else. A letter arrived at the garrison, a list of fugitives, and your name and description are on it. It was posted for viewing before I knew it had arrived. I destroyed it, but it may have been seen by some of my men."

"But—why did Lucius come here?"

Paulus shrugged. "Who can say what's in his mind—other than some mischief."

"We can't trust Megara not to tell Lucius about me. Would she not put aside any fear of you to see me dead?"

"Let me worry about Megara. Believe me, she does not want to be entangled with anything to do with you, because it would involve me and therefore her."

There was a long pause, then Alysia said, "You could have sent a message, instead of coming yourself."

He answered in a low voice, "There are men who are watching the Nazarene—they have been ordered to let me know whenever he enters Judea. Early this afternoon, when I heard he was here, I decided to come. I have been wanting to see him for myself."

A sense of disappointment struck her but she said quickly, "Why? What are you going to do about him?"

"Nothing yet. Nothing . . . as long as he does not gather weapons or speak against Rome."

She shook her head. "He is not going to do that. Besides, he—" She stopped. How was she to tell Paulus what she knew about Jesus, what she had seen? He would never believe her. She still couldn't believe it herself.

"Yes?" Paulus asked, searching her eyes.

"He means no threat to Rome," she said finally.

There was another moment of prolonged silence before Paulus spoke again. "You know that it was you I came to see."

Alysia looked down, alarmed by the violence of her emotions. Happiness flooded over her but she mustn't let him see. She retreated a step and looked at his set shoulders.

"Thank you for the warning, Paulus. My . . . husband . . . would be grateful as well. I must go now."

"I'm sorry," he said quietly. "I didn't mean to distress you. I only wanted you to know that if you ever need me—"

"Thank you," she said again, her voice muffled.

With an effort of sheer will Paulus watched her walk away. He waited for some time, so they wouldn't appear to have been together, and walked the short distance to the house where he had seen the people assembled. He wasn't surprised to see that Alysia had disappeared.

He joined the outer edge of the crowd. Several men had gathered in one place and he knew they must be the special apprentices, or disciples, of the Nazarene. One of them, a man as tall as he with thick, black hair, turned a little toward Paulus to regard him quizzically. Paulus nodded and drifted further away.

He remained only long enough to observe the Nazarene and listen to him speak. A group of children sat around his feet, while adults stood behind them. He was talking about something he called "the kingdom of heaven." The kingdom of heaven was like yeast, he said, when a woman mixes it with flour and it's worked into the dough. The kingdom of heaven was like a merchant who looks for fine pearls, and when he finds one of great value, he sells everything he has in order to buy it.

Paulus thought of a verse he had read recently, out of the Hebrew Psalms: *I will open my mouth in parables—I will utter things hidden since the creation of the world.*

He gazed intently into the Nazarene's face. There was nothing remarkable about his features: large, eloquent eyes, thin nose, high cheekbones, except . . . what *was* the difference? Then it struck him that he was looking at a face that was completely open, one utterly without guile or deception. An honest face.

Paulus' advisors believed that the Nazarene could be dangerous with the large following he had. But whatever his purpose, Paulus decided, it was not to overthrow the government. This "kingdom of heaven" must be some sort of allegory, meant to illustrate his teachings. This man plainly had deep convictions but he was no fanatic.

He glanced over the crowd, wondering if Alysia's husband was present. He didn't see anyone who resembled the wild-eyed man from the Zealot attack. He didn't know for certain that it *was* the same man, for the names were common enough. Paulus had not sought him out, for Alysia's sake, but he could not ignore the man should he be caught in another offense.

"Sir, would you like something to eat?" His thoughts were diverted by a motherly looking Jewish woman who looked up at him expectantly.

He smiled and said in Aramaic, "No, thank you. I was about to leave."

He saw that he had attracted the attention of a group of young maidens, who blushed and giggled when he caught them staring. As he began the walk back to Jerusalem, he thought his heart was very heavy . . . to be so empty.

CHAPTER XIV

A new restlessness seized Alysia during the remaining summer months that she found impossible to put aside. The rainy season began and confined her to her house, as completely as the knowledge of Lucius' presence in Jerusalem forced her to remain in Bethany. She deeply resented this confinement. It was all she could do to present a pleasant mien when Nathan came home at night…if he came at all. His meetings in other towns had become more and more frequent.

Her daily chores became tedious and dreaded; small things began to irritate her. Nathan arrived unexpectedly one afternoon to find her sobbing over a clay pot she had dropped and broken while cleaning the shelves of dishes.

"This is nothing to weep over," he said impatiently. "What is wrong?"

She shook her head, refusing to look at him. He took her by both arms, his face strained. "I want to know what is troubling you."

"I don't know!" She wrenched herself free, walking rapidly into the next room. "Leave me alone!" she cried when he followed her. Nathan whirled and strode irately out of the house and up the steps to the rooftop. When he returned much later, Alysia didn't speak when she felt him slip into bed beside her.

It was almost like watching a play and Paulus was most interested to see how it would end. He stood on the walkway between battlements, looking down into the outer courtyard of the Temple. The Nazarene was there, surrounded by a crowd of listeners. Nearby stood a flock of priests, looking dour and pretending not to listen.

It was another holiday. This one involved the Jews setting up temporary huts, or booths as they called them, made of palm and pine and myrtle trees—and the entire park on the Mount of Olives was covered with them. People stayed in these huts for a number of days, in remembrance of the time their forefathers had spent in the wilderness after their exodus from Egypt. It was all very peculiar and a great annoyance to the legionaries, whose duties were multiplied every time the Jews had one of their "celebrations."

When the Nazarene arrived in the city he had caused quite a sensation, making a scathing verbal attack against the Pharisees and scribes, who were highly venerated and considered authorities on religious law. He openly accused them of insincerity, of teaching one thing and doing another, of exalting themselves and desiring only the admiration and respect of men.

"*Hypocrites*! How can you escape the damnation of hell?" The Nazarene went on to refer to them as "whited sepulchers" and "a generation of vipers."

The religious leaders trembled with outrage at this attack launched on the very streets of the holy city, and by a Nazarene! And the people actually listened to him!

He must be silenced. Pharisees and Sadducees put aside their conflicting opinions on every issue save this one. Their network of spies had failed to trip him in his words in order to establish a charge of treason, for which Rome would promptly execute him, nor had they succeeded in catching him in a phrase that might be construed as blasphemy. To be more exact, they *had* heard him blaspheme—with their own ears!—but whenever they tried to take hold of him he somehow got away. It was as though he actually disappeared, although that of course was impossible. Obviously, Satan temporarily blinded them so that the Nazarene could escape.

Paulus had been informed of all this by his own spy, an "elder" in the Sanhedrin, a wealthy but weak-minded man named Phineas who was terrified by the turmoil caused by the Nazarene. Phineas was certain, as were others, that if Rome believed a rebellion was brewing they would destroy the entire nation. He felt it his duty to relay to Paulus all that the Sanhedrin was doing to check the Nazarene's influence over the people.

That day there had been a meeting presided over by the High Priest and his father-in-law, Annas. Some said that Annas was the real High Priest and Caiaphas only bore the title, for Annas was still the most influential man among the Jewish leaders—though Rome had deposed him from that office over fifteen years ago, and possibly for that reason.

Caiaphas, a small, thin man with skeletal features and a sparse black beard, glared down at the others from his high seat. "Are there any among you who do not understand the plan?" he asked, in a tone that clearly implied they were imbeciles if they didn't.

Receiving no reply, he went on. "The arrangements will be made and will be carried out tomorrow morning. The Nazarene will no doubt be in the Temple area, as he has been these past several mornings. I believe that our plans will at last be fruitful."

"I do not think so."

All eyes turned to old Annas, who sat placidly in his seat and returned the stares from under a craggy, wrinkled forehead and bushy white brows.

"And why not?"

Annas shrugged eloquently. "Nothing else has worked—why should this? The Nazarene has a talent for getting himself out of the most difficult situations, and let us admit, he does have a way with words."

Caiaphas' face flushed darkly. "No matter what he says or does in this situation, he cannot fail to lose popularity with the people."

Another member spoke up. "But suppose we are unable to find a . . . participant . . . in the morning?"

"I have hired two men to supply one. A real one, not someone playing a part. I admit the Nazarene is too clever for that. It will not be difficult. They know where to look."

"If I were a wagering man," said Annas, "I would wager half my house that the Nazarene will come out of this unscathed. And then we will all look like fools."

"And I say that is impossible!" snapped his son-in-law, who rose abruptly. "This adjourns our meeting. Let us pray to the Most High for success."

And, Paulus had asked Phineas, what was the plan?

Phineas did not know; he had arrived too late to hear it, but as usual it would involve trying to get the Nazarene to say something that either his followers or the Romans wouldn't like. One would do just as well as the other.

Yes, it was like a play, a comedy almost, except that it was likely to end in tragedy if the priests had their way. Paulus had to admire the Nazarene's boldness, but didn't he realize his own danger? Just recently Herod had beheaded John the Baptizer for much the same reason.

Well, whatever the plan, Paulus would hear of it. Maybe it *would* be best for the priests to discredit the man and send him back to his little town in Galilee. At least then he would live.

Megara reclined on her silk-covered couch and gazed steadily up at her servant. "Take this note to the woman you found for me—the one who lives in Bethany. Do not tarry; do *not* let anyone see you. No one, especially my husband, must ever know that you delivered this message."

The short, Macedonian slave was mute, which was one reason Megara had chosen him for this particular task. That, and because he was blindly loyal to her. She often rewarded him with money for errands she set him upon that, if discovered, might reflect badly on her. More often than not this involved keeping track of Paulus' whereabouts.

She knew her husband had made a trip to Bethany in the summer and that he had spoken with a beautiful, young woman dressed in the style of the Jews. From her description, Megara knew it was Alysia. It had been easy to send her small, silent slave to spy out the land. Discovering where Alysia lived opened a world of possibilities for her removal, except that Megara didn't know just how to accomplish that particular end without someone ultimately uncovering her role in it. And then a plan had presented itself to her.

After a few more crisply issued instructions, the slave nodded and walked away. Megara let out her breath slowly, concentrating on letting her heart regain its normal rhythm. She was nervous, yet strangely elated. Seeing Alysia captured would be worth all the misery that she, Megara, had endured since coming to Jerusalem. And Paulus would never know how it had happened.

She found herself unexpectedly good at forgery; the handwriting on the note was identical to her husband's, and it bore his seal. That had been a bit harder and involved bribing a guard to "borrow" the seal and then return it without Paulus' knowledge. The note implored Alysia to meet him at a certain time and place, regarding a most urgent matter.

The place happened to be the very room of the inn at which Lucius was staying. It would look like an accidental meeting. If Megara knew Lucius, and she did, he would arrest Alysia immediately and take her straight to Rome without Paulus' knowledge, lest Paulus try to stop him. Of course, there were risks but she had considered each and resolved them in her own mind.

Alysia *could* tell someone about the forged note before she left Bethany, but Megara doubted she would; she certainly wouldn't want anyone to know she was off to meet clandestinely with a Roman legate in Jerusalem. And she would probably be long dead before Paulus contrived to get back to Rome and save her.

Alysia *could* miss Lucius altogether, even though the time had been carefully calculated. Lucius would almost certainly be in his room when she arrived. Alysia would not mention the note to Lucius; she would want to protect Paulus. But if they should fail to meet—well, Megara would have to get rid of Alysia somehow before she had a chance to go to Paulus and ask him why he had sent her the note. Her slave would not be averse to staging an "accident" if offered sufficient motivation. But that would be a last resort; she didn't really want to be involved in outright murder—unless it was necessary. This way, Lucius would accomplish her goal for her. And it wasn't murder. It was justice.

Would the authorities think that Paulus had been hiding Alysia? Maybe, at first. But Megara would swear until she was blue in the face that neither she nor Paulus were aware that Alysia was here when they came to Jerusalem. That much was true. She *knew* Paulus had truly believed Alysia was dead. Never mind that it was quite a coincidence that Alysia should be just a few miles away from her former master—such things happened, such things were ordained by the gods, for reasons good or ill.

Best of all, Aelius Sejanus was dead now, denounced by Tiberius and summarily executed. There was so much confusion and chaos in Rome at the moment that no one would pay any attention to the execution of a slave or the reasons for it; nobody cared about Magnus anymore, and his sottish old father was dead. They were no longer threats to Paulus.

The only possible complication would be that Paulus himself would stand by the slave even after she was dead and declare her innocent. He might even admit to having helped her escape. But why would he be so stupid as to do that?

No, she had thought of everything. Megara's amber eyes glittered with triumph and excitement. Probably this very night Alysia would be on her way to Rome.

Simon approached Paulus' study with foreboding. "Sir, I must speak with you."

Paulus regarded his slave with concern, dismissed the tribune who stood before him and rose from behind his desk. "Come in, Simon. What is it?"

Simon entered and closed the door. "I am sorry to trouble you, sir. It's about your wife."

Paulus said nothing, waiting for him to continue.

"I found some papyrus sheets your wife had discarded. I didn't take them because I thought she would look for them, to destroy them. Besides, she only left the room for a moment but there was something about her—that was why I looked around. It appeared she had been . . ." Simon swallowed nervously. "It appeared she had been practicing at signing your name."

Paulus stood very still. "Go on."

"Yes, sir. Because this was somewhat unusual, I lingered outside the door and heard her order one of the slaves to take a message to someone. I couldn't hear the name but I heard the name of the town. She said Bethany. She was very adamant about secrecy, especially that you must know nothing of it." For a moment, Simon wondered what his fate would be, for it was no small thing to tell a man you suspected his wife was up to no good.

Paulus still didn't move and his face remained expressionless. "How long ago was this?"

"I didn't see you when you came in, sir, or I would have spoken earlier. It was some time ago, mid-afternoon at least."

"Tell me her exact words."

Simon did so, as best he could remember.

Paulus' thoughts raced. He struggled to get inside his wife's mind…it was not a pleasant place to be. It seemed obvious that Megara had written to Alysia and signed his name, for he had no other connection with Bethany. She could only have purposed to bring some harm or trouble to Alysia. How to do that? And then it came to him. Send her to Lucius!

There was no time to waste. As he was running from the room, he placed his hand on Simon's shoulder. "You have done well."

Alysia had been tense and worried ever since she'd been handed the letter by a small man dressed as a slave who had refused to answer her questions and had left without ever saying a word…and with the letter. She was amazed that Paulus had sent for her but it was his writing, which she remembered seeing when he wrote the letter to the captain of the ill-fated ship, and it was his seal.

He'd written that she must come to him at once, that it was a matter of life and death and that above all she must tell no one. He had given directions to an inn. The notion that it could be any kind of trickery gave her only a moment's pause. It *was* his writing, his seal. And because he would never summon her unless it *was* a matter of life and death—he might be wounded, he might be dying!

Nathan was somewhere attending a "political meeting." She didn't know when he would return or even if he would come back tonight. She found a scrap of papyrus and wrote that she had gone to visit a friend. She pulled one of his long, hooded cloaks over her to hide her face and form and began the walk to Jerusalem…knowing all the while that she should not go.

Across the street from the inn, below the Temple and situated at a corner that cut between the inn and a banking house, Paulus stood watching everyone who came and went. He wore only a dark blue tunic without the military trappings in order to be less conspicuous, but he had his dagger strapped to his waist. He was prepared to stop Lucius, at any cost.

He saw no sign of his stepbrother. It would be dark soon, however, and Lucius would no doubt emerge to begin his nightly exploits, as Paulus knew to be his custom. Two hulking men nearby also watched the inn, arousing Paulus' suspicions, but he finally concluded they were only looking for a prostitute.

He had time for doubts to assail him. Had he correctly deduced what Megara had done? Was he too late? Should he go to Lucius' room and see if he was still there, or wait for Alysia to arrive? The most important thing was to protect Alysia, so he decided to wait a while longer. If she didn't arrive within a reasonable amount of time, he would question the innkeeper to find out if there had been any disturbance caused by the tribune.

The longer he waited, the more his ire grew. Megara had done her work well. She had summoned Alysia to the inn at just the right time for a "chance" encounter with Lucius. If Lucius saw her, arrested her, and sent her immediately to Rome, Paulus wouldn't have known about it until it was too late…and he would never have known how Alysia came to be in Jerusalem. He had always suspected it was a great mistake for the male population of Rome to assume that women were mentally inferior to men. However, Megara's shrewdness was outweighed by her lack of common sense, for she often failed to consider the consequences of her actions. And for this, there would be consequences!

His attention was drawn by a slim person engulfed in a hooded cloak. The figure's graceful, elegant carriage assured him it was Alysia, even before she glanced around and inadvertently gave anyone who happened to be watching a glimpse of her face.

Alysia felt a hand on her arm. She jumped and glanced upward. "Paulus!"

"Be quiet." Paulus dragged her into the shadows. At that instant he saw Lucius coming down the outer stairs from the second story, earlier than usual. Paulus pulled her into a doorway of the building, where the innkeeper sat at a low table, counting coins.

"I want a room at once," Paulus said.

The innkeeper looked startled as Paulus thrust money into his hands and began pushing Alysia out again. A stout man with bleary eyes, he ran ahead of them to open a door off the ground level and ushered them inside. The tall man slammed the door in his face.

From the street Lucius regarded the closed door with interest. So, his stepbrother had taken to meeting women at inns these days! It would be amusing to find out who she was. Not a prostitute, surely; Paulus had never resorted to such women when it was possible to have practically anyone he wanted. He gave a mental shrug and hurried on his way, smiling a little. The matter would bear investigating but some other time, for his friends were waiting and he had no inclination to linger about waiting for Paulus and his companion to leave the inn.

As he passed, two huge fellows across the street were talking in low, gravelly voices.

"That has all the looks of a lover's nest," said the heavier of the two men.

"Oh," said the other, "she'll suit our purpose well enough. I've seen her before—you don't forget someone like her. She's married to that stonemason in Bethany. My brother lives there."

"Who's the man?"

"Didn't get a good look at him. Had my eyes on her."

"We were supposed to go around by the booths and catch someone in the act."

"This is better. Close to the Temple. Besides, I know she's married. We wouldn't know for sure about anyone else, and I don't care to go creeping about through the park at night, do you? Find a place to settle down—we might be here all night. If she leaves too early we'll just have to detain her somehow."

Inside the inn Alysia loosened the cloak and let its hood fall down around her shoulders. "Why did you send for me?"

Paulus walked over to the latticed window where he observed Lucius standing across the street. He waited until Lucius moved away, then turned to face her. "Didn't I tell you to stay out of Jerusalem?"

"But—" She paused. "You didn't write the letter."

"Of course not!"

She felt her own anger begin to rise. "I thought something had happened to you, that you needed me. I only came because—"

She stopped abruptly. A feeling of anticlimax gripped her and she realized how tightly her nerves had been wound and how weary she now was. Paulus moved to close the shutters, and as he did so she sank down in a padded chair and looked absently about the room, noticing its spaciousness and the fine furnishings. The close proximity of the inn to the Temple perhaps accounted for its superior quality. The floor was laid with carpet; there were several chairs and a couch covered with cushions and a blanket made of multicolored yarn. The wooden bedstead was high off the ground and on top was a thick mat, also covered with clean linens and blankets. A large, bronze brazier stood opposite the bed for use in the colder months. The scent of aloes and cinnamon permeated the room. Several small tables bore oil lamps and bowls of fresh fruit. Tapestries lined the thick walls, making the room seem closer, more private and intimate.

No, she should not have come here.

"I would not have written you for any reason—even if I were dying. You should have known that, Alysia."

"I'm going home," she said firmly.

"You cannot leave now. We don't know where Lucius is."

She got to her feet. "I *am* leaving. Please get out of my way."

"Alysia, listen to me. Megara wrote the letter, hoping you would run into Lucius which you very nearly did. If her plan had succeeded you would be face-to-face with him at this very moment."

"Megara! I knew she would do something—oh, I have been a fool!"

"You are no fool. Maybe I was, by thinking I could control her. It would be easier to tame a viper."

Alysia stared at him as he stood in the darkened room with the light from the lamps flickering over his tall form. She couldn't stop her voice from trembling. "I won't stay here with you."

Paulus took a step toward her, and stopped. "I'll go and find out where Lucius is and have him watched until you are back in Bethany. I'll have Simon take you there."

When she didn't reply, he asked, "Is that acceptable to you?"

Alysia nodded, not meeting his eyes.

Paulus turned to go. He put his hand on the door and hesitated for what seemed an eternity, and turned again to look at her. Her gaze lifted and fused with his and she drew in her breath sharply. As though with a life of its own, the cloak she had draped over her shoulders slid off and sank to the floor. She wasn't aware of either of them moving, but she was locked in his arms, and he was kissing her with a long-suppressed, ravenous hunger and almost savagery. When he lifted her and carried her swiftly to the bed, her only thought was that no one would ever know…

Sometime in the night she awakened. Paulus had opened the shutters slightly just before they went to sleep and the moonlight pierced the latticework in shafts, falling in a pale glow upon the bed. A light waft of air struck her. It had been unseasonably cold for several days but she was warm beneath the blankets.

This, she thought, *is where I belong*. If only it were Paulus who sat across from her every day and ate the meals she cooked, who shared quiet evenings with her on the rooftop, who lay beside her each night. If only . . .

Alysia released a sigh and rose quietly from the bed. She wrapped the cloak around her and sat down on the couch, wondering how she was to get home and what she would tell Nathan. That her friend was sick and Alysia had stayed the night with her—a friend from Cyprus who had come here for the festival. How she hated the thought of lying to Nathan, and after this! He didn't deserve it, in spite of their trouble. She realized that she was crying.

Paulus stirred and sat up. His eyes, clear and ocean blue in the muted glow of the room, met hers. "What is it?" he asked.

She shook her head. "It is nothing. I'm cold."

He left the bed and began putting on his clothes. "I'll go and get some coals," he said. "It won't take long. Be sure and bolt the door after me. I'll knock twice when I come back."

He slipped his dagger into its sheath and left the room. Alysia slid the bolt against the sturdy wooden door and went to the window. The full moon was high in the blackness; it would be hours before dawn. She pushed the shutters closed.

There was a hand mirror on one of the tables. She glanced into it, wiping the tears from her face. Two knocks sounded on the door and she went to open it, then bolted it again as Paulus poured a bucket of hot coals into the top of the brazier and closed its grated top. "The innkeeper wasn't very happy about parting with these," he said lightly. "I don't think I'm the only one to visit him tonight."

She barely heard him and he asked again, "What is it, Alysia?"

She didn't answer. Gently he took her arm, guided her toward the brazier, and stood beside her. A comforting warmth radiated toward them.

"You're thinking of your husband."

"I shouldn't have married him," she whispered. "Not…loving you as I do. But you've always known that, haven't you?"

He drew her close into his arms. "There was a time when I was sure you hated me. And with good cause."

"I hated your uniform. I hated Rome. But never you."

His voice changed, became low and sober. "Does he treat you well?"

"Yes, but . . . he is not often home."

"Because of his profession?"

"I suppose so, partly. He was away earlier; he may not be home even now. I left him a message that I was with a friend. Paulus, why did Lucius come here? Do you think he believes I'm still alive?"

"No, he has no reason to suspect that. You couldn't have known this, but there's trouble in Rome. Sejanus is dead. Tiberius is busy routing out all his supporters. I think Sejanus and Lucius were acquaintances, if not friends. When Lucius left Rome there were probably already rumors that something like this would happen."

Alysia moved back so she could see his face. "Sejanus is dead . . . but I thought Tiberius had supreme trust in him!"

"Maybe he did once. Something, or someone, opened his eyes to the man's ambitions."

"I'm glad you're not in Rome just now."

"Nobody could accuse me of supporting Sejanus," Paulus said wryly. "But then again, people will say anything to save their own necks. It probably is a good thing I'm not there."

It had grown pleasantly warm in the room. Alysia relaxed against him; she felt him pull her closer, felt his cheek against her hair. Paulus, sure and steady and unchanging. Paulus, who loved her.

"It will be a few hours until daybreak," he said quietly. "Do you want to leave?"

Her head moved slowly back and forth. "I never want to leave."

CHAPTER XV

Morning came, the night was over, drawn down into all the past nights of her life. But this one . . . this one she would remember, always.

She pulled Nathan's cloak over her gown. Paulus had just slipped his tunic over his head, explaining that he would go to the Antonia where he would get Simon and return with him to the inn. Paulus would watch for Lucius, while Simon followed her at a safe distance and made sure she arrived safely in Bethany.

The coals in the brazier had died to ashes and it was cold again. Paulus tied his belt and went to her, taking her arms in his hands. "You must be more careful. You must be safe. I'll find a way to make Lucius leave Jerusalem. I should have done so before now."

Alysia nodded, not trusting herself to speak. He put his hand beneath her chin, lifted her face, and gently kissed her.

Without warning the door crashed open, the wooden bolt flying across the room. Shocked, they both spun to face the door. Paulus reacted with a swiftness the two attackers had not anticipated, and in a single movement pushed Alysia out of harm's way and grabbed his dagger from where he had placed it on a table.

One of the men was a giant, a head taller than Paulus and twice as wide. As Paulus sprang at him, the other man swung a club and knocked the knife from his hand. Paulus' fist smashed into the man's face, slamming him backward against the wall. The larger one struck Paulus from behind with stunning force. He whirled and knocked the breath from that assailant, just before the other man recovered his senses and brought his club down hard on Paulus' head. He slumped to the floor, then groaned and attempted to rise. The larger man struck him with his fist, while the other kicked him in the ribs. Paulus moved no more.

Too stunned to scream Alysia was pulled, struggling, through the door—all the while hanging back and trying to see how badly injured Paulus might be, whispering his name, barely able to speak. Instantly a rank-smelling cloth was stuffed into her mouth. The street was empty as the two men dragged her into an alley and from the shadows emerged four robed and turbaned men. Coins quickly exchanged hands; there was a brief, muttered conversation. One of the attackers had a bloody face and went limping down the alley. The larger one remained, holding her tightly.

Alysia managed to spit out the cloth and found her voice. "Let go of me!"

"Be silent, adulteress," said one of the Jews.

She stopped her wild grappling as the word exploded in her brain.

"The punishment for adultery is death, by stoning."

"I am not Jewish!" she cried desperately. "You cannot judge me by your laws!"

The men, all of whom were bearded and dressed as Pharisees, looked at each other. One of them said in low tones to the man holding her, "You were to make certain that the criterions were met."

"Oh, I know who she is. She's married all right, to that Zealot I've told you about. And that wasn't him she was with."

All four of the Jews then turned and began striding rapidly down the alley, their black robes and broad, tasseled borders flapping, their pointed turbans bobbing beneath the head coverings that were almost as long as their robes. The hired man forced her to follow. Alysia was frantic, choking back sobs. Through the narrow, unpaved streets, past the yellowing limestone houses they went, until she saw they were heading for the Temple.

They are going to kill me! She stumbled against the man dragging her. He picked her up and carried her struggling form under one arm, climbing up the steep flight of stone steps until they came to one of the entrance gates. Once inside the gate, the man shoved her through the dimly lit passageway…up more stairs, and stopped when they emerged onto what was called the royal portico.

The morning sun threw the portico with its innumerable white columns and long pavement, into shadows. Sitting there were a number of men and women, listening to a man who sat on a row of steps before them. He had dark hair tied in the back and alert dark eyes that glanced away from the crowd and directly into her own.

Jesus of Nazareth. This was too great to be borne . . . surely nothing she had ever done warranted having to face this man with her shame!

"Master," called one of her captors in a deliberate, falsely humble tone, "we are sorry to interrupt, but we have a question of the utmost importance."

The four Pharisees had been joined by several other men, clad in expensive-looking robes; they were scribes and other authorities on Jewish law. All were somber and silent and stared fixedly at the Nazarene. None of them so much as glanced at Alysia, whose head was covered by the hood of her cloak. She was in front of the crowd so that no one but Jesus and the disciple who sat next to him could see her face. As she stood there, trembling, her abductor yanked the hood down causing her hair to spill out and over her shoulders. He shoved her forward yet again and turned to disappear among the rows of mammoth columns.

She held her head high, drawing the cloak tightly across her body with trembling hands. Her lips parted and she breathed rapidly; she could see her breath plume before her in the cold morning air. A sudden gust of wind lifted her wildly cascading hair and it played about her head like a cloud of darkness. Bright color stained her cheeks. Her knees shook so hard that the enveloping garment quivered over them.

"The Law," continued the Pharisee, "commands that those guilty of adultery be stoned to death. The woman before you is an adulteress."

They would take her outside the city walls, they would pick up the heavy, jagged rocks...Alysia would steel herself for the first cruel blow and soon her body would be broken beyond recognition. Her scalp tingled, as if anticipating the first stone that would flatten her skull.

"What," said the Pharisee, "do you say?"

They stood there, watching him.

But the Nazarene did not seem to hear them. After his first glance of recognition he had turned his attention away, as though to show his contempt for her accusers. His jaw tightened with what seemed repressed anger. His gaze was on the pavement, which bore a coating of the white dust that covered everything in Judea. Then he leaned over slightly, and with his finger began writing in it.

Alysia could look at no one else. Her hair still shielded her face from the crowd behind her. The people were utterly silent and she could feel dozens of pairs of eyes pinned to her back. All activity at this early hour had ceased—the babble and movement of those strolling across the Court of the Gentiles, the clinking of coins at the Treasury . . .

"This woman," said the same Pharisee, rather testily, "has been caught in the very act of adultery!"

The Nazarene continued to trace a finger in the dust, his brow furrowed as if he were deep in thought.

"Rabbi," called one of the scribes. "Our Law says to kill her! Will you deny the Law? What shall we do with this woman?"

The crowd began to murmur. And at last the Nazarene moved.

He rose, his lean form unfolding with slow deliberation. He drew himself to his full height and under his steady gaze the crowd quieted again and waited for him to speak. His voice came low, but seemed to ring in the stillness.

"Whichever one of you has never sinned, be the first to cast a stone at her."

Silence hung in the air. Alysia held her breath and closed her eyes, but only for a moment. And, unbelievably, Jesus sat down and began writing again. One of the Pharisees seemed about to speak but he stopped and looked at his comrades. He was the eldest, the one of most authority. He turned abruptly and walked away. He was followed by the remaining three, and finally the younger scribes and lawyers. The crowd, too, began to disperse, with puzzled and guilty looks. Only the disciple remained sitting, and he had propped his arms across his knees and was staring at the ground.

Alysia found herself alone. Once again the Nazarene's eyes met hers, and his look of compassion was more than she could bear; it was more painful than the cruelest taunt, the worst insult. There was no accusation in his eyes, no anger, but she saw clearly reflected in them the enormity of what she had done. What had seemed right now seemed terribly wrong—wrong for so many reasons, wrong because she had created a breach in her marriage, and marriage was a sacred thing. Wrong because she had violated the law of God as willfully as if she had stood before him and shaken her fist in his face.

She had only just begun to accept the concept of God. He had no face, no form…whenever she tried to envision him, she could only see the Nazarene. She felt as if she had sinned against *him*, for his teachings about the sanctity of marriage had been all too clear.

A great sorrow clutched her heart, greater than any sorrow of her life.

Once more he rose to his feet and stood before her. "Where are your accusers?" he asked quietly. "Has anyone condemned you?"

She stuttered with cold and delayed emotion. "N-n-no man, Lord."

"Neither do I condemn you." He reached out and touched her arm, and the moment he did so she felt a peculiar energy that seemed to seep strength into her failing limbs. "Go, and sin no more."

Her eyes stung with tears. She took a single, experimental step and found that she could walk. She tried to speak but her voice broke and she turned away. Bringing the hood up to cover her hair and shield her face, she slipped past him between the marble pillars, down the stairs and through the passageway, then down, down the endless steps to the street below. The motion seemed to have a rhythm; every touch of her feet against the earth seemed to say "sin no more, sin no more."

In a deserted alley she fell against the side of a building, leaning her head against its coldness. With rising panic, she thought only of Paulus. Had they killed him? She began to run again with short, dragging steps. She stumbled and half fell, sliding down until she leaned against the wall of the building. Her heart thumped so erratically it was difficult to breathe.

Dimly, she heard the sound of hoof beats as a horse thundered past at breakneck speed. She raised her hand to shield her face from the bits of dirt churned by the racing hooves. A wild neigh came from the horse as it was violently halted, then someone lifted her head. She opened her eyes to see Paulus kneeling beside her.

"Alysia," he said hoarsely, brushing the dirt from her face and smoothing her tumbled hair. "Are you hurt?"

She shook her head. "Just get me away from here."

Wordlessly he lifted her in his arms and settled her upon the horse, pulling the hood of the cloak over her face. He urged the horse forward, passing under one of the arches of Herod's bridge. He guided the horse up the steep ramp of the fortress, passing several surprised guards. He helped her dismount and ushered her through a little-used door of the praetorium. Paulus spoke brusquely to the sentry, who stood at attention and averted his gaze. Once inside he picked her up again and carried her swiftly down a deserted corridor. He entered one of the rooms and kicked the door closed, setting her down gently in a chair.

Her throat was so dry she began to cough. "I was afraid . . . you were dead."

Without speaking he went to a table in a corner of the room and poured water into a bronze cup. Coming back to her, he laid his hand on her shoulder and put the cup into her hand.

"I'll have an ache in my head for a few days to come. I found a horse outside the inn and went looking for you. Are you feeling better?"

She nodded, handing him the empty cup.

"I want to know what happened."

Alysia told him, haltingly, and saw with growing alarm that he had fallen into a cold and silent rage. She read the look in his eyes.

"Paulus," she implored, stretching out her hand to touch his arm. "You mustn't do anything. Whatever you do to those priests will cause them all to hate Jesus more. It will cause trouble for him. And it was he who saved me!"

Paulus turned abruptly and crossed the room, slamming the cup onto a table. "Do you mean they took you from the inn, forced you to the Temple and tried to kill you?"

"By Jewish law, I have sinned."

"Rome is the law here! They have no more authority than . . . than those crows strutting in the field they try so hard to imitate!"

"Paulus."

He stopped his angry pacing at the sound of her voice. "What is it?"

"Please promise me you won't arrest anyone. I don't want him in trouble because of me."

"Alysia, I'm not going to arrest the priests, simply because it would involve *you*. But they will answer for what they did. As for those two miscreants who abducted you . . . I will make no such promise. I should have known that—" He seemed to think for a moment, then gave a harsh, mirthless laugh. "You've been the victim of a double treachery in as many days. First Megara, and now this. I was told something like this would happen."

"What do you mean?"

"It was intended to be a trap, Alysia. The leaders of the Jews want to discredit your Nazarene. Either he had to tell them to disregard the law, or say you had to be killed. Either way, so they thought, he would be finished. He could not evade their law and yet only Rome can order the death penalty. Anyone who does so—an official, a priest, a teacher—risks his own life."

"Yes, it did seem like a kind of test. He seemed to want to ignore them and they wouldn't go away."

"What was he writing on the pavement?"

"I don't know, I couldn't see it. I don't know if that's what made them stop. I only know that they looked guilty and walked away."

"They weren't going to kill you—I'm sure he knew that. They only wanted him to say you *should* be killed . . ."

An authoritative knock sounded on the door leading from the corridor. Paulus flung it open to reveal an agitated sentry. "I am sorry, sir, to interrupt. We have new prisoners, captured last night raiding an army outpost. They've admitted their guilt and pledge that only death will stop them. The officers need you to look them over and sign the order of execution."

"In a moment." Paulus closed the door and glanced back at Alysia. "Are you well enough for me to leave you?"

She nodded, trying to smile. To her surprise he moved to the side of the chair and knelt beside her. "Alysia, forgive me," he said earnestly. "I have done you a great wrong. The only thought in my mind was that I loved you, and wanted you. I can never make amends for what this has done to you."

She put her hand on his cheek. "Paulus, your guilt is no greater than mine. But God help me, it will never happen again." She dropped her hand from his face.

Paulus got slowly to his feet. "Rest for a while. Then we'll find a way to get you home."

She nodded again and with a last look he quit the room, closing the door behind him. Outside, Paulus gave the captives only a cursory glance as he reached for the sheet of papyrus awaiting his signature. But he looked up again with a sharpness that puzzled the young sentry. Paulus fixed his gaze on one prisoner with wild auburn hair, glaring brown eyes, and a face streaked with dirt and blood.

There was something familiar about that face. He looked at the list of names before him.

There it was. Nathan bar Samuel, of Bethany.

"Paulus, you can save his life!" Alysia stared at him with disbelief. "You cannot mean to—" She cut off her words; it was unthinkable.

Paulus laid his hands on her shoulders and looked down at her. He seemed suddenly cold and austere, a stranger to her, and she could not discern the expression in his eyes as deep regret.

"If I release him, he will go on just as he is now. If he kills any more men I will be responsible."

"How can you do this? No matter what I've done, no matter what I feel, he is my husband!"

Paulus turned away without speaking. Alysia looked at him frantically, seeing the sun coming through the window and shining down on his hair. From somewhere outside came the sounds of a man's voice barking orders and the rattle of chains. She didn't dare look out the window, fearing that if she saw Nathan being led away she would lose the tenuous grip she had upon her self-control. She didn't understand the intensity of her feelings. She only knew that Nathan must not die, not now, after what she had done.

"Paulus, you must listen to me—"

"No, Alysia, you listen to me." He faced her again and she was appalled. He *was* a stranger.

"You want him to die," she whispered. "Because of me."

"What you ask is impossible," he said, his voice low and urgent. "Your husband is a rebel and a murderer. He has been identified as one of their leaders—he is the one who arms and trains them. It is my duty to stop him, and all men like him."

"You would put your duty over your love for me?"

"Even if I let him live," Paulus said slowly, "his days are numbered. I could have told you last night I knew who and what he is—I could have told you to warn him against doing what he does. But it would have done no good. Do you think you can stop him? Do you think he will ever stop, as long as he lives and breathes?"

She had no answer.

He looked full into her eyes. "He has brought himself to this end. Do not make such demands upon me, Alysia, and do not question my love for you again."

She knew by the look on his face that any pleading was useless. "But—" She could barely force the dreaded word past her lips, "crucifixion—"

"I do not order crucifixions. My prisoners are shot by archers." He hesitated. "Their aim will be quick and sure, I promise you."

She bowed her head and covered her face with shaking hands. Paulus stood still for a moment, then began to walk toward the door. He stopped as he reached her, and when she looked up he went to her and took her in his arms, holding her close against him.

"Let me take you home."

She pressed her face against his shoulder. "I want to see Nathan."

The entrance to the dungeon was dark as a pit and smelled of mildew and unwashed bodies. When Herod built the splendid fortress he saw no reason to make the prison comfortable; it was only for those awaiting execution. Paulus' footsteps echoed hollowly down the narrow corridor, where torches set in the walls cast weird, dancing shadows. He had put on his uniform and his mantle swung about his boots as his sword clattered at his side. A silent guard saluted him, unlocking a rusty, creaking door to allow him entrance.

Paulus peered through the gloom at the condemned prisoners chained to the wall. "Release that one."

Nathan lifted his head in surprise. The guard obeyed with a noisy rattling of metal as the other prisoners watched apathetically. Nathan stood rubbing his raw wrists and blinking in the darkness.

"Come with me," said Paulus, leading the way into a small, bare room across the hallway. The guard waited outside as Paulus closed the door.

Nathan looked at him curiously. "What do you want with me? Who are you?"

"I am the commander of this fort."

"Yes," Nathan said slowly, watching his face. "I have seen you before . . . somewhere."

Paulus said abruptly, "I have come to offer you a pardon, if you will accept my conditions."

"What conditions?"

"You must swear an oath that you will stop your activities and never commit another crime against Rome. Then you must take your family and move them to a place of safety, a place far from any city, and live in peace for the rest of your life. There's a farming village I know of where you would be able to find employment."

Bewilderment began to replace the suspicion in Nathan's eyes. "Why do you make this offer?"

"Let's say we have a mutual friend. Someone of influence who has intervened on your behalf."

"Whoever my friend may be has wasted his time, and yours."

"So, you prefer that your family suffer for your crimes when you leave them with no means of support."

"I have no family."

"I happen to know that you at least have a wife. Do you care so little for her welfare that you would throw away your life so cheaply?"

Anger flared in Nathan's eyes. "I care for my wife *and* my nation, Commander. I have already sworn an oath, and I will never retract it! I have sworn that I will do my part to abolish Roman rule."

"You Zealots wish to provoke war with Rome," Paulus said, with narrowed eyes. "Do you know what that means—torture and enslavement, the starvation of your women and children? My duty has been to stop revolts before the innocent become acquainted with the horrors of war."

"War may be horrible, as you say, but so is living beneath the heel of tyranny. Tell me honestly, Commander, if you would not do the same in my place."

"Then you refuse a pardon?"

There was a pause. Then, Nathan spat on the ground at Paulus' feet. Their eyes met.

Paulus said, "There is someone who wishes to see you."

He left the room. In a moment Nathan heard light, halting footsteps coming down the hall and the door opened to admit Alysia, still wearing his cloak over her own gown. His gaze went over her, his surprise leaving him speechless. The sight of her left a sickness in his gut that no words of reproach could have brought.

"Alysia," he said hoarsely. "How did you know?"

"I was in Jerusalem this morning and I—I saw you being brought here."

There was a long silence; neither knew what to say. At last he took a deep breath and spoke in a husky voice. "You have been unhappy, Alysia. I once thought I would draw that sadness from you but I wasn't able to do it, was I? I have not been a good husband for you. When I'm gone, maybe you will be happier."

Her hand came out from under the cloak and slender fingers closed over his arm. "You will leave me desolate." She, too, drew in a long breath. "Oh, Nathan, this is all my fault!"

"Your fault?" Nathan smiled a little. "You are not even angry with me? Alysia, I am responsible for this, not you. I have always believed I would be killed in battle, or like this." He hesitated. "It was selfish of me to marry you. I thought I could manage both sides of my life. I was wrong. I'm sorry."

Alysia lowered her eyes, unable to face him. He paused again and said, "I know that Lazarus and Martha will take care of you. I have always depended on that."

"Yes. You need not worry about me."

Another long moment of silence stretched by. He said finally, "I suppose there is nothing more to say. Except that you must be strong and steady, and believe that our cause will one day see victory. Good-bye, Alysia."

Tears streamed down her face. "Nathan, I am so sorry. If I had been a better wife—"

"Stop," he said at once. "What are you saying? You *are* a good wife. You weren't happy and that is my fault."

"No." She shook her head. "I cannot let you say that. You do not deserve this!"

"Who is to say I do not deserve to die? I've killed a great many men, Alysia. Soldiers, yes, for to us it is a war. The commander offered me a pardon if I would vow never to fight again. I refused."

Alysia looked down. He mustn't see how her heart lifted at his words about Paulus.

"Why?" she whispered. "Why did you refuse?"

"It is . . . who I am. And by all that is holy, I can never stop as long as there are foreigners ruling over us."

Alysia said tiredly, "You must do what you must do. Good-bye, Nathan."

She let her eyes meet his, then she kissed him, pressed his hands with her own, and left.

Nathan sank slowly back against the wall, his strength deserting him. After a moment he looked up to see the Roman standing in the doorway as though to give him one last chance to change his mind.

"The guard will take you back now."

Nathan gave a slow nod, walked with a pained, shuffling gait to the door, and stopped. "Can you tell me when—"

"The execution will take place tomorrow . . . at sunrise."

CHAPTER XVI

At Herod's palace Paulus gave a curt command to the enormous, bald Syrian guarding the door to Megara's chamber. The slave stepped quickly aside, reaching out to open the door, but Paulus was already striding into the room. A gale of feminine laughter stopped abruptly and the instant Megara saw his face she was filled with abject terror.

Besides slaves, there were several women in the room engaged in a game of dice. Paulus' gaze fixed on his wife. "I want to speak to you alone, Megara."

Megara found she was holding her breath. She released it slowly and stood up. The brief silence was broken by a young woman wearing a filmy, saffron-colored gown who sauntered toward him, her bracelets and anklets tinkling with the sound of tiny bells.

"Why, it's the legate—and he certainly looks ready to give a few orders." She stopped in front of him. "We're playing knucklebones. Won't you join us?"

Paulus looked down and recognized Herod's stepdaughter, Salome. Her mouth curled up on one side and a frank invitation reflected plainly from her dancing eyes. "Or we could always play something else, if you like."

"Get out," Paulus said. "All of you."

Salome raised an eyebrow. Before she could speak another woman rose, saying imperiously, "Come, Salome."

The young woman looked back and grinned. "Yes, Mother. We shall go, of course. I have envied you, Megara, but not at this moment."

Herodias said something to Megara, then took her daughter's arm. Salome winked at Paulus and allowed herself to be led from the room. The other women scurried out causing a rush of air heavy with perfume. The slaves followed, until Paulus and Megara were left alone.

Megara raised her chin, regarding him with admirable aplomb. "Why have you been rude to my friends?"

Paulus struggled to control his mounting rage. Megara spoke again, quickly, hoping to divert him. "I happen to know you were out all night. Where were you?"

He answered in a cold, impersonal voice, "You will leave for Caesarea today, and you will board the first galley for Rome. I intend never to lay eyes on you again."

Gods forbid, he knows everything! How did he find out? That stupid Macedonian—she would have him flogged, she would flog him herself! Her knees began to quake and she sat down. She looked Paulus squarely in the face. "I don't understand. What have I done?"

"You've done the one thing you were not to do, though your plot failed. And don't try to deny it or it would please me very much to strangle you."

Megara debated swiftly. She wouldn't deny but neither would she confess. "How dare you threaten me!"

"I know what you've done. And do you think I didn't know about that jackal of yours who follows me about? He concealed himself well that day in Bethany, though, for I never saw him. That *is* how you found out where she lives, isn't it, or did Herod tell you?"

Don't confess, don't deny. "You've been with that slave again, haven't you? I suppose you think you have just divorced me. Well, it won't be as easy as that, not with my father's influence. I will see to that! You will never be free to marry that harlot! And she is going to die one day for what she did—"

He took a step forward but Megara perceived instantly that she had gone too far. She sprang up from her chair and slid behind a table on which thoughtfully reposed a marble bust of Socrates. Paulus was before her in two strides. The heavy sculpture crashed to the floor while the table screeched and rasped halfway across the room. Megara flattened herself against the wall and stared at him with hatred and fear in her eyes.

Paulus stopped, grasping at control. He willed the anger to drain out of him. "You have never been happy a day in your wretched life. You like being miserable and you like making other people miserable. You pretended to care for me once—I wonder why you even bothered. You pretended an interest in having a family but from your own lips you despise children. You despise having to care for anyone but yourself."

He paused, looking into her eyes, and went on in a low, ruthless voice. "You have never lifted your hand to do a kind deed or an honest day's work. Tell me, Megara, what has ailed you all these years?"

Megara straightened deliberately. "You wish to know why I married you—I will tell you! Because you were the one thing I could have that others wanted! Yes, even before our betrothal I knew how it would be. Other women could have fine clothes and slaves and anything else, but they couldn't be married to you!"

She paused and finally blurted, "You could be emperor someday, Paulus! You should return to Rome and try to influence Tiberius and get rid of that feeble-minded nephew of his. Sejanus is dead now and Tiberius trusts you. You have supporters in the Senate whether you realize it or not. You have proven yourself an administrator. Besides, the oracle—" She stopped, breathless, wondering how much she should tell him.

Paulus stared at her, unbelieving. "You really are out of your mind." He turned away, his head and his other injuries throbbing, wondering if he would ever feel anything again in his soul...and he wasn't sure that he had one. "Start packing," he said as he placed his hand on the silver doorknob.

Megara moved toward him, regaining her haughty demeanor. "Aren't you afraid that I will betray that woman, now that you are making me leave?"

He looked back at her. "No. For if you do, the entire story will come out and all your friends will know that I preferred a slave to you. Your greatest fear has always been of gossip, of looking like a fool."

"Why should I care about that now? Now that I've lost everything!"

He looked into her exotic, topaz-colored eyes and saw nothing in them but indignation and the raw lust for position and power. "You don't believe that. You could still marry Caligula. I believe he has designs on being the next emperor. He is your junior by some years but maybe you won't mind too much."

"Oh, you would like that, wouldn't you? And I suppose you cannot wait to marry your precious slave! Even if you only keep her as a concubine you will have to leave the army and hide her—you, too, will lose everything."

"Alysia has refused to marry me. She has refused to see me. If you tell anyone that she is still alive you will sign my death warrant, for I did aid in her escape and she is under my protection. And what a scandal that would be, wouldn't it? It would certainly ruin your chances of being the wife of the emperor, the wife of a god, of becoming a goddess yourself!"

Megara grew quiet, thinking. "I will agree to remain silent, on one condition. I will go to Rome, I will not interfere in your life, but I want you to promise me that you will consider what I've told you. You could be regent even now if you made an effort. Why do you think Sejanus hated and feared you?"

"I make no such promise. And I will put a stop to any machinations on your part. Just remember that any scandal attached to me is also attached to you, and your fate will be the same as mine."

He turned to go, stopping at Megara's bitter laugh. "So she has refused to marry you! At least now you can know what it is to want something—to have it within reach—and never attain it!"

"I am sorry to have disappointed you," Paulus said. "Your 'oracle' was wrong." Without waiting for an answer he left, closing the door behind him.

Megara said to the empty room, "No, Paulus. *She is never wrong.*"

Alysia left Jerusalem without seeing Paulus again. She couldn't face him, could not bear another good-bye. She tried to leave secretly but found that Simon had been assigned to follow her to Bethany.

Covering her face, she hurried out to the streets and made her way through the lower city, which by now had come alive with throngs of people. It was easy to slip among them, cloaked and inconspicuous. Glancing back she spied Paulus' slave merging in and out of the crowds behind her. She supposed she should feel relieved, reassured by his presence, but she didn't care. She didn't feel anything except guilt and a sense of doom.

Even the road to Bethany was crowded today and she was able to enter the gate and her own house without notice. Once there, she didn't know what to do. Nathan would die tomorrow, unless his small army could contrive to rescue him, and that seemed highly unlikely. They had probably all been captured with him. His body would be destroyed in a valley south of Jerusalem where fires were always kept burning for the refuse of the city, dead animals, executed criminals, the bodies of the poor.

No! She couldn't let that happen! He deserved a decent burial. Why hadn't she asked this of Paulus before she left? She knew the bodies of criminals were sometimes released to their families. But how was she to accomplish this? She wasn't even supposed to know that he had been captured.

Simon!

Alysia ran outside, all the way to the town gate and started back to Jerusalem. She had gone as far as the great sycamore tree that stood in the sharp curve of the road before she saw him. "Please! Please, Simon, stop!"

The slave turned quickly. The road was not as crowded as before, but enough so that they had to step to the side. She made her request and Simon listened sympathetically.

"I will relay your message," he said, with a kind and sober expression. "Maybe you had better tell the rest of your family now what has happened. Tell them you were on your way home from Jerusalem when you were stopped by the servant of the commander and informed that your husband had been captured. Never mind how this servant knew who you were—let them wonder. Tell them that you begged for the release of the body, but you do not know if it will be done. And I tell you truly, I don't know what the legate will say."

"Very well," Alysia replied, struggling for composure. "Thank you, Simon."

He nodded.

"You needn't follow me back," she said, and turned to walk home again.

But he did follow her. He saw that she stopped at Lazarus' house, a sad and dispirited figure, cloaked in black.

She missed Nathan more than she thought possible. He had been kind to her—most of the time—and even his prolonged absences and his occasional impatience with her didn't seem so important now. His body had been prepared and wrapped for burial by the leaders of the synagogue in Bethany, who had been summoned to Jerusalem by Paulus for that purpose. It was probable that Paulus didn't want Nathan's family to see him, especially Alysia. The body was brought to Bethany on a bier and placed in the family tomb. There was no funeral, no official period of mourning. He had died as a rebel against Rome. People were afraid; no one knew, really, what to do.

Alysia stayed at Lazarus' house, trying to reconcile herself to the fact that she would never see Nathan again. Sometimes she seemed to be in a daze. Sometimes she couldn't remember whether he was really dead or if he was just away on one of his mysterious journeys. Sometimes she thought she was losing her mind!

But, even more, she missed Paulus. In a way it was as if he, too, were dead. She had made a promise to the Nazarene, though unspoken, and she intended to keep that promise. "Sin no more," he had said. And she had looked into his eyes and felt her spirit say, "Yes, Lord."

Her only consolation was that no one seemed to know what had happened to her at the Temple. Either no one who knew her had been there, or she had not been recognized. It seemed too good to be true, and she wondered if Jesus, in some supernatural way, had prevented her from being recognized. *But no*, she thought, *even he couldn't do that* . . . and why should he? She deserved to be punished.

His disciple, John, had been there. The next time she saw him she would know…if he knew.

She tried to numb her feelings but only became dejected and even physically ill, unable to eat, sleeping half the day. Alarmed by Alysia's grief and what seemed to be self-reproach, Martha at last brought in a physician. The stout, elderly man questioned Alysia at length, gave her a quick examination, and turning to Martha announced, "This woman is not ill. She is with child!"

Martha unexpectedly burst into tears at this revelation. "Poor Nathan—he never knew!"

Stunned, Alysia stared at nothing, counting weeks, days. And knew Nathan was not the father of her child.

For the first time in weeks her spirits lifted. As soon as the physician left she got out of bed, began to pack her things, and over Martha's protestations returned to her own house. Her baby wasn't going to come into the world hampered by a brooding, discontented mother. She would make a life for herself and her child and it would be a happy life.

What would Paulus do if he knew? Would he claim the child, would he try to take it from her? No, no, surely he wouldn't. But she would have to tell him eventually, wouldn't she?

The months passed but she didn't send word to him. She busied herself by spinning yarn and making clothes for her baby, as Martha had taught her. Nathan had saved a fair amount of money but Alysia did not intend to be dependent upon Lazarus when it was gone. She would convince him to let her work in his vineyards; it didn't matter if such work was "beneath" her. She didn't care what people said. Martha convinced her to let one of her servants, Judith, move into the extra room in Alysia's house, so Alysia would not be alone. Judith was also a midwife.

Time seemed to race by at first, and then in her eighth month began to drag like a snail and it seemed that her time would never come. But it came at last. One day in mid-summer her daughter was born, long of limb, olive skinned, with a cloud of light brown hair. Martha said proudly, "She's beautiful, Alysia. What is her name?"

"Her name," Alysia murmured, gazing down at the swaddled infant, "is Rachel."

"Rachel." Martha nodded her approval. "It means 'innocent as a lamb.'"

"Yes." Alysia gave a weary smile. "She is innocent."

She recovered quickly from childbirth and grew strong again. She loved Rachel with all her heart and felt almost contented—even though every look at her daughter reminded her of Paulus. She still couldn't bring herself to tell him that he had a child. She didn't really fear that he would take Rachel away, but certainly he would be entitled to some claim upon the baby. And she didn't know what the people of Bethany would do if they found out Rachel's father was a Roman! Everyone had been sympathetic because they believed Nathan had died almost immediately after his child's conception. It was so tragic, so bittersweet. How quickly their compassion would turn to contempt if they ever knew the truth!

She knew Paulus might be sending someone—probably Simon—to watch over her, to see how she was faring since her husband's death. She had been careful not to appear in public when she was great with child. Judith was staying with her indefinitely, so whenever she went out she left Rachel with her…or if they all went out together, she had Judith hold the baby.

Deciding it was time to speak to Lazarus about working for him, she went to his house, accompanied by Judith and Rachel. She took Rachel out of the servant's arms and asked Mary where she might find her brother.

"He isn't well," Mary said, a worried frown on her forehead. "He is resting on the rooftop. He gets so tired of his room."

Alysia expressed her concern, settled Rachel on her hip, and climbed the stairs to the roof. The day was cloudy and cold, with a slight breeze stirring the canopy stretched over the corner where her friend lay on a couch, covered with blankets.

"Lazarus, I'm sorry you're not feeling well."

He smiled. "I'm better now that you have come, and have brought your beautiful daughter to see me."

Alysia sat on a chair next to him, holding Rachel in her lap. "She is seven months old today."

"Well, then, it is like a birthday," he declared. "You must dine with us tonight."

"Martha has already asked me," she said, smiling, but then her smile faded. "They say you are not improving, Lazarus. You must let her send for a physician."

"Physicians have never been able to help me," he answered matter-of-factly. "And if the truth be known I have little confidence in their potions. Some say it is a malady of the heart. Some say a recurring fever due to the bite of an insect—or that I have drunk bad water. Few are honest enough to say they don't know."

Rachel clambered down to the floor, reaching up for her playthings, and Alysia gave her a clay rattle and a doll made of cloth. Without looking at Lazarus she said, "I wonder . . . that is, could you not ask Jesus to heal you?"

"I never thought to," Lazarus replied, with a look of faint surprise. "It seems too presumptive, somehow, to ask such a thing of a friend."

"But surely he would be happy to."

"I am sure he would do so if I asked him."

"Tell me more about him," Alysia urged, settling back in the chair. "What was he like as a child?"

"He was quite a normal child, playing games, helping Joseph in the shop, all the things children do. But the older he got—" Lazarus paused, looking thoughtful.

"Yes?" Alysia prompted.

"The older he got, the more he was resented. By friends *and* by family."

"What do you mean?"

"As he grew up and left childish things behind, he spent more time alone than others, more time in prayer. No one was more obedient or honored his parents more than he. He went to school, to synagogue, but was never mischievous, never quarreled, at least not a serious quarrel. Oh, he loved a good laugh, but never at someone else's expense. He always spoke the truth, but some people didn't want to hear the truth! And though he tried not to show it, you couldn't help but notice that he was . . . wiser than most people.

Even as a child, he astonished the great teachers in Jerusalem with the things he knew.

"There was no doubt that his mother, Mary, favored him over her other children. How could she help it, though of course she loved her children. But his own brothers and sisters began to resent him. His was not always a happy home, I am sorry to say. Although he never behaved as though he thought himself special, his family and friends deserted him. Rejected him. Eventually the entire town rejected him, which is why he spent so much time in Capernaum."

Alysia felt deeply moved. "How unfair! And what of his mother and father?"

"Mary is still close to him. She will never abandon him, you may be sure. Joseph died when Jesus was little more than a youth. Jesus took over the family trade; he is a carpenter, as you know." Lazarus paused for a long moment, looking at Alysia so intently that she almost asked him what was wrong. Then he said, "But Joseph was not Jesus' father."

Alysia lowered her eyes. "I have heard rumors . . . I didn't believe them. Are you telling me that it's true?"

"I only know what Mary's mother told my own mother years ago. She said that an angel appeared to Mary and told her she would have a son. She was betrothed to Joseph, and still a virgin. Mary asked the angel how it could possibly be and was told the child would be miraculously conceived. And then, nine months later, Jesus was born."

Alysia could only stare at him, speechless.

"People often said unkind things about Mary," Lazarus went on. "And later, about Jesus as well. Even though Joseph himself fully believed Mary, and married her."

Alysia was full of questions, but Lazarus had become pale and Rachel was pulling at Alysia's skirt and beginning to fret. She lifted her daughter to her lap.

"I've tired you," she said, in a tone of apology. "Please forgive me. I actually came to ask you something completely different."

"And what was that, Alysia?"

"I would like to work in your vineyards this year. I want to earn my own living. But we can talk later."

"Your place is with Rachel."

"Of course, but Martha begs every day to take care of Rachel for a while. And there is Judith. It will only be for a few hours a day. Lazarus, I must not depend on your charity."

"Alysia, don't you know—" Lazarus stopped whatever he had been about to say and finished, "You are one of the family. We will discuss it later, I promise."

But there was no opportunity later to discuss it. Alysia had little time to even ponder the extraordinary things he had told her, for a servant knocked on her door that night and summoned her back to Lazarus' house.

"He's worse," Martha said, standing outside Lazarus' bedroom and looking helpless. "He has had seizures."

"He won't let us send for a physician," Mary whispered. "He has never been this sick before. What shall we do?"

She said the first thing that occurred to her. "Does anyone know where Jesus is?"

The sisters exchanged glances. Martha said, "I've heard he's in Bethabara, or near there. But can we ask him to come? They say he made some of the priests in Jerusalem so angry they tried to kill him."

"He is not afraid of them," Mary said firmly. "He will come."

A horse was packed with provisions and the largest and strongest of the servants was selected to ride for the town of Bethabara, near the Jordan River. He would have to travel on the Jericho Road, and they pledged to pray for his safety.

The servant returned two days later, without Jesus, but vowing that he had delivered the message. But by then it was too late, for the day after the servant left, Lazarus died.

Weeping neighbors and relatives filled the house, having come to comfort the bereaved sisters, but Alysia, sitting alone in a corner with Rachel asleep in her arms felt little consolation. It almost seemed like losing Nathan again.

It was not much more than a day's journey to Bethabara but Jesus had not come. He couldn't have known that Lazarus had died, yet he had not even sent a message. Martha's own grief was deep, but she fared better than her sister. Mary seemed to feel betrayed by the man she so admired. She wept incessantly and would speak to no one, refusing to be comforted.

Lazarus' body had been washed, anointed with aromatic spices, and wrapped in the most costly of linens. The hands, feet, and chin were bound first, and a separate cloth was placed over his head. It was the custom for the women of the family to do this task, and Alysia helped the sisters and wept with them. Accompanied by hired mourners and musicians, the family and friends had made their way to the large tomb hewn out of rock at the bottom of a hill. All of Bethany had attended the funeral, as did many from Jerusalem and nearby villages.

A loud knock sounded on the door. Quickly Alysia rose with Rachel in her arms to answer it. A small boy looked up at her excitedly. "Jesus is on his way here!" he cried. "He is almost to the gate!"

She heard Martha's voice behind her. "I will go and meet him. Alysia, will you come with me?"

Alysia put the sleeping Rachel down on a pallet beside other small children. The two women slipped out of the house and walked in silence to the gate. It was early afternoon and the wind was brisk, almost cold. Alysia's gown and the mantle that covered her hair fluttered out behind her as she hurried to keep up with Martha's determined pace. She wondered what Martha was going to say to him.

She saw the group of men approaching and Martha began to hang back, until she stopped altogether. Because she did so Jesus met Alysia first, taking her hands in greeting and looking soberly into her face. Feeling embarrassed and awkward, she had to force herself to look at him but there was nothing except warmth and kindness in his eyes, as if he had completely forgotten the spectacle in the Temple. She glanced at John. Yes, he knew. She could tell by his own awkward expression, but he gave her a friendly nod.

Martha came toward them, her lips pressed together, her hand at her heart. "If you had been here," she said, her voice soft but faintly reproachful, "Lazarus would not have died."

Jesus held her gaze steadily. "Lazarus will rise again."

"I know that he will rise again—in the resurrection, when we shall all rise!"

He said slowly, with deliberation, "*I am* the resurrection, and the life. Whoever lives and believes in me, shall never die."

Alysia almost forgot to breathe. What was he saying? What did he mean?

But Martha seemed to understand. He asked, "Do you believe this?"

Martha returned his probing look and answered, "I believe that you are the anointed one, the son of God."

He asked softly, "Where is Mary?"

"I will call her." Martha turned and left so quickly that Alysia was left standing uncertainly by the roadside. The men began walking slowly forward. There was something strangely compelling about the Nazarene, even more so than usual. He spoke to no one else and had a more somber expression than she had ever seen on his face. To her surprise, John came to her side and spoke.

"I must tell you, Alysia, we tried to stop him from coming. He told us Lazarus was dead, somehow he knew, and we didn't see why we should all risk our lives by coming here. You know they tried to kill him the last time he was in Jerusalem. But—here we are. I'm very sorry. I wish we had been in time."

"But why did he delay?"

John shrugged and shook his head. "He said that it was for the glory of God."

Their attention was caught by a large crowd coming toward them from the house, with Martha and Mary leading them. Alysia knew that Martha had meant to summon her sister secretly, but it was obvious the mourners had seen them both leave and followed them, perhaps thinking they were going to the grave. An excited murmuring erupted as the crowd spied the group of men.

Mary halted the moment she saw Jesus, then her feet flew along the path as she passed her sister. When she reached him, she threw herself to the ground at his feet, her slender body shaking with sobs.

"Lord," she cried, "if you had come when we asked, my brother would not have died!"

They were almost the same words that Martha had spoken, but were uttered with such brokenness and pathos that Alysia felt tears in her eyes. Many in the crowd wept openly.

Jesus, too, seemed deeply moved and troubled. He pulled Mary to her feet and gently raised her chin. "Where have you buried him?"

Incoherent, Mary could only put her hands over her face and shake her head. Jesus' eyes filled with tears and a sound like a groan came from his throat. Martha wiped her own face with the hem of her mantle and whispered, "Come and see."

She led the way in the opposite direction and the crowd fell in behind them. Alysia tucked her arm in Mary's and walked beside her, half supporting her.

"Look how he weeps," she heard one woman say to her husband. "See how much he loved Lazarus!"

The man muttered, "If this man has indeed opened the eyes of the blind, why could he not save the life of his friend?"

But he is not weeping for Lazarus, Alysia thought. *He weeps for us all.*

They continued down the winding street until they came to the bottom of the hill. The tomb had been carved out of the rocky hillside, and an enormous, smooth round stone sealed the entrance. As they walked toward the grave, Jesus' countenance had changed. His brow was furrowed, his eyes intense. There was something about him like a barely suppressed rage; he had the look of a man about to do combat with some terrible, unseen thing.

He stopped within a few feet of the tomb. "Take away the stone," he said.

Everyone looked at him with horror. Martha said hesitantly, "But he's been dead for four days. By now—"

"Haven't I told you that if you believe, you will see the glory of God?"

Martha slowly nodded acquiescence. Andrew, Peter, and several others quickly mounted the few stone steps, and after much heaving and grunting rolled the stone in its prepared groove away from the opening of the grave.

Jesus stood aloof, raised his eyes to the sky, and said something Alysia could not hear. Then he paused, his arms outstretched as though he held at bay something of immense power. It seemed that a shudder went through his body. His gaze lowered to the dark, silent tomb and he commanded in a loud, triumphant voice:

"Lazarus . . . come forth!"

Alysia, all of them, stood stricken with immobility. Something, like a soundless wind, passed over the brush that grew along the roadside. There was no other sound or movement; it seemed that no one even breathed. From deep within came a shuffling sound and the rasp of pebbles against the earth. Alysia found herself backing away until she was next to John. Without thinking she clutched his arm, glimpsing his face, as thunderstruck as her own must be.

She saw the man she had watched die, whose stiff and cold body she had helped prepare for burial, the man who had lain in his grave for four days, now walking with slow, measured steps toward the Nazarene. The bands had loosened from around his legs. He was still wrapped in his shroud, faltering, but *alive*.

"Unbind him," said Jesus, "and let him go."

It was Peter who moved first, pulling a knife from his belt and slitting the strip of cloth that encircled Lazarus' neck, tying down the head covering. Peter reached for the covering and stopped, either as if he couldn't force himself to touch it, or didn't want to see what lay beneath.

At that moment Mary gave a sigh and fainted. Alysia tried to catch her as John rushed to help. They lowered Mary to the ground and Alysia knelt beside her. Then all eyes were on Lazarus again.

His hands, whether bound or not, were still underneath the shroud, which had been wrapped over each shoulder and tied at the waist, extending down to his feet. At last Peter reached for the large, square piece of linen that covered Lazarus' head and removed it. Something like a gasp went up from the onlookers.

He was whole, healthy. There was no discoloration, no bloating, no sign of decomposition. It was as if he had never been ill. His dark hair blew back in the wind and he looked before him with amazement. The tableau seemed to freeze in space and time…Martha weeping silently; Alysia kneeling beside an unconscious Mary; the disciples looking at each other, speechless; the crowd awe-stricken; white rays from the sun beaming down on Lazarus before the gaping tomb.

Alysia's eyes sought out the man who had wrought this unspeakable, unbelievable thing. But Jesus had disappeared.

CHAPTER XVII

Paulus eyed his stepbrother with distaste across the table. Lucius had staggered into the praetorium the previous night in an advanced state of inebriation and his bleary-eyed presence at breakfast did little to improve Paulus' surly mood. A servant brought his meal of hot bread, eggs, and cheese, and set before him a cup and a large jug of goat's milk. Lucius paled at the sight of the food and took a hasty gulp of wine.

None of the other officers had as yet joined them in the dining hall. Paulus began to eat, thinking he'd best set about discovering the reason for Lucius' presence.

"You are rising early these days," he remarked. "Especially after a night such as you've obviously had."

"Why shouldn't I visit my noble stepbrother? I've been meaning to do so for some time now. Please excuse my lack of breeding in that I did not come sooner."

"Spare me the satire, Lucius, and I shall ask you plainly—what are you doing here?"

"Very well. It has come to my attention that you have been making inquiries about me in Rome—as to what I'm doing in Jerusalem and who sent me."

"What if I have?" said Paulus. "You've been here for some time and haven't accomplished anything that I can see. I would have done it sooner, but things were in such an uproar last year there was no need to even try. Not that they are much better now."

"I was sent here by the Senate as an emissary and I have a signed letter to prove it. You have no authority to do anything about it, even if you are the senior officer in Judea. Next to Pilate, that is. You would probably like to put me in command of a fort out in the desert somewhere to be rid of me."

"I wouldn't put you in command of anything, as I do have regard for the lives of others. However, if you are an emissary—what is your mission?"

"I do not have to tell you that."

"Spying? On me, perhaps? This would have been before Sejanus' downfall."

"You should know better than that. I haven't the patience for being a spy."

"Do you know what I think, Lucius? You have no mission at all—you simply persuaded someone who owed you a favor to sign a letter, and so you are here having a good time. I hear you spend most of your time at Herod's palace in the company of his stepdaughter."

"It sounds as though you've been spying on *me*."

"It's my business to know who is here, and why."

"Your pardon, sir." A slave had entered the room, bearing a letter. "A messenger has just delivered this and said to give it to you immediately. It is from your father-in-law."

Paulus glanced up at the servant and reached for the letter, then took out his dagger to slit the seal. Lucius grinned crookedly. "Probably wondering when you are going to return to his precious daughter."

He waited as Paulus scanned the letter, noticing the barely perceptible change that came over his face. He seemed to flush under his tan, a muscle twitched in his cheek, his mouth became hard and grim. Lucius congratulated himself upon choosing the right moment to annoy his stepbrother.

"Well?" he inquired. "What news does the senator bring you?"

Paulus folded the letter slowly and placed it inside his tunic. "Megara is dead."

"Dead?" Lucius' wine-dulled mind was unprepared for this announcement. "What happened?"

"She killed herself." He rose and strode over to stare out the window.

"What a cold fellow you are, Paulus," his stepbrother said haughtily. "Have you no tears for your departed wife?"

Paulus said nothing.

Lucius went on mercilessly, "What, or who, could have driven Megara to suicide? I certainly thought she prized herself too highly—for even so sublime a death!"

Again, Paulus didn't answer but thought: loss of ambition, loss of prestige? Loss of *the one thing she could have that others wanted*—a ridiculous statement, but like her. Suicide was usually a selfish act and she had been selfish to the end.

Lucius continued to taunt him. "Have you been seeing another woman? That must be why Megara returned to Rome so suddenly.

Yes, that would have been around the time I saw you in front of my inn with a rather poorly disguised damsel. I never could find out who she was. Why hide your affairs, Paulus? Unless, of course, she is married to someone important. They say Pilate's wife is a beauty."

This seemed to at last penetrate Paulus' deafness and he turned with a look of disgust. "Listen to me, Lucius. I don't like seeing your face at breakfast—or any other time for that matter. You're too lazy and inexperienced to do anything worthwhile, and your rank prohibits you from doing the tasks you might be suited for. Now get out and don't come back—unless it is in the unlikely event that you have business here."

Lucius absorbed the insults with a forced smile but he knew when to retreat. As he left the room he turned and said mockingly, "Please accept my condolences, Commander. I'm sure you are overcome with grief."

Left alone, Paulus sank down at the table and absently ran his hands through his hair. Dismissing Lucius from his mind, his thoughts turned to Megara and he sat for a long time without moving. He took out the letter and read it more thoroughly.

"She had slit her wrists," the senator wrote. "The servant who found her called me immediately. She had left a letter. Be at ease; the servant cannot read and no one else has seen it. Paulus, my daughter accused you of aiding and abetting a runaway slave, the murderer of Magnus Eustacius. She said the slave is still alive and gave the name of the village where she could be found. She stated she could not live with such knowledge.

"Paulus, I have destroyed the letter. I knew my daughter well; I also know you. If what she said was true, I care not. Megara was never at peace. Perhaps now, she will be."

Paulus was alarmed to discover that his father-in-law knew about Alysia. Probably he would never tell anyone—he was a good man who had often been on the receiving end of Megara's diatribes. Still, it was worrisome.

He tried to reason again why Megara had taken her own life. Of course, "suicides" were rampant in Rome just now with all the political furor, but he was quite certain that had nothing to do with it. Well, whatever the reason, she had found a way to preserve the appearance of a dutiful wife scandalized by the behavior of a wayward husband, and to wreak vengeance on him as well. He felt only pity for her, pity for her wasted life, her self-induced misery.

He went to his study and composed a letter to his father-in-law, expressing his genuine regret at the death of his daughter. And as for the runaway slave, he wrote, she was believed to have been on a ship that went down in a storm. That was true enough; let the senator make of it what he would. He sighed as he scribbled his name at the bottom of the page and only then did he allow himself to think of Alysia.

He hadn't seen her in over a year. Acting on Paulus' orders, Simon made occasional trips to Bethany where he watched for Alysia at the market in the center of town. Soon Simon knew what time of day to expect her there. Sometimes she was with another woman, a young mother with a baby. He was to see that she looked healthy, that she was well dressed and didn't seem to be impoverished. From Simon's accounts she was doing well.

Paulus wondered, as he sometimes did, if he had ordered Nathan's execution because he was jealous of him. But if the truth be known he had never felt particularly jealous of Alysia's husband, maybe because he was secure in Alysia's love for him and because he knew instinctively what kind of man Nathan was.

Nathan should never have married in the first place, for his very soul was owned by the cause he believed in. Men like Nathan were willing to sacrifice even their families for their convictions. There was little time to cultivate a relationship with a wife, and even less energy, for it was all used elsewhere. They loved their wives and children, but they hated Rome more.

Still, he couldn't deny that he was easier in his mind when Nathan was dead. No longer was he assailed in weak moments by the vision of Alysia in another man's arms. But if in some small, mean part of his mind he had decided to kill Nathan because he was Alysia's husband, he was not aware of it. He didn't believe it. He had done what he had to do.

But he wished, for her sake, that he had not been responsible for her husband's death.

Nicodemus, one of the older members of the Sanhedrin and one of the wealthiest men in Jerusalem, considered himself a sensible and learned man. He was a Pharisee and had always lived a decent, even exemplary life. But when Jesus of Nazareth began denouncing some of the Pharisaical traditions, he was more puzzled than offended. If their way of life was not the right one, then what was?

Some time ago he had gone to the place where the Nazarene was staying—visiting him secretly at night so that his fellow council members would not know of it—and expressed his need to have this question answered. The Nazarene had replied in a low but earnest voice, telling him things he'd never heard before, things his mind wanted to reject but that his heart knew were true. Above everything was the realization that all his knowledge, and all his good deeds, were not going to earn him a place in heaven. There was something more.

Now, as he reflected on the faces around him at this hastily assembled meeting of the Sanhedrin, he saw that the Nazarene was going to need a friend. One of the youngest council members was frowning at the older man.

"If we leave this Nazarene alone, all of Palestine will begin to follow him. Rome will think a rebellion is brewing and will take away both our place and our nation!"

"Our place!" Nicodemus shouted. "We set too much store by our position and power. How long has it been since we considered the needs of the people? We are just what he called us—blind leaders of the blind!"

The immediate silence was filled with tension. Then the High Priest spoke in a voice thick with disapproval. "Will you not admit the expediency of having one man to die, instead of letting the entire nation perish?"

"I cannot believe what I'm hearing," Nicodemus said, his former timidity vanquished by indignation. "You would seek to put Jesus to death simply because he has dared to criticize us. This would be nothing short of murder! Just as some of you, I happen to know, plotted to murder Lazarus of Bethany so that his raising from the dead could be called a lie. But the plan was never carried out, no doubt because there were so many witnesses to testify that it really happened."

"It never happened!" snapped Caiaphas. "The entire incident was staged. It is unfortunate for all of us that he has gained so many followers by this—this trickery. One would almost think, Nicodemus, that you are one of them."

"I do not believe in judging a man without a fair trial. And Jesus has done nothing to deserve death. As for this man in Bethany, it would be impossible to perpetrate a hoax on such a large scale. There were dozens of eyewitnesses, not only those who attended the funeral of the dead man, but those who saw the actual miracle."

"Are you saying, Nicodemus, that you believe this Nazarene raised a man from the dead?"

Nicodemus did not reply, because he didn't know himself whether he believed it. He only knew that if Jesus were the kind of man he seemed to be, he would not have engaged in chicanery of any sort, so therefore it must be true! Again he looked around the room at the set faces, the expressions of hostility and resentment. Jesus had made some powerful enemies. Was there no one here who would speak on his behalf, other than himself? There! Joseph of Arimathea, also rich and prominent; he had never spoken against Jesus and even now looked as incredulous and indignant as Nicodemus felt.

Joseph saw his look and nodded slowly. "If he is indeed the Messiah, as many claim, he cannot be put to death."

"No prophet comes from Galilee," said one of the elders contemptuously.

"He was born in Bethlehem," Nicodemus replied. "The predicted birthplace of our savior."

"And what proof do you have of that?" Caiaphas demanded.

"It was at the time of the census. There are records. Don't try to tell me, Caiaphas, that you have not thoroughly investigated him, hoping to find some way to discredit him. It would be interesting to know what other prophecies he has fulfilled."

Caiaphas glared at him, remaining silent.

"Yes, I know all about your schemes," Nicodemus went on. "Including the ridiculous spectacle with that woman you had taken before him for adultery. It would be humorous, if there were not such a spirit of malevolence behind your foolishness."

"You would do well to leave, Nicodemus," said the High Priest, his face red with anger. "I trust you want nothing to do with any plans we may form to deal with the Nazarene."

"And you can be sure he will be warned that his life is in danger," replied Nicodemus, striding irately toward the door.

Joseph got to his feet. "He was warned some time ago, but it seems he does not fear you, Caiaphas."

"A mistake," Caiaphas replied.

The two men left the room. The remaining council members looked at each other.

"Bah!" snorted old Annas abruptly and they all started, having thought him to be asleep. "This Nazarene is no more the Messiah than I am! And my son-in-law is right; he is only one man, and our entire nation is at risk. He must be stopped. But you've been going about it the wrong way, Caiaphas. He is too clever for you; he always has an answer for everything. We have all heard him blaspheme, and yet he somehow escapes us when we try to take him. We must capture him first, when he is not expecting it, and then let him blaspheme all he likes. We will have him then . . . Pilate will do the rest."

"How do you propose we capture him?" Caiaphas asked, looking frustrated. "He is always surrounded by his followers. He is so popular with the people they will not stand for his arrest. I tell you we must give them cause; we must make them understand he is not who he appears to be."

"We will, but after he is in our custody. You must find one of his followers who is willing to betray him to us, who will tell us a time and place we can arrest him quietly. Thus far he has eluded us, but it is said he often goes out to pray in secluded places. That will be the perfect time to take him. Send out your spies, Caiaphas. Find someone, even one of the twelve, who can be persuaded to see things our way. Perhaps one of them would be interested in a monetary recompense."

"Yes," said his son-in-law thoughtfully. "It would behoove us to have one of the twelve on our side. But we will continue to watch for an opportunity to arrest him. I still say that destroying his credibility is vital."

"It *will* be destroyed," said Annas complacently, "when he is dead."

In the pearl-gray sky of dawn, Alysia rose and dressed and ate the light breakfast prepared by Judith. A small, demure woman who spoke little, looked younger than she was, and always kept herself busy at some task, Lazarus' servant had proven invaluable in caring for Rachel whenever Alysia wanted to leave the house. And feeling often confined, Alysia left it at any opportunity…to buy food, to draw water, to visit Lazarus and his sisters…though she took Rachel with her on those occasions.

She had thought it would be awkward to visit Lazarus; she hardly knew what to say to him since the miracle. But Lazarus was the same as ever, and his sisters, once they had gotten over their sense of wonder, seemed to accept Lazarus' return as a completely natural event.

Jesus and his disciples had left that same night, traveling by necessity under cover of darkness in the direction from which they had come. Not only were the religious leaders still seeking to entrap him, but everyone knew that once news of the miracle had spread there would be hundreds, if not thousands, of people converging upon him.

Alysia had found the courage to ask Lazarus what it was like—to be dead and raised again. But he only looked thoughtful and said, "Either God has not permitted me to remember, or maybe time does not exist on the other side. It seemed that I had just closed my eyes, and then immediately awakened."

"And did you . . . hear him call you forth?"

"Oh, yes, I heard him. And was compelled to obey. And you know, Alysia, I feel *well* now. He has healed me. I know that someday I will grow old and die again, but not of that former affliction." He paused and looked into her eyes. "There can be no doubt now, can there? About who he is."

Alysia had nodded, somehow both thrilled and afraid. She had to shake off all the myths and legends she'd been taught in her youth and tell herself: this is real; this man, Jesus, is real; he is flesh and blood and something more, something divine . . . And why was he *here*? Why did he not go to Athens or Rome and perform some miracle where the world would sit up and take notice!

She started out for the marketplace to buy meat and vegetables for the evening meal. The shops were already crowded. People milled about and argued with the merchants, who loudly defended the quality of their produce and lamented the low prices they were forced to accept. It seemed a typical, fine spring day, until there was a sudden, concerted murmuring among the patrons, who—just as suddenly—fell completely silent. They began to move, some passing to the right, others to the left, and at last Alysia had a full view of the road.

A company of mounted soldiers was passing through the town. Weary and sweat stained, many of them bore wounds covered with bloody bandages. Alysia stepped aside and watched as they drew nearer, noticing the looks of fear and resentment on the faces around her. Her eyes went back to the approaching soldiers, and with a start she almost dropped her basket.

Paulus rode at the fore, his helmet off and resting on the bar of his saddle. It was the first time she'd ever seen him in full armor. His hair was damp with sweat and there was blood on his arms, though she could detect no injury. His horse bled from the shoulder. He stopped abruptly when he saw her and immediately the entire company came to a halt.

He surveyed the hostile faces around him and said in a loud voice, "I require a man to care for my horse. Where is the nearest stable?"

For a moment no one answered. Even Alysia, who felt no threat with Paulus present, was awed to the point of speechlessness by the appearance of these battle-worn warriors. One of the merchants finally stepped forward and said timorously, "There is but one stable in town, sir, and one man to tend the animals. The owner's name is Lazarus."

"And where will I find the house of Lazarus?"

The merchant swallowed and said, "From this direction, the last house on the right side of the road, sir, before you reach the gate."

Paulus nodded at the man but sat still for a moment, letting his eyes pass over the townspeople as if inviting them to speak their minds. No one did. Paulus' gaze didn't linger upon Alysia longer than any other, but she knew what he wanted her to do.

Everyone watched as the soldiers passed slowly by. At the end of the procession were twenty or so prisoners, bound and soiled with dirt and blood. They were guarded by more soldiers and at last the street had cleared, save for the residents of Bethany. Others had come out of their houses to watch in silence, staring at the prisoners, hoping not to see anyone they knew. Many of them looked at Alysia with sympathy, remembering that her husband had died at the hands of these Roman invaders.

She took a firm hold on her basket and began to walk home, trying not to hurry. She stopped at her house, left the food, and told Judith where she was going. The Romans had disappeared by the time she arrived at Lazarus' house. She didn't speak to anyone but walked the short distance to the wooden building where Lazarus kept his donkeys and mules and his one horse. Still, she saw no sign of the soldiers. The man who tended the animals carried a bucket of water inside the stable.

Alysia followed him, pausing outside the doorway. She saw Paulus' horse drinking noisily from the bucket. The man was carefully washing blood from the horse's shoulder; the flesh along the great animal's side quivered and he stamped his foot. It was dim inside the stable but she could see Paulus wasn't there.

She stepped silently away from the doorway and followed a short path that meandered downward to a shallow brook, fed by a rare spring or two. There were times when it ran almost dry but now it was full, due to the winter and spring rains. It was a secluded spot, for tamarisks and poplars grew abundantly here and the gnarled branches of squat terebinths spread out like grasping hands. Red and white flowers bloomed among the shrubbery.

Paulus sat on the bank in a band of early sunlight that fell slanting through the trees, one knee drawn up, one arm over his knee. His hair was wet from washing his face in the little stream. He was looking out beyond the trees toward the vineyards and as she watched he picked up a stick and poked it restlessly into the earth, unaware of her approach. She could have stood there all day, quietly observing him, but he seemed to sense her presence and turned.

He froze for a moment, then tossed away the stick and got to his feet.

"Are you hurt, Paulus?" she asked quickly, somewhat surprised that she could speak in so normal a voice.

He shook his head. "We learned of a group of rebels camped southeast of here. We rode out last night to take them by surprise at dawn. I chose to return this way in the hope of . . . seeing you. I sent the rest of the men ahead." He raised his hands a little and said lightly, "If I believed in the goddess of fortune, I would thank her most fervently."

The thought struck her that now, perhaps, was the time to tell him about Rachel. What if God had arranged this meeting so she could do that very thing? Paulus had a right to know he had a child. He wouldn't be so cruel as to take her away. But, what *would* he do? How could they arrange for him to spend time with Rachel without everyone knowing of it?

She simply wasn't prepared to make this decision now. She wasn't prepared for this meeting…

Paulus' gaze moved slowly over the loose robe that fell to just above her ankles and was belted at her slim waist. The mantle covering her hair was tied behind her head and framed her face in a way that flattered her high cheekbones and slightly tilted eyes.

"You are more beautiful than ever," he said softly.

"I—I—" Words were sticking in her throat. He didn't seem to notice that she was in a tumult of anxiety.

"There is something I must tell you," he said, and paused. There was really no gentle way. "Megara is . . . dead. I had sent her back to Rome. She took her own life."

Alysia swayed. He made a move toward her but she turned away from him and put her hand against the trunk of a tree. He stopped and stood still, seeming uncertain.

She looked up at him. "I am sorry, Paulus, for your sake."

Her thoughts swirled as though in a windstorm and began to sift themselves with almost no conscious action of her own. What came clear to her, at last, was that she couldn't tell Paulus about Rachel. Not now, with Megara dead.

Without actually being aware of it, she had depended on Megara to keep Paulus from claiming Rachel as his own—not that Megara could have forced him into anything. But it would have been difficult and troublesome for him to do so against her wishes. Without her, what was to stop him from taking the only child he might ever have?

He wouldn't want his daughter raised in the simple manner in which she lived, and as a Jew!

No, she would not risk losing Rachel.

Paulus' voice scattered her thoughts like sunlight upon mist. "Is it safe for you to be here? Can we talk without being seen?"

Her eyes seemed to avoid his, and at that moment a barrier came between them that would not easily be removed. It was the barrier of deception, of a lie told without words.

"I must go. I wanted to make sure you were not wounded."

"Alysia, wait. There is something else. I would like for you to consider leaving Bethany. Megara told her father about you."

"What do you mean?"

"She left a letter, saying you were still alive and where you are living. Her father was the only one who saw the letter. I don't believe he will ever tell anyone, but all the same it is dangerous."

"I will never leave here. All the people I care about are here." She added, looking down at the ground, "Or nearby."

He waited a moment, and when she looked up again, she saw that he understood. But he only said, "Lucius is still in Jerusalem. Supposedly he is here on behalf of the Senate, and I do not have authority to dispute that. I could write Tiberius, but whatever mind he had left a year ago is about gone, from what I've heard. The situation there is still chaotic. All I can do is keep having Lucius watched."

"I will be careful."

He took a step toward her. "This man, Lazarus," he said, unexpectedly. "What is this rubbish about the Nazarene raising him from the dead?"

She answered him quietly but with conviction. "I was there. I saw him die. I saw Jesus raise him four days after he was buried."

Paulus stared at her in disbelief. "Such things are not possible, Alysia."

"It may not be possible, but it happened."

"You—have accepted the God of these people?"

After a moment, she replied, "Because I believe in Jesus, I must also believe in God."

His eyes met hers and it seemed that another barrier leaped up between them, this one of his making. But he fought against it and said impulsively, "Never mind that—it doesn't matter. I, too, am sorry about Megara, but there is nothing anyone can do about it. Marry me, Alysia. Nothing stands in our way."

"Nothing but the man I killed, who still controls my life whether I would have it so or not!"

"It doesn't have to be this way. We could go anywhere in the world. Let me protect you. Don't you know I would give my life for you?"

She bent her head. "Of course I know it, and it is what I fear the most. That you will die because of something I've done. You must not keep waiting for me, Paulus." What she said next had to get past a great lump in her throat. "You should find someone to love, and have a family."

"Alysia, if you think—" Paulus broke off, words failing him. He began again. "Be it known that while you live and beyond that, I will never love another as I love you. And know this—someday we will be together, if I must snatch you up and carry you to the far ends of the earth!"

Tears began to flow down her face.

"Think well on why you refuse me, Alysia, and if it's only because of my life, or my profession, then your reasoning has no merit. These things are nothing to me without you."

"But your life is *everything* to me," she answered in a choked voice. "Do you think it is easy for me to deny you?"

"Don't be a fool, Alysia," he said harshly. "What is it you're really afraid of?"

"I'm not afraid of anything, except what will happen if you're caught with me! Why can't you understand that?"

"I know only that we belong together, and whether soon or late, our time of waiting will come to an end!"

They stared at each other with such intensity that they failed to hear anyone approach until a light cough broke the impassioned silence. Paulus' head jerked up. Alysia whirled to see Lazarus standing nearby, looking apologetic but firm.

"Is anything wrong, Alysia?"

She opened her mouth to reply but it was a moment before she could think of anything to say. "No, Lazarus, there is nothing wrong. This is Legate Paulus Valerius, commander of the fortress in Jerusalem. The night after I was taken by the soldiers to Jerusalem, he—saw to it that I arrived safely in Bethany."

Lazarus said nothing. It was obvious to all of them that there was more to the story than that, considering what Lazarus must have overheard. Paulus glanced at Alysia, who said no more, and easily took command of the situation.

"I assume you are the owner of this property. I would like to thank you for the use of your stable, and your servant."

"Of course. He came at once to tell me of your presence, after he'd seen to your horse. You are welcome to whatever I have. Are you in need of a physician?"

Paulus glanced down at his bloody uniform in some surprise, as if he'd already forgotten the battle he'd fought just a few hours earlier. "No. I will go now if the man is finished with my horse."

Lazarus inclined his head and waited for Alysia and Paulus to precede him. When they reached the stable Paulus' horse gave an impatient snort and jerked at the reins, which had been looped over a fencepost. The injured shoulder had been cleansed and plastered with a strong-smelling salve.

"Again, thank you for your hospitality," Paulus said.

Lazarus humbly bowed his head.

Paulus swung into the saddle and hesitated for a moment, looking down at Lazarus and Alysia. There was an expression of puzzlement on his face as he said, "This rumor that has reached Jerusalem about you—can you explain it?"

"Explain it?" Lazarus smiled a little. "I suppose if it were only a rumor, that would *be* the explanation."

Though Paulus waited, Lazarus made no further comment.

"Well, then," Paulus said, "good day to you." His eyes went to Alysia and somehow conveyed to her what he could not say in the presence of another. They were full of promise and determination. "Farewell, Alysia."

Any words failed to form past the tightness in her chest and she could only watch as he wheeled his horse about, gained the rocky path, and in a moment disappeared over the brow of a hill. She turned a little away from Lazarus, dashed her hand over the tears, and faced him again. Her voice, though she made a great effort to sound natural, was hollow and shaky to her own ears.

"Why didn't you tell him about what happened to you?"

Lazarus glanced at her speculatively, almost as though he were seeing her for the first time. He placed his arm around her, leading her away from the stable, and said, "Because, my dear Alysia, what makes you think he would have believed me . . . if he didn't believe you?"

CHAPTER XVIII

This time he came quietly by night, arriving just after dark with his twelve disciples. Earlier in the day, a messenger brought word to Lazarus and it was decided that a supper would be held at the home of a man named Simon, whom Jesus had healed of a mild case of leprosy. It would attract less attention, at least for that one night. His fame had grown so that everyone in Bethany wanted to congregate at Lazarus' house when they knew he was there.

Martha was to serve, since Simon had no wife or female relatives. She, Alysia, and a servant went to Simon's smaller house and worked all afternoon preparing roasted quail, smoked fish, a red lentil stew spiced with cumin, cheese and bread, and small honey-laced cakes. Simon, a tall, thin man with long, gray-streaked hair, watched their progress with obvious delight. Mary, to Martha's annoyance, did not accompany them.

"She's been no help to me since Lazarus . . . since it happened. Not that she was ever much help in the kitchen, but she did try!"

"She studies a great deal," Alysia tried to explain. "She reads the Scriptures."

Martha did not reply, perhaps remembering the reproof she had once received for criticizing her younger sister. Soon after dark the men arrived and everyone gathered in the courtyard. The food had already been set out and the men ate heartily, but Alysia observed a subtle change in them. None of them were talking and laughing as usual; they were strangely subdued and, with the exception of their leader, almost glum. Jesus made an effort to talk pleasantly with his host, but he, too, seemed preoccupied.

The meal was barely over when someone appeared in the entranceway. Alysia saw that it was Mary, her head uncovered for the first time since Alysia had known her and holding in her hands an exquisite alabaster jar.

When Jesus glanced away from Simon and saw her, his expression changed from one of courteous listening to an intent, serious look that followed Mary as she advanced slowly toward him. Without looking at anyone she broke the flask at its neck and moved to stand behind Jesus.

All conversation halted.

It was like a ritual. In the manner of anointing a king she poured some of the oil on his head. Immediately the breeze from the open door to the outside caught the ethereal fragrance and carried it throughout the courtyard. She moved to kneel before him, and with humility and tenderness, poured the oil upon his bare feet. She wiped his feet with her hair.

Alysia saw the tears streaming down Mary's face and felt tears start to her own eyes. The young woman's movements were so slow and full of reverence that she seemed suspended in time; the moment itself seemed to catch and hold, as if hiding within itself some great and mysterious importance. It was a strange sensation that Alysia felt many times when the Nazarene was near.

And then, uncharacteristically, some of the men began to murmur. "Why, that is pure nard," one of them said—Alysia couldn't see which one. "It's worth a year's wages!"

The cold, unmoved voice that answered belonged to Judas Iscariot, the treasurer of the group. "Why this waste? That oil could have been sold for more than three hundred denarii, and the money given to the poor."

At once, Jesus turned toward him. "Let her alone," he said quietly, but with an intensity that startled everyone. "Why do you trouble her? The poor are with you always. I am not. She has done what she could for me."

He looked at Mary again, whose cheeks were flushed as she kept her gaze lowered to the floor. His voice softened. "She has come beforehand to anoint my body for burial."

Alysia glanced at Martha, then at Lazarus, John and the others—all bore the same look of incomprehension. *What did he mean?*

Jesus spoke again, very low. "Wherever this gospel is preached in the whole world, what this woman has done will also be told, in memory of her."

Judas apparently felt himself rebuked and glared sullenly at his leader's back. Mary retrieved the broken flask and without ever looking up left the courtyard. A silence fell. Martha rose hastily and began gathering dishes. Alysia helped her and as they went back and forth she couldn't help but overhear the men as they began to talk in low voices.

Peter said, "For the last time, will you consider *not* going to Jerusalem tomorrow?"

"We all agree," came another voice. "Remember the word sent by Nicodemus, and others have warned us as well."

"Nicodemus is a paranoid old man," Judas answered. "No one will dare to try to harm you with the whole city full of pilgrims, and a great many of them your followers."

"There is no reason for him to put himself at risk," Andrew objected. "We should go back to Ephraim and wait until—"

Half through the entranceway Alysia couldn't hear the rest, nor did she hear Jesus' reply, though she could tell from the tone of his voice that he was not pleased with his disciples' attitude. Martha and the servant continued their task while she hurried away to her house, to lay out cushions and pallets on the rooftop. It had been arranged that several of the men would sleep there, while she, Rachel, and Judith stayed overnight at Lazarus' house. Others were to remain with Simon.

As before her marriage, she shared Mary's room. Mary was already asleep, or seemed to be. Alysia placed cushions all around her own bed so that Rachel wouldn't fall out during the night…but she could not sleep. She lay there, troubled and burdened by something to which she could not put a name. A cool breeze wafted toward her from the window, and rising, she walked toward it.

A figure stood alone in the courtyard. It was Jesus; she hadn't known he was staying here. His profile was sharply outlined against the night by the brightness of the moon. He walked aimlessly back and forth, his lips moving in silent prayer, his expression so profound that again she felt a vague sense of dread.

She had long wanted to speak with him privately but hadn't found the opportunity. If she were honest with herself, she would admit she lacked the courage to approach him. But thinking of Mary's act of adoration earlier in the evening gave her boldness, and before she could change her mind she threw a shawl over her shoulders, raising it to cover her hair as well, and slipped outside.

She hesitated for a moment. When the Nazarene turned his head and saw her, she felt his silent encouragement and went slowly toward him. "Sir, I wanted to speak with you, and it seemed important to do so before you leave tomorrow."

She paused, but he waited for her to continue and she plunged on, almost whispering, "I must know that you have forgiven me."

He seemed to come back from a great distance, and there was almost a sense of relief about him. He looked at her intently. "Do you then believe, Alysia, that I have the authority to forgive you of your sin?"

"Yes," she answered, without hesitation. "No one could do the things you have done, or teach as you have taught, unless he is of God. I was not raised to believe in God, but I have seen him in you."

He leaned toward her, speaking gently and very clearly. "From the day you stood accused before me you were forgiven, because I saw repentance in your eyes. And remember this—nothing you have suffered has gone unnoticed by your Father in heaven, and he knows every tear you have shed."

Startled, she looked into his eyes and saw full knowledge in them. The face of Magnus Eustacius loomed in her mind and before she could stop herself, she blurted, "Lord, I have killed a man."

His expression didn't change. She rushed on, "He meant to do me harm, but I was filled with rage and hate, and I have never been sorry that I killed him."

"Have you forgiven him?"

"He would not have asked for my forgiveness. He hated me as much as I hated him."

"Alysia, he is gone from this world, but he steals peace from your soul. You cannot have hate in your heart, and love for God."

Again her thoughts turned to Magnus. To her, he represented everything that was evil about Rome; he symbolized every Roman who had anything to do with her father's death and her own degradation. "I want to do as you say," she said, meeting his gaze, which had never wavered from her. "But it is so difficult. I don't see how I can forget what they have done to me."

"Nothing is impossible with God." For the first time that night, he smiled. It began in his eyes and seemed to illumine the darkest shadows of the night.

"Can I be forgiven of murder?" she asked hesitantly. "Can anyone be forgiven of murder?"

"You have heard me say that to hate a man is to murder him. Which deserves the greater condemnation?"

"I—I cannot just suddenly stop hating him, hating them all."

He reached out and took her hand, looking keenly into her face. "When you believe that all hope is gone, remember these words. I will send a helper to you, and He is in me, and I am in Him. He will be your advocate, and your strength, and through Him you can do all things."

She stared at him, bewildered. "Who is this you speak of?"

He looked as if he wanted to explain further, but for whatever reason did not answer. There were so many questions she wanted to ask him but she didn't know how to begin. She had such a tenuous grasp of who, of what, he was. But yes, she would ask him one more thing.

"You have spoken before of going away. Tonight, you spoke of your burial. What did you mean?"

His gaze at last left hers and he was slow to answer. "There are things you cannot yet bear to know. I have told my disciples and they have not understood. Understanding will come to them, and to you, in the fullness of time."

She said softly, "How lonely you must be." She bowed her head and added, still lower, "I am unworthy even to be in your presence."

She felt his hand on her shoulder and another under her chin, lifting her face. "Though your sins be as scarlet, Alysia, they shall be as white as snow."

"Thank you," she whispered. "Thank you for what you have given me . . . peace and hope, and even more than that . . . something I cannot begin to explain."

His smile faded. He looked away and gave a faint sigh. "He sent you to me in this dark hour. Go in peace, Alysia, so that I may thank Him."

She turned to go into the house.

"Pray," he said, and when she turned back toward him, he said again, "Pray that my Father's will be done."

She nodded. When she reached Mary's room, she peeked out the window and saw that he now lay on his pallet on the courtyard, his arms folded beneath his head…looking at the stars.

Paulus swiftly climbed the stairs inside the eastern tower of the fort and looked through the opening to view what his sentries had reported to him. Far below, beyond the deep-cut valley, was a splendid view of Olivet's shoulder with its forest of olive trees and the two main roads that bisected there before entering Jerusalem. On this clear, sunlit day he could see all the way to the sharp curve that led to Bethany. Here and there the hills were dotted with the tents of travelers.

As usual for the Passover season, the roads swarmed with pilgrims journeying to the holy city. The high, stone-covered road from Jericho and the winding pathway from Bethany were two of the popular routes, but what was *not* usual was the behavior of the multitudes that were now pouring toward Jerusalem like a flood-swollen river. They were in a tumult of excitement; they had cut branches from the nearest palm and willow trees and were waving them ecstatically, and shouting so loudly that the hills echoed the word back to Paulus: "Hosanna! Hosanna!" A word that he knew meant, "Save us!"

The object of all this frenzy was a man riding on a donkey. People were taking off their outer cloaks and spreading them on the ground before the man, gesticulating, shouting, bowing, as though they welcomed a triumphant king into his city.

One of Paulus' men approached him from behind. "Sir, what are your orders?"

"Obviously the Nazarene has decided to stop hiding in the desert, but I wonder if he anticipated a reception like this."

"Shall I have him arrested?"

Paulus looked at the tribune. "Has he committed a crime?"

"None that I know of, besides disturbing the peace."

"He rides a donkey instead of a horse, carries no weapon, and my spies tell me that aside from lamenting over some prophecy about Jerusalem, he has not raised his voice to speak. It seems that everyone is disturbing the peace but he."

The officer remained silent. Paulus thought for a moment. "Make sure the entire fort is ready to take action, Tribune. But do not arrest or hinder the Nazarene. I want to see what he has in mind. If he or his followers make any sign toward arming themselves, then we will stop it."

"Yes, sir."

When the tribune had left, Paulus went down the steps of the tower and walked out on the parapet. He still had a good view of the Nazarene, who was now slowly crossing the stone bridge across the valley. The surging mass before and behind him continued to call out praises, their plucked branches a rippling wave of green. Looking out over the rest of the city, he saw people crowding into the streets and leaning out of windows.

He knew what the people thought—that this Nazarene was their promised Messiah. But Paulus was still reasonably certain that this "messiah" did not intend to lead a rebellion against Rome and set himself up as their king. What he did intend remained a mystery.

Almost directly below the parapet, two priests walked across the Temple courtyard and went to peer downward toward the valley. Had Paulus been a little closer he would have heard one of them say bitterly, "We have accomplished nothing! The whole world has gone after him."

Paulus wondered what the Sanhedrin would do next, and in the next couple of days received an answer from his informant, Phineas. It was a sight he would have enjoyed witnessing.

The priests had made a report to Caiaphas.

"It was spectacular!" they declared. "How he dared—"

"What did he say?" Caiaphas demanded. "Tell me everything!"

Upon entering the Temple grounds that morning the Nazarene had walked purposefully among the moneychangers, men who collected the Temple tax and who often overcharged their fellow Jews and pocketed the money for themselves. Then he had been seen observing the Temple rulers and how they refused any sacrificial animals that had the slightest blemish, compelling the Jews to buy animals from themselves at exorbitant prices. The worshippers often paid ten times the price of the first animal for the second.

Jesus made his way past the bleating lambs and cooing doves, bent, and hurled over a table stacked high with coins. The money scattered over the pavement. He grasped one of the cages and shook it until the animals ran out, then thrust it aside to crash to the ground. He splintered a crate with a sweep of his hand, sending the doves into a frenzied rise to freedom. Snatching up a rope he lashed out at the moneychangers, who fled before his wrath.

"It is written," he declared, in a voice that shook with anger, "that my house shall be called a house of prayer, but you have made it into a den of thieves!"

The shocked priests and scribes could only stare, open mouthed, as the Nazarene strode irately from the Temple. His disciples, equally shocked, followed him.

Caiaphas had stared at the priest reporting this debacle with narrowed eyes. "He actually called the Temple *his* house? Blasphemy! This was the perfect opportunity to take him!"

"We were . . . stunned," the priest stammered. "The Nazarene is very . . . dynamic. We were rather afraid."

"Afraid of one man!"

"One of his disciples is quite large and of uncertain temperament."

Caiaphas glowered silently at the priests. After a moment he said, his voice low and clipped, "By his action today he implied to the people that we are not fit to rule. We cannot wait any longer. Find a reason; get him to compromise himself. I don't care how you do it. I want that man arrested!"

The priests had approached the Nazarene—somewhat timidly—as he mingled with the people in the Temple and asked him by what authority he said the things he had said. The Nazarene replied that he would answer their question if they would answer one of his: Did John the Baptizer preach with the authority of God, or men?

The priests unhappily perceived that if they said John preached with the authority of God they would look like fools, for they had all rejected John's teachings. However, if they said John did not receive his authority from God, the people would be angry, since John was popularly regarded as a martyr. They were forced to admit they didn't know and left the Temple grounds with undue haste.

They were immediately replaced by a mixed group of Pharisees and Sadducees, who wanted to know if it was "right" to pay taxes to Caesar. The Nazarene requested to see a coin. When one was displayed to him, he tapped it rather impatiently with his finger and inquired whose image was stamped upon it.

"Why, it is the emperor's likeness, of course."

"Then give to Caesar what is Caesar's, and to God what belongs to God."

These inquisitors quickly withdrew their injured ranks and a scribe stepped forward, desiring to know which of the commandments was the most important. The Nazarene replied, without hesitation, that the greatest commandment was, "To love the Lord your God with all your heart, and all your soul, and all your mind. The second is to love your neighbor as yourself. On these commandments hang all the Law, and the prophets."

The defeated priests skulked away to report to Caiaphas and despite his loudly vented ire refused to ask the Nazarene any more questions. The High Priest had then decided to take his father-in-law's advice.

"We will arrest him quietly and provide a reason for it later. I had not wanted it done during the Feast, but it cannot be helped. We will choose a time when there are no people around him. Find out where he goes at night. In the meantime, if anyone offers information about him—at any price—bring him directly to me."

CHAPTER XIX

Pontius Pilate arrived at the Antonia accompanied by his wife, Claudia. Pilate was not in an amiable mood. He disliked Jerusalem and he disliked turmoil, and the city was definitely in a state of turmoil.

"This is more than the usual holiday fervor," he said morosely to Paulus as they sat at the evening meal. "What is adding so much fuel to the fire?"

Paulus was moody himself, without knowing why. It was a strange and oddly oppressive night.

"The Nazarene," he said shortly.

"Ah, what has he done now?"

"Nothing, except offend the Sanhedrin."

Normally Pilate would find that amusing and make some joke about it, but he fell silent and presently made his excuses, leaving his wife and Paulus alone in the long, private dining hall.

Claudia was short of stature, slightly overweight, and remarkably attractive. Her cheekbones were wide, with hollows underneath, and her thick-lashed black eyes were large and almond shaped. She had a prominent nose, spaced perfectly between her wide-set eyes. Her brows were thick and arched, her lips full, and her black hair fashionably curled. She had an artless, casual manner that usually charmed both men and women.

Now she watched Paulus over her chalice of wine as though trying to read his mind. Seeming to sense her appraisal, he looked up to meet her gaze. He smiled crookedly. "Forgive me, Claudia. I'm not very good company tonight."

"Don't apologize, Paulus." She smiled, and then gave him a serious look. "Forgive me, but we were sorry to hear of your wife's death. I had been looking forward to meeting her."

"Yes. Thank you." Paulus politely refilled her cup.

"I'm sure I saw the famous Nazarene as my husband and I were walking along the battlements this afternoon. He was speaking to the people. Have you seen him?"

"Yes, a few times."

"What do you think of him?"

"I don't know."

"There was something about him. Odd as it sounds he looked up, directly at us, in spite of all the activity around him as if he knew we were there and who we were. I couldn't really see his expression . . . it was just a feeling." She shook her head after a moment, dismissing her thoughts. "I think I shall retire. It has been rather an exhausting day for everyone. Goodnight, Paulus."

He stood up. "Goodnight, Claudia."

She paused for a moment, and with a little shrug swept breezily from the room. Paulus sat down and stared moodily into his plate. Much later he rose again and the lamps cast his tired shadow on the walls as he moved through the corridors to his own room. He threw a glance at the bed but went instead to his writing table where an oil lamp already burned. He sat down, pulling a set of scrolls toward him.

He went through them methodically until he found what he was looking for. His brow furrowed in concentration.

His interest in the prophecies concerning the hoped-for Messiah had intensified in the past few days. He had not been able to put aside what Alysia had told him about the man, Lazarus. Sheer foolishness! And yet she believed it and she was not a fool. Did the Nazarene have everyone mesmerized? What was the secret of his power?

One passage caught his immediate attention: *"Rejoice greatly, O daughter of Zion . . . your king comes to you, lowly, and riding upon a donkey . . ."*

He turned to the prophecies by Isaiah and read on: *"All we like sheep have gone astray, every one to his own way, and the Lord has laid on him the iniquity of us all . . ."*

Paulus came slowly to awareness, realizing he had fallen asleep at the table with his head on top of his folded arms. His lamp had burned out leaving a gray haze of smoke. He rose and walked stiffly across the room. Bending over a basin, he splashed water on his face and changed his tunic, fastening his leather cuirass with difficulty. He missed the aid of Simon, whom he'd sent on an errand out of the province more than a week ago.

Deciding a brisk ride would work the stiffness out of his muscles, he went down the stairs and stepped outside into the gray dimness of dawn. A sentry stopped in mid-yawn to salute him and imperceptibly tried to straighten his stance as the legate stood looking across the pavement.

"What's happening over there?" Paulus asked. He was standing next to one of the pillars on the porch of the praetorium. Below, down a long row of marble steps, a flock of priests obstructed from view all but the dark hair of a tall man.

"The Jews have arrested the Nazarene preacher, sir," replied the sentry. "They're waiting for the prefect to come out. They won't come inside because it would defile them during their holy season, or something like that, sir. So they say."

Another of their stupid, hypocritical rules, Paulus thought irritably, starting down the steps. His gaze moved over the grim faces of the priests, who weren't speaking. There seemed to be an air of secrecy among them, a sense of urgency. One of them looked up to see Paulus coming toward them and nudged the priest next to him. A quick, whispered consultation ensued. Paulus realized that if they were waiting for Pilate they must be demanding the death penalty. He had been half-expecting this to happen, though not so soon, and certainly not on the eve of the Passover Sabbath—one of the most sacred holidays of the Jews. The movements of the priests gave him a better view of the Nazarene.

He stood under heavy guard as if he were the most dangerous of criminals. His wrists had been chained together before him. Blood ran from the corner of his mouth and into a bare, bleeding spot on his chin, where it looked as if someone had viciously jerked out a handful of his short beard. Paulus' glance fell on a captain of the Temple police, who stood nearby.

"By whose order was this man arrested?"

The man spoke rapidly, seeming eager to justify his own part in the matter. "The High Priest sent us to bring him for questioning late last night, sir."

"Why in the middle of the night? Could it not have waited until morning?"

The officer shrugged. "The priests and elders seemed to think there might be a riot among the people."

Paulus walked casually toward the prisoner, feeling anger rising in him as he observed how severely he had been beaten. Though the Nazarene's head was slightly lowered and he didn't look up, Paulus could readily see that the right side of his face was swollen and his eye had partially closed. His nose was also swollen and bloodied.

He turned to the cluster of priests, holding his anger in check. "Who beat this man?"

One of them replied, "He has received the treatment he deserves. We have found him guilty of blasphemy."

Paulus stared at him so contemptuously that the man took a step backward. "Do you expect the governor to condemn this man on a charge of blasphemy?"

Another priest stepped forward placatingly. "What my colleague meant to say, Legate Valerius, is that we have found this man guilty of blasphemy *and* sedition against Rome."

Paulus recognized him. "Caiaphas—this must be an important case for you to appear in person. Where is the old man who's really in charge?"

Caiaphas remained stoic. "If you refer to my father-in-law, he became ill last night and was unable to accompany us."

"You must have conducted this trial in the last few hours. Correct me if I am mistaken, but isn't it one of your laws that a trial cannot take place at night, and should carry over to a second day in order to give the accused every chance to defend himself?"

Caiaphas' nostrils flared. "You are correct, Legate, in saying that this is an important case, an unusual case, involving a man more dangerous than any of you suspect. This is why we have acted so expeditiously." He stopped and drew pointedly away as Pilate marched out onto the portico amid his surrounding bodyguards and gazed down at them.

It was barely dawn. To the east, pale fingers of light pointed downward toward the fortress, and at that moment bugles sounded from the main tower, marking the time. When they stopped, all was quiet except for the murmuring of a small group of spectators waiting on the level below them, down a wide set of steps. Paulus gestured to one of his men, who gathered up several legionaries. They took a stance in front of the crowd, spears in hand.

The disciples of the Nazarene were nowhere to be seen. Paulus wondered if they were incarcerated somewhere. Pilate stared hard at the prisoner, then noticed Paulus standing near him, but his eyes slid back to the Nazarene with no change of expression.

"Well?" he said, looking much annoyed. "Who has presented the charges, and what are they?"

"If this man were not a criminal," Caiaphas said loudly, "we would not have brought him to you."

His words were spoken with none of the respect, albeit grudgingly given, with which he had spoken to Paulus. His entire manner had changed somehow, had become more hostile and almost challenging. It seemed a strange development; the High Priest had always been extremely cordial toward the governor.

Pilate was still annoyed. "Take him and judge him according to your own laws."

"As you well know," Caiaphas answered, "we have no authority to put a man to death."

One of the other priests said, "We have found him guilty of perverting the people, refusing to pay taxes to Caesar, and of calling himself a king."

The prefect's glance went slowly over the prisoner, taking in his plain, homespun robe and rough shoes. Then he looked at Paulus and said crisply, "Legate, escort the prisoner inside. I wish to speak to him alone." He turned and withdrew from the portico to the inner hall. Paulus approached the Nazarene, who gazed at him solemnly from out of his good eye, and took a firm grip on his right arm. He didn't have to exert any pressure; the Nazarene willingly walked up the steps with him and into the hall.

Pilate waited in the vestibule, which was lined with statues and with colorful mosaics on the walls. He looked at Paulus for a moment, seeming to sense his resentment at the treatment of the Nazarene. He addressed the prisoner directly. "Are you king of the Jews?" he asked, with more than a hint of sarcasm.

The Nazarene answered slowly, having to form his words through a bruised and bloodied mouth. "Do you ask because you want to know, or simply because others have said this of me?"

"Am I a Jew? I care not what they say about you! I am concerned about what *you* believe. Your own people and religious leaders delivered you to me—what have you done?"

The Nazarene regarded him soberly. "If my kingdom were of this world, I would not be standing here before you. My disciples would have fought to prevent my arrest."

"So, then, you *are* a king?"

"To this end was I born, that I should bear witness to the truth."

Pilate shrugged and said with mock gravity, "What is truth?"

The Nazarene didn't answer, but his gaze never left the prefect's face. Frowning, Pilate stepped back and made a gesture of impatience. He stalked back to the outer portico, leaving Paulus to follow with the prisoner.

"I find no fault in this man," he announced.

On the pavement below, Caiaphas' jaw hardened with anger and he said at once, "We have found him guilty of sedition! He has urged the people not to pay their taxes to Caesar! He seeks to liberate us from Rome and has a huge following."

Paulus knew that the charges were not true and was amazed that the Nazarene didn't attempt to defend himself, considering what was at stake. Pilate, too, seemed taken by surprise.

"Do you not hear what they are saying against you?"

Silence.

"Caiaphas, you have made accusations but have offered no proof. Where are your witnesses? I repeat, I find no fault in him."

The High Priest, and the other leaders surrounding him, all wore the same expression of fierce determination. Just below and within hearing distance the crowd of onlookers began to mutter.

"I tell you, Prefect, he has stirred up the people from Galilee to Judea!"

Angry now, Pilate said, "Send him to Herod, then. This man is a Galilean, is he not? He falls under Herod's jurisdiction. Take him away!"

After a brief consultation among the priests, the prisoner was prodded and shoved toward the elevated walkway to the Temple area, where they would enter the arched bridge leading to Herod's palace. Pilate turned wordlessly to enter the praetorium, noticing that Paulus followed him.

"I know of your interest in the man, Paulus. We'll both benefit by having Herod decide the matter."

"It's a waste of time. This man is immensely popular in both Galilee and Judea. Do you think Herod will jeopardize his position by ruling the Nazarene guilty? They will return."

The governor shrugged his heavy shoulders and gave an order for his breakfast to be prepared. "The man is crazy—thinks he has a kingdom not in the world. Where is it then, Mount Olympus? But he is not out to conquer Rome. I recognize those fanatics when I see them."

A short time later his breakfast was brought and he made a show of eating. Paulus declined Pilate's invitation to join him and stood at the window, his face tense and alert. Pilate finally pushed away his plate and stared at it until they both heard rapid footsteps in the corridor. An inner door opened and Claudia entered the room in a dressing gown, her hair uncombed, her face pale. "Claudia!" Pilate exclaimed.

"The Nazarene," she whispered urgently, going to her husband and placing a plump hand upon his chest. "What have you done with him?"

"Why?" he asked in amazement.

"I haven't slept peacefully all night. I kept having dreams—you must have nothing to do with this Nazarene!"

Pilate could only stare at his wife, astonished at her words. "Dreams, Claudia," he said at last, attempting a laugh. "Surely you—"

"I know this—if you allow the death of this man, yours will indeed be a black name in the history of Roman rule!"

"History!" Pilate exploded, his patience pushed to the limit. "By the eternal gods! This entire affair will be forgotten in a few weeks at the most!"

"Paulus." Claudia appealed to the silent commander.

"There is nothing I can do, Claudia."

"But you are a legate!"

"I agreed to the terms of my command before I came here. Pontius Pilate has full judicial authority."

The prefect appeared on the verge of apoplexy for a moment as he realized that his own wife would, if she could, wrest his power from him and place it in the hands of another. The situation was growing more complex by the moment. But with the discipline of the skilled politician he brought his emotions under control and smiled a little. "Come, Claudia. How can you be so concerned about a man you don't even know? Let's forget this sorry business. Herod will take care of it."

Paulus didn't share his sudden amiability. "The man has already been through at least one trial, two if Annas tried him as well. The Jews have one of the fairest legal systems I've ever encountered, but I've seen none of it displayed here today. Rarely is anyone sentenced to death—first there must be at least two witnesses, who must swear an oath before they even accuse the prisoner, and the judges are supposed to act as advocates, not executioners! Who actually heard him say the things he's alleged to have said? My sources reported that he said the exact opposite."

"You should have been a lawyer, Paulus," Pilate said sourly. "It's none of my concern—what sort of investigation these Jews have conducted!"

"Paulus is right," Claudia said. "You should call in the magistrates and let them vote on the Nazarene's guilt or innocence. What right have these priests to come to you, making demands upon you?"

Pilate crossed the room, turning his back on them, then turning again. "Tell me, Paulus, who do you have in prison awaiting execution?"

"Barabbas, for one, along with some of his men."

"An insurrectionist?"

"Yes—thief and murderer as well. You're not considering—"

Before he could finish, a soldier appeared in the doorway. "Sir, the Jews have returned. The prisoner refused to answer any questions from the tetrarch. Herod made sport of the prisoner and bade the priests bring him back to you for judgment."

Pilate swore. Claudia bit her lip, and rising, fled to her apartments as her husband and Paulus went outside.

It was still early in the morning but word of the Nazarene's arrest seemed to have spread. Below the portico, a large group of men stood apart from the rest of the crowd and were shouting excitedly among themselves, as though deliberately trying to create noise and confusion. They were watched by a solid line of Paulus' soldiers.

Pilate had to shout to make himself heard. "You presented this man to me as a criminal—as someone who attempts to incite the people to rebellion. Yet on examination I have found no basis for any of these charges. Nor has Herod. The prisoner has done nothing worthy of death. I propose to chastise and release him."

He proposes! Paulus thought. *He is still vacillating. Why doesn't he just release the man?*

Suddenly, the unruly men in the crowd shouted, "Away with him! Crucify him!"

The Nazarene's head remained slightly bowed as before. Sweat and blood dripped from his face. He must have been up all night, had been paraded all through the city. Paulus had to admire his stamina but why did he not speak? Why did he not defend himself?

Crucifixion, that unspeakable, barbarous practice of nailing men to wooden crosses . . . surely the Nazarene realized what it meant. Criminals hung on crosses on public highways throughout the country as a deterrent to seditionists. To the Jew, crucifixion signified something even worse than physical suffering; their law stated that such a man was cursed by God.

"We have a custom," Pilate was saying, "that we release a prisoner during your Passover feast. We have Barabbas, a rebel, a thief, and a murderer. Who would you have me release, Barabbas—or Jesus, who has not been found guilty of such charges?"

Paulus started forward; he didn't intend to release Barabbas, who had been difficult to catch and was as cunning as he was violent. But before he could speak the crowd took up the cry, "Barabbas! Release Barabbas!"

The vehemence of the men calling for Barabbas' release and Jesus' death made Paulus think they were being paid by the priests. What reason would they have to hate the man so fervently?

Pilate spoke to one of his own soldiers, who marched away toward the prison. Well, Barabbas might be released today but Paulus would catch him again tomorrow!

As they waited for Barabbas to be brought out Paulus watched the Nazarene closely, pondering what he knew about the man. He had never shown any signs of violence, except when he threw the moneychangers out of the Temple…that must have been particularly upsetting to old Annas, who controlled that function of the Temple authority. The Nazarene stood quietly, bloodied and bruised with a haunted look about him, and yet there was also a sort of majesty, a *kingliness*.

Paulus could have liked this man, a man of obvious intelligence, well-spoken, a man of action as well as words, who wasn't afraid to speak the truth. He was supposed to have performed miracles, but if that were true he wouldn't be standing here, silently accepting insults and false accusations and the vilest physical abuse. He would make himself invisible, or something! Paulus felt disappointed somehow, and at the same time scoffed at himself for even considering the man might be capable of such things . . .

A soldier approached him without warning. "Sir, the prisoner, Barabbas, misunderstood why he was being taken and grabbed a weapon from the guards. A centurion was called and he was attacked as well."

Paulus scowled. "I will see to the prisoners. Stay here and tell the prefect I wish to be informed before he takes any action concerning the Nazarene."

"Yes, sir."

Paulus strode across the pavement, speaking sharply right and left until he was accompanied by a score of armed legionaries, and descended the steps into the dungeon. Two wounded guards huddled on the floor, along with the man Pilate had sent to free Barabbas. Though the cell door stood open, all the prisoners but one remained chained to the walls. The one who was loose, a large man with a heavy beard, held a dagger against the throat of a centurion.

"Barabbas, the prefect has just offered to free you in honor of the Jewish holiday. But if you harm this soldier, I swear I will kill you myself before I allow you to be released."

"Free me?" The man laughed harshly. "Since when have I believed the word of a Roman?"

"Whether you believe me or not, you would do well to put down that blade. There's no escape for you—I have twenty men behind me. And I will be the one to choose the manner of your death. What will it be, Barabbas? The arrow, or the cross?"

After a long, suspenseful moment, the prisoner swore obscenely and pushed away the sweating centurion, throwing the dagger after him. More guards surrounded him. Paulus ordered the wounded men to be tended and removed, then drew the centurion aside.

"How did this happen?" he demanded.

The centurion rolled his eyes and shook his head. "Sir, I cannot say. One of the Caesarean tribunes came and told me that Barabbas was to be released, so I took him to the prison. When the guards were unlocking the prisoner's chains he somehow overpowered them and got a weapon, and struck them down along with Pilate's man, and then I swear someone pushed me—only one of Pilate's men would have done it! They don't like us, don't like coming here. And so Barabbas got me as well."

"Are all the prisoners accounted for?"

"I think so, sir."

"Make certain of it." Paulus turned to a tribune standing behind him. "Take Barabbas, show him to the people, and release him. But my orders are these—I want Barabbas followed; I want to know with whom he stays and with whom he has contact. The next time he is arrested he may have even more company."

"Yes, sir."

"By the way, Tribune, tell the cohort commanders and have them spread the word—this fort will have nothing to do with what happens to the Nazarene prisoner today. Let it be on the head of Pilate and his own men."

"As you say, Legate."

Paulus left the dungeon, ascending the long flight of stairs swiftly. He had an uneasy feeling that he had delayed too long…and soon knew it to be so. When he reached the praetorium he saw that the Nazarene had been taken to the level below and was tied to the whipping post. His clothes had been removed. Two soldiers, both as muscular as young bulls, wielded the flagella, one after the other. The lead balls hissed through the air to plummet into the prisoner's back and buttocks, and over his shoulders to his chest. The prisoner, though powerfully built with well-defined muscles, had collapsed against the post, his back and legs a bleeding mass of torn flesh.

Paulus saw, in one seething glance, that the soldiers involved were those who had escorted the governor from Caesarea. They must have just reached the maximum number of strokes; they dropped the flagella onto the blood-spewed pavement and untied the prisoner. The Nazarene hit the ground hard on both knees, half conscious.

Paulus went up the steps into the praetorium and stalked toward Pilate, who stood staring blankly out a window. "By all the gods," he gritted out, "why did you scourge him? Your men have torn him to pieces!"

"Then perhaps it will satisfy Caiaphas and spare his life! You have no right to question me, Legate!"

Paulus struggled with his sense of outraged justice. "Now I understand," he said harshly. "You've never missed a chance to antagonize the Jews, Pontius Pilate—even the Sanhedrin itself. But you have lost your ally. Aelius Sejanus is dead. There is no one to support or defend your actions. And if these priests write a letter of complaint to the emperor, your career is finished."

"I do not fear the priests!" Pilate retorted. "I fear an uprising, and so should you, Legate. Listen to that! Do you hear the crowd?"

"Men employed by the priests to intimidate you and everyone else."

"You do not know that. Caiaphas has no such power."

"He does, and Annas even more. You're a fool if you think otherwise."

When there was no reply, Paulus said heatedly, "The Nazarene is innocent. You believe that. Be fair and just for the sake of humanity, Governor—not for Jew or Greek or Roman. If you are not, the emperor will hear of it, from me!"

"And so," Pilate said, in a low but angry tone, "either the priests will report I failed to kill a seditionist, or you will say that I killed an innocent Jew. Which do you think he will deem the worse?"

"Who can say, with Tiberius? But you must consider how you will live with your own conscience."

"Men in my position cannot afford a conscience, Paulus." The prefect seemed weary, suddenly drained of anger and resentment. "I am sure you know that."

A knock sounded on the door and Pilate's tribune entered. "Sir, they have brought the prisoner back to the judgment hall."

Pilate's chin lifted and he seemed to take a deep breath. Without looking at Paulus he walked slowly out the door. After a moment Paulus followed, stopping short when he saw the Nazarene standing unsteadily at the bottom of the steps.

The soldiers had made a mockery of him, throwing a scarlet cloak over his shoulders and cruelly pressing upon his head a spiked cap made of some thorny shrub—no doubt someone's idea of kingly attire. Crooked lines of dark red blood poured from his brow. Except for the cloak, he wore only an undergarment and heavily bleeding scourge marks showed on his chest and the front of his legs where the metal pellets had curled around him from behind. He was deathly pale, his facial muscles lax with pain and shock. Paulus could tell he was making a supreme effort to stand upright.

Sickened, Paulus thought, *I should have seen to it that this didn't happen!* His own men would not have been allowed to treat a prisoner this way. Obviously, Pilate's were not so disciplined.

But even Pilate was speechless. The priests avoided the spectacle, standing in a circle and whispering together. The crowd had stopped shouting. There was a long moment of involuntary silence.

Then Pilate called, "Behold—the man!"

CHAPTER XX

Paulus moved to stand close behind the prisoner where he could see the faces of Pilate before him and of the priests to the left side. His senior tribune and a centurion stood just behind Paulus, along with a few of his other officers—who seemed interested in the proceedings and somewhat confused by this display of animosity toward a man who had thousands cheering his entrance into the city just a few days ago.

"What?" said Pilate, into the heavy silence, "shall I do with this man?"

At once the roaring began, like Romans in the arena. "Crucify him!" The men worked themselves into the frenzy of a mob, shouting and shaking their fists. The supporters of the Nazarene could not even be heard.

Pilate walked down the steps, lifted his hands to no avail, and raised his voice to speak to the priests. "What has he done to warrant crucifixion?"

"By our laws he deserves it, for he calls himself the son of God!"

Pilate spoke directly to the Nazarene. "Who are you?"

He was met with no answer.

"Why don't you talk to me?" Pilate urged. "Don't you know that I have the power to release you or crucify you?"

The Nazarene lifted his head and spoke hoarsely. "You would have no power at all over me, unless it was given to you by God. Those who have delivered me to you have the greater sin."

Looking over the Nazarene's shoulder, the governor met Paulus' eyes. He made one last attempt. "It is my wish to release this man."

"No! No!" the priests cried vehemently. Their faces worked; they all but spat with rage. "The Nazarene makes himself a king! If you let him go, you are no friend to Caesar!"

Paulus knew then that it was over. "Friend to Caesar" was a title coveted by every administrator—its denial was poison, in more ways than one. Pilate tried to manage a sarcastic laugh but it was little more than a grunt.

"So, shall I crucify your king?"

"We have no king but Caesar! Away with him! Crucify him!"

Unaware that he had even been debating with himself, Paulus reached a decision. It would surely be a suicidal move in regard to his career, even to his life, and all for a penniless Jewish carpenter who was saying nothing on his own behalf . . . but to remain silent in the face of so great an injustice was to ally himself with these fanatical priests. The Nazarene might be insane, for all Paulus knew, but he had done nothing to deserve crucifixion and Paulus didn't think he could live with himself if he allowed it to happen.

He would exercise the full authority of his rank and demand that Pilate release the man. Even if it meant ordering his own men to arrest Pilate, even if it meant a full-scale battle, he must do something to put an end to this farce, this torture and murder of an innocent man. His hand was on the hilt of his sword when, unexpectedly, the Nazarene turned and looked directly into his eyes. The message struck him like a physical blow, as if a voice spoke into his mind.

Put away your sword.

Slowly, his hand dropped to his side. Gradually his accelerated heartbeat returned to its normal rhythm. The Nazarene had not spoken but Paulus had heard his voice. For a moment he doubted his own sanity.

The Nazarene held his gaze, his breathing labored, then he raised his bound hands to wipe blood out of his eyes and turned away. A servant hurried down the steps and handed the prefect a small sheet of papyrus, which Pilate read with a heavy scowl.

"From my superstitious wife," he muttered, and once more seemed to waver. He was not immune to superstition himself. He looked up. The mob was shouting incoherently; here and there the words "Caesar" and "traitor" could be discerned. The priests waited expectantly for the final word, angry and tense.

Turning abruptly, Pilate climbed the steps to the portico and called for a basin of water. When the servant brought it, he dipped his hands in the water and raised them for all to see. He meant it to be a symbolic gesture—certainly the Romans and priests knew that it had no legal meaning and was merely a dramatic way for Pilate to declare he wanted nothing further to do with the matter.

"I am innocent of the blood of this man," the prefect called down to the priests, glaring at them. "See to it yourselves."

The Nazarene was to be crucified.

Pilate had no choice but to place his own staff in charge of the execution, for it was obvious Paulus would have refused. He ordered that two other condemned men be crucified as well—perhaps it would be a slight diversion, at least. He then disappeared into the praetorium.

Paulus took it upon himself to order the cap of thorns removed from the prisoner, as well as the scarlet cloak. Then he followed Pilate, who was sitting limply in a chair staring once again at his half-eaten breakfast.

"Legate, will you—" Pilate stopped and had to force himself to meet Paulus' eyes. He was sweating profusely. "Will you go and control the mob? I don't know what will come of this, or how the people will react."

Paulus glared at him. "You are still the governor, Pontius Pilate. You have two choices. You may alter your decision before it's too late, or you can abide by it and be prepared to accept the consequences."

At Paulus' sharp tone, the frightened look began to leave Pilate's face. "You are quite right, Legate." He cleared his throat. "Since your presence might prevent a riot, you will accompany the prisoner to the execution site."

"I will accompany the prisoner," Paulus said coldly, "but not for that reason. If there *is* a movement to free the Nazarene, I will make sure that neither your men nor mine interfere."

He went outside and ordered his horse saddled. When it was brought to him, he traveled at a brisk pace down the almost empty street and passed through the gate which opened onto the place of execution.

The path led up a gradual incline, ending on a cliff that looked down upon two highways, one parallel with it, the other extending northward. The Jews called it Golgotha and the Romans, Calvary—

the words meaning "the place of the skull." When viewed from the two highways, the cliff face had contours and cavities eerily resembling a human skull. Executions were carried out here in full view of travelers, thus emphasizing Rome's punishment of wrong-doers and at the same time not offending the city with the smell of death...for the victims were usually left there to rot.

Now that it was mid-morning the news of the Nazarene's arrest had spread over certain quarters of the city. Dozens of people began to converge on the barren, rock-strewn plateau. Some wept or appeared to be dazed. But no one seemed to be on the verge of rebellion. None of the disciples had come to fight off the crowds, to shield their master from harm. None were there to comfort him; none had come to die with him.

The Nazarene walked with slow, agonized steps. The crossbar to which he would be nailed, the weight of a small man, had been placed over his shoulders. Legionaries flanked the crowd on horseback, while others surrounded the prisoner. When he was forced to stop as soldiers cleared a path for him, one of them lashed at his legs with a leather whip until he began to trudge on again. A group of women cried piteously, reaching out to touch him as he passed. He paused and said something to them but was driven on by a vicious lash from behind.

Paulus glanced down at the northern road and saw a man walking toward the city, watching the activity above with bewilderment and horror. It was Simon, returning to Jerusalem. Paulus guided his horse to the edge of the precipice and caught his eye, gesturing. Simon immediately walked around the base of the rock "skull" and gained the path leading upward.

The Nazarene stumbled, falling heavily on his knees. He attempted to shift the great crossbeam that chafed against his raw wounds. Behind him, the soldier sneered and raised his whip, then a hard jerk upon it nearly pulled him off his feet. He let go and a stinging burn appeared on his hand. He swore and whirled in fury, only to look up and meet the formidable glare of the Antonia's commander.

"You fool!" Paulus snapped. "Return to the fort and report to Pilate that you gave a good account of yourself—beating a dying man!" He threw the whip at the soldier, who caught it deftly and turned, sullen but obedient, to walk down the incline toward the city. Lowering his gaze, Paulus saw the Nazarene slumped on the ground.

He twisted in the saddle. "Simon!"

"Yes, sir." The slave appeared amid a sea of faces.

"Help the man carry his cross."

"Yes, sir!"

Dropping the bag he carried, Simon made his way to the Nazarene, who seemed to have reached the end of his endurance. Stooping beside the prisoner, he took the wooden beam upon his own strong shoulders and carried it the remaining distance. The Nazarene staggered after him, his head lowered, seeming not to hear the lamentations of one group or the taunts and jeers of another.

"He saved others—himself he cannot save!" The men curled their lips and shook their heads. Even people on the roads stopped to look up and shake their fists. Someone yelled, "You led us to believe you were going to save us—look at you now! You are nothing but a fraud! We called you Messiah, and now you will hang on a tree—accursed of God!"

The priests who had followed the cruel procession also derided him. "See if God will help you! You say you are the son of God—he doesn't think much of you, does he?"

Simon paused as they reached the flattened area of the execution site. A soldier relieved him of the crossbar. Simon turned to inquire of Paulus what he should do next. Paulus indicated with a movement of his head that he could leave, if he chose.

Simon looked at the Nazarene. He had straightened to look up into the sky; it seemed to the slave that he was involved in some tremendous inner struggle that had nothing to do with what was going on around him. It was as if he gazed at some other world . . . it was as if he saw something in the sky that Simon could not see.

Then the prisoner drew his gaze down and looked at him, and Simon knew he couldn't stay. He swung about and began descending the knoll.

Paulus' eyes scanned the group of mourners who stood apart from the main crowd. He still didn't recognize any of them as being one of the twelve disciples. But wait—there was one of them. The youngest one. And there stood Lazarus and several women. His attention was drawn by a woman of middle age who bore a slight resemblance to the Nazarene. The look on her face, as though her soul had been torn asunder—surely they had not brought his mother here! This was a sight that even the most seasoned soldiers, if they had a shred of decency in them, found difficult to bear. Paulus followed her agonized gaze with his own.

The team of skilled executioners went quickly to work. The Nazarene was stripped of his garment and forced to lie on the ground, with his shoulders resting against the crossbeam. He was offered a drugged wine by women from a charitable organization who were present at every execution, but he shook his head, refusing it.

A soldier held down one arm, placed a spike over the prisoner's wrist, and hammered it quickly into the wood. The Nazarene wrenched his head. His hand clenched and spasmed. The soldier nailed the other wrist. The crossbeam was raised with the aid of ropes and pulleys and attached to the center post, which was already set in the ground. His left leg was roughly rotated and the foot placed over the other. A single spike drove through both feet and into the wood of the center bar. The entire procedure, designed to inflict the worst pain and misery imaginable, had taken only a few moments.

With difficulty the Nazarene spoke, as though to some invisible presence: "Father, forgive them, for they know not what they do."

The legionary who had done the nailing stopped his business of gathering up tools and stared at the man on the cross. Whether or not he understood the words was not clear—something in the tone had reached him. But the Nazarene was silent now, closing his eyes and rolling his head back against the wood, his body writhing.

"If you are the son of God, come down from the cross!" screamed one of the priests.

As before, Paulus was surprised by the depth of their hatred and hostility toward this man. Especially when he hung nailed to a cross, no longer a threat to either their doctrine or dignity.

Now would come the hours, sometimes days, that such victims would wait to die. His body had been forced into an unnatural position, the hips thrust to one side, the knees bent in the opposite direction. The chest was constricted and in order to breathe or in an attempt to take pressure off of his wrists, he would raise himself only to increase the pain in his impaled feet. He would release his weight, and the pressure would again be on the wrists. He could shift himself in such a manner as long as he was able, but the only relief was death. Some victims were driven mad by the pain.

In that moment, Paulus was ashamed of himself, and his heritage. Though he considered this form of punishment so cruel that he never used it, it was a Roman punishment, and he was a Roman. Why had he not done something? What if he had misinterpreted the look on the Nazarene's face—what if he'd only imagined those words he thought he had heard?

Well, it was too late now to save him. The man would never survive, even if Paulus had him taken down from the cross this very moment. He was too badly wounded, he had lost too much blood, the beating had been too severe. And that could be attributed to two Roman soldiers who didn't even know him and yet hated him. There was something almost diabolical about all this animosity, if one believed in such things.

"Legate, the prefect has requested your presence immediately at the praetorium, sir."

Paulus' head jerked around at the unexpected summons. One of his own men had approached him on horseback.

"Very well."

The young soldier avoided looking at the three crosses and left. Paulus lingered, offering in his mind a respectful farewell to this courageous man. Then he turned his horse and walked it slowly away. From the two thieves who had been crucified on either side of the Nazarene came almost inhuman moans of agony, but from the man on the central cross, there was no sound.

He found, on his return, that Pilate seemed to have regained control of himself and was involved in a dispute with some of the priests over the wording of a sign he had ordered to be posted over the Nazarene's cross. It was the custom to post such signs over the heads of the condemned so that the public might be aware of the nature of their crimes.

One of the priests complained, "The sign says— 'This is Jesus, King of the Jews.'"

"I know what it says," Pilate replied flatly.

"But he is not our king! The sign should read, 'He *claimed* to be King of the Jews.'"

"What I have written, I have written."

"But there was no need to put it in three languages . . ."

Paulus, who had not yet entered the room, felt a bitter urge to laugh. He walked briskly through the doorway.

"Legate." Pilate gestured to him wearily. "Come here."

Paulus complied, eyeing the priests with an expression falling short of friendly interest.

"I think you know Annas, of the Sanhedrin, and Caiaphas, the High Priest."

Paulus nodded curtly at the older man. "I heard you were ill. It seems you have made a remarkable recovery."

Annas shrugged. "I was merely indisposed after a long and arduous interrogation. I have not your youth and vigor, Commander."

Pilate interrupted. "Paulus, these men have come to me with a request, and for once I can see the wisdom of it. I am going to assign you to do it."

"If you mean taking down the sign, it remains."

"Yes, the sign remains. There is another request. Annas, you will explain."

"We want you," the old man said, "to make certain, beyond any doubt, that the Nazarene is dead. Then we want guards posted by his grave for at least three full days."

Paulus was intrigued, in spite of himself. "For what purpose?"

The priests were silent. Pilate made a careless gesture with his hand. "It seems that this Jesus told his followers some time ago that he would be killed, but assured them that within three days he would rise again."

"Of course," put in Caiaphas quickly, "the disciples will more than likely attempt to steal the body and present the empty grave to the world, proclaiming the man had risen. Or they may try to take him down before he is dead and revive him, so that he may appear three days hence claiming to be resurrected. It would create a disturbance, and that we must avoid."

"Yes," said Paulus. "You killed him for creating a disturbance."

"He was a blasphemer!" Caiaphas asserted with sudden balefulness. "In my very presence he declared he was the son of God!"

"And for that you would nail a man to a cross?"

The High Priest drew himself up proudly. "It is notorious, sir, that you Romans take your religion lightly, but with us it is not so. And for a man, a Nazarene, to claim he is the son of God is the utmost profanity!"

"Can you prove," Paulus asked, with a raised eyebrow, "that the man is not the son of a god? After all, he is said to have performed many miracles—among them ridding the Temple of your thieving moneychangers."

Caiaphas stared and began to sputter helplessly. His father-in-law came to his rescue.

"Lord Valerius." Annas gave him a placating smile. "Possibly you are not familiar with our religion—and why should you be? We hold our God in the deepest reverence. For a man to claim he is God's son is the same as saying he is God himself. That is contrary to our most important commandment, which says, 'Have no other gods before me.'"

"It seems there has been a difference of opinion on which is the most important commandment, but you are welcome to yours. I do know a little of your religion, Annas, and I know that much has been written of the promised Messiah. Suppose you have crucified him?"

"We, as Sadducees, do not hold to the idea of a Messiah."

"But you can hardly deny he was an extraordinary man. How do you explain his miracles?"

"Tricks," said Annas, without blinking an eye. "We do not deny he was a master of illusion."

"And the bringing of a dead man back to life?"

"Impossible. It was nothing more than an elaborate hoax."

Paulus was enjoying himself. "Can you be sure of that? There are many witnesses who will swear that the man called Lazarus was dead and in his grave before the Nazarene recalled him to life."

Pilate interposed at that moment, saving the old man from racking his canny brain for a reply. "Paulus, please, enough of this. I would prefer that you handle this duty, so I can be certain it is well done. They have their own Temple guards, but they want trained men, real soldiers."

Paulus answered, "I am impressed by the piety of your priests, Pontius Pilate—although it surprises me that they have entered the house of heathens when they are about to begin their ceremony." He looked at the sullen priests. "Or is this just another law you've bent to accommodate yourselves?"

Annas seemed truly offended. "That is a *Pharisaic* law! We, as the heads of the Sanhedrin, are not required to abide by it."

"I see." Paulus' look of disdain was not lost upon the priests. "I suppose there are any number of laws you, as heads of the Sanhedrin, are not required to 'abide by.' Very well, then. I will confirm the death and wait with interest to see what happens—in three days."

No sooner had he left the room than another of his men approached and saluted him. "Sir, they are about to free the prisoner, Barabbas. The document requires your signature."

"I thought he had already been released."

"There has been some confusion, sir. Some of the tribunes thought you opposed the release."

"As I did, but Pilate has ordered it. I gave specific instructions regarding Barabbas."

The legionary said nothing and looked uncertain.

"Bring the prisoner and whoever is in charge of him to my reception room."

"Yes, sir."

Paulus swore and entered the empty dining hall, where he poured himself a generous draught of wine. A stale loaf of bread had been left on the serving table. He tore off a piece and ate it, though he wasn't very hungry. Crucifixions tended to dull the appetite.

When he reached his office the bound prisoner and his three guards were there, along with the apologetic tribune who came smartly to attention.

"I am sorry, sir. I know what your orders were to me, but some of the staff believed you had changed your mind. I did not wish to release this prisoner until I was sure of your wishes, due to the nature of his crimes."

"If I had changed my mind, I would have made it known to you, Tribune. My order stands. You do recall the exact words?"

"Yes, sir."

Paulus looked at the prisoner, whose expression was half smug and half disbelieving.

"I wouldn't say you are a free man, Barabbas. We will find you again, should you resume your former activities."

The man grinned. "That won't be so easy. But if I may ask—why did you choose today to make use of that old tradition? It hasn't been done in years, has it?"

"I wouldn't know, nor was it my decision. I find it stupid and irresponsible. Give me the scroll, Tribune."

The officer handed over the document. Paulus sat down at his desk and signed it, saying, "Take him outside and release him."

The five men turned to leave. Then Paulus said, "Barabbas, have you no curiosity about the man dying in your place?"

The scraggly man turned, his grin fading. "What did he do?"

"Nothing. He was innocent."

Barabbas quirked an eyebrow. "Roman justice," he said.

There were other matters needing his attention but Paulus found it difficult to concentrate. It was unusually quiet in the praetorium. He wondered what Pilate was doing.

Suddenly, the entire room went black. It was as though a shade had been put over the window. He groped his way to it and looked out…and saw nothing. Slaves shuffled in, lighting lamps, their faces reflecting fear and alarm. Paulus said nothing to them, doubting they could explain the sudden darkness. An eclipse? He went outside. There was no storm, no clouds that he could see, no wind. The sun had been completely blotted out.

Lamps and torches had been lit all around the fort. Paulus called for his horse. For some reason he felt drawn to the place of execution, as if the Nazarene could explain this phenomenon. Rumor had it he had once stopped a terrific storm in mid-blast—did he have power over the sun as well? Or were the gods mourning over his ill treatment? Paulus couldn't believe such thoughts were actually running through his head.

There was a rational explanation for everything. This had to be an eclipse of the sun, though the Greek and Egyptian astronomers residing at Herod's palace had failed to predict this one—something they had accomplished in the past with phenomenal accuracy. Nor had he ever heard of an eclipse lasting for more than a few minutes. There was no aura around the sun, no glow from anywhere. Just total blackness, pressing down like a blanket.

His horse pranced skittishly. Few people walked in the street, and those who had ventured out held oil lamps and looked frightened. A group of soldiers perched on jittery horses talked and laughed loudly as if to prove themselves unconcerned with the strange darkness. It had grown much cooler.

The plateau was lit with torches, giving it a weird, underworld quality. Fewer people stood there now. The mob had either wearied of reviling the Nazarene or had grown fearful of the darkness. Some distance away Pilate's soldiers, all in various stages of intoxication, played with dice and waited for the men to die.

Standing together the mourners remained in almost the same position as when Paulus had left them. The woman he thought was the Nazarene's mother was down on her knees, her head bowed. Her courage and self-possession almost matched that of her son. The two thieves still twisted and sobbed; one cursed intermittently. The Nazarene was still, his head limp, his eyes closed. Maybe he was already dead. He looked dead.

The flickering torchlight played over him with a red glow. Brutally beaten and disfigured, he scarcely resembled a human being. His ribcage jutted out, giving him a distorted appearance; it looked as though his bones were ready to pierce through his skin. His entire body dripped profusely with blood and sweat.

"My God, my God, why have you forsaken me?"

Paulus' head jerked around when he heard the hoarse voice of the Nazarene. There was immediately a stirring among the mourners, and only when someone began quoting the remaining verses did Paulus recognize that the Nazarene had called out a portion of the Hebrew psalms. He seemed to try to speak again, but looked as if he were gagging. Paulus watched as the centurion said sharply, "You heard the man say he was thirsty—give him something to drink!"

Another soldier ambled forward and lifted up a stick attached to a sponge soaked in vinegar. After barely a swallow the Nazarene lifted his head, and looking at the black sky, he cried out, "It is finished!"

There was something triumphant, almost victorious, in the way he spoke. Then he said, in a lower voice, "Father, into your hands . . . I commend my spirit." His head drooped forward again, and he hung motionless.

It was almost as though he had deliberately willed himself to die—though certainly he was a dying man. But it was the other thing he had said that intrigued Paulus; the Greek word he had used for "finished" more implied the payment of a debt than the completion of something. There was a key to that word, he thought, the key to the secret of the Nazarene's very life . . .

At that instant a tremor shook the ground; Paulus' horse neighed and reared, rolling its eyes in fright. Most of the remaining people scattered with alarmed cries and shouts. Paulus fought to control his horse but the tremor stopped as unexpectedly as it had begun.

One of Pilate's centurions appeared beside Paulus, staring at the Nazarene. "Surely this man was innocent. Surely he is the son of God!"

Shaken, Paulus didn't reply. Everything was utterly still but for the nervous stamping of his horse. Suddenly light appeared, as though a giant mass over the sun had finally passed over. People stood blinking, frowning in bewilderment and looking at each other.

Another soldier approached the centurion, holding a long, stout club. "The prefect has ordered their legs to be broken to hasten their deaths. He said to make absolutely certain they are all dead." But he didn't move, looking up at the Nazarene with an expression of dread.

"Do it," the centurion said grimly. "It will be a mercy."

The soldier obeyed. The first thief convulsed as the club swung heavily against his legs with a sharp crack, then he went limp and sank into unconsciousness. The second thief only stirred and moaned slightly as he received the same treatment. No longer able to raise themselves to suck air into their lungs, they would soon suffocate.

The soldier raised the club to strike the Nazarene.

"Wait," said Paulus, gazing intently into the blood-streaked face. "This man is already dead."

He carefully edged his horse to the center cross. There was no longer a free flow of blood from the man's wounds. He was not breathing. One eye was still swollen closed but the other was partially open and unblinking. Paulus nodded toward one of the sentries standing by with a javelin. "Make sure."

The sentry hesitated for a moment, then plunged his weapon deep into the unresisting flesh. A flow of blood and clear fluid ran out, but there was no movement.

Paulus looked down and met the centurion's gaze. "Release the body to his friends."

"One of the Jews has already asked Pilate for the body, sir. That one. They want to bury him before their holy day begins." He nodded toward a wealthy-looking man who stood near the young disciple and Lazarus. The women had moved further away, weeping quietly. A black-garbed member of the Sanhedrin, a Pharisee, also stood with the mourners.

"Bring the ladder," Paulus ordered. "Help them take the body down."

The centurion quickly went about securing a ladder and giving directions to the Nazarene's followers. Paulus waited on his horse. His gaze went over the deserted area on the other side of the crosses. After the earthquake several of Pilate's soldiers had fled.

The centurion had climbed on the ladder and was working to free the Nazarene's hands. The dead man's head rolled to the right, his cheek resting against his shoulder.

Paulus dismounted and stood quietly beside his horse, some distance away. He was sure these people must hate the sight of him. He heard Lazarus say, "Please . . . put something over his head."

The wealthy-looking Jew approached the women, one of whom held in her arms a white burial shroud made of a costly linen. She lifted a smaller cloth away from the larger one and handed it to the man, who carried it back and climbed up the wide ladder, positioning himself just below and to the right of the centurion.

Paulus watched as the man spread the cloth over the Nazarene's head and face. One of the other women stepped forward, having taken the pins from her head covering, and handed them up to the man on the ladder. The man pinned the cloth in place as best he could. The sweating centurion finally succeeded in releasing one of the hands from the cross. The body rolled to one side. Another soldier stepped forward to help hold it in place. The centurion worked on the other hand.

Lazarus, the young man, and the Pharisee picked up the ropes lying on the ground, looped them over the drooping body, and handed the ends up to the Jewish man on the ladder. When the second hand was released, he held the body up while the centurion descended the ladder and set to work releasing the feet. At last the Nazarene was free and lowered slowly to the ground.

Jesus of Nazareth lay for a moment on his right side, and the cloth covering his face was now soaked in bloody fluid. The Jews gently turned him onto his back. One of them tried to staunch the flow from the nose and mouth. The woman Paulus believed to be the man's mother began to sob.

He couldn't bear to watch any longer, couldn't bear the looks on the faces of these people who loved this man. He motioned to the blood-soaked centurion, who came to him at once. "Follow them," he said. "Take these other men with you. You are not to leave the body for one moment. Watch where they bury him and stay there until you are relieved. I'm sending out a company of men to guard the grave. And I want no one interfering with his burial—especially the priests. He deserves that much."

The centurion looked mystified, but nodded. "Yes, sir."

Paulus mounted his horse, tugged gently on the reins, and turned onto the path to the city gate. It was almost evening, and by the Jews' reckoning would be the beginning of their Passover Sabbath. The day after that was their regular Sabbath, so there would be no activity on the streets by religious Jews for two more days.

He felt deeply depressed. *Someone should tell Alysia*, he thought. She was probably alone in Bethany. But . . . how to explain why he had let something like this happen, when he knew the man was innocent? How to explain the fact that the events of the day seemed to occur in such a chaotic and yet cohesive way, and completely outside his or Pilate's control?

How to explain thinking he had heard the Nazarene tell him to put away his sword!

Hours earlier Alysia had stood in her doorway, a look of apprehension on her face. The sky had turned completely dark. She could see nothing, not even the outline of the distant mountains. She went inside, closed the door, and slid the bolt into place. She found the one lamp that was always kept burning and went about lighting the other lamps. She had heard about eclipses of the sun…could this be one?

She looked at Rachel, who had just been put down for a nap. Her daughter was sleeping peacefully. Alysia returned to the table where she had been making bread but she kept stopping to listen, not knowing what she listened for, and heard only the anxious thudding of her own heart. She wished Lazarus and his sisters hadn't gone to Jerusalem. Judith had gone as well. The only people left in Bethany were those too old or too sick to attend the Passover. There weren't even any travelers on the road outside.

She didn't like being alone today. It frightened her, this darkness hanging over the land like a cloud of doom. But, no, it was not like a cloud. It was like a blanket, heavy and oppressive, bearing down in suffocating folds of fear and alarm and an indescribable sorrow.

It was like the end of the world.

CHAPTER XXI

Paulus found it impossible to concentrate on his duties. He decided to ride to the city of Emmaus where workmen were building a small Roman fort. Emmaus was a picturesque city, sitting on a hill and accessible by a newly paved Roman road. When finished the fort would fall under his supervision and would be staffed with part of his own legion. For two days he watched the construction and consulted with the carpenters and stonemasons. He tried not to think about what was happening in Jerusalem, having confidence in the men he had set to guarding the Nazarene's tomb. Besides, what could possibly happen? The Nazarene was dead; there was no threat of any rebellion by his followers…who, in fact, all seemed to be in hiding. And the priests' idea that the disciples would try to steal the body was ludicrous. How could they hope to even carry out such a plot, much less convince people that their leader had risen from the dead?

But on the morning of the next day his restlessness had only increased, so after one final meeting he departed for Jerusalem. On the road he passed several travelers apparently returning from there, some of them serious and quiet, others walking together in animated conversation. He noticed three men in particular, for the man in the middle was taller than the others, and though his outer garment covered his head there was something familiar about him. The men were talking earnestly and the man in the middle looked directly at Paulus. Intent on his thoughts, Paulus only glanced at him and rode on.

He was standing in the doorway of the stable stamping dust from his boots when one of the tribunes approached him and saluted gravely. "Greetings, sir. The prefect has heard of your return and instructed me to tell you he wishes to see you at once."

"Very well." Paulus preceded the tribune into the praetorium, not even pausing to wash the journey's grime from his face. Pilate sat in the library, his elbows braced on a table and his head in his hands, rubbing as if to blot out some pain. Claudia perched on the edge of a chair near him, white-lipped and silent.

Pilate looked up and gestured weakly. "Come in, Paulus. Close the door."

Paulus obeyed. He glanced at Claudia, who would not look at him.

"Paulus, just how reliable were those guards you placed at the Nazarene's grave?"

He felt a strange quiver inside him. "Completely. They had orders to change guard every three hours. Sirius, one of my best men, was in command." He paused, and though he knew the answer, asked, "What happened?"

"The Nazarene's body is gone!" Claudia cried. "He is gone, and it is the third day!"

"Please, Claudia." Pilate continued to rub his aching head. "The body has been stolen, Paulus. The Sanhedrin is outraged, saying your men were asleep on duty."

Paulus looked incredulous. "They were not asleep! Every one of my men is aware of the penalty for sleeping on guard duty."

Pilate leaned forward and said in a cold, clipped voice, "They have admitted that they fell asleep. When they awakened, the body was gone. The Jews say that if this news spreads, the people will become convinced the Nazarene was a god. Then they will turn against the Sanhedrin for crucifying him. All of this could be disastrous, Paulus, for the Jews and for us. That is why I want you to find the body."

"That should be simple enough. And if I find that this is true, I will have the guards executed."

"No, you are not to punish them. Caiaphas has already convinced me that this is the best handling of the matter."

"What do you mean, don't punish them?"

Pilate and his wife exchanged looks of uneasiness. "Very well—here it is. Caiaphas paid them to say they had fallen asleep and promised them immunity from prosecution. I realize he went beyond his authority—and so does he. However, executions of Roman soldiers over a dead Jew's grave! What would that do for our army's morale? Besides, it makes us look like fools."

Paulus' eyes speared the governor to his seat. "Were they, or were they not, asleep when the body was stolen? By the gods, Pilate, there were twenty of them!"

Pilate's own gaze shifted away. "They had to be. They had some wild story . . . Caiaphas didn't want to tell it, sounds like a hallucination of some sort. Nonsense. But we must prove once and for all that this miracle-worker from Nazareth is nothing more than a decaying corpse."

"I warned you," Claudia said in a despairing tone, which was so uncharacteristic of her that both men stared. "I warned you to have nothing to do with that man!"

Still half in a daze Paulus went to his room, where he washed and donned a clean uniform. Then, immediately, he confronted the captain of the guard.

"Do you think I believe this rubbish about your falling asleep? I want the truth. What happened out there?"

"That—that is the truth, sir."

Paulus stared at the officer with contempt. "You know that the penalty for sleeping on duty is death. If you persist with this story, I will be forced to carry it out—with or without Pilate's permission. I have only to consult with his superior officer."

The captain turned pale but made no answer.

"Sirius, I've known you a long time. You are not a simpleton, nor are you a liar. You are the best soldier I have, which is why I put you in charge. And since I wrote the orders myself, I know that you were on duty this morning. Tell me what happened."

Sirius licked his lips, eyeing his commander nervously. "Sir, you will not believe—"

"Never mind what I believe!"

"We—we came upon the priests as we were running away. They were going to the tomb, I think, to see if anything had happened. And they paid us all a great sum of money to say that we had fallen asleep and the body had been stolen. They said they would arrange with Pilate that we would not be punished."

"Running away from *what*, Sirius?"

"I—had just come out to join the morning watch, as you ordered. There were twenty of us. Nothing at all had happened the previous two days . . . the guards had seen no one anywhere near the tomb. I suppose we were all wondering why we were even there. And then—"

He stopped to run a hand over his face. "And then, the earth shook, sir, as if a giant beast had set his foot upon it. There was a sound from inside the tomb, like . . . a huge chorus of singers. We saw a light coming from around the stone, so bright that I think we would have been blinded if it hadn't been blocked by the stone. Just that much of it hurt our eyes. There was a . . . man, dressed in white. He came from nowhere. He rolled the stone away, as if it were nothing—a pebble. Sir, no mortal man could have done that! Then he sat down on it and just looked at us. That was when we ran, sir. We didn't look back."

Paulus stared at the officer for so long that Sirius cast down his eyes and almost began to squirm. "What else did you see?"

"Nothing, except . . . there were some women approaching from a distance."

"And the Nazarene's body? What happened to it?"

"Sir, I am not trying to make myself appear any better in this thing, for I know it is inexcusable. But I was the last to leave. When everyone else ran, I . . . well, I was the last. I looked into the tomb. And there was nothing there."

"How can you be sure of that? You have said you were almost blinded by a bright light!"

"The tomb was not dark. It was . . . glowing, as if the light inside were slowly growing dimmer. I could see perfectly. And there was no body inside."

"Who was this man in white? Why did you not confront him, fight him?"

"I don't know. His strength . . . the way he moved. The way he got to the top of the stone to sit on it. We assumed he was a god."

"Then you believe, Captain, that one of the gods came and rolled that stone away so that you and the world could see that, by some supernatural means, this Nazarene had come back to life and just . . . disappeared?"

Sirius winced at the sarcasm in his commander's voice. "I don't know what to believe, sir. I only know what I saw. No one, nothing, was in the tomb except the Nazarene's body when the entrance was sealed. We examined it thoroughly. It was an ordinary tomb."

Paulus' mind flew; he told himself again there was always a rational explanation for everything. It was a fantastic story, told by a man not given to fantasy, an honest and intelligent man that Paulus had respected...until now.

"You have brought disgrace upon this legion by your cowardice," he said sternly. "And by your willingness to lie, and by accepting a bribe from the Jews. Pontius Pilate has ordered your pardon from execution, but I will not be so lenient. I will find a way to punish you and your men. Now tell me where I can find this grave."

Sweating, Sirius gave him directions. Paulus went for his horse and rode northward, to see the gravesite for himself.

Below and slightly west of the cliff face that so eerily resembled a human skull, the tomb was apart from the city and carved from the sheer rock wall. Paulus left his horse close to the road and walked down the graveled path. The massive boulder that had covered the rectangular opening stood some distance away. Spikes had been driven into the stone on either side of the entrance to hold the thick leather strap in place. This was the seal protected by Roman law; to break it would invite severe consequences. The strap now dangled at one end.

He saw an upraised area of rock-covered earth to the right, where the soldiers would have stood guard. A square of pavement graced the front of the tomb. Flowers in full, riotous beauty—white lilies, roses, tulips, crimson poppies—grew in large clay pots bordering the pavement. Their scents filled the cool spring air. The evening sun was ready to descend and its last rays surrounded the place with a nimbus of golden light.

Paulus stood perfectly still for a moment, staring at the darkened entrance. He didn't for a moment believe in a resurrection . . . but something had happened here, something that had so frightened twenty hardened soldiers that they had risked their lives by running away from their post. He was about to enter, to see if there was some evidence that had been overlooked when a small noise came from within, as of a pebble scraping against a shoe. He hesitated and in spite of himself a shiver wound along his spine.

"Who's there?" he called in a tone of authority.

There was no answer. Paulus drew his dagger and went down the stone steps, bending his head as he cautiously entered the sepulcher. A waft of cool air struck him, bringing a smell of mustiness and something else, something like the scent of earth after a storm of thunder and lightning. He didn't move as his sight adjusted to the dimness. Another sound, like the rustle of clothes, came from his right. He stiffened and cautiously turned his head in that direction.

"Who are you?" he demanded.

A clear, feminine voice replied. "I am called Mary, the Magdalene."

After a moment's pause, and with an unmistakable sense of relief, he replaced the dagger in its sheath and stepped closer to the woman. He could see that she was tall and wore a black cloak that also covered her hair.

"What are you doing here?"

"I came here to pray," she said simply.

"How did you get in here? This tomb was under the seal of the Roman army."

Her eyes went over him for a moment, taking in the crimson mantle clasped at his shoulders, the mail cuirass and pleated kilt of his uniform. "Are you going to arrest me?" she asked softly.

"Not yet," he said, trying to curb his impatience. "But someone broke the seal and stole the body of a man buried here three days ago. What do you know about that?"

The woman made no reply. He felt that she was debating what she should say to him.

He said quietly, "Who was it—the fisherman they call Peter? Were the others involved also?"

Again, she didn't answer. She lifted her arm and pointed across the small chamber. "That was where we put him. There was so little time, for the Passover Sabbath was beginning. We wrapped him in the linen and laid him there."

Paulus turned and looked where she pointed. There was a long, gently sloping groove along the floor. There was, of course, no body lying there now, and once again a strange shuddering swept over him.

"What happened to him?"

The woman began to weep softly. He strove again to control his impatience. The peculiar smell was making him light-headed and he touched her arm. "Let's go outside," he said gently.

She allowed him to lead her up the steps and out into the diminishing sunlight. She stumbled once, as if she too were dizzy. When they stood in the garden he looked intently into her face.

She was about his own age. The black cloak had slipped back, revealing auburn hair that seemed aflame in the setting sun. He remembered seeing her at the crucifixion. Tears streamed from her brown eyes but he saw with some surprise that she wasn't weeping with grief . . . instead, she seemed filled with some deep, inexpressible joy!

She's insane! was his first thought and her next words confirmed his suspicion.

"Jesus is alive!" she said rapturously, her arms spread at her sides and her fists clenched. "You will not find a dead body, sir, though you may search for a thousand years because I have seen him! I was the first to see him, and to speak to him."

Paulus stared at her, knowing that his face revealed his disbelief, but he said calmly, "When you saw him, what was he wearing? Was he still in his grave clothes?"

She shook her head, smiling, and closed her eyes for a moment as if to calm herself. "No. He wore a robe. Like gardeners wear. He must have borrowed it from the caretaker of this tomb. We found his shroud lying there, where his body had been."

He tried to make sense out of what she had told him. There was no doubt in his mind that she had succumbed to the distress of seeing her friend and teacher killed and completely lost her reason!

"You said you were the first," he remarked. "Who else has seen him?"

Again she smiled a little. "Sir, I cannot tell you that."

"Who rolled the stone from the grave?"

She turned and looked at the great, circular stone. "Maybe it was the men we saw when we first looked inside the tomb."

"What men?"

Her face was lit as with some inner flame. "I think that when we got there, it had just happened. I had come with a few other women to finish placing the herbs around his body. As I told you there was not time on the day of his death to see to these things. This is our custom, but we had to wait until the Sabbath was over.

"We wondered what we would do about the stone. We even considered asking the Romans to move it. But when we got there, it was already moved. The guards were gone. When we looked inside—"

She stopped as her voice broke, and continued, "When we looked inside, the air seemed strange and . . . crackling with some kind of current, and there was a smell . . . it's going away now. There were two men inside whose faces were like . . . like lightning. And one of them said, 'Why do you seek the living among the dead? He is not here. He is risen.'"

For the third time that day something touched Paulus, touched him intimately this time in his heart, but he shoved it away as one might shove an outstretched hand.

"Who were these men?" he asked. "Where are they now?"

Her gaze was direct. "I didn't realize it then, but I do now. They were messengers from God. We call them angels." She added softly, and unnecessarily: "They are not here now."

"Where, then, was the Nazarene when you saw him?"

"I will tell you. We ran to tell the disciples what had happened—I was the one who actually told them. They did not believe me at first. But Peter and John ran to the tomb and looked inside. I followed them. There was nothing there except his grave clothes—the shroud and the cloth that had covered his face. The cloth had been quite neatly folded and set aside. They are gone now, as you can see.

"Then Peter and John left, but I stayed behind. I was distraught; I still didn't understand. When I looked inside again the two angels had returned and they asked me why I was weeping. I answered that someone had taken away the Lord's body and we didn't know where to find him. And then, I heard someone outside. I turned and saw a man. I supposed him to be the gardener. And he, too, asked me why I was weeping and who I was looking for."

A hushed silence fell. Paulus noticed that it was now completely dark except for the moonlight that gleamed off the woman's uplifted face.

"I said, 'Oh, sir, if you have taken him away please tell me where he is and I will go and get him!' I really don't know what I meant by that; I just wanted to know where he was! And then the man said, 'Mary.'"

She paused again but Paulus refrained from prompting her.

"When he said my name, I knew who he was. I hadn't really looked at him. But then I did look at him, and it was Jesus."

He didn't believe it but it was obvious that *she* did. "What did he look like? Just the same?" he asked, curious to see how far her imagination would carry her.

"No, not as he did when he died. There were no bruises or swelling. But the wounds on his hands and feet, places where there would be scars, are still there. And his hair is white."

Paulus said, surprised somehow by that detail, "You are certain it was the same man? How well did you know him?"

"A few years ago, he healed me of something—something quite terrible. I have been a follower ever since." She went on hesitantly. "How can I explain it? He is different, and yet the same. Before, there was a vulnerability about him like that of any other man. And now he looks . . . transformed. Indestructible."

"What do you mean—indestructible?"

"You have heard of Lazarus, how Jesus raised him from the dead? Everyone has heard of it. Well, Lazarus is still mortal. He looks like any other man. But Jesus' body is different. I cannot explain it. This is the only word I can think of. *Indestructible.*"

"Did you touch him?"

"He asked me not to touch him. I think there was something he needed to do before anyone could touch him. You would not understand it."

She seemed to rein in her thoughts and for the first time looked at him intently. "I saw you . . . that day. You didn't like it. You knew he was innocent."

Paulus frowned. "I need to know where his disciples are. They are in danger from the Sanhedrin perhaps, but not from me. I only want to know where the Nazarene's . . . where he is. Will you take me to him?"

"I know you think I'm insane," she said clearly. "You can take me to jail and torture me or whatever you Romans do to make your prisoners talk, but I will not betray my friends. Besides, I do not know where all of them are at this moment. Do what you must do."

Silently he cursed her stubbornness, thinking that she reminded him of Alysia. He looked into her eyes and knew that any further questioning was useless. Whatever she knew, she was going to keep it to herself . . . and maybe she knew nothing at all. Maybe she had been waiting here for him, or anyone else who might come to investigate, to fill his ears with some bizarre tale in order to give the disciples more time to dispose of the body they had stolen.

He tried once more. "I only want to question them. Will you tell me where I might find one—the leader? If this matter can be settled quietly, maybe the Sanhedrin will leave your people alone."

"The matter has already been settled, sir. I don't think it will be kept quiet for very long."

"Who has the burial shroud? Who took it?"

"I don't know who has it now. You see—" She lowered her head. "That is all I can tell you."

There was nothing more to say. He hesitated, then nodded solemnly to her and walked down the graveled path toward his horse. He had almost reached it, his footsteps grinding on the rocks, when he heard her say, "Sir?"

He turned. "Yes?"

"You asked me if I would take you to him. If I knew where he is right now, I would do it. But, perhaps, he will come to you."

He stood poised there in the moonlight until she turned away and disappeared into the shadows.

CHAPTER XXII

Paulus went to work with a zeal that surpassed anything he had ever done. He cared nothing about the dilemma of the Sanhedrin, or even Pilate, but finding the Nazarene's body became almost an obsession.

Never mind that there were things about his conjecture that the body had been stolen that did not make sense. He would concentrate on finding it, then unravel the mysteries. First there was Sirius, and what he and the other guards claimed they had seen. He had interrogated all of them and they all told essentially the same story, in different ways and with emphasis on different aspects—but still the same story. Since it was unlikely that they were all lying, especially since they had to admit to running away, then somehow they had been tricked into believing what they *thought* they had seen.

Second, there was the matter of the burial shroud. Why had the woman, Mary, placed such emphasis on the shroud, and why had the head covering been placed neatly aside? And third, the woman's story had been sincerely told—if only it weren't impossible to believe! The only conclusion he could draw was that an elaborate plan had been concocted to make it seem that the Nazarene had risen from the dead, involving sophisticated trickery and well, never mind all that. He would unravel that later, as well.

The thing that bothered him most was . . . why? Who had anything to gain by faking a resurrection? Not the Romans, not the Jews, and certainly not the disciples. Even if they had stolen the body, they could not endue it with life. Their leader was still dead. If *they* wanted to live they would disappear quietly into the country and never speak his name again.

These were difficulties, but not insurmountable. The alternative was impossible.

And as if all this weren't enough, he was forced to deal with Pilate and Herod. The two men had always disliked and distrusted each other, but they had formed an uneasy alliance when it came to the Nazarene. Which one approached the other first Paulus never knew but they had hatched a plan, deciding it would be a good idea to use the body of some other crucifixion victim and claim it to be the Nazarene's—after all, one dead and beaten Jew looked very much like another. It would prove to the people that the resurrection rumors were false; it would pacify the Sanhedrin and avert a great deal of unpleasantness.

"Do you think the Nazarene's followers are stupid?" Paulus all but shouted at them when he learned of it. He had called them both together and castigated them like schoolboys. Herod fumed in silence. Pilate only stared at him, concealing his sudden fear, and cursed the day he had ever heard of the Nazarene.

An intensive search began for the original twelve disciples, but no one would admit any knowledge of where the men were hiding. Rather, that was *eleven* disciples—one of them had supposedly killed himself. At last someone reported that they had been seen in Galilee. Paulus dispatched some men at once, but they returned after a few days saying the disciples had put out in a fishing boat and couldn't be found. It was thought that perhaps their boat had sunk. Paulus promptly sent the soldiers back to Galilee with a stern admonition not to return until they had proof to support their theories.

Mary the Magdalene was not seen again nor did anyone else venture to the tomb, which was being secretly watched. Each day that passed brought increasing frustration, with the knowledge that the Nazarene's body was decomposing to the extent that it would soon be impossible to identify.

But . . . he didn't necessarily have to have the body, if he could get one or more of the disciples to admit they had taken it.

Almost two months later, Paulus heard of a disturbance at a place in Jerusalem where the Jews were celebrating still another of their festivals, this one called Pentecost. The chief instigator was said to be the disciple, Peter. It was Peter's first public appearance since the night of the Nazarene's arrest. A worship service had somehow turned into such pandemonium that first the Temple police, then the Romans, were called in.

Thousands of people were involved. Reports came to him of a mysterious wind and flame, and people being able to speak in languages unknown to them. When Paulus arrived, the crowd had broken up and Peter had disappeared. A dozen or so people were brought to the Antonia, among them a man named Jonas who had been caught uttering loud praises and prayers to the Nazarene. Paulus himself interviewed the man, for his initial inquisitors had considered his story so unlikely that he was slapped around a bit before Centurion Marcus Terentias intervened and referred him to Paulus.

"I have said these people are not to be harmed," Paulus said, observing the red marks on the man's face. "Inform the men again of this order, Centurion, and punish those who do not obey it."

"Yes, Legate." Marcus left the room. Two guards remained at the door and Paulus dismissed them also.

When they were alone, he looked closely at the man before him. He was short and heavyset, with long, stringy hair and a wart on his chin. Not a pretty sight, to be sure . . . still, there was a certain radiance about him.

"Your name is Jonas and you are from Jerusalem," Paulus said. "How do you know the dead Nazarene?"

"Before he died, he gave me sight," replied the man, with equal directness. His speech was slightly affected by noticeably bad teeth.

"You mean you were blind, and he healed you."

"Blind from birth. I never asked him to—never thought it was possible. He just did it."

Paulus was, by now, accustomed to hearing reports of miraculous goings-on and it was easier to hide his skepticism. "And *how* did he do it? Simply by a word?"

"No." Jonas scratched his head. "They say he often healed with a word, but this time he made clay and put it on my eyes and told me to go to the Pool of Siloam and wash it off. When I did, I could see."

"So, what did you think of him? That he was a healer, or a god?"

The man looked faintly amused. "The Pharisees asked me the same question. Then they went and got my parents and made them swear I'd really been born blind. I'll tell you the same thing I told them . . . if this man weren't of God, he couldn't have done it!"

"And what did they say to that?"

Jonas grinned. "They said I was a miserable sinner, and how dared I try to teach *them* anything and then they threw me out the door."

"So, they didn't believe it?"

The man shook his head. "When Jesus heard about what had happened, he came looking for me. He asked me if I believed he was the son of God. He said he had come into the world to give sight to the blind and to take it away from those who could see."

This caught Paulus' interest. "What did he mean by that?"

Jonas scratched his head again. "There was more to it than that, but I can't remember all the words. Seemed to me like he was talking about those Pharisees. They think their spiritual eyes are wide open, when they're really as blind as I was. And those who are blind of the spirit but really *want* to see, that are seeking the truth—those eyes he will open."

Paulus asked, "What did you answer when he asked if you believed he was the son of God?"

The man looked amazed. "Said I believed it, of course. But my answer won't do *you* any good! You've got to answer it yourself."

"Never mind what I believe. Where is the Nazarene now?"

"I don't know."

"Where do you think he is? Have you seen him lately?"

"No. I never did see him after the crucifixion. But I know people who did."

"Where can I find them? I would like to speak with them."

Jonas eyed him from under bushy brows. "Don't want to get anyone in trouble."

"Why do you people keep doing this?" Paulus said, exasperated. "Why do you insist on speaking his name, and preaching about him, and even worshipping this dead man, when all it means is getting into trouble with the Sanhedrin? I hear they've already thrown several of you into jail."

"Well." Jonas smiled at him again. "I suppose it's because we're either plain stupid, or we're telling the truth. And if we're telling the truth, we can't help but worship him, can we?"

Failing to get any further useful information from the man, Paulus released him. Two more weeks passed. Some of the disciples were seen in various places but had a way of vanishing before they could be seized—as if they were under some sort of protection, divine or otherwise.

As a last resort, he decided to go to the one person who might trust him enough to help him.

Having drawn a lamp close to the table, Alysia yawned over the scrolls she was reading and wondered at the lateness of the hour. She was alone, with Rachel asleep in the next room. Now that Rachel was old enough to walk, Judith had moved back to Lazarus' house.

The scrolls belonged to Lazarus; they were copies of the Jewish history books and some of the prophets. Her interest in the subjects had increased in the last few months—ever since it had happened. The unthinkable, the unknowable…the tragic and yet wonderful thing…and though she had not witnessed the tragic part, she had seen the wonderful!

She started when a light but urgent rapping came on the door. Putting the scrolls aside she walked to the barred door. "Who is it?"

"Alysia, it's Paulus."

She pressed a hand over her heart and took a deep breath, then quickly unbolted the door and swung it open. She couldn't speak, her eyes wide and flying to meet the vivid blue ones that gleamed from the familiar, sun-bronzed face.

His gaze flicked swiftly about the room as he came in and closed the door behind him. "You are alone?"

"Yes." They stared into each other's eyes for a long, searching moment, then as though by some unspoken and mutual understanding each looked away, Paulus at the scrolls she'd been reading and Alysia at nothing in particular. She tried to avoid a nervous glance toward the room where Rachel was sleeping.

"Paulus, what's wrong?"

He relaxed somewhat and looked at her closely, this time avoiding her eyes. She seemed tired and the skin was drawn tightly over the high planes of her face. Her head covering was down about her shoulders with her rich black hair tumbling over it. The homespun robe she wore was dyed a dark green and fell to her ankles, and he noticed her thinness even under the loose folds of her gown. Her feet were bare.

"Have you been well?"

"Yes, and you?"

He nodded, glancing at a bench. "May I sit down?"

"Of course."

He pulled out the bench and she sat down across from him. The lamplight cast shadows over the contours of his face and burnished his hair to dark gold. His brown tunic clung to his broad shoulders and his eyes glittered with a strange intensity.

Before speaking again, Paulus glanced around the room. Simon had told him where Alysia lived and it was the first time he had seen her house. He was surprised by its smallness and more than a little displeased by its bareness. Alysia was meant to live in a mansion, not a hovel; she was meant to wear gowns of silk, not rough homespun!

But she seemed content, and rather than risk offending her he swallowed his indignation and said nothing about her humble state.

His emotions, more compelling, more forceful than he had expected, demanded closer contact than a table's breadth apart. In fact, the taxing of his self-restraint was so severe that he wondered how he would endure this meeting. He should not have come.

She was waiting, toying with the edge of her mantle, noticing his reluctance to speak.

"Alysia," he said finally, in a slow, careful way, "I did not want to do this, but I need information. I thought you might help me."

She looked puzzled. "I will try."

He paused, and then went on. "This Nazarene—Jesus. I'm sure you know that he is dead?"

She said as carefully, "I know that he was crucified, and died, and was buried. That's been months ago. Everyone has heard by now."

"And what else have you heard?"

She raised her eyes to meet his. "That he rose again."

"The Sanhedrin is claiming that the body was stolen by his followers. Pilate has asked me to find some evidence of a hoax before this rumor gets out of control."

"The—rumor—is already all over Judea, and probably Galilee," Alysia said calmly.

"Then why has there not been a revolt? Do the people believe in this—resurrection?"

"A revolt against the Sanhedrin would accomplish nothing. And yes, many of us do believe."

Paulus stared at her. "*You* believe it?"

"Yes. I saw him."

She noticed with dismay his expression of incredulity, mixed somehow with disappointment as if she had let him down in the uttermost way.

Paulus' hands gripped the edge of the table. "You saw him?"

Alysia nodded slowly. "Just a few days after the crucifixion. And then twice afterward. Scores of people saw him, Paulus."

"How can you be sure it was the Nazarene you saw? What did he look like? Did he speak to you?"

"I'm sure. He looked exactly the same, except—"

Her words seemed to hang in the air as she considered how she would convey this to him and Paulus found the suspense more than he could stand.

"Except—"

"I didn't know what had happened until after I saw him. And so, the scars were something of a shock to me. And his hair is completely white."

That detail alone, first revealed by the woman of Magdala, would have been enough to convince him—had it involved anything but the bringing of a dead man back to life!

Paulus got to his feet and stood with his shoulder lightly braced against the wall, staring at her, almost looking through her. He was thoroughly disconcerted to see her certainty, her confidence. There was indeed a radiance in her eyes that had never been there before—the same radiance he'd seen in the Magdalene and the man named Jonas, and countless others.

"If he is alive, why does he not show himself in the streets of Jerusalem? Why not prove to the priests he is a God?"

"He has shown himself—to many people—hundreds of people. Why should he do so to the priests who crucified him? They will never believe in him, even if they should see him!"

"Where is he?"

She lowered her eyes. "Neither would you believe me, if I told you."

Exasperated, he asked, "Where are his disciples?"

"I am his disciple. He has thousands, all over Palestine."

"I mean the original twelve. Or eleven. I hear one of them is dead."

"Paulus, are you asking me to betray them?"

"I will not harm them. I only wish to talk to them."

Alysia gazed at him, troubled. "Do I have your word that you won't arrest them, or threaten them?"

"You have my word."

She drew another deep breath. "There is to be a meeting in a fortnight at Lazarus' house, just after the sun sets. I don't know where all the disciples are but I know that some of them will be there."

He looked into her eyes. "Thank you, Alysia."

"You had better come dressed as you did—that other time. They have no reason to trust a Roman."

"I will." He sat down again and continued to look at her, until she dropped her gaze in confusion. Since that matter was settled, Paulus decided to cast discretion to the wind and asked, with a rough edge to his voice, "Alysia, are you happy here?"

She lifted her head and a smile touched her lips. "Sometimes I dwell too much on the past, but I am at peace here." A look of joy and wonder crossed her face and she said, "Paulus, if only you could have seen him—if only you knew!"

Again he was reminded of the woman, Mary, for the expression on her face had been exactly what he now saw in Alysia's. A feeling of helplessness seized him. He couldn't call Alysia a liar, nor did he think she was mad. He didn't know what to think.

She reached out and touched his arm. "Please listen to me, Paulus. I used to wonder why it was so—so galling to me to be a slave. I actually believed it was a fate worse than death. And it was simply because I was so proud. Too proud to actually have to *serve* others.

"And that is what will stop you from following Jesus. Pride will hold you back because you must surrender—everything. But it's not slavery. It's liberation *from* slavery. It's freedom from yourself and all the chains that have ever held you—like selfishness and hatred and anger and fear. Not that you would never feel those things again, but he carries them for you and helps you to overcome . . . oh, it's too difficult to explain!"

"Alysia," he said, trying to speak gently. "I can respect your feelings for this—this new religion but don't try to convert me into it."

"It's not a religion. And it isn't new. It has all been planned since before the creation of the world."

Confused, he met her eyes. She went on. "He waited until the time was right, and he came."

"It sounds like a hopeless tangle of Jewish superstition to me."

"Then watch what happens. See if it survives and what price men and women are willing to pay for their belief. If it's all over, Paulus, why haven't the disciples gone back to their homes, to their families and professions? It would be so easy to do that. Especially when the Sanhedrin is threatening to kill them. Why is the fire spreading, instead of dying out?"

He shrugged. "Men have always been willing to die for some ill-conceived cause."

"For a cause perhaps, but not for a dead man!"

Alysia paused, and added reluctantly, "You are not ready to hear this. Maybe we should speak of other things."

"Yes," he agreed. "Let's do."

"I will tell Lazarus to expect you. I feel certain he will recognize you but he won't say anything. Is there anyone else who might have seen you—that day?"

"The young man, the youngest of his followers, was there."

"That was John. He's in Nazareth now, helping Jesus' mother settle her affairs. She is moving to Jerusalem."

"What about the Pharisee? And the other man—I think he was a member of the Sanhedrin as well."

"Nicodemus and Joseph. Neither of them will come. This meeting is for people who want to know what happened that day."

Paulus felt uncomfortable. "How did you know I was there?"

"Lazarus told me. But he said you didn't seem to have anything to do with it."

"Alysia, I would have released him, if I could. The whole thing seemed . . . out of control, somehow."

"I have never blamed you. They said that Pilate conducted the trial but it was the priests who condemned him."

He shook his head; he had had enough talk of the Nazarene. He reached across the table and placed his hand over hers. "I miss you."

She wanted to tell him she missed him too. She wanted to tell him that not a day went by that she didn't dream of what it would be like to be his wife. She opened her mouth and never knew what she was about to say, for at that moment sounds came from the next room…a stirring, a whimper. Alysia's face seemed to drain of color and her hands clenched. Paulus moved his own hand away and became perfectly still, staring fixedly at Alysia.

Rachel tottered into the room. She went to her mother, held up her arms to be lifted, and twisted about to look at Paulus. Her tousled hair was the color of honey, her eyes dark blue, and she looked remarkably like his sister, Selena.

He could not speak. Her age . . . her looks! The truth and all its implications crowded upon him without mercy. As through a fog he saw Alysia's stricken face and was aware that she carried the child back to her bed. She was gone for some time. When she returned he was still sitting in exactly the same pose of stunned disbelief.

"Why," he said, over something large and oppressive in his chest, "didn't you tell me?"

Alysia tried to draw a deep breath. She sat down at the table and stared at her folded hands. Oddly, she felt as if she herself had just received a stunning blow.

"I was afraid," she said quietly. "I was afraid to let anyone know who her father was and I knew you would want her. I was afraid you might take her from me."

He swore and got to his feet. She had never seen him so angry. He didn't shout but the effect was worse than if he had begun tearing down the house.

"What kind of man do you think I am?"

All at once she felt sick—sick in her very soul. She'd been wrong, terribly wrong. He would never have been so unfeeling as to take her child from her! In her heart she had known that. Why, then, hadn't she told him?

"I'm sorry," she managed to whisper.

He made a tremendous effort to calm himself. He strode backward and forward across the room and finally sat down again, across from her. After an eternity he said, "I don't know if I can ever forgive you for this."

The old spirit of defiance brought her chin up. "You must forgive me! I have forgiven you everything—and there was much to forgive! I don't know why I didn't tell you. I didn't really believe you would take her away, but it would have made things so much more . . . difficult. I was confused, and alone." She didn't add *why* she was alone; she would not throw that in his face.

After another long pause he asked, "Is she well?"

"Yes."

"What is her name?"

"It is Rachel."

"I don't want you to think that I'm not . . . happy to have a child." He started to say more, and then looked as if he couldn't bear to. He stood, not looking at her, and strode to the door. "I suppose I will see you at this meeting of the disciples?"

"Yes." She rose quickly to stand beside him. "Paulus, don't go. We must speak of this—"

He looked down at her, his face close to hers. "You say you believe in this Jesus, who prized the truth, and all the time you lied to me by your silence. And you believed a lie, as if I could hurt you that way or willfully bring shame upon you and our child."

"I don't know why I was afraid, Paulus. I couldn't give her up, even for a little while. She is all I have of this world. It was not an easy choice to make. Don't think it wasn't painful for me!"

He asked, in that quiet, impersonal voice, "Do you still love me, Alysia?"

Tears stung her eyes and she could barely squeeze the words past the lump in her throat. "You know I do."

He paused and said evenly, "But you didn't trust me with what you hold most dear."

The door closed and he was gone.

When Paulus returned to the Antonia he went at once to the room Simon occupied next to his own. Not bothering to knock, he flung open the door so that the lamps in the corridor flared and dimly illumined the cubicle.

Simon started up, half falling out of bed, and seeing the legate got quickly to his feet. He couldn't see Paulus' face with the lights at his back but the cold tone of his voice confirmed Simon's suspicion that something was greatly amiss.

"Simon, did I not ask you to report on the welfare of a certain young woman in Bethany?"

"Yes, sir."

"And you knew who she was because you had seen her before, spoken with her before?"

"Yes, sir."

"Then why, in the name of every god that man in his stupidity ever imagined, did you not tell me she had a child?"

Simon stared into the darkness where Paulus' face must be. He looked completely baffled, Paulus thought…but how was it possible that he didn't know? At last Simon spread his arms out helplessly.

"There was a woman with her who carried a child, sir. But I had no idea it was *hers*! Now that I think of it, there were times I went to Bethany and she was nowhere to be seen—I suppose women do hide themselves when they are with child. But I inquired about her among some of the townsfolk, pretending to be a relative, and was always told she was doing well. I think they might have been somewhat suspicious of me and didn't say much. The idea that she had had a child never occurred to me. I never saw her holding one."

"Well, Simon, it seems we've both been remarkably slow witted."

"Yes, sir."

"I'm sorry I disturbed you. Goodnight."

Simon watched him leave the room and heard the legate pacing in his own, far into the night.

After Paulus left, Alysia made certain Rachel was asleep and then sat down again and put her head in her hands. Her feelings alternated between regret for her own actions and anger at Paulus. After all the things she had forgiven and forgotten, or tried to forget, he had the effrontery to say what *she* had done was unforgivable! And Paulus' offenses extended over the entire time she had been a slave until he ordered the death of her own husband—even if it had been in the course of his duty!

She lifted her head and stared indignantly at the wall. Then her eyes fell on the scrolls she had been reading earlier, and suddenly she thought of *him*, and what *he* had taught about forgiveness. Her resentment began to leave her. She remembered the night she had spoken to him of her own need for forgiveness.

And then she thought, as she did over and over, of the last time she had talked alone with him . . .

It was the first day of the week in the days following the Passover. Many people were still in Jerusalem; Lazarus and his sisters had not returned. She'd been walking toward the well in the center of town, alone, enjoying the solitude and the early, clean beauty of the day. A man had fallen into step with her, and when she glanced at him, she was struck by the familiarity of his form and the way he walked. Men never walked next to women. Except . . .

Now she looked at his face, noticing the almost startling contrast between his flowing white hair, black eyebrows, and dark eyes. His short beard was white, too, against skin that was smooth and tanned. When she finally looked into his eyes she stopped abruptly and dropped her water jar. Miraculously, it did not break.

He stopped, too, and he was smiling at her, his eyes kind, the same and yet different, filled with some indefinable quality that rendered her speechless.

"Greetings, Alysia," he said, in the same clear voice.

At last she whispered, "What has happened to you?"

"I saw you walking here and wanted to speak with you. You haven't heard of what happened in Jerusalem."

"You mean, the darkness?"

"Yes," he said, "but the darkness has turned to light."

She stared at him, bewildered. He bent and retrieved the water jar and handed it to her. When he did so, she noticed the rounded holes in his wrists. She would have dropped the jar again if he had not closed his own hands over hers.

"Lazarus and his sisters have not yet seen me, but they will. Tell them. And I tell you truly, there is a man, a man you know well, who will do a mighty work in my name. As will you. You would have believed without seeing me, but for him it will be more difficult. Pray for him."

He released the jar into her hands and was gone. She stood immobilized for a long time. Had he just disappeared into thin air? She doubted her own senses; she sat down on the great stones encircling the well and looked down the road, this way and that. It was as though he had opened an invisible door and walked through it!

She still, at that time, did not understand, had not known what happened until Lazarus and his sisters returned to Bethany the next day. She had been shocked and dismayed to hear about his crucifixion, but not surprised to hear the rest of the story. She already knew.

A man who would have trouble believing, and yet would do a great work in his name. She had known, even then, who Jesus meant. But how could that ever be? Why couldn't Jesus have just appeared to him? It would have made things so much easier . . . it would take much, much prayer. It would take a miracle.

CHAPTER XXIII

Shades of magenta and gold touched the western sky, interspersed with wisps of purple clouds. A light breeze stirred as Alysia walked the short distance to Lazarus' house. She was strangely excited; knowing that Paulus would be there made everything seem different, somehow. It would be difficult to act as if she didn't know him.

She knocked on the door, waiting nervously until it opened, and Martha took her past the courtyard and up the outer stairs to the roof. She quickly scanned those who were present and saw that Paulus had not yet arrived. There were several residents of the town that she knew to be believers, among them Simon, the former leper. Peter was there, with Andrew and James. She was introduced to a man named Stephen. She had heard of him; he was a Hellenistic Jew, as everyone believed *her* to be. Mary sat at a small table with a pen and sheets of papyrus, as if she intended to make a written record of the meeting.

Lazarus nodded and smiled a greeting, and went on talking in low tones with the other men. She had told him that Paulus was coming, that he would not be dressed as a soldier, and there was nothing to fear from him. She could only hope it was true, considering the seriousness with which he took his duty! Lazarus, she thought, must have guessed the truth about them after seeing Paulus and the strong resemblance her daughter bore to him. Yet he had never said or implied anything to cause her embarrassment.

Burning lamps sat on top of the low wall surrounding the rooftop, and beneath the gaily colored awning were several comfortable cushions. Alysia sat down on one of them, next to Mary, who smiled and asked, "Judith has Rachel this evening?"

"Yes. What are you writing, Mary?"

"It is a record of many of the things Jesus said and did. It will be in Aramaic, of course. I thought that, when you have time, you could make a copy in Greek."

Alysia stopped in mid-nod as she saw Paulus come up the stairs onto the roof. He wore a rust-colored robe and might have been Greek, Roman, or even Galilean—many of whom had fair hair and blue eyes. He had let his hair and beard grow; if she didn't know him well she might not have recognized him herself! Lazarus went immediately to meet him and Paulus responded in perfect Aramaic.

Lazarus turned to the others. "This is Paulus, a friend from Jerusalem."

After a brief exchange of greetings, she saw Peter eye Paulus a little skeptically, as if he sensed something about him, or as if he might have seen him before. Lazarus caught Peter's eye and nodded a little. Peter raised his black eyebrows but said nothing as Paulus took the seat shown him by Lazarus. His eyes met Alysia's briefly, then each sought to avoid the other's gaze.

Everyone became quiet and attentive. Peter stood before them, outlined against the setting sun.

"I have called this meeting for one purpose. All, or most of you, were close to Jesus while he was here. You ate with him, talked with him, and walked throughout the country with him. It is important for each of you to know everything that has happened since we entered Jerusalem for the Passover. Some of you—Andrew and Lazarus and James—already know most of it. They are here to confirm what I am going to tell you. Some may find it difficult to believe." His glance fell on Paulus, who returned his look unwaveringly.

Alysia was noticing the change in Peter. His former brashness had become a more humble, but still bold, aura of confidence. It seemed that even the contours of his face had altered, becoming sharper and more pronounced, so that he had the stern, implacable countenance of a rock. But his eyes were kind in spite of their wariness, displaying a compassion and patience in which he'd been found lacking until now.

Paulus made a conscious attempt to dismiss Alysia from his thoughts. It was difficult, for he'd thought of little else for the past two weeks but her, and the child she had kept a secret from him. This had even crowded out his thoughts of the Nazarene. But now, as he listened to Peter, his own problems began to recede and his interest heightened until he was no longer aware of anything but the story unfolding before him.

The words penetrated into his deepest being; it seemed that a ray of light had somehow pierced a crevice of his soul and was shining in, exploring . . .

"That night he tried to warn us of what was to come. He said that we would all be scattered, that one of us would betray him, and that I—before morning came—would deny three times that I even knew him." Peter stopped then and looked away for a moment. His voice grew a bit gruffer. "Of course, I swore it would never happen! I was ready, I said, to die for him. Even if everyone else deserted him, I never would!

"We—that is, eleven of us—went to Gethsemane, the place across from the valley. Part of it is a public garden and there's an olive grove there, where we often went at night when he wanted to be alone. Jesus asked James and John and me to stay close, and he walked about a stone's throw away from us. And he...began to pray. But not as we had ever seen him pray before. He seemed to be in great anguish. There was a huge rock there, and sometimes he knelt beside it. Sometimes he lay prostrate on the ground. He would come to us and ask us to pray, but we were awed and almost horrified...we hardly knew what to pray for. There was a sense of great oppression. I cannot describe it. We waited for so long that we finally fell asleep.

"Then we heard voices shouting. We woke to see the place filled with the Temple guards armed with spears and cudgels and carrying torches. Even a few Roman soldiers. Everything was lit with a red glow. And Judas was there in the midst of them. Judas, the betrayer."

There was utter silence for a moment. Peter's listeners found themselves leaning slightly forward. He went on, steadily. "The signal was, we discovered later, that Judas would give the kiss of greeting to the man they were to arrest. There was so much confusion and moving around...there were so many of us. When he did so, Jesus said something to him—I didn't hear the words, but I think John did. John could add much to this. I wish he were here. But even after Judas identified Jesus, they made no move to arrest him. They just stood there.

"Jesus asked them who they were looking for. They said, 'Jesus of Nazareth.' He answered that he was that man. But still they made no move toward him. Some of them even fell to the ground, as if... in awe."

Peter looked intently at the faces before him. "I cannot explain this, except to say that there was something about Jesus at that moment...so majestic, and God-like, that even we who knew him were overwhelmed. Again, he asked them who they were looking for, and again they answered, 'Jesus of Nazareth.' Jesus said, 'I told you that I am he. Let these others go.'

"When Jesus said that, something happened to me and I became like a wild man. James and I both had swords with us. I struck out at the man closest to Jesus, aiming for his head, and cut off his ear. Whether I meant to kill him or not I cannot say, even to this day. Jesus put out his hand to stop me and said, with great emotion, 'Put away your sword. Shall I not drink the cup my Father has given me?' There was a great deal of pushing and shouting around us, and during the commotion Jesus touched the man's ear and healed it.

"By then, we were surrounded by the guards. But they only took Jesus. They bound him and led him away. We all stood for a while in the dark, trying to think what to do. Yes, we had deserted him. Judas had already left us; he went and tried to give the money back to the priests, the money they had given him to lead them to Jesus. He said that he had . . . betrayed innocent blood. But the priests wouldn't take it. He went out and hanged himself from a tree, though we didn't know all this until much later. The branch had broken off the tree and the body fell down into a ravine."

"Why, Peter?" called out an old man, who had tears rolling down his face. "Why did Judas betray him?"

The disciple shook his head. "Some say greed. Some say he believed Jesus was going to lead a rebellion against the Romans and was trying to force him to take a stand. Some say he was possessed by Satan. But only Judas really knows. And Jesus."

Darkness had fallen and now Peter stood against a backdrop of stars, the lamps flaring and smoking around him. His voice thickened and he spoke slowly, as if reluctant to go on.

"Finally, John and I began to follow Jesus—at a distance. The initial hearing was held at the house of Annas, the former High Priest. Little was accomplished there. I'm sure I need not tell you that so many laws were broken by the Sanhedrin during these trials that it was all a complete travesty. It was the only way they could deal with an innocent man! From there they took him to Caiaphas' house. Only certain people were admitted, and John was one of them. Caiaphas knows John and his family. But I don't believe the High Priest knew John was there—a servant let him in. I stayed in the courtyard. There was a fire and several people around it.

"John said that the interrogation was very severe. That they beat Jesus and spat on him and treated him with the utmost contempt. I could hear some of it, when they were yelling at him. One of the servants, a young woman, accused me of being one of his disciples. All I could think of was being dragged in there and treated the same way. I said . . . I didn't know him."

Someone said, "Oh," in a sympathetic way, but Peter seemed not to hear.

"Another woman began talking about seeing me with Jesus, and so one of the men accused me. I denied knowing him—again. Then, someone else who turned out to be a relative of the man whose ear I cut off, looked at me and said, 'I know I saw you in the garden with him.' And, I cursed at him. I swore, 'I do not know the man!' At that exact moment, two things happened. A rooster crowed for it was almost morning, and they pushed Jesus out onto the courtyard. He looked directly at me."

Peter stopped. He turned slowly and sat down on the wall, looking again at the faces around him. "I need not tell you of my remorse. I need not tell you how bitterly I wept. I hid the rest of the day, hid and wept like a child." He paused, and his eyes seemed to blaze in the lamplight. "I will never deny him again."

Lazarus stood and laid his hand briefly on Peter's shoulder. He took up the story.

"Andrew came to the house where my sisters and I were staying and told me Jesus had been arrested. I arrived at Caiaphas' house after the first interrogation. They took Jesus down to a room beneath the house and left him tied there while certain members of the Sanhedrin discussed what they would do—behind closed doors. None of us except John heard anything, but I don't think they were quite prepared. They hadn't wanted to do this during the Passover but Judas had gone to them and made his offer.

"At last they brought Jesus back out, in chains this time; they really believed he was going to elude them as he had in the past. They took him to the Antonia Fortress to be sentenced by Pontius Pilate. They had not the authority to condemn him to death. But Pilate was a bit more stubborn than they expected. He tried to put it off on Herod, but Herod couldn't get Jesus to say anything at all and sent him back to Pilate. The prefect wanted to release him."

Paulus sat back a little; Lazarus had thrown the barest glance in his direction. Lazarus spoke lower than Peter and with less intensity, yet with the same calm assurance.

"Pilate had Jesus scourged. The Romans dressed him like a king and mocked him. With great cruelty, I might add. All the time he said not a word of rebuke. He only answered the questions Pilate put to him. Again, John was there through it all. But the prefect gave in to the priests, and the crowd. They crucified him between two others."

Here Lazarus seemed overcome by emotion; he stopped for a long moment. Many of his listeners were wiping tears.

"He spoke several times from the cross. You know the things he said, for they have been repeated many times. Mary, you know them—write them. You know of the darkness and the quaking of the earth as he died. And he was *dead*, my dear friends. A Roman lance thrust into his side made certain of it. And then two men who were secret followers, Joseph and Nicodemus, came forward to help bury him. They purchased linen and spices to prepare his body. Joseph offered the use of his own tomb."

Now Paulus leaned forward again. His heart began to pound in his head and in his ears so that he had to strain to hear.

"As they were doing this and discussing arrangements, so much time elapsed that it was almost the beginning of the Passover Sabbath. I think everyone here knows that, according to our law, the handling of dead bodies is not permitted on the Sabbath. Someone, an officer, ordered the soldiers to help us get the body off the cross. We carried him to the tomb, in the garden near Joseph's house. We wrapped him in the linen cloth and put the few spices they had been able to buy around his body and left him there. The entrance was then sealed and guarded by the Romans.

"After three days, Mary of Magdala and some other women went to the tomb with more spices, intending to complete the burial. But they found the tomb empty and the guards nowhere in sight. Mary ran to tell the disciples, but they didn't believe her. At last, Peter and John went to the tomb and found it as the women had said.

"When I heard about it, I went to the house where the disciples were staying and I was there when Jesus appeared to them that evening. At first we were afraid, thinking he was a ghost. But he wasn't a ghost. He let us touch him; he spoke to us and reassured us."

Peter nodded. "It is hard to believe. But we *saw* him. He was seen here in Bethany. He was seen that very day on the road to Emmaus. He has been seen in many places by many people. And most of you saw him on the day he left us, on the Mount of Olives not far from here. You heard what he said; you saw him taken up by what appeared to be a cloud. And you heard the two men—angels—say that he would return in just the same manner."

It was over. No one said anything for a long time. Looking from one person to another, Paulus saw that his was the only pair of dry eyes. He alone remained bereft of something wonderful and glowing that shone from the faces around him. Whatever questions he had wanted to ask were forgotten. Any questioning at all would have seemed incongruous in this atmosphere of reverence and quiet elation.

He frowned a little, still looking from person to person. Many were nodding at Lazarus' words. The man named Stephen was looking up beyond the edge of the awning into the night sky and he seemed apart from them all, as though he understood something even Peter and Lazarus had not yet grasped. Alysia, too, brushed at her tears; she, too, wore an expression of serenity and of some ineffable knowledge.

I really don't know her at all, he thought, and a vast loneliness engulfed him.

The others began talking in low voices. It seemed clear to him that he did not belong; he quickly said something to Lazarus and took his leave. Later, he would have no memory of the walk back to Jerusalem.

Then he remembered something—something that Peter had said, and it burned within him like an inner fire that didn't consume, but instead cleansed and comforted. Peter had repeated Jesus' words: *"Put away your sword."* For the first time since that terrible day Paulus felt an almost insupportable burden begin to shift. He had not imagined those words. In some inexplicable way, the Nazarene had imparted that same message to him.

Somehow it was not meant that he should intervene in the events of that day. But if that were true, if there were indeed some "divine" plan being carried out, he would have to admit the existence of God. And if he went that far, he might as well admit that the Nazarene had exhibited all the qualifications a god might have…except that Paulus knew he was human.

Paulus had seen him bruised and bleeding, torn literally to shreds and nailed to a cross.

He had seen him die.

All the guests departed except for the three disciples. Martha, yawning, went down the steps to enter the house. Alysia remained sitting next to Mary, who continued to write, her brow furrowed with concentration. The men had gathered close by and were talking.

"Who was that man, the one called Paulus?" Peter asked, and now they had Alysia's full attention. "You called him a friend, Lazarus. Yet he's not one of us."

"I know him," Lazarus replied, without hesitation. "I think he *will* be one of us, someday. Perhaps soon rather than late."

"He seemed troubled," said Andrew. "How do you know you can trust him?"

"What does it matter who we can trust?" said Lazarus mildly. "We need only trust God."

Peter looked thoughtful. "He had the bearing of a soldier. He *is* a Roman, isn't he? He could have arrested us all. Just to satisfy my curiosity, why did you bring him here?"

"He asked to come. And there were things he needed to hear."

CHAPTER XXIV

"What? Is my stepbrother actually taking time out from his duties? The world must be coming to an end!"

Lucius' mocking voice interrupted Paulus' thoughts as he swam another length of the huge, marble pool. He pushed his hair back from his face and looked up to see the tribune, in full uniform, standing above him. Maybe if he ignored him, he would go away. Paulus kept swimming, feeling the stretch and pull of muscles and tendons as he ploughed expertly through the cold water.

The Antonia's gymnasium was new and immaculate, resounding with men's voices and their hollow echoes. Paulus had had the building constructed soon after his arrival, for though Herod the Great had lavished his attention on luxurious details he had not provided a place for those inclined to more athletic pursuits. Gymnasiums were not as popular in Rome as they were in Greece…Rome preferred the baths, which Paulus considered an inexcusable waste of time. He saw to it that there were rooms equipped not only for swimming, but for the practice of swordplay and mock fist fighting.

Lucius didn't go away. At last, Paulus emerged from the pool. A slave handed him a towel and he sat down on a bench, rubbing the linen over his face and hair. "Do you wish to speak with me?" he inquired, none too pleasantly.

"If you don't mind," said Lucius with exaggerated politeness.

Paulus rose and walked to the other end of the room toward the dressing chamber and began to put on his clothes. Lucius strutted after him.

"Well?" he prompted impatiently.

"I want to know," said Lucius, "what you are going to do about this new cult."

"Cult?" Paulus repeated with indifference, pulling his tunic over his head and fastening the belt around his waist.

"The followers of this Nazarene—the one they call Christ." A thinly disguised look of hostility crept into Lucius' gaze. "They've actually begun preaching in the streets. The Jews cannot control them. Who wants to hear their drivel?"

"You don't have to listen to them," Paulus said shortly as he tied his dagger into place.

"They are a nuisance! They're disturbing the peace. Jerusalem hasn't been the same since this Jew was killed. Even some of the largest and oldest businesses are suffering, the wealthiest men in the city, because so many of these stupid Christ-followers won't patronize the shops of those who opposed their leader!"

Paulus gave him a cool stare. "For someone who has always criticized my intolerance of certain things, you seem to have acquired a large measure of it yourself. You are free to leave anytime, Lucius."

"So, you're going to do nothing? I'm sure the emperor would be interested in learning what is happening here, how these people prattle that the Nazarene is their king!"

Paulus sat down to put on his shoes. "It is not Rome they object to. They don't think of him as an earthly king; it has to do with their religion. But by all means, go ahead and write the emperor. Maybe he will appoint you to get rid of these . . . troublemakers."

"It seems I am wasting my time. I would almost believe you are sympathetic to the fools." Lucius began to stride arrogantly from the room but turned to say over his shoulder, "You've had something on your mind for a long time now, Paulus. Don't think I'm not watching you."

"It's regrettable that I am your main source of entertainment—your life must be exceedingly dull. Maybe it *is* time for you to leave Jerusalem."

Lucius stopped. "I seem to be the only Roman in Judea with any sense of alarm over this new movement. Pilate has washed his hands of it, literally, and Herod is so afraid of seeing ghosts he won't come out of his palace. The Jewish Council can only beat them and put them into prison, which hasn't discouraged them in the least! You are the one to stop this, Paulus, before it gets out of hand."

Paulus stood up. "Do whatever you feel is your duty, Lucius. As long as it falls under your authority—which, correct me if I'm wrong, I believe you have none."

Lucius' eyes bore into his stepbrother's. "I came here to express my concern over a faction that is growing more rapidly than anyone would suspect. You show no interest; therefore, my next step will be to write the legate in Syria."

"He and I have already discussed the matter. These followers of the Nazarene are not violent. Neither of us feel it necessary to restrain them at this point."

"If it is not stopped it will reach all the way to Rome! Violence is not the only precursor to rebellion, Paulus. There are more subtle ways of invasion, of change and corruption."

Paulus laughed outright. "Corruption? There are not many ways left to corrupt Rome!" Inclining his head toward the door, he added, "Sentry, escort the tribune back to his lodging."

Lucius drew back his shoulders and glared at the approaching legionary. "That will not be necessary. I'm going and I won't return—until you no longer command this fort. And that, Paulus, might be sooner than you anticipate."

If Lucius were just an irritation, like a mosquito only noticed when it's buzzing around one's head, Paulus would have dismissed his stepbrother from his mind and left him to his own foolish devices. But he continued to be a danger to Alysia and now he had focused on the followers of the Nazarene. He would have to be dealt with. Paulus would have to expel him back to Rome and with a good enough reason to convince either Pilate or the governor of Syria to agree with him, not to mention Lucius' high-ranking friends in Rome. Why Lucius liked Jerusalem so well was a puzzle, or maybe not, now that he thought about it. There were enough Roman influences here to please any urbane young man. And there was Salome, Herod's stepdaughter, with whom Lucius spent many obviously enjoyable hours.

He also happened to know that Lucius had often been seen in the company of Servius, one of the legionaries who had kidnapped Alysia three years ago. When Servius was not on duty they frequented the same gambling and drinking halls and other places of ill repute. Paulus had sent Servius to work in the salt mines for a year as punishment; Servius had objected to this unfair treatment and hated Paulus accordingly. Lucius was probably using him to keep up with Paulus' comings and goings. They were quite a pair—one, intelligent and shrewd, the other not so intelligent but loyal to any authority figure who might pay him a bit of attention. And both unscrupulous enough to be dangerous.

But Lucius was right in saying Paulus had something on his mind. There were many things that drove and distracted him . . . and the main quandary was not Lucius and, surprisingly, not Alysia. It was the Nazarene.

The autumn moon showed its ghostlike face through a bank of clouds touched with silver. Its rays reflected palely off the stone houses and chalky dust of the streets, barely lighting Paulus' way as he rode his horse aimlessly over the city. It had become a habit, this nocturnal ride of his, that took him always the same route...from the Antonia to the house of Caiaphas, with its cedar trees lining the drive and its gates grown over with yellow henbane, then northward again, and finally to the gate that led to Golgotha.

Usually, at that point, he returned to the fortress. But tonight he was more restless than usual, his nerves drawn tighter, and he knew he wouldn't be able to sleep. He went through the gate, its watchman staring at him silently, and turned his horse in an easterly direction, steadily climbing hills and crossing bridges until he found himself in the enclosed garden known as Gethsemane.

What a lovely, tranquil place it was, this forest of twisting olive trees. Thick groves of palm, too, and myrtle bushes and pine trees sloped gently upward. In the places void of trees, there were benches and large grassy areas where pilgrims put up tents during holidays and festivals when there was not a spare room to be found in the city.

Paulus dismounted slowly, not sure why he did so. It was dark now, the moon hidden in the clouds. His eyes discerned something huge and misshapen as a large boulder; it could have rolled down from the hills a hundred or more years ago. Paulus could envisage the Nazarene praying there, before his arrest, as Peter had described that night in Bethany.

He took a step toward the great stone. Suddenly, it seemed as if a shout rang through the trees: "I have betrayed innocent blood . . . innocent blood . . . innocent blood!" So loud were the words in his own mind that Paulus looked around, half-expecting to see someone slumped on the ground in misery. Where had he heard those words before?

Then he remembered. They had been spoken by Judas, the betrayer.

Paulus' heart pounded. His breathing became labored and uneven. Looking back, he could see the northeast corner of Jerusalem, strangely still and quiet, as though it waited for something. Between was an undulating length of the Kidron Valley. The Nazarene would have been able to see the flickering torches of those who were coming for him long before they reached the garden.

There was only one conclusion. Paulus had resisted, he had denied, he had tried not to think, he had called himself a fool.

No living person had broken that Roman seal in the presence of armed soldiers. No living person had moved that massive stone out of its groove and set it against the wall of the cliff. Nor had the Nazarene somehow survived the cross, spent three days in a guarded, airless tomb and walked out, managing to convince his disciples that he had miraculously risen from the dead. He wouldn't have been able to crawl or croak, much less walk and talk.

Paulus' mind groped reluctantly on. The disciples were no longer afraid. Something had changed them, and for that "something" they were willing to suffer, even die. There were eyewitnesses, people who claimed to have seen the Nazarene alive. Paulus himself had spoken to many of them. They had no reason to lie.

And the priests! It occurred to him for the first time that the priests had never asked him to find the dead body. That had been Pilate's idea. They had never expressed any interest whatever in the body, once it was reported to be missing. Because they *knew*! They had seen firsthand the terror of the guards; they may have even looked into the tomb and seen the man-like beings called angels. And yet, perversely, they denied the truth and were determined to stamp out any vestige of the Nazarene.

Paulus took another step toward the great rock, unmindful of the rain that was now falling from the black sky, gradually increasing in intensity until the raindrops slapped into him like needles. He fell to his knees and his hands reached outward. This was where *he* had knelt. *His* hands had touched the roughness of this stone, just as Paulus' did now. The touch was one of awe and reverence because he knew that he, too, had seen him . . .

Ever since that night in Bethany something had been gnawing at him. Someone—he couldn't remember if it was Peter or Lazarus—had mentioned a certain road. The road to Emmaus. Jesus had been seen there.

Paulus had been on that road. He remembered several men walking together, the tallest in the midst of them. The tall man's head had been covered but now he remembered the white hair, barely seen beneath the mantle. The man had looked directly at him. He remembered being struck by a sense of familiarity; he had felt some sort of pull, a magnetism he had ignored.

What did it all mean? If Jesus of Nazareth had risen from the grave as he had said he would, then it stood to reason that everything else he had said was true. That he was the son of God, that he had come into the world for the purpose of dying for it.

No, he could no longer deny it, ignore it, or reject it. For weeks he had tried to convince himself he was mistaken, that it couldn't be, that all the disciples and followers were either liars or lunatics. But there were too many of them. He had heard their stories and seen their faces. They *believed.* Alysia believed; she had not only seen him but had talked with him.

He had to give up, he had to surrender, or he would have no peace…in this world or the next. His heart ceased its wild thumping and he could breathe again. He fell prostrate to the ground, his hands balled in fists beneath his forehead, the rain surging over his body. "Forgive me," he said out loud, "for *I* have betrayed innocent blood."

Something broke inside him, something he had held rigid for so many years that the breaking of it was a long and painful thing. It ripped him, laying him open so that the tears coming out of his eyes felt like blood flowing out of his heart. It was the first time he had allowed himself to weep since his childhood. A sense of emptiness, an old, familiar restiveness, began to leave him, and he was filled with peace . . . and an unshakeable assurance.

"What is truth?" Pilate had asked, and refused to admit that the truth stood before him.

The man entered the room slowly, glancing back when the guard closed the door behind him. He was lean of build, with dark hair and a voice that was deep and clear. He looked at Paulus, who stood quietly beside the window.

"Stephen, you may not remember me. I met you a few months ago in Bethany."

The man appeared wary but unafraid. "Yes. I remember you. Though you looked different then. Longer hair, and a beard."

"My name is Paulus Valerius. As you probably know by now, I am the commander of this fort. I am not trying to spy on you or harm your cause. Though I have listened to you speak, without your knowledge. You seem to have a greater understanding . . ." Paulus seemed unsure how to continue and finally said, "I want you to tell me . . . how I can become one of you. That is, one of *his*."

The man's surprise was so evident that Paulus had to restrain a smile. "I thought you would speak to me more freely than the others. There are things I need to have explained to me."

"I—I hardly know what to say, sir. Tell me, please, how you came to believe in Jesus."

"Yes. Would you like to sit down?"

Stephen moved across the room and sat in a chair. Paulus leaned back against the window, still not sure how to proceed. Then it seemed as if an unseen force prompted him and he began by telling Stephen how he had become interested in the Jewish religion after he'd been mysteriously saved from death, and how he'd studied the history books and prophets. He told all he knew of the crucifixion and the empty tomb.

"The evidence for his resurrection has been too strong for me to deny. I've read the prophecies concerning the Messiah, and have seen how he has fulfilled them. But even conceding all of this, it wasn't until I—" Paulus stopped for a moment and cleared his throat. "It wasn't until I confessed to him that I believed, that something happened to me, and changed me forever. It's as if . . . he has come to reside within me."

Stephen was staring at him. "Sir, you *are* one of his."

"Do you mean . . . the only requirement is belief?"

"Yes, belief in the full sense of the word, which connotes action. Acting on your belief. You will need to be baptized, sir, which Jesus commanded for all believers. If you will allow me, I will be happy to baptize you."

"Of course. And then what?"

"There is much for you to learn. You need to learn Jesus' teachings, and follow them so that you may tell others. That is our cause—to tell others of him so that all might be saved."

"Saved from what? Hades, the underworld?"

"Saved from eternal death, to eternal life. Saved from that place we call hell, separation from God, to that place of glory where Jesus dwells and where God will wipe away every tear."

"I want to be of use to your cause. That is why I've decided to resign my position. Persecution is coming to your people, Stephen, and Rome will be part of it. Now it's only Caiaphas, and possibly Herod. But eventually Rome will become opposed to the idea of this new kingdom. I can be of no use here. I could be ordered to imprison believers, or worse. If it becomes known that I'm a follower, it might be either prison or death . . . and then I would be of no use anywhere."

"Where will you go, sir?"

"I don't know . . . yet."

"I agree with you that the danger to us is increasing, rather than lessening. The danger to you, a person of importance, will be even greater."

"I can never do enough for him," Paulus said earnestly. "Even to die for him would be poor payment for what he's done for me."

"You could never earn what he has freely given."

"Tell me, Stephen—tell me why Jesus had to die. Why could he not come and simply set up his kingdom on earth?"

Stephen didn't answer for some moments, gazing beyond Paulus as if into some distant place. "That is a question we all asked ourselves. Jesus tried to tell us but we didn't understand, until it was all over."

He paused again and Paulus nodded for him to continue. "Say what you will, but every man is born with knowledge of a creator. He only suppresses it, or ignores it, or calls it something else. Sir, there's not a man alive who hasn't sinned—broken God's laws. And even if we are ignorant of God's laws, there is our *conscience* to tell us some things are right and some things are wrong. And almost always, when we do wrong, we do it willfully."

Stephen waited to see if Paulus was following his words.

"Go on."

"We were created with spirits as well as bodies, spirits that will live forever . . . somewhere. And there's no way that we, being sinful, can enter into the presence of a holy God. God will not co-exist with evil. It must be punished, eradicated."

There was a long silence. Then Paulus said, "And he took the punishment. He was the offering, because he never sinned. The lamb of God."

"Yes. But there is more to it than just *dying*. God turned his face from him. Those hours of darkness—I believe that was when God laid the sins of the world upon him. From the smallest act of rebellion to the most horrific crime you can imagine…all laid upon a guiltless man who *offered* to do that very thing."

Any lingering doubt Stephen might have had about the legate's conversion disappeared when he saw tears in the Roman's eyes. "Death and hell were the price he paid for us, sir. God's justice demanded it. Yet God wept for his son. I have no doubt of it. And never forget what Jesus went through in Gethsemane. I believe *that* is where the greatest battle was fought."

"Do you mean . . . he could have decided not to go through with it?"

Stephen's own eyes lit as though with some inner fire. "Jesus could have, at any point before his death, summoned ten thousand angelic warriors to his aid! The entire host of heaven would have been ready. Even all the legions of Rome could not have stood against him, had he decided to fight. He had only to say the word, and he could have wiped man off the face of the earth!"

"What it must have cost him," Paulus said, as if thinking aloud, "knowing he could do that and not doing it . . . why would God love us so much? Why not just destroy mankind since we are so rebellious and have made such a mess of things?"

"I don't know how to answer that, sir, except to repeat what a friend of mine said…that mankind was created to be a companion, if you will, for the Son of God. That was the intent from the beginning. You see, Jesus has always existed, and he knew before the first man and woman were created what he would do to redeem us."

"Redeem," Paulus repeated. "That was what he meant when he said, '*It is finished.*' It means *paid in full.*"

Stephen nodded. "There is a mystery involved in all this, sir, that we may never completely understand."

"And what about those who died before Jesus came, or those who die without hearing of him? Have they no hope of heaven?"

"God is just," Stephen answered. "We can trust him to deal justly with everyone."

A stillness fell over the room and both men grew quiet. Paulus felt overwhelmed by what he had heard.

Stephen spoke again. "I can arrange to meet with you, to teach you. There are others—Peter, John, James. Any of them. And Lazarus as well. We will help you in any way we can."

"Thank you, Stephen. You have already been of much help. I am indeed grateful."

Stephen turned to go, then seemed to hesitate. He looked again at Paulus. "This road will never be easy, sir, whether persecution comes or not. The old nature will always struggle with the new. That is why only the innocent blood shed by Jesus the Christ can save us. We cannot save ourselves, no matter how hard we may try."

"I think . . . I understand that."

"I knew, sir, that night in Bethany, that you were seeking something. I'm glad you found it."

"It wasn't what I expected, Stephen. But I found it."

Paulus looked up as Simon entered the room. Slowly he laid aside several sheets of papyrus on which he'd been writing.

"You sent for me, sir?"

"Yes." Paulus leaned back in his chair and handed the documents to his slave. "I have something for you."

Simon took the sheets and his puzzled expression changed to one of disbelief. "What—" he began and stopped, staring at Paulus.

"It's perfectly obvious, Simon. A record of manumission, and a letter to help you find employment. And a little money . . . think of it as back wages."

"I am . . . free?"

"As free as I am."

Simon was speechless. When he found his voice, he could do little more than stammer his gratitude.

"There is no need to thank me, Simon," Paulus said soberly. "I should have freed you long ago, when you first came into my possession. I'm sorry. But you were also a friend to me; I became used to your companionship. Of course, you can stay and work for me. I will pay your wages. Or you can return home . . . or do anything you like."

Simon still had a look of stupefaction on his face. "I will go back to Cyrene," he murmured. "Back to my wife and sons."

Paulus was grave. "You realize, Simon, that things change. People change. If things are not what you expected, feel at liberty to come to me. I'll help you in any way I can. I'm not sure exactly where I'll be, though. I may be difficult to locate."

"What do you mean, sir?"

Paulus got up slowly from his desk. "I am resigning."

"But . . . how can you do that? I thought the emperor gave you this appointment."

"The emperor won't know—until after I've disappeared. I may have to go into hiding."

Simon stared at him, looking into his eyes as if he'd never seen him before. "You are a follower of the Nazarene?"

"What makes you think so?"

"You look . . . different. Like them. I've seen them, heard them talk. I don't know what to say, sir. I had not expected this of you."

"I'm not 'sir' any longer, Simon. Call me Paulus. And you know almost everything about him that I know. I believe in him. I hope that someday you will come to believe in him as well."

If Simon was confounded before he was doubly so now. "But this is nothing but a myth! I agree that he was a remarkable man, maybe even a great man, but a god? There are no gods! He was just a man—who died the death of a common criminal, and you would worship him?"

A small frown appeared on Paulus' brow. "You surprise me, Simon. I thought you had more compassion for him. I thought you felt, as I did, that there was something different about him."

"I do think he was different, and it did grieve me to see him mistreated! I will never forget how he looked at me that day, after I had carried his cross. He . . . thanked me, if you can believe that!" Simon shook his head in perplexity. "He might have been the bravest man I ever saw, but he was just a man. He was in agony—anyone could see that. I can't explain this talk of a resurrection, but it's just talk! No, I cannot call him God, and I'm amazed that you can do so!"

"Well, I amaze myself, Simon," Paulus said, a little more lightly. "But I do call him God. I call him savior, and friend. I'm not ashamed to say that I love him and would die for him."

"And you *will* die for him, if you will forgive my saying so. Once this is known, they will give you no peace…until you have recanted before the emperor himself!"

Paulus looked at him oddly. "I may one day be called before the emperor. But God willing, I will never recant."

"Well, it's about time you brought this precious child to spend the day with me!" Martha exclaimed, adding with a chuckle, "I think I'll teach her how to bake bread. After all, she is over a year old!"

Alysia laughed, as Martha added, "Come inside. You are going to stay a while, aren't you?"

"If you don't mind, Martha, I would just like to walk around the grounds. I'll come for Rachel soon."

"You needn't hurry, Alysia. Enjoy yourself and do whatever you like. We'll be busy for a while, won't we, little one?"

Rachel nodded happily and spun about to smile and wave at her mother.

"Be good, Rachel. I'll be back soon."

Alysia walked behind the house and thought for a moment about which path to take. Almost at once she chose the winding trail behind the stable, leading to the brook where she and Paulus had talked—it seemed a hundred years ago! The brook was brown and low, showing the rocks at the bottom; the rainy season had barely begun and there had been only one rainfall in weeks. Blue water lilies floated limply on its surface.

That's how I feel, she thought, *brown and low.*

Most days her newfound faith upheld her, in spite of the unresolved matter with Paulus that grew heavier every day. But there were times when she wondered if she would ever see him again. After all, he had made no attempt to see *her*, or even communicate with her. Probably he thought that was what she wanted. But it wasn't… not when they had parted so bitterly. A dozen times she had decided to go to him and then hadn't done it, either out of cowardice or because something had occurred to stop her.

She should sit down on the ground, right here beside the sluggish little stream, and have a long talk with God. Maybe he wanted her to forget Paulus. Maybe she was just making herself miserable. Maybe . . . she should marry someone else. No, that was unthinkable. Not while he lived! But then, couldn't God change her feelings, if she let him? Did she have enough faith to even ask for such a thing?

She kept walking. It was warm this October morning. She reached up and removed her mantle, letting it drop to the ground. She gathered her hair in one hand and brought it over her right shoulder, enjoying the sudden coolness against her neck. Overhead the branches of the trees leaned forward and touched each other, forming a tunnel of dappled light. A path trod by animals had formed near the brook and disappeared into the trees.

A stirring of bushes and the sound of twigs snapping made her turn to look at the path. Startled, she saw a lone figure come into view…tall, clad in a light brown Roman tunic, with hair almost the same hue. He held the reins as he walked his horse, his face alert and watchful.

"Paulus!"

He stopped, his eyes meeting hers. He let go of the horse, which walked toward the little stream and halted as though affronted by its lack of depth.

Alysia stared at Paulus, aware of the marked change in him. A certain hard look of cynicism had gone and in his eyes were no clouds of bitterness. The years had made their mark on his face, for it was lined about the eyes and forehead, and more than a few strands of silver threaded through his tawny hair. But that *other* change, that new look in his eyes, held her spellbound.

He took a step forward, and all at once they rushed to each other. Paulus drew her against him and, bending a little, enveloped her in his arms. "Alysia," he said, half-choking from the constriction in his throat. "My dearest love."

Her arms were tight around him; her cheek pressed against his hard shoulder. She couldn't believe he was really here. This must be a dream…and yet his body was warm against hers and she felt his hand on her hair. She smelled the clean linen of his tunic; she could hear the swift thudding of his heart and behind her the shuffling of the great horse, the rustling of leaves, the twittering of birds. No, it was too real to be a dream.

She lifted her head and he kissed her, gently, with hard-won restraint. At last it was she who pulled away and stood looking up at him, trembling. What did this mean, why was he here? She backed up against a tree and braced herself against it.

"How did you find me?" she whispered.

His eyes were intense and penetrating, his muscles taut, his own voice full of emotion. "I went to see Lazarus. There was something

I wanted to tell him. Martha told me you were out here. I came another way—in case anyone was watching."

"Why have you come?"

"To tell you how sorry I am, Alysia, for everything. To beg your pardon for my stupidity and hard-heartedness. In your place I would have done the same. About Rachel, I mean. Will you forgive me for what I said?"

"I have forgiven you. I was angry," she admitted. "I felt that you didn't understand."

"It took some thinking," he said, with a smile. "But I do understand. And I came—"

The pause grew long, and she said, "Yes?"

"To tell you that I am going away."

His words pierced her as coldly as a shaft of metal and she lowered her eyes so that he wouldn't see the acuteness of her disappointment. Whatever she had expected of him, it hadn't been this. Her eyes filled uncontrollably with tears.

"Alysia," he said quietly. "Did you think I would leave this place and not take you with me?"

She held herself back, standing stiffly before him, not knowing what to say.

"I'm going to ask you a question," he told her, "and I want you to answer with complete honesty."

She nodded, putting aside her confusion.

"You refused to marry me after Megara died because you thought I would lose everything I care about, and you were afraid of what would happen if we were caught."

Paulus hesitated again, watching her expression closely. "But what if I told you that I intend to give up my profession anyway, for something that has nothing to do with you, and become something of a fugitive myself? Would you marry me then?"

Alysia was looking at him in bewilderment. "Paulus, what do you mean?"

"I am . . . a believer. Stephen baptized me, and he and others have been teaching me. I'm resigning my command and leaving Jerusalem. I want you and Rachel to come with me."

Her mind seemed half-frozen, her thoughts turning sluggishly in her brain. Paulus, a believer! It was the answer to a prayer, to hundreds of prayers! As if coming from underwater, she realized he was still speaking.

"I intend to go to Rome. I know that Rome is probably the most dangerous place in the world for both of us, but I believe that is where God wants me to go. We will have to be very careful. But God will protect us until our work is finished."

Still, her voice failed her. Why couldn't she say yes . . . why couldn't she smile and show him the joy she felt at his words? This meant that they need never be separated again! But something, some feeling she didn't understand, restrained her.

Paulus saw in her eyes the great happiness she felt, seeing also something baffled and uncertain. He had told himself he would accept her answer; he had tried to prepare himself for the possibility she might still refuse. But now, unexpectedly, he was filled with near desperation, with a fear he could hardly control.

But he said evenly, "It will take some time to get things in order. I must see to a replacement. I have a man in mind that I believe will be fair to the believers in Jerusalem. Pilate will have no choice but to accept my resignation. And by the time Tiberius hears of it, he won't be able to find me."

Alysia reached out and touched his face, still saying nothing.

Paulus placed his hand over hers. "Beloved," he said softly, "what is your answer?"

She withdrew her hand, took a deep breath, and turned slightly away. "You want me to be your wife. You want me to stand beside you and go with you to tell Rome of Jesus Christ. This is an honor I do not feel worthy of, Paulus."

"Worthiness has nothing to do with it," he replied, a rough edge to his voice. "God has forgiven our past."

"I know he has forgiven us. And yet—"

"Are you thinking of Magnus' death?"

"Oh, it's more than that. It's you and me, it's . . . don't you see how we could hinder each other? Don't you see how our message could be harmed and distorted if the truth about our past, and about Rachel, were ever known?"

"That was before. People will understand—"

"No." She shook her head. "Some people will not understand! Some will brand us hypocrites, liars. Our credibility would be . . . in doubt. We would bring shame upon all believers, shame upon him!"

"Alysia." Paulus strove for patience. "Do you mean to say we cannot be together because of what people might think? I tell you God has forgiven your past, and mine."

She said stubbornly, "But it's still there! Oh, I don't know what to do!" She closed her eyes for a moment and looked away. "Have you prayed about this?"

"Of course." He didn't add that, unlike the matter of his mission to Rome, he had never received a clear answer about Alysia. Yet he had come to her anyway.

"My sins are a hundred-fold greater than yours, Alysia. But they are under his blood. If everyone who wanted to tell others of Jesus had to be perfect, there would be no one worthy to do so."

"I cannot answer you now," she said, with an imploring look on her face. "I want to be your wife, to go anywhere with you. But—"

Her gaze dropped. Her fists clenched and she slipped them behind her, scraping them painfully on the bark of the tree.

Paulus stood tall and straight, then it was as if a breeze stirred and something came into his face. Even had she seen it, it passed so quickly she could not have read it.

At last he said, "I must go to Caesarea. I will be gone about a week. When I return—"

She raised her eyes to his.

"Whatever your answer is, I will accept it."

CHAPTER XXV

Lucius peered over the heads of the men seated in the fortress' dining hall. Spotting the one he sought, he entered the room and dragged out a bench. Pulling a platter toward him, he grabbed a hunk of goat meat and began chewing it.

"Tribune," said Servius, looking surprised.

"Greetings, Servius. You may well show your astonishment but my stepbrother is not here to throw me out. I've heard he's left Jerusalem and I'd like to know why."

"I'm not privy to information concerning the commander," Servius said, but with a hint of a smug smile on his face. "However, the word seems to be going around that he has resigned."

"*Paulus* has resigned his post?"

Servius nodded and abandoned his pretense of ignorance. "He went to Caesarea, allegedly to tell Pilate. It was supposed to be a secret, but someone let it out. Pilate will be glad to see him go, mark my words. I think your stepbrother intimidated him." He soaked up gravy with his bread and stuffed it into his mouth. When he could speak around his food, he added, "He's due back here any day now."

"Why does he do this?"

Servius shrugged. "For that matter, why did he ever come here in the first place?"

A soldier from the next table made an observation. "The legate is a changed man. His expression, his manner—it's as if he found a whole new reason for living!"

"A woman, no doubt," said another, raising a few guffaws. "He's been too closemouthed for my liking. It's said you don't really know a man until you know the kind of woman he consorts with."

"Speaking of women," said the first, dourly, "mine just left me. For an Arabian camel driver, no less."

The room echoed with laughter and the sardonic retort, "Likely she prefers the smell of camel!"

There was another spurt of laughter. The soldier went on, "She was a comely one. It won't be easy to replace her! There aren't enough Roman women to go around, and the Jewish ones won't even speak to me."

"There are some beauties among them," Servius commented, reaching for more bread. "I'll never forget that one we brought to the barracks for a bit of fun a few years ago. Only Marcus spoiled it all. Remember her, Quintus? She had the face and figure of a goddess. And her eyes . . ."

Quintus was nodding. "Violet, like amethysts. I never saw such eyes. And her hair was full and black as night. She was a lioness . . . scratched me so hard I had the scar for weeks."

"Her name," Lucius interrupted, thinking of only one woman who matched so remarkable a description. "What was her name?"

Servius raised his eyebrows. "Athena, Alysia, or something like that. A Greek name."

Lucius took a napkin and slowly began wiping grease off his hands. "Where does she live?"

Servius and Quintus looked at each other. Quintus shrugged and answered, "We found her on the road to Bethany."

Lucius stared straight ahead, his eyes narrowed. So that was how it was, was it? Somehow the slave had escaped from Rome and survived the shipwreck—*if* there had ever been a shipwreck—and had sent for Paulus to come for her. All this time she had been practically under his nose! How they must have been laughing at him!

He felt a pressure in his chest, as if his heart were going to burst. He said to Servius in a low voice, "How would you like to be promoted in a very short time?"

"How?" Servius asked blankly.

"By helping me bring in a murderer," Lucius replied. "The murderer of Senator Eustacius' son. Alysia of Bethany."

Pontius Pilate had been strangely apathetic when Paulus visited him at the governor's palace in Caesarea. It was rumored he spent most of his days sitting on a bench staring out over the sea. Apparently, the rumors were true; he had to be summoned to his office by a clerk, and when he arrived only gave Paulus a fleeting glance and sat down wearily behind his desk.

"Well, I haven't seen you since . . . since—" the prefect stopped, frowning.

"The crucifixion in Jerusalem," said Paulus, although he had actually spoken with him a time or two since then. He thought he knew what was eating at Pontius Pilate.

"The—oh, you mean that Nazarene business." Pilate avoided Paulus' eyes and began shuffling things on top of his desk.

"Has he been on your mind as much as he has mine?" Paulus asked frankly.

At last the prefect looked up. "What? What do you mean?"

"We both knew he was innocent."

"And you heard those demented Jews claim responsibility for it—no, it wasn't my fault. Is that what you came here for? I will not discuss the matter."

"As I matter of fact, I came here to inform you of my resignation."

Pilate lifted his brows. "You cannot simply abandon your post, Paulus. You were appointed by Tiberius."

"I am not abandoning my post; that's why I'm here. Tiberius and I had an understanding. In addition to my own letter, I would like for you to write the emperor and tell him what I've done, and tell him that I'm recommending a man to replace me, one that I believe will be responsible and fair minded—Claudius Lysias, who is in Syria at the moment."

"I know him. But this is most unusual, Paulus. As governor I should, perhaps, place you under house arrest and charge you with desertion."

"*Perhaps*," said Paulus, with a flare of annoyance, "you shouldn't."

Pilate got to his feet and for the first time since Paulus' arrival looked him fully in the eyes. Something the prefect saw there had a strange effect, for his gaze shifted and he walked toward the window where he pretended an interest in something outside. Then he turned again.

"I suppose I should be grateful you didn't report that matter to Tiberius. Why didn't you?"

Paulus shrugged. "What good would it have done?"

"I keep expecting . . . well, let's just say that I know Sejanus was responsible for my having this position, and Tiberius has never particularly liked me."

"With things as they are in Rome just now, I wouldn't worry too much. He doesn't want to be bothered with our problems. That's why I'm reasonably certain he won't oppose the suggestion to appoint Lysias."

"If he doesn't fly into a rage and kill the messenger," said Pilate wryly.

"I don't think he's going to care very much. But I also don't think he will want to hear that you arrested me. Will you write the letter? I'll leave my own letter of resignation for you to send with it. I intend to tell him I came here and spoke with you."

There was a long pause, and Pilate said, "As long as you understand I am not giving you permission to leave. I will take no responsibility for it."

"I understand—perfectly," said Paulus, and almost asked him if he wanted to wash his hands.

That night he dined with Claudia in a small, private room. The prefect claimed a severe headache and remained in his own chamber. His wife looked lovely in a gown of midnight blue, over which she wore a white stola edged with the same shade of blue. Her dark eyes were clear and candid. Claudia told Paulus how worried she was about her husband, who hadn't been himself since "that day," and she was full of questions about what was happening in Jerusalem.

"I know there are many people who believe he rose from the dead," she said, with a serious look replacing her normally amiable expression. "And you never found the body. If anyone *could* have found it, Paulus, you would have."

He didn't know what to say to that.

"Well, what do you think happened to it?" she asked.

How much should he tell her? Could he trust her not to reveal all to Pilate? He hesitated for so long that she began to look at him strangely. Well, she had put him on the spot and he wasn't going to lie to her. He watched as she dismissed all the servants and then turned to him expectantly.

"I think that Jesus is alive," he said.

"But . . . you mean, of course, that he somehow survived the crucifixion?"

"No."

Claudia blinked. "You mean . . . you believe—"

"Yes," he said. "I believe."

She was silent. Her earrings began to clink as though she were trembling; in fact, she was visibly shaking. Then she whispered, "My husband would put you into prison if he knew. He would send you to Rome on the first ship out of here!"

Paulus nodded. "Are you going to tell him?"

Slowly, Claudia shook her head. "No. I will not tell him. But I want you to tell me *why* you believe it! You are the last person I would expect to . . . to be taken in by such a story."

He told her. She listened with great attentiveness, sometimes interrupting to ask questions. It grew late and he began to wonder what the ousted servants must be thinking. At last he said, "The evidence is so overwhelming that it almost takes more faith *not* to believe it."

"I can see why you would say that," she answered. "And yet . . . it is a very large leap, you must admit!"

"But once you've taken it, there's no turning back."

She placed heavily ringed fingers on top of one of his hands. "Be careful, Paulus. I don't know what you intend to do, and I won't ask you. But I would hate to see something happen to you. If you speak with everyone as freely as you have spoken with me, you won't live very long. My husband has many sides to him and he can be cruel. I think he likes you, as much as he likes anyone, but he would not tolerate a Roman legate joining some sort of sect that calls their leader a king."

Before he could reply she lifted her hand and whisked away, slipping out the door and closing it softly behind her.

He left the next morning, not yet pressed with any sense of urgency. He hadn't seen Claudia again but he felt confident she would say nothing of their conversation to her husband. Pilate had eaten breakfast with him but had eyed him rather guardedly; Paulus wondered if the servants had been talking about his and Claudia's prolonged time alone together in the dining room. That would be unfortunate. However, the prefect seemed sincere in wishing him well and promised to write the emperor on his behalf.

The city was only half a mile behind him when he caught sight of a tall man in an ill-fitting brown tunic walking along the roadside. There was something familiar about him. As Paulus' horse approached, the man turned his head and Paulus recognized his former slave.

"Simon!"

Simon halted and stared up at him. Dismayed, Paulus saw that his friend's face was thin and haggard, showing a stubble of black beard, and his eyes were sunken and dull. He dismounted quickly, leading his horse to the edge of the road as travelers flowed by on either side. Simon followed him slowly.

"What are you doing here?" Paulus asked. "I thought you had gone to Cyrene."

Simon nodded. "I have been back," he said, his voice hoarse. "My . . . wife . . . I didn't see her. I inquired among the neighbors without letting them know who I was. She remarried, saying she thought me dead. When I saw my sons they were standing in the street, talking with their friends. They have grown tall and strong." There was pride in Simon's wounded dark eyes. "They . . . did not know me. I didn't expect them to, but it wasn't a very good feeling. I couldn't tell them. I couldn't stay. I took the first ship back and it was stopping here rather than Joppa."

Paulus said nothing, but reached out and grasped his friend's arm for a moment. After a moment, he asked, "Why have you returned?"

Simon looked away and shook his head. "I don't know. I suppose I intended to try and find you. I need work."

"I don't think it is a coincidence that we have met here today, Simon. Come with me to Jerusalem and we'll talk. I don't think you should give up so easily. But first, let's go back and get a horse for you...and you look as though a good meal wouldn't hurt."

"Yes," was Simon's only reply, but a glimmer of hope had appeared in his eyes. With Paulus leading his horse the two men turned and reentered the crowded city of Caesarea.

Alysia swept the floor one last time before nightfall. Rachel played in the bedroom, waiting for a story before time to go to sleep. Alysia kept on sweeping even after the floor was clean, for her thoughts were not on her task.

Why was she holding herself back from Paulus? Why hadn't she said she would go with him to Rome? Did she hate and fear Rome that much? Was her assertion that her past might harm their cause only an excuse? Was she afraid of failing Paulus because of some deep-seated feeling of inadequacy?

It all seemed so complicated...and yet it was so simple. Either she would marry Paulus, or she wouldn't!

She listened absently to Rachel in the next room and like a thunderbolt the thought came to her that she was being unfair to her daughter. Rachel deserved both her parents. She *needed* both her parents. She thought sorrowfully of her own father, trying to be both parents to his child. She remembered the feeling of incompleteness after her mother's death, the sense of loss that never really went away.

She stopped and thought, poised with broom in hand, *I should have married Paulus after Megara died! I've been selfish. I wasn't trusting him, or God.*

The pounding on the door came with no warning. A voice commanded: "Open in the name of Caesar!"

Swiftly she put down the broom and closed the door to the bedroom. She put her hand over her heart as though to still its painful, hard thumping, and before she could move again the door crashed open. She looked into the smiling face of Lucius Aquilinus.

"I was hoping you would be at home," he said, with mock courtesy. "I must ask you to accompany me to the Antonia. There is a certain *matter* to be resolved."

Alysia slowly drew air into her lungs. What would she do about Rachel? No sooner had the question entered her mind than Rachel came out of the bedroom to grab Alysia's legs, staring at the uniformed stranger in alarm.

"What's this?" Lucius made a great show of surprise. With narrowed gaze, he said, "A brat for the slave and the legate?"

Alysia closed her eyes, pleading silently, *Oh, dear God, have mercy on us both . . .*

"There is a cart waiting outside. It's almost dark so you will forgive the need for haste."

"This child means nothing to you," Alysia said. "Let me leave her with someone."

"Anything that concerns my stepbrother is of concern to me. Now, if you'll go first—"

She lifted Rachel in her arms and walked slowly through the broken doorway. A donkey and cart stood outside, with a soldier sitting in the cart. He, too, was smiling at her.

"We meet again," he said, his head tilted sardonically.

Recognizing Servius she had to bite back a retort, knowing it would only increase his hostility. She managed to get Rachel and herself into the cart and sat down with her back against the driver's seat, drawing Rachel close against her. Lucius climbed upon his horse.

"Cover your face, and the child's," he said sharply.

She did so but there was no need; there was no one on the road at this hour. They drew near to Lazarus' house and she hoped against hope that someone would be outside, that someone would see them. But though the windows glowed with lamplight she could see no one looking out. There weren't even any lights burning on the rooftop.

Suddenly, the donkey stopped in its tracks and gave a series of ear-splitting brays that fairly rent the night asunder. On and on it went, so indignantly that Alysia looked around to see if someone had thrown a rock. Rachel covered her ears.

"What's the matter with that infernal beast?" Lucius demanded, his horse skittering over the path.

Servius helplessly slapped the reins to no avail.

Lucius edged close to the cart, grabbed the reins from Servius, and struck them hard against the donkey's rump. "Stop—that—bellowing!"

The donkey ended its outburst as suddenly as it had begun and jigged forward. Servius reclaimed the reins with an irate look at Lucius, who cantered ahead of them. He said over his shoulder, "Hurry, before that mule wakes up the whole town!"

Alysia couldn't be sure but she thought someone had come and leaned over the wall surrounding the roof, as if to peer down into the street. It was not completely dark; there *had* been a shadowy figure. But though she herself might have been seen, it would have been as barely more than a shadow.

They clattered up the hillside and passed through the town gate. The night watchman had not yet taken his post, and there was no one to witness their swift departure. They started on the too-short road to Jerusalem.

After a slow, three-day journey avoiding the congested highways, Paulus and Simon remained some fifteen miles from Jerusalem when they stopped for the night in a wooded area and built a fire. The air had cooled rapidly once the sun went down and a strong easterly breeze turned the night almost cold. Simon seemed eager to talk, and Paulus listened. He talked about his family, his business…and about the day the Romans arrested him.

"I was a wool merchant," he said in a matter-of-fact way, as they shared a meal of dried meat and water. "I was very successful, if you'll pardon my saying so. I even had my own small fleet of ships to deliver the wool. One day as I was traveling on one of my own ships a Roman tribune stopped us at the port of Alexandria. He tried to take over the ship for his own men, who he needed to send immediately to Rome.

"When I protested, he struck me. When I was about to return the favor I was overpowered by some of the other soldiers. I woke in prison—and very shortly to be sold as a slave. As you know I was sent to Rome, where your wife's father purchased me."

"Yet you never seemed to mind your slavery," Paulus commented. "You were never angry or seemed to resent us."

Simon smiled a little. "I was angry. But I had learned my lesson and tried not to show it. But truthfully, I didn't mind working for you—as that was my lot. I always believed that someday I would be free to take up my life again. I believed, foolishly, as it turned out, that my wife would wait for me."

Paulus shook his head with a look of deep regret. "Can you ever forgive us?"

Simon said thoughtfully, "I think the blame lies not so much with people, as with the fact that the practice of slavery has become so commonplace that no one ever really thinks about it. It's 'just the way things are.'"

"Yes, Simon, we do think about it. A great deal." Paulus tossed more dead branches onto the fire. "The problem *is* with people, and I used to think that people couldn't change. Now I know we can."

Simon said quietly, "I wish I could believe as you do."

"If you really mean that, there's only one thing that keeps you from it."

"What is that?"

"You," Paulus said, with a smile.

Simon shook his head and suddenly gave a great yawn. "I'm too tired to think about that, or about anything just now. That was too rich a meal you bought me earlier today, Paulus. Wake me when you're ready to go."

Long after Simon had stretched out and gone to sleep Paulus sat before the fire, staring into the flames. For the first time in weeks a feeling of heaviness, of some oppressive burden, came upon him. He thought at first it was simply a sympathetic reaction to the state Simon now found himself in, but gradually he realized it was more than that. It was almost like the sense of disaster he had gotten that day on the road from Jericho.

Finally he slept, but it was a restless sleep. Somewhere near a jackdaw gave a hoarse cry of alarm. He woke and now the feeling of impending doom hung over him like a fog.

No sooner had he begun to ready his horse than Simon stood up and began to do the same. "What is it, Paulus?"

"Something is wrong," Paulus said. "We ride tonight for Jerusalem."

Alysia stirred slowly, conscious of acute discomfort and a throbbing ache in her head. Had she been sleeping? How much time had gone by? She shivered in the damp murkiness of the cell and found herself huddled in a corner with Rachel asleep in her lap, wrapped in Alysia's mantle. A heavy chain, attached to the wall behind her, encircled her ankle. If there were other prisoners nearby, they made no sound. All she heard was the muffled scurrying of mice or rats somewhere within the walls.

She knew they were below ground, in the prison of the Antonia. Lucius had brought them here by skirting the eastern edge of the city and entering through the north gate. All the way, the word WHY reared before her like some great, immovable mountain. *Why* did this have to happen . . . why now, when at last she and Paulus could be together?

But words had come to her, soundless words that were somehow breathed into her mind. She had known, then, that she and Rachel were not alone. There was someone else riding in that cart with them.

She had heard him say, as though *his* spirit were speaking to her spirit: "My peace I give you. My strength is sufficient for you."

She still didn't understand, but slowly the gathering storm inside her had begun to abate. She didn't have to be strong because he could be strong for her. She didn't have to be afraid because he was in control. She had only to trust him.

"I do trust you, but I'm still afraid," she had answered silently, her eyes closed, her face lifted to the night sky. "I am afraid of what's going to happen. Please, please help me to keep trusting you—no matter what. And I beg you to spare my daughter."

The rattle of a key in the lock brought her to full awareness and wakened Rachel. The door swung open. First a hand with a torch appeared, then Servius strode into the cell where he stood looking down at her with disdain. He set the torch in a hook on the wall, then bent and unlocked the band around her ankle.

"Get up," he said coldly.

As soon as she managed to get to her feet, he reached forward to take Rachel out of her arms. "No," Alysia whispered, refusing to release her. She must try not to panic; she didn't want to frighten Rachel.

Lucius' voice came from outside the door. "Do you want her to die with you?"

Alysia stepped quickly toward the entrance to the corridor so that she could look into his face. "What are you going to do with her?"

Lucius shrugged. "You are the one guilty of murder. I don't want her. In fact, I shall just hand her over to Paulus when he returns and he will know without a word what has happened to you." He smiled, seeming amused by the idea.

She fought to keep her voice low and steady. "I cannot let you have her."

"Give her to him. Servius won't harm her, I'll see to that—unless of course you refuse to do as I say."

Alysia slowly bent her head and kissed Rachel, saying into her ear, "I love you, darling. God will take care of you. Everything will be all right."

She let go of her daughter, permitting Servius to carry her away. Rachel's wails of protest grew fainter and died away. It was more than Alysia could bear. Her mind wanted to retreat, to deny it all… this could not be happening! Yet she *was* bearing it, she was being carried, uplifted, and she had to hold on to this invisible hand and not let go.

Lucius stepped forward and took her hands, pulling them in front of her and deftly tying them together. He bent his head so that his face was close to hers. "You are very calm," he said, "for someone who is about to die."

She dropped her gaze, refusing to look at him. He laughed lightly and prodded her forward. They climbed a long stretch of curving stone steps and walked out onto the mosaic pavement. She was surprised to see that it was morning. A mist floated eerily among the pillars of the various buildings, shining white from a pallid, dawning sun that offered little warmth.

She saw that Servius stood nearby, watching her with a curiously avid expression. Where was Rachel? Her gaze went swiftly from one direction to the other. There were several soldiers standing about, and others she could hear on the parade ground some distance away.

There was her daughter, being held by one of the sentries near the praetorium. She was still and quiet, as though she had gone to sleep again. Lucius began to argue with one of the senior centurions…a man Alysia knew rather well.

"You have kept me waiting all night," Lucius said harshly. "I happen to know that Tribune Fabius is too sick to get out of bed, and the others have not yet returned from wherever their duties have taken them. That leaves you, Centurion, and you are going to have to make a decision."

Marcus studied him with a look of disgust. "I know nothing of this matter. A man came to see me last night, to speak on her behalf—a Jew from Bethany. I've already told you I will do nothing until the legate returns."

"He may not *be* an officer when he returns, if he ever does!"

Marcus looked closely at Alysia and she could tell that he recognized her. "Did you murder this man, Magnus Eustacius?"

She answered quietly, "He was about to . . . take me by force, and so I killed him. I meant to stop him; I do not know that I meant to kill him."

The centurion gave her a long look and turned to Lucius. "And you want to put her to death without a trial?"

"She is a slave! A runaway slave! My stepbrother aided in her escape and he will have to answer for that."

Marcus' voice was unmoved. "I will not put her to death until I have spoken with the legate, and you have not the authority to do so without a sealed order from him."

"Or from you, the temporary commander. Or shall I go and pull Fabius out of his sickbed?"

"He would tell you the same. You can either wait for the return of Paulus Valerius, or take her to Rome and let her face the charges there."

Before Lucius could reply, the sound of hoof beats on pavement rang throughout the fort. Everyone turned in that direction. Slightly below them, riding up an incline from the first level and barely visible beyond the mist-shrouded colonnade, came two horsemen. They dismounted swiftly and climbed the steps to the upper court. Alysia swayed, almost dizzy with relief.

"What are you doing, Lucius?" Paulus' low tone masked an inner fury.

"As you can see, I've caught a fugitive. The one you've been hiding, quite successfully, for a few years." Lucius swept his hand toward Alysia. "She is not so beautiful now, is she, after a night spent in the dungeon?"

Paulus glanced contemptuously at Servius, who guarded Alysia closely with drawn sword. "Let her go."

"No." Lucius seemed undismayed by his stepbrother's unexpected appearance, and even wore a look of satisfaction. "You are not in uniform, Paulus. I must presume you are no longer commander of this fort."

"Let her go," Paulus said again, without taking his eyes off Servius.

Servius began to sweat. He hadn't bargained for this! One look at the legate's face and he saw his chances for revenge, and promotion, slipping away. It seemed improbable that anything good would come of this situation. Silently he cursed Lucius, and lowering his sword began to move discreetly away. Lucius observed the movement and stepped closer to his prisoner.

"Sir." It was Marcus who spoke. "Are you, or are you not, in command here?"

Paulus looked for the first time into Alysia's face, who stared back at him with anguish in her eyes. Her relief upon seeing him had turned into deep dismay, for all that she had feared had come to pass. These men knew that he had helped her escape. Even now more soldiers were coming out of the barracks to see what was happening.

He withdrew a letter from the front of his tunic and handed it to Marcus. "Where is Tribune Fabius?"

"Sir, the prefect of the camp is sick with a fever and has placed me temporarily in charge. The other tribunes have not returned from their inspection of the fort at Emmaus."

"Then you are in command until the arrival of my replacement, who will be appointed pending the approval of the emperor."

Marcus broke open the letter, his face expressionless. Paulus said, "Release this woman. She is not guilty of a crime."

"Since when is murder not a crime?" cried Lucius. "I am an eye-witness! If these men let her go, their guilt will be the same as yours."

Paulus took a step toward Alysia but Lucius was quicker. In a single, fluid motion, he grabbed her arm and held the point of his dagger against her spine.

"Hold, Paulus, or I'll kill her."

Paulus came abruptly to a halt. Studying Lucius, it seemed he was too assured, almost smug. That could only mean that he was certain Alysia was going to die, one way or another…even if he had to kill her himself. There was a look in his eyes Paulus hadn't seen before, as though his malice had turned to madness.

Paulus exchanged a brief look with Simon, who gave an almost imperceptible nod of understanding. On Paulus' signal he was to act. Simon began to inch closer to Alysia. Paulus was still, making no sudden movements.

Alysia, too, knew without doubt that Lucius meant to kill her. Just as she knew somehow that this was *not* about her; it was about Paulus. Lucius didn't care that Magnus was dead. He didn't care that Alysia had killed him. He hated Paulus, had nurtured a venomous jealousy of him for years, and this was a way to inflict the maximum pain upon his stepbrother.

"Have you ever had to beg for anything, Paulus?" Lucius asked, freely gloating now. "Then go down before me, and beg me for her life!"

Nile blue eyes clashed with shining black, and hatred flared in both pair. Slowly Paulus went down on one knee, holding his hands out from his sides. A murmuring went through the watchful soldiers. They didn't like seeing their commander thus humbled, and though they knew Lucius was out of control there was nothing anyone could do as long as he held Alysia at knifepoint.

"I'm begging you, Lucius. Release her, and you can have anything you want of me. Property, money, my life, whatever you want."

"No," said Alysia, almost inaudibly. "No, Paulus."

Lucius laughed. He whirled around and gestured with his free hand. "Behold the brave and noble legate, reduced to begging for the life of his harlot!"

But no one joined Lucius in his laughter. Even Servius was silent. Lucius made a swift, angry movement and pushed Alysia forward.

"Then here she is, Paulus. See to what avail you have lowered yourself!"

She felt the cold metal in her back, and only a moment's pain before awareness left her. The last image emblazoned upon her mind was a memory of Magnus' incredulous face at the moment he died, for she felt the same sense of disbelief. She fell upon Paulus before he could rise from his kneeling position. He caught her, not knowing what Lucius had done, and tried to help her rise. Feeling something warm and wet on his hand, he held it up and saw that it was blood.

"Alysia—" Dazed, Paulus pressed his hand over the wound in her back as though he could stop the flow by sheer force of will, but still the warm blood seeped through his fingers. Holding her with one arm he took his dagger and released her bonds, his face filled with some dark extremity of emotion. He lifted her in his arms and began to walk past Lucius, but Lucius drew his sword.

"You want to kill me, Paulus. I have always desired to test my skill against yours! I won't let you pass. I'll finish her, and you as well."

Paulus stopped, his gaze seeking out Simon. Two other men were standing beside him now—Lazarus and Stephen. All three rushed forward to take Alysia from him.

"Find the physician," Paulus said, inclining his head toward a nearby building. "Over there."

She was bleeding so freely they had to stop. Simon and Stephen placed Alysia gently on a cedar bench, beneath a tree that grew from a square of earth left in the midst of the pavement. Lazarus started to go toward the physician's residence, but at a call from Stephen stopped and went back. Paulus had no time to wonder what was happening.

"Sir!" The centurion walked toward him, withdrawing his sword. "Let me place him under arrest until this matter can be investigated."

"No." Paulus shook his head. "This is between Lucius and me . . . and here it will end."

Marcus held out his sword, giving him a salute of respect. Paulus nodded and took the sword. He turned to his stepbrother.

"You will pay dearly for this blood upon my hand."

Lucius said, through clenched teeth, "Alysia will die."

"And so will you."

CHAPTER XXVI

The two swords met with a heavy clash. The soldiers of the Antonia knew of Paulus' skill with a sword, but they didn't expect to see Lucius almost match it. Lucius excelled in two things…gambling and swordplay. But, unlike Paulus, his experience had been limited to practice sessions with slaves and gladiators who knew they were not to harm him. Never had he faced a man of such controlled strength and ruthlessness, for Paulus had replaced his fear for Alysia with rage.

Metal rang against metal as their bodies leaped nimbly from side to side. Blood appeared on Lucius' arm, then on Paulus' shoulder through a rip in his tunic. Paulus had, for a moment, underestimated Lucius' ability; he would not be so careless again. The soldiers watched in silence, moving out of the way when necessary. They had seen such exhibitions in the arena but never at close range…and in battle there was no time to look at anyone else.

Lucius was tiring; he was neither as strong nor as fit as Paulus. Forced to retreat, he backed over the pavement, around pillars, up and down steps. Paulus pursued him, agile, and quick as a lion would stalk its prey. Lucius stumbled and caught himself. His right arm began to ache…if it cramped, he was finished. All his concentration was on parrying the heavy blows that rained on him unceasingly. Now it took both arms to swing the blade. Again he lost his footing, and his concentration faltered as he struggled to right himself.

His hatred and contempt for Paulus were forgotten in his efforts to defend himself. Somehow it had not occurred to him that Paulus might best him. His imagination had carried him no further than the attack…and Lucius had supreme confidence in his own prowess.

I'm losing, he thought, drawing from the dark tangle of thoughts that spun in his head. *I am losing this fight, and I am losing my life. He will kill me, he will have his revenge, and I will be a laughingstock.* His strength returned at such an odious notion and, surprised again, Paulus had to fall back for an instant before bounding forward and reasserting his advantage.

Paulus felt as if he had become possessed by all the rage he had ever known. He was conscious of nothing and no one else. The desire to kill his stepbrother was so powerful, so demanding, that he could see Lucius only through a haze. His strength doubled and he seemed unstoppable. With one swift movement he brought his sword crashing against the other and sent it flying from Lucius' grasp.

He tossed aside his own sword and, reaching out, closed his hand around the throat of Lucius' tunic and jerked him forward. His other hand went crashing into Lucius' face. Lucius reeled backward and forward, so drained he could do little more than grunt each time

Paulus struck him. His attempts to shield himself were futile. He began to moan incoherently.

Then through the haze, Paulus saw the blood...Lucius' blood on his hands, all over Lucius' face and splattering on the front of his tunic. It seemed to become the blood running down both sides of a cross. At that instant the rage evaporated, was gone as completely as if it had never been...because he knew that Lucius was already dead, dead in his soul. He stopped as suddenly as he had begun, dropping Lucius onto the pavement.

Crawling laboriously on his hands and knees, Lucius retrieved his fallen sword. Paulus watched him, breathing hard, bent slightly forward with his hands braced on his knees, preparing to kick him aside.

"You will not leave me worse than dead!" Lucius rasped through cut and swollen lips. "You lose, Paulus! You do not destroy me, and Alysia will be with *me*—in death!"

He fell upon his sword, collapsing onto his side. Of the soldiers surrounding them, not one moved or spoke. Lucius' sightless eyes were fixed on the sky, his mouth open in silent protest.

Paulus turned to run toward Alysia. He stopped and stared in disbelief. How was she able to sit up? She looked as if . . . His gaze fell on Stephen, who was walking away, leaving the fortress. Lazarus sat next to Alysia with his arm half around her, and Simon was nowhere to be seen.

"Remove this body at once," Marcus ordered some of the men. Then he, too, became aware of Alysia.

Paulus went slowly toward her. She stood up and went to meet him. He took her in his arms. "Forgive me," he said, his voice hoarse. "It's my fault. I thought I could protect you. I was sure—"

"Hush," she said softly. "There is no need."

He pulled back, looking into her face. "How can this be?"

She glanced at Lazarus, who said simply, "Stephen healed her. I mean, the Lord healed her, through Stephen."

Alysia shook her head. "I don't remember anything after he struck me. Until Stephen's voice called to me."

Paulus' brows drew together in wonder. His hand slipped behind her back, found the rip in her gown and touched her bloodied but unbroken skin. A feeling came over him much like that of the night of his conversion—unworthiness mingled with intense gratitude, regret and relief, and the utmost peace. For a moment he couldn't speak. He looked into Alysia's eyes and suddenly they smiled at each other. She went again into his arms, and he held her there as if he would never let her go, his face against her hair.

At last he pulled away and looked at the man sitting on the bench. "Lazarus, how did you and Stephen come to be here?"

Lazarus, seeming much moved, cleared his throat. "I saw her being taken past my house last night. I heard a donkey braying and when I looked, I could see a cart and someone in it, a woman and a child. Although I couldn't see her face, I could tell by the way she sat and held the child that it was Alysia. I got on my horse and followed them, without them knowing. I explained to the centurion that, whatever was happening, it was his duty to protect this woman. He refused to let me see her but gave me his word he wouldn't do anything until he had talked to you. I went and found Stephen. We prayed through the night, or most of it, and decided to return here this morning."

"Has Stephen ever . . . done anything like this before?"

"Stephen has something I have not even seen in the disciples. The eleven, I mean. It is not to say that his faith is stronger, but he has . . . an understanding that the rest of us don't seem to have. Not yet."

Paulus reached out and grasped his forearm. "Thank you, from the bottom of my heart."

Alysia looked around the courtyard, saying anxiously, "Where is Rachel? One of the guards was holding her, just over there!"

Paulus turned and surveyed the area behind him. They had taken Lucius away and several men were scrubbing blood from the pavement. The other soldiers had resumed their posts; others were going into the dining hall. Servius had disappeared and so had the sentry with Rachel. Marcus began to walk toward them.

"I need to get you out of here," Paulus said. "Right away."

"I won't leave this place without Rachel!"

"Alysia, your life may yet be at stake."

She shook her head and Paulus saw that she was not to be persuaded. He turned as the centurion approached them.

"Sir," he said, his eyes on Alysia. "I thought she—can someone explain—"

Paulus hesitated. "There is one among us who has the gift of healing."

"I see." Marcus appeared doubtful but did not pursue the subject, since the young woman must not have received the mortal blow he believed she had. He looked somewhat embarrassed and avoided her steady gaze, remembering all too well the last time they had met. "Will you swear to me, Paulus Valerius, that this woman did not commit murder but only defended herself against rape?"

"I swear it."

"Then I will not detain her. I have seen no official dispatches concerning this matter."

"I destroyed them," Paulus admitted. "What happened was no fault of hers and she has suffered much because of it."

"Then I cannot add another wrong to those she has already endured. In my opinion, your stepbrother became deranged, and engaged you in a fight to the death. I will report this to Pilate just as it happened, and that I saw no reason to hold the young woman in custody. I realize he may question this, but . . . because of my own past misdeeds, I cannot do otherwise."

"This is good of you, Marcus. But there may be trouble. For whatever good it will do, I will write the governor and tell him I destroyed the notices and that I convinced you that she was innocent."

"There is no need, sir. I'm prepared to take the consequences." Marcus glanced at Alysia, his face reddening. "Was *my* life in danger that night?"

"Truthfully, I do not know. Although . . . I had prepared to defend myself. But for this, I do thank you, Centurion."

He gazed at her for a moment, his lined face pensive. Then he said, "You are all free to go."

"We cannot leave until we have found our daughter," Paulus said. "She was being held by one of the guards. Do you know which one?"

"Your daugh—that is, I'm sorry to say I paid no attention once Lucius marched out with the young woman. I did see Servius with the child at one time."

"Can you describe this sentry?" Paulus asked, turning to Alysia.

"No, only that he was tall. He was too far away to see clearly."

Marcus straightened, falling habitually into a military stance. "I'll have some of the men start searching."

As he hurried away, Lazarus said, "Alysia, let me take you home. I'm sorry, Paulus, but I still don't trust these Romans."

"No offense taken," Paulus said lightly. "He's right, Alysia. You should leave."

"Not without Rachel!"

"Very well . . . come with me." Paulus put his arm around Alysia's waist and led her up the steps and into the praetorium, with Lazarus following. A slave was passing through the corridor. Paulus said to him, "Take this woman upstairs and bring her something to eat and drink."

"Please," Alysia added, with a reproving glance at Paulus.

Simon entered from behind them. When everyone looked at him inquiringly, he explained, "After Alysia was . . . healed, I noticed that the man carrying the child was gone. I didn't see him leave. I've been trying to find him."

"What does he look like?" Paulus asked.

"Tall, light hair. He could be anywhere. I came back for help."

"We're going now and the centurion has started a search." Paulus looked into Alysia's eyes, bent his head, and kissed her forehead gently. "Do not worry. We'll find her."

Alysia nodded. As she started up the stairs, Lazarus said, "Alysia, last night Mary and Martha went to your house and packed your clothes, and Rachel's. We didn't know what was going to happen and thought you might need them. They're in a bag I left on my horse."

Paulus briefly touched the slave's arm. "Cassipor, find the horse and take the lady her clothes, after you've seen to her comfort—please. Lazarus and Simon, come with me. We need to find Servius. He may know something of this mysterious sentry."

"Paulus," Alysia whispered, pulling him aside. "I didn't see it all . . . did you kill Lucius?"

"No," he answered soberly. "He killed himself. But I wanted to kill him, and almost did. I most definitely have some repenting to do."

"I'm sorry it happened that way."

"He hated me, Alysia, not you. We must put this behind us now."

"Find her, Paulus! Find our daughter and bring her back to me."

The slave showed Alysia into a room with comfortable-looking couches and chairs, and a large window that overlooked the entire west side of the fortress. Once inside she felt overwhelmed with emotion. She collapsed to her knees and began to sob, great wracking sobs that tore at her throat and took away her breath. She had gone from fear, to pain, to a strange, dreamless sleep . . . then to awareness and gratitude, and now fear again. An intense and so utterly helpless fear that she could only cry out to God.

"Please take care of my child! Thank you for what you have done for me, but please don't let anything happen to Rachel. You know I would rather be dead than to know something had happened to her! Oh, I beg you to be merciful once more."

She couldn't remember her wound, couldn't remember anything, as she had told Paulus. *Something* had happened; she shouldn't be amazed, for she had seen such things, such miracles… but why it should be done for her she didn't know. It was too vast a thought, too much for her at this moment.

She was kneeling with her head bowed and her palms pressed against her eyes when the slave entered the room with a tray of food. Cassipor, an elderly man, thin and short of stature, set down the tray and put his hand on her shoulder. "The Lord will take care of your daughter," he said quietly. "And if she is harmed in any way, he will be with her. His ways are not our ways. Whatever happens, he will *always* be with a child."

Alysia got to her feet and held out her hand to the slave. "You are a believer, and you speak words that he has given you. I'm very grateful."

"You must eat," said Cassipor, pressing her hand and releasing it. "Please sit down."

She did so, first washing her hands and face in a basin he provided. He left the room and after some time returned with the bag of clothes Lazarus had brought her.

"I will pray for you," he said, as he left again.

Alysia felt comforted but her qualms had not subsided. Who was the man with Rachel, and why had he disappeared? It didn't make sense!

She rummaged through the clothes, took out a gown with its matching cloak and removed the torn and bloodied one she wore. She was soon dressed; she combed her long hair with her fingers and covered it with the mantle. It seemed that a long time had gone by.

She went to the window and could see several buildings—the residence of the tribunes, the infirmary, the stable on the first level, and the workshops of some of the artisans—immunes, they were called. She could tell there was activity among the soldiers and assumed they were searching the buildings. Many of them she could still hear drilling on the parade ground.

She pulled up a chair so that she could watch. She knew it wasn't safe for her to go down and look for Rachel herself, but she was half inclined to do it. Her head drooped; she rested it for a moment against the sill and exhaustion pulled at her until she fell into a strange half-sleep.

The sound of hooves on pavement and the voices of men brought her to her feet. The sun was high and warm on her face. She leaned out the window and saw Paulus, Lazarus, and Simon riding up a ramp from the first level of the court. They dismounted slowly and began walking toward the praetorium. He did not have Rachel!

She turned, flung open the door and ran down the stairs. Paulus entered the vestibule and the look of deep concern on his face filled her with dread. Simon came in behind him. Lazarus must have lingered outside.

"Servius was hiding in the barracks. He says he doesn't know who the man was, that he just took Rachel away from him. We haven't been able to find them yet, Alysia, but we will—if we have to tear this place apart and search the entire city."

"Do you mean . . . she's nowhere in this fort?"

A sound, an unexpected dimming of light from the end of the corridor where they stood, made all three of them turn their heads. The window at that end of the building was partially blocked by a tall figure, its outline clear, the rest indistinct due to the light from behind. As the figure drew closer, they saw it was a soldier . . . a soldier who carried a child in his arms.

He came slowly toward them. The others stared, strangely immobilized, as he walked. There was not a sound but his footsteps. At last he entered into their own sphere of light and they could see Rachel curled against his chest, sleeping.

The man stood taller than Paulus. His hair was blond and cut short, his eyes a blazing light blue. He wore the uniform of a Roman sentry.

"You of little faith," he said, with a rueful smile. "How soon you forget what great things the Lord has done for you."

He handed Rachel gently into Alysia's arms. Tears of overwhelming relief started from her eyes. Paulus had not yet looked away from the soldier.

"I know you," he said, with conviction. "You are the one who brought me here when I was wounded on the Jericho road."

The soldier nodded, but did not speak.

"I know you, too," Alysia whispered. "You were one of those with Jesus, that day on the Mount of Olives when he went away."

"And so he will return, in like manner."

"Why did you take the child?" Paulus asked.

"I was told to. She was not to witness the things that happened. I've been here all the time . . . but you could not see me until the time was right."

"I don't—" Alysia began, but then she did understand, or thought she did. It looked as though Paulus did, too, but Simon was bewildered.

"There are things done for you, for all those who belong to him, that you cannot see. Things like—" He looked at Alysia and almost seemed to wink "—pulling a donkey's tail."

She stared at him in amazement, remembering the indignant brays of the donkey on the way from Bethany.

He gazed back at them, smiling, and they watched as he turned and walked away. As soon as he stepped into the shadows, he disappeared. He might have turned to the right or to the left, except that there were no retreating footsteps; there was no movement of air to mark his passage.

They stood motionless. Then Paulus said quietly, "May God have mercy on my wretched soul…I have not yet thanked him for all he has done here today."

"I—I want to thank him too," said Simon. "For what I've seen and heard, and . . . I want to tell him that I believe."

They drew close and knelt together, bowed their heads, and prayed.

Outside, they found Lazarus in conversation with the centurion. Both men turned and looked astonished to see Alysia carrying her daughter. Paulus attempted to explain.

"The sentry was inside. We're not sure where he had been before, but . . . he's gone again."

"I want to question him," Marcus declared. "Where did he go?"

"Truthfully, Marcus, I do not know. You can search for him if you like—very tall, light hair, blue eyes."

Marcus addressed one of the other centurions who stood nearby, ordering him to assemble another contingent of men to search the fort. Paulus looked at Alysia and shrugged a little. He said in a low voice, "It will keep them busy—until we get out of here."

"I won't ask where you're going," Marcus said, turning his attention back to Paulus. "But how will you travel? I can provide an extra horse."

Paulus' brow furrowed; where *were* they going? Alysia hadn't yet said if she would marry him. There had been no time for any such discussion. But whether she married him or not, she would still have to leave Bethany.

He felt her hand slide into his. "I had already decided," she told him. "The answer is yes."

He clasped her hand, smiling into her eyes. "My horse, then…all three of us."

Marcus said, "I'll have the horse readied, and will provide food for your journey."

"You've been very kind," Alysia said to him, with a puzzled look. "What has changed you?"

He looked embarrassed again. "The legate set me straight, on a lot of things." He nodded at Paulus and walked quickly away.

"What did you say to him, Paulus? Is he a believer?"

"Not yet, but I think he will be. As for traveling, we'll stop as soon as we can and buy another donkey and cart, and a mat and some blankets for the back. But we need to get out of here as quickly as possible, and Asbolus is the best way."

"Oh," Alysia said suddenly, "I left my clothes in that room . . . here, Paulus, take Rachel. And I must speak to Cassipor. I'll only be a moment." She placed Rachel in his arms and hurried back into the praetorium. Simon offered to go and pack some of Paulus' things as well.

For the first time Paulus held his daughter. In fact, he couldn't remember ever having held a child before, but she seemed to be suffering no ill effects. Awake now, she stared solemnly into his eyes, her small hands tugging on the cord at the throat of his tunic. She gave a great yawn, smiled at him, and laid her head trustingly on his shoulder. Paulus placed his hand on the back of her head, and felt something catch at his heart that he knew would never let go.

He turned to see Lazarus waiting quietly, his attention discreetly fixed on something in the distance. "Lazarus, we both owe you a great debt. I'm grateful for everything you've done for Alysia. I hope there will not be any trouble over your helping her."

"Alysia and Rachel are part of our family. And now, so are you. There is no need to thank me, Paulus."

"Will you tell Stephen—" Paulus hesitated, and to his vague surprise felt tears sting his eyes. "Stephen has been more than a brother to me. I regret that I didn't get to tell him good-bye."

"I will tell him of your words. I know that he feels the same toward you."

"About that . . . exhibition with Lucius," Paulus said ruefully. "I was wrong, and I'm sorry you had to witness it."

"A mistake. We all make them. And unfortunately, usually pay for them in some way. I hope you will not be bitter toward him, Paulus."

Before he could answer, Alysia came quickly down the steps with Simon behind her, who carried her bag as well as one for Paulus. Paulus looked around and saw some of the soldiers eyeing them surreptitiously, and he didn't like it. He had thought, before all of this happened, that he might call the men together and say something to them before he left, but there was no time now. Too many of them had heard what Lucius said about Alysia. Some would believe it… some would begin to talk among themselves and wonder if there was a reward for her capture. Tribune Fabius would eventually hear of the matter and who knew how he would react? It was time to leave.

"Let's go to the stable. I think that's where they took our horses." Paulus led the way down a flight of steps and found Marcus outside the long, narrow building, watching as slaves strapped satchels of food and some blankets onto his horse.

"I'd like to pay for these things," Paulus said, handing Rachel to Alysia and untying a small moneybag from his belt. "You've been helpful enough as it is, and the men are going to talk."

Marcus seemed to follow his train of thought. "I don't think you have anything to fear from most of these men," he said, taking the coins Paulus offered. "But . . . there are many, and word will get around to them all. The cohort commanders will have to explain your absence to their own men, and though they are loyal to you it is best that you leave as soon as possible. I wish you good fortune, sir."

"Again, thank you for everything, Marcus."

The centurion gave another nod, dismissed the slaves, and left them. Lazarus said, "I see they have my horse ready as well. I know my sisters are very anxious to hear what has happened."

Alysia caught one of Lazarus' hands in hers.

"How can I ever tell you how much you've meant to me? You and Mary and Martha."

"There is no need," he said gently. "But I take it you won't be returning to Bethany—for a long time?"

"Paulus and I are going to be married. I do hope to come back, someday. I'm sorry I wasn't truthful about everything, Lazarus. But I—I didn't know what else to do."

"Please . . . again, there is no need to speak of it. I wish you happiness, Alysia. May God be with you."

Rachel stretched out her arms toward him. He took her from Alysia, held her for a moment, and kissed her cheek. "Good-bye, little one."

Turning to the other men, he grasped the reins of his horse and said with a smile, "Is there anything else I can do to help you?"

"No, but may God reward you for what you've already done," Paulus said. They all bade him goodbye and watched as he rode his horse onto the long avenue leading out of the fortress.

Paulus asked, "Simon, what are your plans? You are welcome to come with us."

"Thank you, sir—I mean, Paulus, but I've decided to go back to Cyrene. I'm not sure yet about telling my wife, but I want my sons to know me. I know I can find work there. First, though, I'm going to see Stephen, or some of the others. I have much to learn, about *him*."

"A wise decision, I think, but take care. You are known as my slave and there are going to be questions asked."

"No risk is too great—" Simon stopped and said a little ruefully, "Well, it seems I've heard something like that before . . . from you! I'm sorry that I spoke as I did that day."

"You said what you thought at the time, and can't be blamed for that, Simon."

"I'd like to ride with you as far as the gate."

Paulus nodded. "It will seem as though you left with us, and they won't know where to look for you."

He already had the route in mind—not to the coast, which would be expected. They would travel north, through the country, and then through the region known as Asia...by land rather than sea. It was possible that fast-riding soldiers would be sent to watch for them at the ports, and ships were too confining, with all sorts of passengers who might know or recognize him, or even Alysia.

He lifted Alysia and Rachel onto his horse, then mounted behind them as Simon mounted his own horse. They left the fort slowly, trying to make as little noise as possible. Turning right, they made their way to the Damascus gate, passed through it, and came upon one of the highways beneath Golgotha…the Roman "Calvary." As if compelled, they turned back to look at the skull-like rock. The flattened terrain at the top bore several wooden crosses, sharply outlined against the afternoon sky. In Pilate's absence there were no victims writhing upon them.

They were moved to a deep silence. At last Alysia said softly, "The cross is going to change the world."

"Not just the cross," Paulus answered. "But that he *lives*. If the cross had been the end, he would be just a man to admire, just a man whose teachings were followed for a while and forgotten. It's the empty tomb that changes everything."

They all looked at each other, reluctant to part, but at last Simon turned his horse to re-enter the city. "This is farewell, but something tells me we'll see each other again, someday. It didn't occur to me to ask before now…where are you going?"

Alysia tilted her head back to look at Paulus; her eyes were shining.

"We're going to Rome," she said.

AUTHOR'S NOTES

Although Alysia's story is fictional, the "woman of sin" was real, and the brief mention of her occurs in the eighth chapter of John in the Holy Bible. Many have assumed this person was Mary Magdalene. There are no grounds for this supposition; Mary Magdalene was never referred to as a "sinful woman" or prostitute. The Bible states only that Jesus "cast out of her seven demons." She became a devoted follower.

The woman in the book of John is unnamed; her identity has always been a mystery. John is the only writer who mentions her.

If you enjoyed this book, it is the first in a series with the sequels entitled *Man of God*, and *Child of the King*. I have written other historical novels with more in the planning stage. I'm currently writing a novel in the paranormal/supernatural genre.

Thank you for reading my books! Feel free to connect with me through my website, www.debradiaz.com or by email at debra@debradiaz.com.

ABOUT THE AUTHOR

Debra B. Diaz is the author of the *Woman of Sin* trilogy, and has written several novels in the historical and romantic suspense genres. She is retired and enjoys spending time with her family, doing research on biblical topics, and writing books. Her goal as a writer is to not only entertain, but to challenge and inspire! For more information, visit www.debradiaz.com.

OTHER BOOKS BY DEBRA B. DIAZ

Man of God: Book Two in the *Woman of Sin* trilogy

Child of the King: Book Three in the *Woman of Sin* trilogy

Shadow of Dawn: A Civil War Romantic Suspense Novel

On This Night: A Civil War Mystery

Place of Peace: A Post-Civil War Romance

Summons From a Stranger: A Young Adult Mystery

OTHER TITLES IN THE *WOMAN OF SIN* TRILOGY

In Book Two, **Man of God**

Paulus Valerius, former legate in the Roman army, and Alysia, the woman he loves, face danger and betrayal—and the maniacal emperor, Caligula—as they seek to spread the word of God from Jerusalem to Rome. From its suspenseful beginning to its violent and inevitable finale, this sequel to *Woman of Sin* is an unforgettable story of those who choose to share the atoning power of the cross, no matter what the price.

In Book Three, **Child of the King**

The daughter of Paulus and Alysia is grown now and ready for a life of her own. But Rachel is unable to rise above her past, and something that happened in Rome ten years ago. Metellus, former tribune in the Praetorian Guard, has been commissioned by the emperor, Claudius, to bring Rachel from Jerusalem to Rome. It is a journey that will affect both their lives…in ways they could never have imagined.

EXCERPT FROM MAN OF GOD

PROLOGUS, AD 40

Tiberius Caesar was dead, supposedly of natural causes, but it was rumored that he had been murdered. The story began with his traveling about in Campania in defiance of an increasing physical weakness; he finally stopped at a villa on the southern coast of Italy, where his physician informed Sutorius Macro, the Prefect of the Praetorian Guard, that the emperor was about to "breathe his last." Hiding their exultance, Macro and the emperor's grandnephew, Caligula, sent out dispatches and laid their plans.

When the old man expired, Caligula gravely made the announcement to a group of his own admirers, who were also thrilled—and didn't hesitate to show it. The young man was still tearfully addressing them when an irritable voice rang out from the imperial bedchamber:

"Where is everybody? By the gods, I want something to eat!"

Panicking, everyone scattered, but the emperor's recovery was short lived. Caligula sought out Macro, who calmly proceeded to smother the old man under a pile of his own bedclothes.

It was, however, just a rumor.

The nickname, Caligula—meaning "Little Boots"—had been bestowed upon Gaius Caesar by soldiers of his father's army, when at the age of two or three he had gone strutting about the campgrounds in a tiny but authentic uniform. He'd been popular even then, and now was hailed with delight as the new emperor. At last, grouchy old Tiberius was dead! Here was the young and noble son of Germanicus—Germanicus, who had been loved by everyone, except by whoever killed him.

True, the new emperor had an odd and feeble appearance, with a wide forehead, wispy pale hair, high cheekbones, a weak chin, and a sad and drooping mouth that could harden into a line of abject cruelty. But few saw the cruelty, at first. At the age of twenty-five he gave the impression of great promise. In spite of his look of frailty, he had a strong voice that served him well onstage, for he had a passionate love of theater.

He declared, in that fine, orator's voice, that Rome should never again fear the sort of despotism that had taken place during the reign of Tiberius. A year passed, during which he improved the tax system, increased pay to the army, sponsored spectacular events in the arena, gave free food to the masses, and brought about many other reforms that solidified the public's approval of him.

But the following year, something happened. Caligula fell victim to a mysterious illness, and when he recovered, he had changed—though many who knew him well said he did not change at all; he only stopped putting on a show of goodness. No one could decide whether he was indeed mad, or if he was simply running amuck, having gone in such a short time from obscurity to being the most powerful man in the world.

He began a reign of terror that made Tiberius' treason trials look like the antics of schoolboys and embarked upon such sexual abandon that even Rome was outraged. There was only one man who could give him pause once he set his mind upon some frantic and incomprehensible course of action, and that was his uncle. His old confidant, Macro, had gone the way of many others—stripped of his position two years ago, after which he and his wife committed "suicide."

Uncle Claudius was as unlike his brother as it was possible to be. Germanicus had been handsome, affable, an excellent soldier. The unfortunate Claudius was unprepossessing in appearance, limped, stuttered, and was generally regarded as a fool. It was, however, a calculated effect, for Claudius had a keen intelligence and did not mind if it was underrated, since if he'd been considered a true threat to the throne he would no doubt exist only as a heap of ashes, like most of his other relatives.

Caligula would never confess it, but in spite of his scorn for Claudius' physical and presumed mental shortcomings, he had a grudging respect for the practical advice his uncle could give him on occasion—after all, even idiots could have a degree of common sense, could they not? Claudius was well acquainted with politics and human nature, and had watched, with a jaundiced eye, all the happenings in Rome from the time of Augustus.

"Tell me, Uncle," the emperor said one day, pretending to yawn with boredom, "what do you think of this new sect that calls itself the Nazarenes, or whatever it is?"

Claudius' mouth sometimes worked and twitched a few times before anything came out. "I—I don't think anything about them. After all, they worship another god instead of those of Rome and Your Divine Maj—Majesty. It is wise to ignore them and most likely the whole thing will die out eventu—ally."

Caligula rose from his marble, cushioned bench and strode to the edge of the palace balcony where he struck his habitual pose, bending a knee, grasping the finely embroidered edge of his toga. He cocked his head and rolled his eyes thoughtfully. "I don't know about that. Look at the Jews. They worship another god and we have very graciously allowed them to do so. Perhaps that has been a mistake. I can only imagine what they would do if I required them to bow down to me. In fact, I decided some time ago I would put a statue of myself in their Temple over in Jerusalem."

Claudius tried to conceal his horror. "It wouldn't be worth the consequences, Your Majesty. You know they would fight to the death before allowing such a sac—that is, what they consider a sacrilege, my lord emp—orer."

"That's just the problem, Uncle," Caligula said softly, with small pouches puffing out on either side of his mouth. "And the Nazarenes are just as stubborn. They worship the same god, I hear, but somehow this dead Jew is mixed into it, and they think he is on equal footing with their god. I don't like it. It doesn't make sense. It would be better all the way 'round if everybody stopped this twaddle and admitted there is only one Lord, one King!"

"One Lord, one King," Claudius intoned. It was Caligula's favorite appellation for himself.

Caligula turned and strode toward his uncle, who sat beside a small potted tree and seemed to be trying to hide behind it. "I am going to call for an assembly. Rulers and chieftains from all over the empire. We shall see how widespread this problem is and decide how to deal with it. Well, actually, I have other reasons for this gathering, but that one will do well enough. And now for that other matter that concerns me. You remember Paulus Valerius, do you not?"

"We met several times, years ago. He was always k—kind to me."

"Kindness is weakness, Uncle! Paulus Valerius Maximus is not weak. It was pity for your wretchedness you saw. Tiberius was most anxious to find him, before his—death. And I have often wondered what became of Valerius. He has recently been seen here in Rome! Someone reported it to me. But we can't find him. When we do, you can be sure we will have some questions for him to answer."

"Questions?" Claudius repeated, reluctantly.

"Yes, questions!" The emperor's eyes became fixed; his tone softened again. "Such as, why did he abandon his appointment and leave Jerusalem? Why has he remained hidden these seven years? And where is that woman he supposedly rescued, the one who killed Magnus Eustacius?"

"Why such an interest in Valerius?" Claudius was afraid to ask, but knew his nephew expected it.

"I liked him," Caligula almost whispered. "He reminds me of—someone. Why is his statue not in the Forum of Augustus?"

"He never p—permitted it, Your Majesty. It seemed he lacked the pa-patience for such things."

"I want him as head of my bodyguard. Flavius will have to take second place."

Claudius didn't think that was a good idea. "Even though he helped the woman escape? Even considering he has broken his oath and is no longer a soldier?"

"We shall see about that. As for the woman—well, who cares about Eustacius! He was a bumbling sot, like his father. But he was an aristocrat, after all; therefore, she must die."

Caligula jerked his head around as if listening, then turned back to his uncle, who now sat with alarm bells ringing in his own head. "Jupiter has spoken," the emperor declared, with a familiar, wide-eyed expression that Claudius could never decide was comical or one from which to flee as speedily as possible.

"We will start a search for the woman. We have a description; she is quite a beauty, I've heard. Indigo eyes, hair like a black waterfall. Whoever said that is a poet! She's Greek, an aristocrat herself, before her father was executed and she was sent off as a slave. I am certain that when we find her, we will find Valerius as well. And both of their fates will be up to me—not to the dead Nazarene, not to the unknown God, and not even to Jupiter. Don't tell Jupiter I said that, Uncle. One Lord, one King!"

RECOMMENDED RESOURCES

Graham, Billy. 2013. *The Reason for My Hope*. Nashville, TN: W Publishing Group.

Lewis, C. S. 2001. *Mere Christianity*. New York, NY: Harper Collins Publishers.

Rogers, Adrian. 2014. *Believe in Miracles but Trust in Jesus*. Collierville, TN: Innovo Publishing LLC.

Strobel, Lee. 1998. *The Case for Christ*. Grand Rapids, MI: Zondervan Publishing House.

Made in the USA
Monee, IL
03 August 2020